Vanilla Salt

ADA PARELLADA

Translated by
Julie Wark

ALMA BOOKS

ALMA BOOKS LTD
London House
243–253 Lower Mortlake Road
Richmond
Surrey TW9 2LL
United Kingdom
www.almabooks.com

First published in Catalan by Editorial Planeta, S.A. in 2012
Translated from the Catalan by Julie Wark
This translation, based on a revised text, was published by Alma
Books Limited in 2014
Translation rights arranged by Sandra Bruna Agencia Literaria, SL
All rights reserved

© Ada Parellada, 2012
Translation © Julie Wark, 2014

The translation of this work was supported by a grant from
the Institut Ramon Llull

**institut
ramon llull**
Catalan Language and Culture

Cover design: Jem Butcher

Ada Parellada asserts her moral right to be identified as the author of this
work in accordance with the Copyright, Designs and Patents Act 1988

Printed and bound by CPI Group (UK) Ltd, Croydon, CR0 4YY

ISBN: 978-1-84688-333-0
EBOOK ISBN: 978-1-84688-342-2

Vanilla Salt

1

BITTER

Except for the incarnation and death of the Creator, the greatest event since the creation of the world is the discovery of the Indies.

Historia general de las Indias
FRANCISCO LÓPEZ DE GÓMARA

Àlex could really do with some help in the kitchen. It's now a week since the last bloody moron walked out on him. "You know what I say? Go and stick turnips up every one of your orifices, including the smallest one," he bawled at the kitchen hand who, also enraged, flung down his apron on Table 3.

Since Moha left six months ago, things have gone from bad to worse. Everyone's broke, that's true. Àlex, owner of the Antic Món restaurant, hardly speaks or listens to anyone, but even so, he can't avoid the news that a lot of businesses are closing down. Crisis.

Well, that's not quite the case for everyone. Can Bret is just opposite Antic Món and they've got plenty of work. More than that, they're flat out. On weekdays it's full of workers from the industrial estates around the town of Bigues i Riells. Well, they're not exactly workers in blue overalls but the so-called white-collar lot, who don't have a cent of their own in their pockets. If they're lunching with a supplier they'll go for a Priorat red, one of the pricey ones. If they're eating with clients and have to pay themselves, they order the house wine,

3

saying, "It's from a great boutique winery I've just discovered." Slick bastards!

Weekends are pure madness at Can Bret. Its customers even invade Antic Món's car park! Àlex can't stand it. When this happens, he usually rushes out of the kitchen like a raving lunatic, no matter what he's doing at the time. If he's filleting a sea bass, he flies out with the fish in his hand, brandishing the weapon at his neighbour's customers. Sometimes, however, he gets tired of yelling at them and lets them park wherever they bloody like. Anyway, it's ages since he's needed all the spaces in his car park.

Ever since Can Bret joined the *calçotada* craze – churning out charcoal-caked mountains of barbecued spring onions smothered in romesco sauce, which diners are then supposed to eat with their fingers – people have been coming in hordes. Those bastards are doing fine. Each of the owner's daughters drives a brand-new Mini, and one of them is pink. Poor girls, they look so damn ridiculous, Àlex thinks as he peels apples and stares out the kitchen window. This is one of his main distractions when he's cooking: slyly checking out the competition's customers. He finds them all horrendous, just like he thinks that everything they have and do at Can Bret is utterly despicable.

Now, Àlex is different. He really knows the trade. He's pure. He's honest. He never studied in any catering school but, for anyone who lives it intensely enough, life is as good as a PhD from Harvard. It's extremely demanding, but if you see it through to the end you come out on top. The rest fall by the wayside. Àlex graduated with honours from the University of Life, but he's a little rusty in Diplomacy. He'd be lucky to get five out of ten for that.

The apples are ready. He sautés them in a little butter with a sprinkling of sugar until they glow with the golden tones of the setting sun. He then puts them aside in a bowl and, as usual when he makes this dish, can't resist having a taste. They're divine, and their intense fragrance pervades the kitchen. The feeling is difficult to describe, but it takes him back to the family kitchen, when he was a little kid and the house rang with laughter.

In a medium-sized casserole he browns the chicken thighs in olive oil and then adds the chopped onion and a clove of garlic. He turns the heat down and lets it all cook slowly. Now it's time to add a generous dash of brandy and, as part of the recipe, have a tipple himself, because his communion with the chicken must be complete, body and soul. Perked up by the brandy, the chicken starts singing, at first with great gusto, then finishing with the sweet murmur of a little hymn to spring. After tipping in the brandy and draining his own glass Àlex sings too, his rendition of Lluís Llach: "Pull, pull together and we'll all be free…"

This is a strange ritual he often indulges in. Each dish has its own song and Lluís Llach is great for chicken with apples. Now he covers the chicken thighs with broth and keeps them simmering. "If we pull together, the tyrant will fall, and bad times will end in no time at all."

The phone rings. It would bloody have to be right now, when he's happy cooking and singing 'L'estaca'. Who the hell's trying to bother him this time?

Half an hour, half a bloody hour this woman's had him on the phone. It's the third time she's called this week. Yes, yes, don't worry, on Sunday he'll cook macaroni for her grandson and, yes, he knows the boy's only six and is allergic to every kind of food on the planet and, yes, of course he'll put flowers on the table, and the cava will be properly chilled, just as a good sparkling wine should be… and two or three other requirements that have completely slipped his mind because he hasn't made a note of any of them. If the customer knew that by the time he put down the phone he'd forgotten everything she said, she'd have a fit.

All this crap really winds him up. His customers, in Antic Món, are supposed to come here to eat, not to sniff flowers. Flowers, smells... What he can smell now isn't flowers, that's for sure... It's chicken! Fuckfuckfuck! The chicken's burning!

He runs into the kitchen but it's too late. The chicken's burnt to a cinder. The broth's all gone and the casserole's pitch black. Bloody woman!

He sits at the kitchen table, staring at the wreck and the dark smoke rising from it. He pours himself a glass of brandy, right to the brim, and sips at it as he eats the cooked apples one by one.

Tomorrow he'll phone Òscar and will take on that friend of his as a kitchen hand. He's got no choice. He needs help. He can't do this all by himself. Well, if she's no good he'll boot her out on day one. He's had a gutful of trying to help out losers.

When Moha was here, everything worked better. Or at least it was easier. They even had a good laugh sometimes. His Moroccan kitchen hand turned up dirt-poor and holding out not just one hand but four. That was their joke, tirelessly repeated. It was always the same, because that kid really could do four things at once, and in a split second too: wash a saucepan, keep an eye on the fillet, stir the custard and turn out a pear *tarte Tatin*. He'd developed these skills because he frequently had to manage the stove, the dishwasher and a practically full restaurant all by himself, while Àlex, slumped over the kitchen table, slept off the effects of half a bottle of gin.

Moha didn't drink, of course. He was a fervent Muslim. He observed Ramadan and prayed a lot in that strange position, half stretched out on the floor, facing Mecca with his bum pointing at Àlex's *pernils de gla*, the very best hams from the most pampered acorn-fed pedigree pigs.

Àlex couldn't handle that. When he saw him in that snail-like posture, he just had to kick his arse. It was a kind of therapy. After the well-aimed kick, his spiced loin of venison always turned out absolutely fantastic.

6

Moha laughed too, because every kick would be repaid in eight days, he said, and he worked on his revenge all week. His imagination was boundless. One day he got a friend of his to phone, pretending to be the secretary from the Moroccan embassy. She informed Àlex that a government minister would be coming to have lunch at the restaurant. All the staff would have to wear traditional Moroccan dress in order to receive him: a white djellaba, pointed-toe slippers and a red skullcap. Moha's friend went so far as to say that he needn't worry about the attire, because everything was being sent from the embassy and he'd have it all very soon. The telephone conversation ended with: "We hope you will comply with the wishes of His Excellency the Minister." The next day the finery arrived, and Àlex got all decked out in ceremonial dress to await the big shot. Moha's friend rang at the restaurant door and, when Àlex went to open it, her camera didn't stop flashing. The photos are still on all the social-media sites. Àlex nearly pissed himself laughing. He thought it was hilarious, but Moha had to pay. And he certainly paid! He had to cook dishes with sausages and other pork-based delicacies for two weeks.

Moha was worth his weight in gold. They'd made a great team.

"Boss, my dad's sick. I've got to go to Fez to look after him and take care of the goats."

"Tell me another one, you bloody liar! You've never seen a goat in your life! And your dad lives right here. I see him every morning in the bar, breaking the Ramadan fast with a glass of cheap brandy," Àlex said fondly.

"OK, you caught me out again. You're right, boss. My dad doesn't live in Fez and he hasn't got any goats and he's healthy enough to chase all the skirts in Bigues i Riells. But, yeah, I'm going to Morocco. I'm getting married and my fiancée wants to go and live there. I'm going to work in a luxury hotel they've just opened in Fez. I got through the selection process," Moha said, avoiding his boss's eyes. Basically, he felt bad about leaving Àlex in the lurch.

"Fuck the selection, Moha. In Fez they'll pay you a pittance, and here you've managed to get a decent wage and status. You're important to this restaurant."

This was the first time Àlex ever had a serious conversation with his kitchen hand.

"Yeah, but my fiancée—"

"You're already henpecked, but you're old enough to make your own mistakes. Come back when you're ready. I'll be here waiting for you. Good luck."

As a joke, Àlex gave him a bottle of Aromes de Montserrat, a nice little herbal liqueur supposedly invented by the Benedictine monks. But he also presented him with the best cookbook of his collection, Brillat-Savarin's *The Physiology of Taste*. In order to avoid any excessive sentimentality and to spare himself any emotions that might arise from the situation, he couldn't help adding: "I'm giving you this book so you'll learn to read and stop being such an ignorant bloody scarecrow."

Since Moha left, Àlex hasn't found anyone who's shown the least bit of interest. And of course it's always ended in a fight. A cook must be rigorous. OK, some idiot might overlook a bone in a gilt-head bream. That he can live with, but there's no way he'll tolerate gluey risotto.

That was what caused the row with the last lad to leave, a week ago now. With an outsize knife in his hand and jabbing the tip of the blade in the direction of the risotto, Àlex, his face red with rage, screamed at his kitchen hand.

"Give me the phone number of your first-year teacher at the cooking school. I want to ask him about the blow job you gave him. It must have

8

been bloody good if he passed you. You cretin! Have you actually looked at this shit you're trying to pass off as risotto?"

Àlex believed that the odd spat like this was part and parcel of moments of stress in the kitchen, but of course his assistants didn't see it quite the same way. He's had three in the last two months and as soon as he had them slightly trained they pissed off.

Things are even worse in the dining room. This is a strange world for Àlex. He can't imagine how anyone could possibly enjoy that kind of work. Of course, the turnover for dining-room staff is very high, as even the newspapers point out, and a restaurateur just has to get used to the fact.

This kind of news report soothes Àlex, cushions him. That's why he doesn't get too worked up when his waiters only last two weeks.

On their first day, waiters are punctual and seem keen to work, but that doesn't last long. The first time they have to stay the whole afternoon serving a food critic who wants to drain a whole bottle of whisky, they start getting huffy, and they stay huffy until one day they tell him they're leaving. They're even less enchanted when they have to escort the critic in question to his car, bearing not only his weight but also his rambling account of the latest bickering over Michelin stars.

Restaurant workers nowadays don't understand that this is a trade that requires you to listen, serve and forget about it the moment you get home. With such a high staff turnover, Àlex chooses not to remember the waiters' names. He calls them all, male and female alike, by the same name: Gabriel. That was what his first waiter was called, the one who stayed for three years. That one really was good, as good as Moha, who was with him for eight years but, in the end, decided to go back to Morocco.

Dammit, he feels so bloody lonely.

A few days ago, Àlex's friend Òscar, who has a very popular food blog, dropped in and asked him a favour. It was difficult to say no, especially because he's such a good chap, though this world is full of good chaps and Àlex couldn't give a shit about them. What he greatly appreciates about Òscar are their conversations and the classes – though Òscar calls them tutorials – where he learns how to manage a computer and about this crap they call social media.

His friend is infinitely patient when coaching him about tweets, hash tags and TripAdvisor, but Àlex quickly loses interest, saying that he's not only unfit for logic but also computer illiterate. Then he jumps up from his chair and starts cooking, his way of showing his gratitude for Òscar's help.

Òscar's thirty-five, fifteen years younger than Àlex, and adores cooking with him.

Today they're going to do sautéed vegetables with king prawns and onion cream. Snow peas, carrot and asparagus, all julienned. A splash of oil in a very hot pan in which the vegetables are shaken with a few flicks of the wrist, so they fly up and fall back again, tinged with gold outside and fresh and crunchy inside. Next, king prawns, well cleaned and, most important, the intestinal tract removed. They need just a touch of heat and then you let the sea fragrances seep into the vegetables, after which you enhance the flavours with a dash of soya sauce. Finally, the onion cream, made with juicy purple Figueres onions. The onions are browned, and then cooked in the juices of the vegetables and a touch of cream until all the flavours mingle and it is reduced to a satiny texture. It then has to be well puréed to become a light, aromatic sauce.

They eat the sautéed vegetables and Àlex quaffs almost a whole bottle of Terra Alta wine. Òscar tells him how he makes Parmentier potatoes. He thinks they'd go very well with the vegetables.

"This Parmentier nonsense might please a few farm animals," Àlex snaps. "It might make great pig slop, but people with any decent level of gastronomic culture would never stoop so low as to eat potatoes. Potatoes are for barbarians, like those pigs, that rabble over there in Can Bret."

Àlex spurns all food coming from the Americas. It's not that he's exclusively into local medieval cuisine, because he uses products from other cultures and cutting-edge techniques. He believes that Catalan cuisine was rich enough in ingredients before Columbus came along, so he's not going to serve imported food pillaged from a continent subjugated by firearms and rape and thus steeped in blood. Furthermore, in his stringent view, these items have no culinary merit. He doesn't want to know about them.

This stubborn determination has earned him considerable prestige among connoisseurs because of the problems it entails. It has also lost him a large number of customers. After all, Antic Món is in Bigues i Riells, a nondescript town of second homes, and these families don't understand why he can't do fried potatoes to go with little Johnny's veal cutlets, even if he offers caramelized turnip instead.

What use are Àlex's prizes if he has no customers?

The previous night, after having to wait on the single table of a pair of architects, he locked himself in his cubbyhole of an office and started to do the sums: income, overheads, suppliers, wages, social security and all the rest. He can no longer afford to pay an accountant, so he has to do the books himself. Truth to tell, he hasn't got a clue. To begin with, he couldn't give a damn about management and, to cap it all, there's not a drop left in the gin bottle. By two in the morning a bass drum is pounding in his head. His mum always said "Don't mix", but he's gone and mixed sums and gin, a lethal combination. His head is foggy, but the conclusion is crystal clear: his clientele is

11

dwindling fast and the Antic Món's coffers are getting emptier and emptier by the day.

He's had the restaurant for ten years. Business used to be quite good, but he's having a lean time of it now. He's too outspoken, he knows, and inflexible and unapproachable too but... but isn't this about cooking? Why should he be friendly? What does sociability have to do with good food? People come to the restaurant to eat, not to have someone running after them, hovering over them and licking their arses. The food critics, yes, they know how to value his work. They love his kind of cooking and are always impressed by his daring, innovative ideas. In fact, he's been awarded numerous prizes and is always being asked to speak at food congresses. Hmm, well, he used to be, perhaps. It's quite a while since they've phoned him. Thanks to the prizes and other forms of recognition he's managed to attract customers from far away, gourmets who would never have set foot in Bigues i Riells otherwise. They've come expressly to taste his dishes and they've left very well satisfied.

People love his food, dammit! But this type of customer, the epicure, tends not to return. Normally they only come once, because they like flitting round all kinds of restaurants and are loath to go back to one they've already tried. The second-home owners in the town are more faithful, but they don't feel comfortable in Antic Món. Àlex is all but alone, without clients and without staff.

Òscar asked him a favour, namely to take on a friend of his. This is one of these strange acquaintances that bloggers make, a borderless friendship with someone he met in the online community, as he puts it. The girl is called Annette, she's from Quebec and Òscar met her on Facebook, Àlex seems to recall, or one of those social networks, the usefulness of which escapes him. And what the fuck is a virtual relationship anyway? When Òscar raised the matter, Àlex tried to get him to understand that he couldn't afford to pay a professional, but Òscar assured him that Annette wasn't motivated by money. She needed to work, that was true, and she wanted to settle in Catalonia. She'd decided to learn the language and embrace the culture. That was her goal.

"Annette's a foodie," Òscar innocently remarked.

"Listen, lad, you come up with a new word every day and I can't stand it. I haven't got a clue what you're talking about and, frankly, I couldn't give a shit. I don't want to know about computers! I have no idea what a foodie is and I don't give a damn. As for your friend, I only want to know if she's willing to work, if she's not in a hurry to be paid, where she's going to sleep and if she's a proper woman with tits and all."

"Must you always be so crass? She's a friend of mine and, even if I haven't seen her in person, I can tell you she's a proper woman. Yes, she does want to work, and yes, she'll have to be paid something. But money isn't her priority, as I told you."

"OK, but what's this 'foodie' bullshit about?"

"A foodie is someone who likes anything to do with food – keen on cooking, eating in restaurants, discovering gourmet boutiques, exploring markets, tasting different products, gastronomic tourism, reading recipe books, and so on and so forth. Basically, anything to do with food. Hence the word 'foodie'. Well, Annette's a foodie, so she reads my blog and we chat from time to time. She likes eating and says she's a great cook too. She's done lots of courses on food from all round the world, so she's mad about discovering new spices, different products and special dishes. That's why I thought of you. You're the most special among the special."

Àlex wasn't sure about all this but couldn't think of a riposte. Nothing occurred to him, no withering remark, no smart-arse comment. The words just didn't come, and, to cover up, or to change the subject, or because he was hungry, he downed two bits of carrot and a king prawn.

13

"Before you fill your mouth with claptrap, fill it with tasty morsels," he reminded himself.

Recalling the encounter, Àlex thinks he wouldn't lose anything by contracting this woman, especially right now when he has no one to help out in the restaurant. That can't go on.

While he himself washes the dishes from a lunchtime table of five, the only people who've turned up the entire Saturday, a strange fragrance sneaks through a crack in one of the windows. Perfumed portents, airs wafting in to turn his life upside down.

2

SOUR

*The discovery of a new dish does more for
human happiness than the discovery of a star.*
JEAN ANTHELME BRILLAT-SAVARIN

Àlex is jumpy. The truth, the pure truth of the matter, is that he's never had a female kitchen hand. Something tells him it's not going to be easy.

The two of them are sitting facing one another at a table in the restaurant.

She's different, this woman – or should he say girl? She must be about thirty-five, and she's got long red hair. Her curls are eye-catching, as are all those freckles on her face. There'll be hairs in the soup for sure... and who's going to fish them out? Maybe she should get it cut... And he's not at all sure about this citrusy fragrance of hers. It's going to spoil the aroma of his dishes.

Yes, well, she's got lovely round tits.

"I'll get to the point. I've got some kid roasting in the oven and I've got to keep an eye on it. I'll sum it up in a few words. In this restaurant, cooking is king. That's the essential thing. I'm not in-terested in fancy stuff and this frivolous froth they're churning out all round the country. Here, the food is sound. You cook things as slow or as fast as needed, so that every dish is pure perfection. It's hard, rigorous work. Everything you make has to be impeccably brought off, with an exquisite presentation. It must be served at the

15

table without delay. If you agree to these conditions, you can get to work right now."

"I sorry, Senyor Àlex. Mon Catalan très petit. I only study half-year in Quebec. C'est pareil à French, little bit, but I mix with English. No understand conditions."

This is too bloody much, Àlex thinks indignantly. This damn woman can't understand Catalan and doesn't speak Spanish either. This really complicates things, but cool it, cool it, he tells himself. It's no big deal either. Moha hardly knew any Catalan when he started to work in Antic Món, but after Àlex yelled at him enough he soon caught on.

"OK, I'll speak slowly and say it in just a few words. There's one condition: hard work. You get it?" The veins in his neck are bulging.

He hasn't realized that he's switched from the familiar *tu* to the formal *vostè*, but it's a sure sign that he's enraged. He only uses *vostè* when things get out of hand. It expresses a mixture of indignation and uneasiness.

"I no fraid work hard. I very worker. Today premier day, Senyor Àlex?"

"Yes, yes, right now. Have you got your chef wear? I'll take you to the changing room and show you the restaurant."

"I bring suitcase ici. Òscar say I sleep ici. I no have house."

That's true. Òscar had asked him if he could let Annette have a room, as she had nowhere to stay and no money to rent somewhere. Àlex had forgotten this, because when Òscar was telling him his brain was swirling in the aromatic mists of the sensational Terra Alta wine. He was also sleepy by then so he'd said yes. In fact, the restaurant is in a big old house and there's a sort of spare room on the second floor. It's not exactly luxurious, but it's well ventilated and even has a small bathroom with a shower. It'll do for the two weeks that this woman will last in his kitchen.

"Right. Òscar told me. First of all, I'll show you your room. It's very simple, but I'm sure you'll be able to give it a personal touch. Good cooks like to live in pleasant surroundings, and I'm told you're a very good cook."

There is a challenge lurking in the final comment. While they were talking at the table, Àlex looked at Annette's hands, which betrayed the truth: this woman has never cooked. She might have cooked at home, but she's no professional. A chef can easily spot hands which have cooked, and Annette's show no signs of war with the stove, or scars of old burns inflicted by the oven, no souvenirs of deep cuts or of fingers martyred by icy water, no flesh made rubbery by handling fatty meat and, most important, he doesn't see the light movements of a chef's hands.

"I like a lot cook. I no know Catalan cook. I want learn," Annette replies, avoiding his gaze.

Àlex sees it all too clearly. She hasn't got a clue about professional cooking. What's more, she doesn't speak Catalan. He's never worked with a woman and, to make matters worse, this one's going to be hanging round the restaurant all day long. This whole bloody thing is a nightmare – or, still more alarming, it's going to end up as a nightmare! Well, there's no way around it: he has no choice. He has no help in the kitchen, no waiter, no dishwasher and, in fact, no customers. Maybe this inscrutable, freckled redhead Annette has brought a bit of happiness tucked away in her pocket, an idea or two in her suitcase, a kiss of life for the cemetery that Antic Món has now become.

They go upstairs to the bedrooms, Annette leading and Àlex, who has the good manners to offer to carry her case, behind her. What the hell has this woman got in there, a male mannequin? No, a male mannequin is light, and this suitcase weighs more than a Girona bull! He's about to come out with one of his more oafish remarks, but bites his tongue, surprising himself. What's going on? Has he gone soft all of a sudden?

Why is he being nice to Annette? He addresses her with the polite *vostè*, carries her bag which weighs a ton and refrains from cussing. Shit, this is no good. This woman will have to get used to him and not the other way round. But this bum, so round, soft and generous, the bum of a proper woman, of a woman who's slept in feather beds and sleeping bags in tents, who's familiar with other cultures… this bum climbing the stairs, reminding him somehow of busy beaters whipping up egg white, this bum right before his eyes, so close it's almost touching his eyelashes and eyebrows, lighting up desire, this bloody bum that's making him feel so damn flustered.

Annette is shocked into silence when she sees the grotty room. Although, owing to her present circumstances, she'd settle for living in a wardrobe, this hole-with-a-window in which she'll have to live is hardly reassuring. It needs a thorough clean and a coat of paint. For the time being, she'll hang up the photos she's brought from home. She's also packed half a dozen of her favourite books, which will help to transform this tiny, gloomy dump into a sanctuary for memories of her beloved Quebec.

"Remember, you're here to cook, and we open the dining room in two hours. I'll wait for you in the kitchen. I've got to go and check the kid in the oven." Àlex's hospitality comes to an abrupt end.

Annette needs a moment to get her emotions under control and decides to open up her suitcase and take out a couple of things. It's a way of giving herself time to digest Àlex's behaviour. After the few blunt words they've exchanged, it's clear that this relationship's not going to be easy. Àlex isn't willing to make it easy but, on the contrary, wants to set off the spark that will ignite the conflagration, after which he can watch her leave. Out the door. Lugging her heavy suitcase.

What Àlex doesn't quite understand is that Annette literally has nowhere to go, which is a powerful reason for her to put in some time decorating the unwelcoming room to make it her own, as a kind of declaration of intent. Like the Canadian maple, she wants to put down deep strong roots in Antic Món. Photos and books come out of her suitcase, and also a Mayan rain stick, an album of pressed flowers, a box full of all kinds of spices, a Quechuan mate gourd and a peanut necklace. The most highly prized item of all is placed on the rough-hewn table: the computer with which she can connect up with her friends all round the globe, follow the most interesting food blogs and chat on Facebook. The computer is her window onto the world, and the anonymity afforded by the screen is her way of amusing herself. Hiding behind keyboards and pixels, she is Madame Escargot. She'd love to connect right now, but she has to go down to the kitchen.

The kid's been slowly browning in the oven for the past hour and a half. The most important part is the marinating process, with garlic, onion and mustard, which took all last night. Then it is condemned to solitary confinement in the oven, where all the aromas blend together. Àlex watches over it adoringly. Seeing how the colour keeps changing reconciles him with the world. The kid perfectly expresses his idea of the way things should work. There are certain determining factors: kid, oven, time. And an evident result: beautifully browned kid. If everything was so wonderfully reasonable, so empirically simple and logical, life would be comprehensible and he'd learn to love it. But things don't work like that. Even if he invests the necessary factors, his milieu is hostile and consequences are unpredictable.

Àlex is so absorbed by the kid that he doesn't hear Annette silently entering into the kitchen.

Àlex jumps. "Shit a brick! You scared the wits out of me," he yells.

"Sorry, Senyor Àlex."

"And don't bloody call me senyor. Just call me Àlex," he grumbles.

19

Then he bursts out laughing. What the fuck is she wearing? What a sight she looks! What the hell does she think she's doing dressed like that?

Annette's wearing her cooking apron, the one she wears at home. It's patchwork with frills. She looks like a country singer disguised as one of the Tatin sisters. He's never seen a woman in such a ridiculous get-up.

"Er, excuse me, this thing you're wearing... is it some kind of traditional dress in your country? Hang on a minute, I'm going to get my shepherd's pouch, clogs, sash and red cap and we'll dance the *sardana* while you sing country. This is a joke, right? You don't really think you're going to cook like that, do you? For Christ's sake, this is a high-class kitchen!"

Annette hasn't understood much of the tirade, but Àlex's face says it all. It seems he doesn't like the apron she's brought from home. He throws a white chef's apron at her saying, "Go back to your room, take off that gaudy rag and come back in jeans and a clean T-shirt if you've got nothing better. I'll lend you my chef's gear, and as soon as you can you'll have to buy your own."

"Sorry, Senyor Àlex, clothes no important. Important is work. I want work. I no take out apron." She is very dignified.

Now she's done it. This is intolerable! Àlex is incensed. "Listen, who do you think you bloody are? I'm the boss in this kitchen! You get it? You will dress, cook and eat as I tell you. Go back to your room and get changed immediately."

"No," she replies firmly. "Cook, yes, je suis agree. Eat, aussi. Dress what like me."

Luckily the phone rings and saves the day. Àlex looks daggers at Annette and leaves the kitchen to put a stop to the infernal, nerve-jangling racket. This woman's really pushing her luck. When he's answered the phone he'll give her a good earful, tell her a few home truths. There's nothing to stop him kicking her out right now. But something does stop him. He won't stand for Annette's defiance, but then again he really likes the grit she's shown with her answer. There's no explanation for it, it's not rational, but the woman's got something that makes him feel small, like a little pea next to a watermelon. It's not the tits or the bum, no, not that. It's the sweet smile, the eyes, blue, sincere, but also slightly disturbing, as if they're hiding something. A mystery.

He hangs up and goes back to the kitchen. He hears a voice singing "So long, it was so long ago. But I've still got the blues for you." A lovely voice, singing to the kid.

Delighted and bemused, Àlex watches her from the doorway, knowing she can't see him. He does that too. He also sings to the kid. Discovering that he's not the only lunatic who sings to food is comforting, and so too is knowing that he's got the other lunatic from the opposite side of the planet right here next to him.

"Kid have soul of blues," Annette explains when she realizes that Àlex is watching her.

"More like Aragonese jota, I'd say." His snigger punctures the little bubble of tenderness that has formed in the kitchen. "Come on, woman, that's enough nonsense. We've got to open up right now and we're really behind today. Do you know how to make cream-of-asparagus soup? Here's a bunch. I don't use cream. I make it with vegetable broth and cream cheese. It's possible we won't have many customers for lunch, but tonight we've got the Antic Món Gourmet Club. Some important people are coming. Have a look at the menu. It's there, printed out on the table."

They've only had one customer for lunch, a travelling salesman who's turned up at Antic Món because Can Bret is full up and he doesn't have time to wait for a table. Without even looking at the menu, he's asked for a good salad with tomato and red pepper, steak with potatoes and vanilla ice cream.

Àlex has offered neither response nor explanation, but has simply thrown the menu at him saying he hasn't got anything the man's asked for: no tomato, no peppers, no potato and no vanilla ice cream. He must choose from the dishes that he, the chef, cooks for the Antic Món menu.

The salesman, hungrier than when he came in, runs off as if pursued by a thousand demons after paying a hefty sum for eggs scrambled with black chanterelles, turbot with pickled radishes and honey-and-cardamom *semifreddo*. The poor chap hasn't understood a word on the menu. He'll never set foot in Antic Món again. A sandwich by the roadside is much better, the gentleman thinks.

"We have to stay back to cook this afternoon. The Gourmet Club people are finicky and we've got to come up with something to surprise them. They've been coming once a month for the past five years."

"A lot persons?" Annette asks, feigning interest.

"At first there were plenty of people, up to twenty at times. Not so many recently. Everyone gets tired of everything, and the woman in charge, the one who invented the club, Pilar, is always busy, so she doesn't send out the information about their meetings until the last minute. Ten would be the maximum now, even on a good day. I'd like to take over the publicity side, since it's in my interests more than anyone's that they continue to like my cooking, but the fact is I'm hopeless when it comes to emails... Come on. That's enough chitchat. We've got to get the tuna marinating and make the peach mousse."

The gourmet dinner is spectacular. They've made six dishes, all of them technically complex, with harmonious flavours and intense aromas. The crowning achievement is a kind of tartare made from tuna which has previously been marinated with lime juice, ginger and pink pepper. It's a shame that only three people turned up for the gathering and one of them, who wasn't feeling well, asked for boiled rice.

"No much gastronomique persons in dinner," Annette observes, trying to suppress a yawn. She doesn't want Àlex to see that she's so tired she can hardly keep her eyes open, and that she's not terribly interested in the state of health of the Gourmet Club.

"No, not many. Well, three three-toed tree toads, to be precise."

"Toads? Where toads?"

"Forget it. It's a tongue twister. I mean only three people have come, but the thing is, the economic crisis in this country is doing a lot of damage and people aren't really in a festive mood."

"Many toads this night they go Can Bret," Annette replies.

Ouch! She couldn't be more hurtful. But it's true. They've had a lot of custom at Can Bret tonight, so the crisis is a shabby excuse that no one's going to buy. He doesn't know how to deal with this situation. He's cut back in every area of the restaurant's costs and he cooks well, bloody hell, he cooks extremely well, and everyone, especially the food buffs, tell him so. He's not very nice to people, that's true, and never has been. It's precisely one of the reasons why he became a chef, so he could work in intimate communion with the stove without needing to have much truck with people. It's his food that should speak for him, something everyone can understand. Àlex has the soul of an artist, but believes it would be too pedantic even to think about what that means. As far as he's concerned, it's the audience that makes the artist, the people who know how to value and consume the work. Only idiots go round saying they're "artists". He's foul-tempered, bitter, a man who's lost his bearings – plus a few more defects – but nobody can say he's an idiot.

However, even if he'd like everyone to understand his work, he has to accept the evidence that he's an artist for niche tastes, judging by the few people who come to eat at Antic Món. A restaurant can't keep going on niche tastes and it's not just a question of economic sustainability. You have to work with fresh food and, if you can't use it, everything, the cooking, the staff and the whole atmosphere, starts smelling stale. An empty restaurant stinks of decay.

Frank always says, "A good restaurant is a full restaurant."

Frank Gabo is the fish supplier. Well, he's the delivery man. He brings the freshest fish, the most succulent turbots, the finest prawns, the loveliest, most transparent squid… which Àlex is going to cook right now, even though it's almost midnight. He's been cooking all day long, without a break, and he's hardly had time to sit down, either for lunch or dinner. He's exhausted, but those squid are going to soothe away all his despair and dark thoughts. Actually, he doesn't need calamari stew, so who's going to eat it? Moreover, these squid are too delicate to be stewed. They're ideal for grilling or tossing in the pan with a few vegetables. That's what he had in mind when he chose the daintiest ones. But his spirit's begging for a stew. He needs a couple of hours to think, get his thoughts in order, find a way out of this situation, work out whom he's let into his space in the form of this woman, confront the present and dream up a rosier future. So tonight he's going to make stewed calamari.

At night, you take your time cooking, with contemplative pauses, a long way from the trials of the day, with no traffic noises coming in from the road, no telephone, no demands, just the colours of the night and the hushed darkness of its whispered words. Only his own breathing will caress the slow caramelizing of onions.

"Just a rover, just a rover," sings Lluís Llach as he cleans the calamari.

He browns them in a large casserole and puts them aside on a plate. He peels and chops the onions, more than he needs. He likes chopping onions. At first they make him cry. He needs tears. They are tears that mix sorrow and onion. They are well-justified tears that can fall without restraint, without his feeling foolish because they're cleaning out his soul.

24

The pity of it is that tears dry up very quickly. "If you move onward in life, further than I can go..."

He lets the onions cook as he chops three cloves of garlic – "I won't stop being the best rover of all, or the greatest athlete strong and tall" – adds marjoram, bay and a sprig of thyme. Slow, easy does it, and now, yes – "the depth of the rivers that will not wet my feet" – a generous dash of white wine.

He has to wait till the onion absorbs the wine. Now it's time to have a ceremonial glass, sipping carefully to savour the suggestive acid notes of the simple Xarel·lo, shared by a casserole and a rough-mannered chef. He returns the calamari to the casserole and covers them with fish broth – "the immensity of a sky I shall never fly".

A few almonds, a bit of fried bread and a touch of parsley. This is the great moment, furiously grinding these ingredients in the mortar to make the *picada* for thickening the stew – "I'm jealous but not sad at all the luck you've had" – mashing the nuts, forcing them into a paste with the bread and parsley. The *picada* will be the imperceptible soul of the stew, dissolved in its juices. He observes its binding power, turning the liquid into a gloriously consistent sauce, which then prods at his most damaged memories. A tiny touch of salt – yes, always light on salt, because the calamari have to play the leading role in bearing the smell of ocean waves to his taste buds.

Cooking the calamari has been balm to his muscles and mind. If only everything was so sure, so clear, so predictable. Fine raw material gives excellent results. But life stubbornly refuses to stick to a logical script. He doesn't know how he's going to face the future, and the present is telling the truth, overwhelming him with evidence that Antic Món is an old, decrepit dump, despite its youth.

Annette went up to her room a while ago, immediately after their only clients that night, the three Gourmet Club diners, left. She must be asleep, Àlex imagines. However, walking past her door he sees light filtering through the crack. Maybe she likes sleeping with the light on. He'll have to tell her to watch her electricity consumption. He can't manage extra expenses and, anyway, people should sleep with the light turned off.

Annette is tired, but also jet-lagged, so she can't sleep. It's hard adapting to this new time zone. She tries to entice drowsiness sitting at her computer, reading her friends' latest blog posts, having a look to see what's happening on Twitter and checking out her five thousand Facebook friends.

She uses the social network to express her feelings in writing. This has been her first day's work at Antic Món. Àlex is a cantankerous man who hardly speaks to her and won't let her cook much. Her work in the kitchen has been peeling vegetables, stirring the odd casserole and doing a heap of washing-up. It's taken her less than a day to catch on that her boss refuses to recognize that the restaurant's not working. He cooks a dish as if he's expecting fifty people to eat it. He receives his raw materials with great ceremony, cleans them impeccably, and quickly and rigorously transforms them, fretting about opening hours even though the pages of the reservation book are impeccably white, immaculate, unsullied by the scrawling of any name or table number.

Annette is now wide awake. Her tiredness has evaporated and her brain has lit up as if with a revelation. Most of her Facebook friends and Twitter followers are foodies, like her, lovers of all kinds of cuisine. They come from all over the world, but lots of them are Catalan. She'll do a web page called Friends of Antic Món and liven it up with offers and suggestions. In fact, from what she's seen today, Àlex doesn't employ any waiters, so she had to serve all the dishes. If she offers a free tot of liqueur, he won't know. He's only got eyes, ears and nose for the food and doesn't care about anything else, as expressed by the distressingly thick layer of dust mounting up on the bottle shelf, which she'd set about cleaning. That dining room is so pathetic.

But how can she create a Facebook page in Catalan if she hasn't got the faintest idea of the language? She has a look to see who's on Chat. Yes, Òscar's there. She tells him about her brainwave.

"You're crazy, Annette. He'll never forgive you. And if you don't ask him first, you might as well pack your bags now. You've got to understand that you've only just landed in Antic Món and you're already want to make waves on the social networks. Aren't you rushing things a bit?"

"Il n'y a pas clients. No customers, he must to close restaurant. If you no help I do sans aide."

"You're right. Not many people go there. The Bigues i Riells people think he's rude and unfriendly, a weirdo. The ones with weekend houses won't go near the place. He refuses to make potato chips for the kids, let alone throw a bell pepper, an aubergine and an onion on the grill to make a nice *escalivada* for the adults. His food's too complicated for families."

"What's weirdo? Vegetarian? Why he no make chips? C'est vrai, no potatoes in kitchen."

"No, a weirdo is a strange man. You have to hurry up and learn Catalan, Annette. Hasn't Àlex told you yet that he won't serve any food that comes from America? It's forbidden in his kitchen. He says it's barbarian food, for people with no culinary culture. It's precisely this exquisiteness that makes the critics – and me too – so interested in his cooking."

"Exquisiteness?…"

"Exquisiteness… It's hard to explain. Well, it's something delicate and difficult to achieve. OK, let's leave it. Àlex is an oddity, as I warned you. He's got hardly any friends and he's never even told me if he has a family, but he's always treated me very well."

"You help me ou non, with page?"

27

"Don't worry, I'll help. But Àlex will kill us, the two of us. So what do you want to say?"

Luckily, Òscar decides to help. After some hesitation about the text and the name of the page, they finally launch a page on Facebook.

Antic Món. Unusual restaurant at Bigues i Riells. Special, succulent and sybaritic food. Closed Mondays. Become a Friend of Antic Món. We invite new customers to a taste of Caol Ila single malt.

Annette has seen the Caol Ila on the malt whisky shelf. She's mad about it. It's an exceptional, legend-laden whisky. Her foodie friends will read between the lines and see that this is a truly special restaurant, not like the ones that, without a single gourmet's taste bud, invite you to a cheap limoncello. She has to get the message across that this is a highly select, very discerning restaurant which, if it invites you to something, offers only the very best. Tomorrow she'll post photos of the dishes, write down some of Àlex's recipes and suggest a virtual flavours game in which contestants have to guess the secret ingredient in each of Àlex's recipes. Well yes, maybe she's taking things a bit too fast in devising this offer. As usual, it's a case of getting down to business straight away. She's gutsy, dynamic and impetuous. And very generous. She can't resist helping if she thinks she can. More than anything else she wants people to know that a great chef is waiting to cook for them in a restaurant in Bigues i Riells.

In bed, covered up to her nose with the childhood quilt she's somehow managed to cram into her suitcase, a niggling question keeps her awake. Why won't Àlex use food from the New World. Why?

3

SALTY

"Good morning. How're we doing, family?" shouts Frank Gabo as he brings the fish into Antic Món. Sardines today.

He's a good young fellow and carefree by nature. His only education is what life has dished out to him. His Mozambican parents were in the first group of African immigrants who came to the Maresme region a couple of decades ago. His Catalan is impeccable. He doesn't even get the weak pronouns wrong. He laughs with gusto, mouth open, and his incredibly white teeth seem to spark flashes off the omnipresent, gleaming stainless steel of the kitchen.

"Good morning," Annette answers.

Àlex doesn't bother to greet him. He's too busy rolling out fresh pasta.

"Hey boss, got a new girl in the office then?"

"Mind your own business, Frank. What have you got for me today? Sardines? Local, I hope. Let's check the eyes. I don't trust you as far as I could throw you. You're too fishy."

Àlex loves scrapping with Frank. They get on well, though no one would guess it judging from the barbs flying back and forth. They're just playing, no harm intended.

"Àlex, I need to talk with you… and, er, I'd prefer not to do so in front of this girl here."

"Don't worry, Frank. She's a foreigner and her Catalan's worse than an Eskimo's. Say whatever you like but don't try to fool me with those sardines, telling me they're from the Gulf of Roses when I can see they've been dredged out of the Llobregat Delta, right next to some damn factory."

"Listen, friend, I'm not here to talk about sardines. It's a problem with the boss. He says we're not bringing you any more fish because you've got unpaid bills mounting up from six months ago. He can't keep supplying you if you don't pay, Àlex. Unless you pay at least a part. I'm really sorry. You know I—"

"I hope your boss chokes on an umbrine bone, you fucking lackey!" Àlex yells. "Damn it, I've been wanting to change my supplier for a while now. Your fish stinks. It's the worst in the whole region. If you can't appreciate the fact that you're working with the best bloody cook in this godforsaken country, you can bugger off."

Àlex, red-faced, waves a knife around as he's shouting.

Annette is a horrified witness to all this. She stares at the sharp knife without knowing what to do. Maybe a murder's about to happen, right here. Should she call the police?

In less than a minute her boss goes from the most histrionic raving to total composure, his face fading from puce to waxy pallor as the violent storm subsides into the balmiest calm. He puts the knife back on the table and keeps rolling out pasta as if nothing has happened.

Frank leaves, feeling distressed. Having to tell Àlex that he can't deliver there any more is like stabbing him in the heart. Things aren't going well at Antic Món. Everyone in the town's talking about it. The restaurant's had its time of glory and now it's going to rack and ruin. Only a few of his friends have been eating there and even they've stopped coming.

Everyone knows that, with the first sign of any problem, friends desert like rats from a sinking ship.

No one comes for lunch that day either, but everything is ready to serve in the kitchen. Àlex can never have enough of cooking. The burners are always lit and he's never still. The fridges are bursting with cooked dishes, stews, side dishes, sauces and basic preparations.

Although Annette's only been there a few days, she's seen him emptying the rubbish bin full of food that was going off, not just once but plenty of times. Food that isn't in the least bit dodgy also goes into the bin, including the cream-of-asparagus soup she so carefully made. Obviously Àlex didn't like the way she made it. He didn't lift a finger to help her and neither did he tell her how she was supposed to prepare it, or offer any comment once it was made, but he made sure she saw him throwing it out, which he did with all the pomposity of some old ham doing *commedia dell'arte*.

Annette was hurt, but understood very clearly that he was making a statement about their relative roles in this show. It was also a ploy on Àlex's part to see how much she could take of his offensive behaviour. A kind of exam. Annette pretends she hasn't noticed, so she keeps chopping garlic, because her goal is to pass this test with flying colours. She knows she's not going to win in this duel, but there's no way she's going to be a loser either. The war has only just begun.

The first week has been gruelling, what with jet lag, frayed nerves, settling in, putting up with Àlex's tantrums and sleeping very little. She's spending her nights at the computer trying to find ways of resuscitating Antic Món. She's posted comments about the restaurant on all the gourmet guide sites, even outside the country, but the pages of the reservation book remain stubbornly unmarked, the purest pristine snowy white. She can count on her fingers the total number of lunch and dinner customers.

31

She doesn't know what else to do. The Friends of Antic Món Facebook page is starting to fill up with content. With Òscar's help, she's posted recipes – with a few invented touches, to tell the truth – and there are photos of the restaurant too. There is some interest in the virtual flavours competition in which contestants have to guess the secret ingredients of a recipe, but no one's come to try the fabulous offerings of the chef at Antic Món. People say it's a great game but nobody wants to play.

In any case, she thinks it might be better that nobody's come in the last few days, because the dishes are emanating doom and gloom. The first one to stop supplying raw materials was Frank Gabo, but now deliveries of meat and eggs have stopped too. Àlex has been going to the supermarket in town, but the quality of its products is very inferior. He's humiliated by being seen there and can't stand "mingling" with the people of Bigues i Riells. He's putting up a front, trying to mask his dour and lugubrious mood, but his cooking gives him away in excessively strong tastes, radical flavours, over-spicing and too much salt.

"Take that *gratapaller* to Table Two!" How was she supposed to know he meant chicken?

If Àlex needs to specify the impeccable pasture-raised pedigree of the roast fowl, there is no need to give the number of the table at which it is to be served, since it is the only one that is occupied. Decked out in her frilly patchwork apron, Annette takes the chicken to Carol.

At present she's a kitchen hand doubling as a waitress. They have to save every last cent. Although she'd prefer to work only in the kitchen, she's happy enough waitressing, as it's a way of getting to know the customers and check out how they're enjoying the meal.

"Madame, Table Two, Carol, is good client?"

"Is she ever! She's a top food critic. She's very influential in this country. She's a friend of mine. She comes here a lot and often gives Antic Món a good write-up in the media. Well, it's been a while since she's done

32

that, because there are lots of new restaurants she has to review," Àlex tells the empty kitchen as Annette's back in the dining room serving Table Two and hasn't heard him.

When she comes back to the kitchen, she says, "Àlex, Carol she wants speak with you."

"Tell her I can't now. I've got to keep an eye on these morels. This is a highly delicate moment."

"Carol she wants speak with you," Annette insists.

Cursing and swearing, Àlex marches out of the kitchen to see what's going on. When Carol's had a glass or two – and today she's worked her way through a Les Terrasses red, 2001 – she gets garrulous. And she would bloody want to talk right now. She should know that morels are terribly temperamental, and if you take your eye off them for a second, they turn into a mess, with the taste and consistency of cork.

Carol's features faithfully express her personality. They sum up a long-ish life, lots of experience and a permanent itch to learn. Her aquiline nose has sniffed out the most complex bouquets of all the wines she's tasted over the years and her wide, wrinkle-free forehead suggests a frank, sincere mind. She has a long, luxuriant mane of black hair, scattered with a few grey ones, each one a little cache of memories representing some moment or other of her fifty-three years, whether it's one of happiness or disillusionment, a battle won or an instructive failure.

Her clothes also talk. Carol doesn't dress. She dresses up, drawing attention to her chameleonic nature. She's someone who can easily split into a host of characters, revelling in every role she plays.

"Àlex, I love you heaps, and you've always been my favourite chef, but this free-range hen or haystack-scratcher or whatever you want to call it is inedible. It tastes like a factory worker's idea of salt cod."

Carol doesn't like saying this. She's implacable and extremely scathing as a critic, and certainly doesn't mince her words, but today she feels sorry for Àlex and saddened by the run-down state of Antic Món and all its unoccupied tables. She's the only client, alone in the whole restaurant.

Standing there in his apron, Àlex grabs a bit of his well-bred chicken and puts it in his mouth. He drains the gourmet's glass of red to wash it down, his blue eyes roving around the emptiness of the restaurant, the chicken and Carol.

Without a word, he pulls off his apron and throws it on a table. The Arcimboldo reproduction trembles on the wall and almost falls off as Àlex storms out of Antic Món, slamming the door behind him.

Annette, transfixed, watches the scene from the kitchen doorway, with the casserole of morels in her hands. She's so shocked that she almost drops it. Her nerves are stretched to breaking point. What kind of restaurant has she landed in?

Gourmet writer and kitchen hand stare at each other, both completely dumbfounded.

Just then somebody rings at the door… Whatever next? If someone stabbed her now she wouldn't shed a single drop of blood. It's frozen in her veins. At the door she finds three Internet foodies who are keen to try out the virtual-flavours game Antic Món has announced on its web page. Oh my God!

Annette pulls herself together and escorts the clients to the best table, the one in the corner. In a flash of lucidity she announces that tonight they're doing a tasting menu.

"Today, surprise!"

Luckily Carol has finished her dinner – or non-dinner, depending on how you look at it. It seems she doesn't want dessert and is contentedly sipping at a double shot of Lepanto. She's old-fashioned in this. She likes her brandy.

"Brilliant idea," a girl, the youngest of the three customers, gushes. "Today we're going to try the very best creations of Àlex Graupera! We

34

can't wait to meet him and especially to work out the hidden flavours. We might even win the competition!"

Annette is about to faint. She's tough and courageous, but the problem is she doesn't know where to start. Terrified, she runs into the kitchen, opens up the fridges to see if salvation resides therein, some dish she'll only have to warm up... Her brain is boiling. She looks for solution number one, something she can serve them immediately so she'll have time to think about what to do next.

Ah, the morels!

Yes, the first course will be morels à la crème. She tastes them, and they aren't bad. She doesn't know if Àlex meant to cook them like this, or whether they're the whole dish or a side dish. Not a clue. She puts them on three aperitif plates and, full of dignity, goes out to serve them. Whoops, she hasn't given these people bread or water or wine yet... What a mess! But at least they can start eating something. She quickly supplies the bread, water and a bottle of Trepat Foraster, a lovely red *denominación de origen* from the Conca de Barberà.

"Today he marry menu with wine," she murmurs.

The clients don't understand anything, least of all Annette, but they're happy to go along with it and open to whatever surprises the night might bring.

"I think the waitress said that it's a tasting menu with specially chosen wines," the boy in the group says.

Annette wants to get back into the kitchen to invent some dish, to let the food inspire her, to give the best she's got, or simply cook something edible dressed up as haute cuisine.

She's on the point of bursting into tears.

All that effort to pull in customers, all those hours at the computer, all the accumulated stress is now hitting her. She was so thrilled at the idea that someone might respond to her promotions on Facebook, but they would have to come today, of all days. Her hands won't obey her. Her brain's at a standstill. She's done for.

Then a divine apparition, in the form of Carol with Àlex's apron in her hands, descends on the kitchen.

"I'm going to give you a hand, my girl, if you'll let me. If you have to cook and serve a tasting menu to the only customers who've set foot in here all week, you'll need a bit of moral support at the very least. I don't know much about cooking, but I've eaten plenty of things in my day, and between the two of us we'll come up with something decent."

"Thank you, Carol." Annette is weeping.

They cook, side by side, for three hours. It wouldn't be easy to reproduce what they served up to the clients. They've dreamt up everything on the spot. They've switched sauces. A shellfish base has been used to make a sauce for the roast kid, and the saffron sauce has landed on the chocolate delights for dessert. The stewed squid has been a star dish.

The plates have come back empty, except for the last one, which the foodies have hardly tasted: hot raspberry soup with green-pepper ice cream. They've apologized, saying they can't eat any more, but when Carol tastes the "creation", she nearly throws up. It's horrible. Now Annette remembers that the green-pepper ice cream has almost no sugar in it. It was supposed to go with baked turbot, and they've used it for a dessert. What idiots!

Just before Annette goes to see if the clients want coffee, Carol opens up a couple of nice cold beers and offers her one. She's only too happy to accept. They've earned this! They clink bottles and drink directly from them, glugging almost the whole lot in one mouthful. Their eyes meet for a few seconds and they burst out laughing. This has been such a thrill!

The three customers are happy. They don't know what they've eaten, but they think it's all been daring, different and very entertaining.

They've tried to guess the secret ingredient in each dish and now it's time to see if they're right. With the serious face of a professional chef, Annette tells them they've got it almost all correct, except for the secret ingredient in the meat, which wasn't sesame seeds but toasted pine nuts. Actually, there were no sesame seeds and no pine nuts either, but she has to say something.

She invites them to a shot of Caol Ila. She leaves the bottle on the table and tells them in her outlandish French-laced Catalan that Àlex Graupera has had to dash off to appear on a television programme about the latest trends in gastronomy.

Carol, now minus the apron, comes out of the kitchen and returns to her table, where she calmly sips the brandy left in her glass. She waves Annette over to join her.

Annette accepts the invitation, although she still has to clean up the kitchen. She's well aware of the fact, because the whole place is a complete mess, as if they've been cooking for forty. Nothing has been spared. Not a single casserole, stirring spoon or plate. Everything has to go into the dishwasher. Right now, it's pure hell, worse than anything Dante could have imagined, but she's dead on her feet, because of the culinary adventure and all the drama she's had to endure this week. It will be nice to chat with a friendly voice, and it seems that Carol is in the mood for talking.

In a melange of English, French, Catalan and Spanish, they settle into a surreal conversation. Carol is worried about Àlex, as everyone's given up on him, she says. The critics, the gourmet writers and the connoisseurs are all saying he's not doing anything interesting now, he's outmoded, and that his pig-headedness in refusing to cook any food coming from the Americas doesn't make sense. He never had a lot of fans in the wider public, but at least the gourmets respected him and kept track of what he was doing. But he's finished now. It's not enough to be a great chef.

He has to make sure people like and understand his food. His success hitherto has been based on his technique, but he's got to improve his communication skills and apply a touch of diplomacy. If he doesn't get his act together, he'll end up having to close the restaurant.

The conversation with Carol after that is hazy in Annette's memory, and she can't remember how the night ended. She sees through a rip in the grubby curtain of her room that the sun's high in the sky and it's late. Her brain dredges up few blurry images: young customers, bottle of Caol Ila, the five of them dancing tangos, other tomfoolery, and her "criminal" Catalan, which had them laughing so much they were almost rolling around on the floor. She has no idea of what time they left. Maybe it was four in the morning.

Now it's ten o'clock and she has to get out of bed, but she fears what will be awaiting her in the kitchen and restaurant, as she didn't clean up last night. If Àlex comes back early, he'll make mincemeat of her and throw her in the soup. She'd better get moving right now and do the tidy-wash-wipe-shine circuit faster than a Formula One driver.

Her head is heavy, but that's not the worst of it. Everything disgusts her and she wants to vomit. She'll have to pull herself together, be strong and try to get through the morning with the help of some Vichy Catalan mineral water, Coke and a few aspirins. She'll feel better this afternoon, so she just has to get through three or four hours. This she knows from experience. It's not her first hangover.

She has no regrets at all. It was a fantastic night and she had a great time. She needed to relax her muscles and head after a very tense week and, more than anything, she needed a friend. But, ooh, this is a headache and a half!

She goes downstairs, and the sight of the dining room is a slap in the face. She gets a tray and starts cleaning up. She'd better get moving and sort this out. She's terrified that Àlex will see the deplorable state of his restaurant. What's that noise? Is that someone in the kitchen? Mon Dieu, he's in there! What colour coffin does she want?

"Good morning, Annette. I imagine you'll be able to tell me what went on last night here in my restaurant. When I left, everything was in order in the kitchen and dining room."

This is it. Now he's going to cut her open and stuff her with olives, mincemeat and breadcrumbs. She doesn't know Àlex very well, but this exceedingly polite tone he's using doesn't augur well. She was expecting shouts, a brandishing of knives and offensive gestures. His measured words are tissue paper covering an imminent earthquake, she's sure of that.

"Three clients come when you leave."

"So what did they eat, eh? You're crazy, girl. Who the hell do you think you are? How dare you serve my customers when I wasn't here? Needless to say, you don't know how to cook, so what did you give them? My God, what a disaster… This little girl thinks that by filling the bellies of three poor bastards she's also going to fill the coffers of this calamitous restaurant. What's this I've got here, for Christ's sake? Ah yes, of course, it's Mother Teresa of Calcutta dressed up as an enlightened lass from Quebec! Listen, my girl, stuff your charity up your arse. There is only one cook in Antic Món and that's me. Got it?"

Now, yes, Àlex is ranting, striding up and down the kitchen with a knife in his hand.

Annette does nothing. She doesn't know if she's transfixed by the threatening knife or because Àlex has gone from the formal *vostè* to the familiar *tu* again. This change of register is significant. She's still not sure what it means, but something is happening in Àlex's head. For him, *tu* is a sign of closeness, a way of saying he likes the person, of wanting to be friends. She's seen this with his suppliers. He addresses Frank as *tu* and uses *vostè* for the butcher, the dairyman and all the drinks people, whether they're bringing wine or water.

She hasn't known him long, but she's starting to predict his reactions. This is exactly what happened a few days ago when Frank told him he wasn't bringing any more fish unless he paid off his mounting debt. She knows he's going to yell a bit more and, immediately afterwards, will devote all his attention to some painstaking culinary task of the sort that locks away all kinds of rage and murderous thoughts, as if absolutely nothing has happened. So, despite her paralysed muscles, Annette isn't afraid. So she serenely replies, "I no want you leave me tout seul, Àlex."

He doesn't answer. He's gone to open the door. That's odd. Annette can't hear him talking with anyone, just the sound of the door closing. He returns to the kitchen looking baffled and carrying a polystyrene box full of all sorts of small fish. He looks at them one by one and mutters to himself, "This must be Frank's doing."

Whatever the case, the fish have turned up at Antic Món, or someone's left them at the door like a Christmas present, and Àlex's face has changed. It seems he's completely forgotten his outburst. While Annette is washing all the pots, pans and plates from last night's party, he's cleaning fish and singing a Paolo Conte song about pissed-off French people, flapping newspapers and going to the cinema.

Tra i francesi che s'incazzano, e i giornali che svolazzano, e tu mi fai – dobbiamo andare al cine – e vai al cine, vacci tu!

Annette lets out a big sigh of relief. If Àlex is singing, she's safe. It's a clear sign that he's forgotten about the mess his kitchen was in and the state of the dishwasher, and now he's showing how happy he is.

The fish are small, perfect for serving with romesco sauce or in soup. Their flavour is intense, delicious. You need three saucepans for making fish soup, one for the garlic-and-onion base, one for the broth and the last one for the soup itself. You have to use onion, garlic, bay leaves and a lot of fish. A couple of red prawns as well. Yet the soup is always too pale.

"Àlex, my home cook he put in soup tomato. Colour red. And small pepper, also give red colour." Annette's trying to help.

"Madame top chef, I'll have you bloody well know that no tomato and no pepper will ever darken the doors of this house. Do me a favour, will you, and get on with the job of cleaning up everything you messed up yesterday before the first clients arrive. Ah yes, and how much did those kids pay last night?"

Pay? Annette wonders who had to pay. Oh dear, the customers, those three young people!

She let them off paying for their dinner because they got the ingredients of the flavours game right... An image flashes back, the moment when she's saying, "In me the dinner is today. I pay!" She remembers Carol's giggles as she echoes, "'In me the dinner is today. I pay!' Annette means it's on the house. You're invited!" Another flash: the amazed expression on the faces of the three clients when they realize it's on the house. They hadn't left a drop in the Caol Ila bottle, had no idea of the price of the "surprise" menu and were terrified they wouldn't be able to pay the bill. And then the opposite happened. It was gratis! But how will she wriggle out of this one? How is she going to tell Àlex there were no takings yesterday? Carol didn't pay either. Carol never pays.

She opts for the deep end. "I invite them last night."

"Ah, that's so kind of you! That's really lovely. So, first of all you sabotage my prestige. You don't even know what you're going to serve up, but of course it's got nothing to do with my cooking. Then you create bedlam in my restaurant, leave the kitchen looking like a rubbish dump and, to cap it all, you give away my food and drink! Are you completely mad?"

Annette stares at the floor like a kid in primary school being ticked off by the teacher. The phone saves her. It's Carol, who wants to say hello and then speak to Àlex.

"How are you, love? Are you alive? I feel like something the cat threw up. I've only just dragged myself out of bed but, before anything else, I wanted to phone and thank you for the wonderful time we had last night. It's ages since I've enjoyed myself so much. It was, to tell the truth, the best night I've spent in many years!"

"Me also. I'm tired, very much. You come today?"

"I can't today but I'll be back very soon. I really want to talk with you again and, if Àlex lets us, cook together too. Now, put Àlex on please. I'm going to tell him off a bit, which will give me a lot of pleasure, and I need to start the day with a bit of oomph. You look after yourself, sweetheart."

Àlex cusses a bit before taking the phone and stumbling through an apology. "Carol, er, sorry I walked out on you like that last night. I was in a state."

"Listen, laddie, you excelled yourself, with me and with Annette. Let me tell you that this little foreign lady you've taken on is worth her weight in Sevruga caviar. If you don't look after her, if you bully her just for the pleasure of feeling superior, if you keep making everyone around you feel like shit and if you apply any single one of your strategies of psychological sadism, I'm going to saw your balls off, nice and slowly with a rusty knife, purée them with barbed beaters, make patties of them and fry them in hot oil. You choose. By the way, when is that lovely girl's day off? I want to invite her out to dinner. She needs to discover there's a bit more to life than hanging around your run-down hole."

Carol's going for the jugular today. The most intelligent strategy is not to fight back too much, Àlex thinks. He says, "She has the same day off as I do, when the restaurant's closed, which is on Mondays. I'm free too and can come and have dinner with you. It'll be good for me to have a bit of a break."

"No way! I'm going to punish you for quite a while. Let's see if you can learn not to leave me stranded with my mouth gaping open, not because I'm in the grip of some kind of culinary rapture, but because you storm out in the middle of a conversation. Anyway, I must say that I was overjoyed, absolutely overjoyed that you pissed off like that, because I had the chance to get to know the girl and do something I've always wanted to do, which is cooking Lord-knows-what, in a top-ranking restaurant – well let's say in a whatever-ranking restaurant, as it is nowadays."

"Carol, I know this may sound trite, but I'm determined to get Antic Món back to the top. I'm in especially good spirits today. I found a box of the freshest fish imaginable at the door. It's a gift and also a sign that not all is lost. I imagine Frank's involved in this, but the thing is, I'm cooking with top-quality fish again, even if they're small fish that wouldn't bring in much on the market. If I bone them and cosset them a bit, you'll get the finest Mediterranean fish right here at my place."

"It's not a matter of fish, or raw material, or quality, Àlex, as you very well know. It's about good manners, understanding the customer, making an effort, being nice to people, teaching tactfully, being an elegant host and knowing how to explain your dishes. You fail on every count. You do what you like, but let me repeat, it's not enough to be an excellent chef. You have to listen to your customers. I have to leave you now. I'm going to throw up, because I drank almost a whole bottle of Lepanto on a virtually empty stomach last night. Let me remind you that your chicken was all but inedible. Give that lovely girl from Quebec a kiss from me. She has the hands of an angel, a heart of gold and the brains of a Nobel laureate."

43

"I hope the sour bloody cow drowns in her own vomit," Àlex mutters to himself as he returns to the kitchen. "And that she doesn't bloody try to get off with Annette." He promises himself that he'll slam the door in her face next time she comes to Antic Món.

He's well and truly convinced that, thanks to him and him alone, without the toxic advice of any critic or any other arse-licker for that matter, his restaurant will soon shine again.

4

SWEET

If God had intended us to follow recipes,
He wouldn't have given us grandmothers.
LINDA HENLEY

It's a month today since Annette arrived in Antic Món. Àlex hasn't mentioned a salary or payment of any kind, but she's not bothered by this. She's happy. She knows it's a question of patience – the patience of those who have no choice.

The Friends of Antic Món Facebook page has almost five hundred followers and people sometimes turn up at the restaurant wanting to take up one of the offers or try their luck at the guessing games Annette posts on the page.

Things seem to be looking up. The restaurant hasn't been empty for more than two weeks. Occasionally they even have more than one table. It's nothing to get too excited about, but at least they're not standing around twiddling their thumbs, although it must be said that, whatever the case, Àlex never stands around twiddling his thumbs. He's always on the go, constantly busy in the kitchen. When there is no more cooking to be done, he goes off to his office to do the books. This is a cross he has to bear. He's always moaning about it, saying it's difficult, a pain in the arse, and that doing an accountant's work is a waste of his talent. But the way things are going, doing the books is actually quite easy: very little income and expenses galore. Although since he can't pay most of his suppliers, even the expenses side is skimpy. He doesn't have to worry about a payroll: just the two of them are working in the restaurant and Annette doesn't have a contract. Neither has she been paid for the month she's been working there.

A couple of days ago Àlex asked her to give him a hand with the books. He must have wanted to pass on the crappy job to her, or why else would he be making her go up to his office, she now wonders, as she's following him upstairs up to the tiny room where he keeps his paltry takings. Once installed, Àlex pours himself a glass from the first bottle he finds to confront his trials with a little more verve.

When she first arrived, Annette thought gin was his favourite tipple, but she's since discovered that his taste varies depending on what's within reach. Anything's good as long as it has high alcohol content. He's funny when he decides to justify what he's drinking, always downing it with the same words: "I love this. It's the best drink in the world, my favourite of all." It doesn't matter whether it's gin, vodka, cognac, whisky, wine, cava or Bonet herbal liqueur. Àlex believes you can't lock yourself in an office without having a nice glass of something strong.

"What are you going to do tomorrow, Annette?" he suddenly asks.

She takes a moment to answer. She wavers, surprised by such a personal question.

"I do nothing. Rest. I always rest the Monday. I need. You, what you do? Where you go the Monday?"

"Doing what I have to do… getting away from it all. You should do that too, get out a bit, see Catalonia, move around and meet people. What about Òscar? Don't you see him? You're friends, aren't you?"

Àlex wants to find out a bit more about Annette, but doesn't seem keen to tell his own secrets. She, however, has no hang-ups.

"With Òscar, we the virtual friends. Just meet one time. We chat very much with computer. I very tired for to see more persons. Maybe later."

"Two loners, we are," he says, trying to imitate Bogart. "Two sociable loners. That sounds like a contradiction, but it isn't. We need to be alone and we need to share. Why did you leave Quebec?"

"Quebec cold place... I want see Barcelona."

"You're a dab hand at changing the subject, girl! Good work. Well, no one gives a damn about what you did or what you're doing. It's a bit like old photos. They're fascinating because they're mute, and then you can imagine their stories. Stay as you are, carrot top. The mystery you're cloaked in makes you even more alluring."

With a skinful of highly alcoholic Basque sloe berries in liquid form, poured from his bottle of patxaran, Àlex is getting a little maudlin.

Annette pours herself a glass and adds some ice. She likes this liqueur, which she considers "indigenous", traditional and authentic.

"When I will go Barcelona, you also come?"

"I don't like the city. If you want, we'll go to the Maresme and look at the sea one day. One Monday night."

"And we no can go Monday in day?" Annette asks, trying to find out what he does on his days off.

"Maresme is cold place..." he mocks.

Strange as it may seem, Annette hasn't left the restaurant in all this time. Apart from the supermarket, she's seen hardly anything of its surroundings and, of course, has never been to Barcelona. It doesn't bother her, because she's not here to go sightseeing and right now she's giving her all to the project of reviving the restaurant.

On Mondays, Àlex heads off wherever he goes and she enjoys some peace and quiet in her small room. She spends the day resting and working on the Friends of Antic Món Facebook page. Àlex hasn't found out about it yet. He thinks social networks are teenage crap. However, thanks to this crap, quite a few tables have been filled with people wanting to taste "the fabulous cuisine of Àlex Graupera".

"Want to see a film with me tonight, girl?"

Àlex doesn't want to sound tender, so he always addresses her as "girl" when he comes out with anything she might interpret as a come-on. Annette understands this as a distancing manoeuvre, a way of putting years between them, as if he's much older and sees her as a little girl who could never aspire to be a friend, let alone a lover.

"Oh yes! What film?"

"One of my favourites. I've seen it at least ten times: *Big Night*."

"In what cinema?"

There is no cinema in Bigues i Riells, which means they'll have to go to Granollers or even to Barcelona, Annette thinks. But nothing is further from Àlex's intentions.

"In my room."

Annette finally opens her eyes at about eleven in the morning. She's slept for hours, but badly. She drank too much last night. Both of them drank too much. The film, *Big Night*, was great. She loved it, and she loved relaxing with Àlex just as much. Lying in bed, she recalls details of the film and her evening with the boss.

She was surprised by his room. She imagined it would be baroque, full of mementos, but instead she found an austere space with badly distributed old furniture, dominated by a huge television set and an even more impressive stereo system. Not a picture on the walls. The only personal touch was a set of shelves full of old LPs, CDs, DVDs and videotapes, all set out in perfect order.

They sat on the bed because there was no sofa. Annette was both re-laxed and edgy, however contradictory this may seem. She was relaxed because he was relaxed, and edgy because she was expecting some sign from Àlex that might be interpreted as an overture.

But no. And it was better like this. They didn't talk much, but laughed a lot. She was surprised that Àlex knew how to laugh. This was something she'd never seen.

When the film finished and she was leaving, he said. "I've got lots of films and I enjoy watching them over and over again. We can do this again, if you like."

These words were even more comforting than sitting by the fire with a cup of tea on a cold winter's afternoon in her beloved Quebec, watching snowflakes gently drifting down outside the cold-misted windows.

Annette goes down to the kitchen, hoping to find her boss there and relive the story of the film about two Italian brothers who open a restaurant in the United States with exquisite food and not a single customer who understands it. A customerless restaurant with exceptional food, just like Antic Món.

He's not there. She's completely alone in the restaurant and this is disconcerting. She wants to talk about their nice time last night. They were getting on well, starting to feel closer. She's surprised that she wants to see him and spend more time with him when on previous Mondays she'd enjoyed precisely the opposite, which is Àlex's absence and the fact that he leaves early in the morning.

She's got a headache. She cuts a huge slice of bread, covers it with thin rounds of cucumber, some roast chicken, apple, mayonnaise and a sprinkling of oregano.

Then she goes upstairs. Turns on the computer. A whole world is waiting for her out there beyond the screen: the blogs she likes, the friends she wants to read in English and French. It's such a relief to forget about Catalan for a while! She opens Facebook and posts some photos of Antic

Món on the restaurant's page. They're very enticing: pictures of forks in a row, a box of bright-red strawberries, the brilliant colours of a salad, the dust that's collected on a venerable bottle of cognac, a golden roast just out of the oven... She's so engrossed that she almost misses Carol, who's chiding her from the chat window.

"What are you doing today, love?"

"Hallo Carol. I do nothing. I rest."

"I want to see you. Let's go and have lunch somewhere."

"I eat now a sandwich."

"Leave your sandwich. I'm coming to get you. I'm going to take you to a fabulous restaurant, legendary. It's in Granollers. We'll eat proper Catalan food there. I'll be with you in a couple of hours. Get yourself dolled up. It's an important day today..."

Annette doesn't know how to say no. She doesn't want to go, but can't think of a remotely convincing excuse. She doesn't understand why it's an important day, but she's always been obedient.

She gets dressed, runs a comb through her hair and clumsily applies some eyeliner. She still has more than an hour before Carol comes to get her. She whiles away the time surfing the web and can't resist typing "Atlantic Viandes" in the Google search box.

She's already seen plenty of pages where the name of the company is prominent in the news. Suddenly she finds a new one. Oh no! What's this? More problems? Now very alert, she reads the note. It seems that a new gang of criminals has been caught fattening pigs with anabolic steroids. A few lines into the article she reads:

This is the first food safety scandal in Canada since the ATLANTIC VIANDES clenbuterol poisoning tragedy. The Canadian police have not yet arrested the director of the latter company.

Annette starts dry-retching, trying to vomit, but she can't. She undresses and gets in the shower, as if to wash away the memories. She needs to dissolve her tears, burn away her rage in scalding water.

She loses all sense of time. She has no idea of how long she's been under the shower. The skin on her fingers is as wrinkled as it used to get when she was a little girl splashing around in her parents' swimming pool.

The doorbell rings insistently, three times, but she ignores it. She's lost in thought.

Then she reacts. The doorbell! Carol's here! There's no time to dress. She wraps herself in a towel and runs downstairs to open the door.

Carol smiles ecstatically. She couldn't ask for more. Annette, barefoot and wearing only a towel is a heavenly sight.

"Well, well, well! I never imagined you'd welcome me in such a sexy way."

"Sorry, Carol, I shower late."

"I'm charmed, love. Let's go upstairs while you get dressed, OK?

"No, no… I come down soon as possible. You drink aperitif."

"I'm coming with you… Then we can keep talking. I'm sure you have lots to tell me."

"Carol, I like for you wait here. Just one minute."

Annette's embarrassed about Carol seeing her humble, poky little room, but Carol is not to be dissuaded, so they go upstairs, each armed with glass of cava.

Carol is entranced by the photos hanging from rusty nails driven into the wall, thrilled to be able to snoop and check out Annette's mementos. She asks where she got the rain stick and the mate gourd and runs her finger along the spines of her books on the shelf. She asks about her travels and Annette happily offers her a string of anecdotes. Reliving the moment of buying the rain stick on a trip to Mexico, or the hilarious moment when she was presented with the Quechuan mate gourd helps her forget the anxiety caused by the news she read on the Internet. Annette's quite comfortable wandering around dressed in a towel and pleased to share her pressed-flower album, a collection of memories in which each petal is a little scrap of her life.

"I love hearing your stories," Carol says happily. "But you'd better get dressed now. It's after two, and they'll close the kitchen in La Fonda if we don't hurry up and get ourselves to Granollers."

Carol opens the wardrobe to look for something worthy of the occasion, some sexy dress, but she can't find one.

"You've only got jeans, white T-shirts and jumpers for climbing mountains. Where on earth did you imagine you were going to live? Livingstone's jungle? Did you think we're still cave dwellers rubbing stones together to make fire? Haven't you got anything stylish?"

"I work no stop all the day. I no need the luxury dress."

"In between luxury and woolly caps there's a world of possibilities. There are some very good shops in Granollers. I'm going to buy you a dress this afternoon so you can wear it when you come out with me."

"Thank you, Carol, but I no need nothing."

"Listen, sweetheart, if I want to buy you a dress, I'm going to buy it. Now you just be a good girl."

Annette doesn't know what to make of these last words. She doesn't get a lot of the nuances in Catalan, but something tells her it's better to keep quiet.

She drops the towel on the floor and bends over to put her knickers on. When she's doing up her bra she finds warm hands helping her.

She thinks Carol's being very attentive.

"Remind me to get you some underwear too. What you're wearing is fine for going to war, but I like ladies in lovely lacy lingerie. You'll be gorgeous in garnet red."

Annette still doesn't catch on, but she wants to get dressed quickly and leave. She's hungry and is keen to see Granollers and the legendary Fonda Europa. And something strange is thickening the air in the room.

In the car, almost yelling, they sing Nat King Cole's Spanish songs: "*Luna que se quiebra sobre las tinieblas de mi soledad, adooooonde vas…*"

They giggle.

When they arrive at Fonda Europa, Annette's astounded to see so many people. The place is bursting at the seams, with tables of customers tucking into large casseroles of rice, massive fillets and immense salads. They have to sit at the bar as there is no free table. A couple of glasses of cava help to while away the time.

They end up waiting half an hour, after which they've quaffed four glasses each, talking non-stop. Carol is particularly loquacious. She tells stories about Fonda Europa, her meals at luxury restaurants all over Europe, superstar chefs, exotic flavours and other aspects of her occupation as a gourmet.

Annette greatly enjoys the conversation and the meal. They order the restaurant's most famous dishes, namely those based on offal: calf's head and foot and pig's head, belly, ears and trotters. They round off the feast with the celebrated *pijama*, an endurance test for the staunchest of stomachs consisting of a plateful of preserved peaches, caramel custard, whipped cream and two rolled wafers.

"Wow! Go for it!" Carol exclaims, laughing. "It's really worth knowing about this place. Fonda Europa is a classic of Catalan cuisine. It's belonged to the same family since 1714. Canada didn't even exist then!"

"Yes, it exist."

"I'm teasing you, gorgeous. I just said it to make you angry. I want to see what you look like when you're angry, but I'm not having any luck. You're so sweet…"

"I no get angry."

"What do you mean? We all get angry when people attack us."

"I before in my life very angry. I no want feel bad. I want easy life."

"Hmmm. Well, I'll get you a little bit irate one of these days. Then I'll have the pleasure of consoling you in my arms," Carol says, gently stroking Annette's curls.

Annette goes with the flow. She's happy with Carol. They're laughing a lot and the conversation is interesting. She likes being treated with so much deference. She's like a wounded animal and needs a friend, understanding, cherishing and affection. And Carol's willing to give her all of this in abundance.

In the afternoon they stroll around Granollers. They go to see La Porxada, the sixteenth-century portico that once sheltered a grain market, and wander through the main square and its surrounding alleys.

They enter Can Montañá, an elegant dress shop where Carol insists on buying her a party dress.

"Thank you, but I never put this dress."

"Of course you'll wear it! You're going to wear it next week because we're going to have dinner in a great restaurant, in Barcelona. That and the lingerie we're going to buy for you right now."

"I have already the lingerie. You no waste the money."

"This isn't wasting money. This is an investment in what I like most: enjoying life's fleeting pleasures. You'll never catch me laying out money for a house, or a car, or even clothes for myself. I don't need material things. But to see you dressed up and looking so sexy is a huge pleasure. I won't take no for an answer. This is my priority now."

They're in the lingerie shop and Carol insists on selecting Annette's underwear. Annette's resisting. "No, I no like the red brassiere with exquisiteness," says Annette, showing off the word Òscar taught her a few days ago.

"Well I do like it and that's what counts. You're so gorgeous."

Carol says this in a croaky voice, the way she was speaking a few hours ago. It's a voice that surges from her depths, a darker, silkier, slowly throbbing voice. Her eyes are shining. The bottle of cava, their lunch and the image of Annette in this underwear have inflamed her. She wants to touch her, here, now, in the fitting room.

"I'm tired, Annette. What about you? I'd love to have a siesta. Shall we see if they've got a free room at the hotel?"

"Now? I no want the siesta. Is good the coffee."

The prospect of going to a hotel for a siesta terrifies Annette. She's started to realize what Carol's intentions are and certainly doesn't want to play any dangerous game that would jeopardize their friendship. She values Carol very highly as a friend. Her life's already too complicated without getting tangled in difficult sentimental situations as well. The timing's all wrong. Anyway, she's never been attracted by women. No way.

They have a coffee and Carol calms down.

They're silent on the way back to Antic Món. The atmosphere is tense. Carol's upset by Annette's rejection and ashamed of having been so up front. She should have been more subtle, she thinks, but the gelatinous sensuality of the *capipota*, its melting tenderness of calf's cheek and foot, combined with the cava's tingling zing, has stirred up her most hidden carnal desires.

They say goodbye. A kiss on each cheek and a hand caressing Annette's thigh. Carol once again feels she's spinning out of control. The luxuriance of the red hair, the beautiful curving hips and the pale sprinkling of freckles on dimpled cheeks are driving her crazy.

Annette goes up to her room. She leaves the bags in a corner. She doesn't want to put away Carol's purchases. She'll do that later. Right now she needs to rest and sort out her emotions.

She turns on the computer and tries to do some work on the Facebook page, read the blogs and sort out some photos, but she can't concentrate. Images of her day in Granollers keep parading through her head. Contradictory feelings are making her dizzy. Maybe she should have been more compliant with Carol. Should she have let her have her way? But then she might have lost a valuable friendship. It's been a bittersweet day. She wants to speak with Òscar and looks for him on Facebook. Right now, he's the only friend she has, or at least the only one who's not trying to push at the limits of friendship, wanting something else.

"Annette, are you OK?"

"Yes, yes, Òscar. Many emotions only."

"I was thinking I might come and visit you and Àlex tomorrow. I have to go and see a client in Granollers and, all being well, I could come and spend bit of time at Antic Món around mid-afternoon."

"Please come. For me is good. I need very much speak."

"I think it would be a good idea if we tell Àlex about the Friends of Antic Món page tomorrow. He mustn't be kept in the dark about this. If I'm there, he won't get so angry."

"Tomorrow, perfectly. Or no, maybe. I no sure. It depend of Àlex mood. I have sometimes fear with him."

"I know. Don't be afraid. Basically, he's a good fellow but he's got a lot of hate seething inside him. Oh, and by the way, remember that carrot-cake recipe of yours? My girlfriend wants to make it and I can't find pecans. Could she use our local walnuts instead?"

"I think yes. Of course."

It's completely dark outside. Annette's cold, but it's the type of cold that comes from within and makes your very thoughts shiver. She's terribly, intensely homesick for her own home, her country, her friends and carrot cake.

She knows that Àlex will be back late, boozed up and tired, so she takes her little notebook of recipes from the drawer of the bedside table and goes down to the kitchen, where she dons her patchwork apron and lights the oven. As if performing some sacred liturgical rite, she gets out all the ingredients, ready to make her cake.

In a large bowl she beats two eggs with brown sugar until the mixture expands. She adds the half-melted butter, two grated carrots, a handful of walnuts, a generous spoonful of cinnamon and finally the flour and baking powder. The trick is to fold in the flour, not ill-treat it with beaters.

Half an hour, an oven on low temperature, and the fragrance is floating in the kitchen. "Summertime, and the livin' is easy," she sings to Ella Fitzgerald. She can't help it. She's singing and crying at the same time. "Fish are jumpin' and the cotton is high."

Sitting on a stool and using the shelf of the serving hatch as her table, legs swinging, she eats the cake hot from the oven, breaking off little morsels with her fingers, just like she did as a little girl at afternoon tea time, when her mother made her sit at the kitchen table under her watchful eye. "One of these mornings you're going to rise up singing." She keeps a hefty slice for Òscar.

Àlex and Annette meet up in the kitchen early next morning. He isn't at all pleased to discover she's made a carrot cake on her day off. He doesn't even say hello.

"The day off is for everyone, right? Agreed? Is that clear?"

"Yes, that clear," Annette answers automatically.

She's fed up with Àlex's tongue-lashings. He seems to revel in conflict and is always looking for a fight. Annette's had a couple of rows with him, but now she prefers to roll with the punches. He'll soon get tired of trying to provoke her.

"The oven has a day off too," he raves on. "On Monday the restaurant equipment has a rest. On Monday you have to get out and clear your head, my girl, and I don't want you messing around in my kitchen."

She'd love to point out to Àlex that, without a cent to her name, her choices are very limited. She hasn't been paid her first salary yet and has no idea of what her monthly wage is going to be, because the boss hasn't deemed it worthy of mention. But she merely says, "OK. I go out the Monday."

Àlex can't stand the fact that she doesn't answer back, that she's so concil-iatory, that she's always trying to keep the peace. He believes that the kitchen needs shouting and arguments to whip up adrenalin and strengthen bonds, because when the thunder and lightning have passed a soothing sun appears. Flowers and violins are what you get in wishy-washy kitchens. This must be a female thing, he tells himself, because all the kitchen hands he's had so far have been males who've responded to his yelling and insults with even louder yelling and more offensive insults. That's how it's supposed to be.

Resigned, he focuses his efforts on making the spinach-and-walnut filling for some cannelloni he's going to cook. He fills the sink with water and tips a big bunch of fresh spinach leaves into it. He pounces on them mercilessly, shoving them well under the water and shaking them around vigorously.

"Look at the way I'm doing this. You've got to get them right under the water. They're full of this bloody soil stuck to the leaves. If you don't wash them properly, the customers are sure to bite on the dirt and all your work goes into the rubbish bin."

"Why you make so many cannelloni?"

"This is a restaurant, in case you haven't worked it out yet. We've got to be prepared for whatever comes up."

"Tuesday it is quiet day," Annette comments, because she hates to see such large amounts of food thrown away at Antic Món. There have even been dishes that have not sold as much as a single serving and been tipped intact into the bin.

"What the fuck would you know? Get on with your work unless you want to run out of here screaming."

"Yesterday I lunch with Carol," she suddenly remarks.

"What! What's this you're saying? I don't think I heard you rightly."

"I yesterday lunch with Carol in Granollers. We talk about you and restaurant. Taster menu is best. No à la carte. We say this."

"Yesterday you went to have lunch with Carol in Granollers. Well, well, well... and you had a little chat about me. And my cooking, I suppose. So now you're suggesting that I should forget about the à-la-carte menu and offer a taster menu instead."

"Yes, exact."

"Oh, that's lovely, so lovely... So, you decide to go out for lunch together and, since you've got nothing to talk about, because you're a pair of bitter, twisted spinsters, you while away the time organizing my cooking and my life. That's bloody marvellous! You can stick the degustation menu right up Miss Carol's arse, my girl. Make sure it all goes in, right down to the last dish."

Annette knows that what will wind Àlex up more than anything else is her remaining silent and calmly getting on with the job. In the time she's worked with him, she's learnt that this is something he can't stand, because he doesn't know how to react. Then again, she's hurt and she's had enough of his shouting.

She takes off her patchwork apron, carefully folds it, gazes steadily at him and says very firmly, "I finish. Thank you for all. I no want nothing. You no pay even salary. You no have money. Antic Món is finish. Game over!"

She goes up to her room, throws everything into her suitcase and leaves.

She's in the street, dragging the heavy suitcase. She has no money except for twenty euros she's taken from the cash register at the restaurant.

She doesn't know where to go. She must make a decision. She doesn't want to phone Carol, no, not Carol. Òscar? No, not him either, poor fellow. He's already done enough to help her.

She walks aimlessly down the road and then goes into a bar to have a cup of tea. It will give her time to think about how to deal with this new situation. She's in a country she doesn't know, where she has no real friends.

She sits down at a small table, asks for her tea, which she sips, staring at a corner of the bar with the unfocused look of someone who's lost their marbles. Frank Gabo comes in, an apparition bearing a huge box of fish.

"Hello, what are you doing here with that mad look in your eye? Has something happened to you?" he asks, flashing his incredibly white teeth.

"I drink tea."

"Yes, I can see that. Are you OK? Are you going back home?" He points at her suitcase.

"I'm OK, but no sure what I must to do. I think."

"Aha! So you've had a row with that damn cook, have you? Like everyone else."

"Yes, he intolerable."

"Can I sit down with you?" he asks, sitting down opposite her, perfectly at ease.

"I no know what I must to do, Frank. I alone and no have money. I no can to go home."

"I can't do much to help, but if you need a roof over your head you can come to my place. There are eight of us and the flat's tiny. You can stay a couple of nights till you decide what to do. You can sleep in the dining room. We'll put a mattress on the floor. That's where my cousins sleep when they come from Mozambique, and they stay a whole month! Of course, they're used to roughing it. I'll give you my phone number and, if you have no other option, just call me. My wife makes a millet soup to die for."

"Thank you Frank, thank you so much… and thank you so much also for fish."

"What fish?"

"Door of restaurant. Every day the box. That you!"

"Àlex is OK. He's had lots of bad luck. Then again, my boss is rich and hasn't even twigged that a couple of kilos of small fish go missing every day. It's cheap fish, but it's better that nobody finds out about this, OK?"

"OK. Nobody. I no know nobody. Fish very good. Clients like very much. Àlex cook very good and fish very tasty, very good."

"I have to go. I've got a horrific list of deliveries to get through. Come to my place. We'll be expecting you."

Àlex tastes the carrot cake. "Bloody hell," he thinks, "this is impressive. Very rustic, very authentic. Mmm, delicious!"

5

DEATH

*In general, mankind, since the improvement of
cookery, eats twice as much as nature requires.*
BENJAMIN FRANKLIN

The last thing Annette could have imagined was that she'd be taken in
by an African family. Frank's wife's Catalan is very rudimentary, and
Annette's even more so. Their conversation would be the source of some
great gags for a comedy film.

This is an outlandish situation. For all Frank's efforts to tell her who's
who in his family structure, Annette can't work it out. The house is filled
with a tangle of children of brothers and sisters, children who are his
wife's uncles, children who don't seem to belong to anyone in particular,
and brothers and sisters passed off as offspring.

Frank is practically Catalan. He came as a small child, but his wife
arrived in Catalonia relatively recently and, thanks to her, he's gone
back to the old Mozambican ways of doing things. Graça wears brightly
coloured dresses, typical of her country. She's a woman of ancestral
traditions, even though she's adapted quite well to living in Catalonia.
The hardest thing for her is finding the ingredients she needs for cooking, and when she does get hold of them she stows them away and ekes
them out like priceless treasures.

Annette can think of nothing more enjoyable than going to the market
with Graça. Then they cook together for all the children in the minuscule

space reserved for the stove. She's sure that they don't see her as an extra mouth to feed, but doesn't want to outstay her welcome. She hates feeling that she's a burden, as she has no money to contribute towards her upkeep. Moreover, the awkwardness of sleeping on the floor and sharing the miniscule flat with so many people is beyond her capacity for adaptation, despite the wonderful hospitality of the Gabo family. Privacy is non-existent, and her large suitcase gets in everyone's way. She can't even get out her computer for the simple reason that there's no space on the table. She's got to come up with some solution.

Meanwhile, things aren't going well for Àlex in Antic Món. He has no help whatsoever, no waiter, no cleaning lady and, naturally, no kitchen hand. He tries to do everything himself, but isn't up to it.

Surprisingly, despite all the problems, more and more people are turning up, day after day. Business is looking better but, if he doesn't take on someone soon, they'll never come back again. The service is bad. He can't be slaving at the stove, recommending a wine, and putting new paper in the toilet all at once. That's physically impossible.

He needs a waiter right now! A waiter who'll also clean the dining room, manage the cash register, see to public relations, do the books, decorate the place, wash up, manage all this stuff about social networks, cope with payroll, and be a polyglot to boot. Actually, he needs someone like Annette or, more specifically, he needs Annette. But he can't even think about that.

Today, when he's done the lunchtime shift, he'll phone his contacts and try to sort it out. Right now, he's too busy. He's got to finish the artichokes he's cooking with some clams he found in the box of fish that lands on his doorstep every day. Frank Gabo has never let him down, always bringing some small, bony fish, but from time to time he throws in some delicacy, like the clams he's found today. Then Àlex prepares a feast.

Now he's cleaning the artichokes, the noblest of vegetables despite their apparent Carthusian austerity. They are flowers, but they don't resort to the wily strategies of the species, seducing with bright colours and assertive perfumes. Artichokes don't exhale fragrances because they don't have any, and their colour is a sort of matt greenish brown. They seem to be dressed for war... or survival maybe, Àlex thinks. Not even the name is beautiful. ARTICHOKE. He spells it out slowly to confirm the vegetable's unmelodious nature. You have to close your eyes and believe in an artichoke. It's not about appearances, not a question of looking like a hand grenade about to explode, or of judging it by its stiff, stringy outer leaves. You've got to believe in it, probe it and find its heart. It's just a matter of time to remove the tough fortress of its outside layers. There inside, protected from all of life's buffeting and blows, lies the gift, a bonus of bliss, a tender, tasty, intense and honest core. No surprises, no tricks, a refined heart. If you eat an artichoke heart and drink a glass of water with it, the flavour is doubled. Two for the price of one. That's how generous it is, if you know how to find its heart.

What kindred spirits they are, Àlex and the artichoke.

The telephone's ringing, interrupting his train of thought. It's Òscar.

"Hi, Àlex, how are you?"

"Very busy, mate... I've got a lot of work and don't know how to manage it all."

"What about Annette? Isn't she pulling her weight? I'm phoning to see how you are, but also to have a chat with her. I've called her number but she's not answering. I'd feel bad if she's upset because I didn't turn up the other day. Not that she'd have any reason to be angry with me. I don't know why, but I'm a bit worried about her. She hasn't been on Facebook for days, or updated the Friends of Antic Món page. It's very strange."

"What do you mean, the Friends of Antic Món page? What the hell are you talking about?" Àlex asks in a tone somewhere between aggrieved and intrigued.

Oops. Òscar's let the cat out of the bag. Evidently, Annette still hasn't said anything to her boss. Now he's really put his foot in it.

Àlex starts putting two and two together. Those comments from customers that he didn't understand, when they asked for a free whisky after correctly guessing the ingredients in his dishes... They said they'd read about it on Facebook, and he, being so busy, didn't pay much attention. Of course he didn't give away any drinks. The customers were quite irked when they left, but at least they congratulated him on his cooking.

"Àlex, I see that Annette hasn't told you anything. I can't fill you in because I think she's the one who's got to tell you. But when she tells you, don't blow your top or patronize her, because she's done this with the best of intentions," a contrite Òscar says.

"I can't ask her. Annette's not working here now. She got upset. She was interfering too much in my work and I told her so. I don't think she liked hearing this, even though I was well within my rights. She packed her bag and left, more than a week ago. Tough luck for her and I told her so."

"Come on Àlex, I know you. Are you trying to tell me you told her patiently and clearly what the problem was?"

"Well, in the kitchen words take on a different tone. It's different from the world you move in, where everything's so watered down. Here it's about straight talking, no beating about the bush. This is because we work with knives. We leave the fancy words for all the PhDs and BAs."

"I see. So you did a hatchet job, right? You didn't mince your words and spewed it all out. Your idea of 'no beating about the bush' means swearing and insults. Well done, Àlex, you've gone and lost a real gem. For your information, Annette's a highly cultivated, well-educated woman who's done everything possible to breathe some life into the restaurant. She was sleeping very little because she spent hours working for you on Facebook. She wrote wonderful things about your cooking, posted some beautiful photos, responded to the comments of visitors on the social network and did everything she could to entice people to come and eat at Antic Món. Anyone else would have left you high and dry after not being paid the first month's wages. But she, who's committed to the project and from a very good family, by the way – which anyone can see from a mile away – didn't even mention it. Have it your own way, but I recommend that you go and find her and get her back."

"Listen here, you bloody keyboard-and-pixels wuss, I'm fed up with your advice, and everyone else's for that matter. All you wankers, constantly banging on about what I have to do or undo! Well, guess what, now I'm going to eat a *llonganissa* sandwich because I feel like some lovely cured-pork sausage, and I'll shit it out when I bloody well feel like it. Get it? I pay a high price for my freedom and I'm going to use it however I damn well like. Right now I'm going to use it to tell you that I hope that this virtual world you inhabit will suck you up and turn you into a hologram, so you can skulk around like a soul in purgatory. Now fuck off."

"I'm not going to give you any more advice," Òscar says. "But I'm sorry that you've gone and trampled all over a fantastic woman like Annette. And I'm also sorry that, once again, you're going to be more alone than an anchovy in a banana split. Bye-bye. Have it your own way!"

Antic Món opens its doors at one thirty sharp. Actually, this is in a manner of speaking, because in order to cross the threshold, customers must ring the doorbell, whereupon a helpful member of staff – and, now, none other than Àlex himself, as the only staff member – welcomes them as if they were guests at the chef's home.

This was Àlex's wish. He wanted a doorbell at the entrance of Antic Món to give the sensation of its being a private home, while at the same time the staff would show the courtesy of opening the door for the customer. He thought it an elegant touch. Now, when he's got no one to help him, the damn bell's God's gift to Àlex, because he can keep working in the kitchen or anywhere else, right up to the moment when his customers arrive.

The doorbell rings. It's a group that's reserved a table for three. They look at him and one of them whispers, "This must be Àlex Graupera, the chef himself."

"Good afternoon. Come in. Have you booked a table?"

Why the hell has he asked that? As if it made any difference! If they're the ones for the only table written down as reserved in the book, that's great and, if they're three passers-by, so much the better! There's no risk of overbooking.

"Yes, we have a table for three reserved in the name of Armengol."

"Would you like this table?"

Àlex realizes that he's opened the door in his white chef's jacket, which is spattered with grease stains. Worse, he hasn't shaved today. He looks like a tramp. He's got to smarten up. He can't wait on people looking like this. But the fact is he simply can't manage everything.

"Would you mind if we had that one over there on the right? Last time we were here we sat at that table and we have very good memories of it."

Àlex doesn't answer. He merely nods and jerks his chin in the general direction of the table so they can go and sit down.

"Here's the menu, and the wine list too."

"Menu?" asks the younger of the two girls. "We thought you offered a taster menu with wines to match. That's what we had last time, which was a huge surprise. And what about Annette and Carol, aren't they here? They looked after us so well. They're such great cooks and were so friendly! We'd like to see them again today, if that's possible."

"Annette's not working here any more, and Carol only cooked here once and won't be doing it again. The kitchen and restaurant are mine. I've never offered a tasting menu. On that occasion, they offered it because I wasn't here and they couldn't think of anything better to do. Here you have an à-la-carte menu. Choose the dishes that appeal to you most. They're all excellent."

"What a drag having to choose!" protests the older girl once Àlex is out of earshot. "That chef isn't very nice. What a shame that Annette's not working here now. Shall we go?"

They think about it for a while, but end up giving a vote of confidence to the chef. They'll stay and order one dish each.

They've eaten very well, but there haven't been any surprises like the last time and it's been nowhere near as amusing. The chef is run off his feet, because he has to look after a couple of other tables as well. A grand total of eleven people. Àlex can't look after his customers properly and practically throws the plates on the tables. He's rushing all over the place and, to cap it all, the phone hasn't stopped: bookings, suppliers, people offering information and a mobile-phone salesman who doesn't even know what advantages he was supposed to be offering. Àlex doesn't shove the phone down his auditory canal, as he's about a thousand kilometres away, but he'd love to give him half a kilo of a new kind of ear decoration.

When they finish their meal, the three friends call Àlex over. "We've eaten very well. Is cumin the secret ingredient of the black-sausage lasagne?" the young man asks.

"Yes, there's cumin in it, but that's no secret."

"Well we want to know if cumin is the ingredient so we can get our free Caol Ila, as promised. And since we've already guessed two secret ingredients, we'd like our free dessert. Warm fondant chocolate cake, please." The young man insists.

"I don't know what you're talking about, but I understand it's some rumour on Facebook," Àlex says, his face as sour as vinegar – stale vinegar, that is.

"Man, I wouldn't call it 'some rumour on Facebook'. It's on the official Friends of Antic Món page. We're among the very first followers, and that's how we got to know about the restaurant. It's been our favourite ever since and we've recommended it to all our friends. By the way, the page says that if you return to the restaurant within a month you also get a free glass of cava. To recap: you owe us three shots of Caol Ila, our dessert and three glasses of cava."

Àlex massages his chin, trying to curb the impulses he's feeling in his arms. He'd love to indulge in a bit of assault and battery.

"Let's see now... I think it's all very well that you've played, you've won and you're owed after playing, but I don't know what game this is, and I don't know anything about this page, and I don't know what kind of imbecility this social-network stuff is. This is a serious restaurant, not a bloody Christmas raffle. Here you pay for things, because everything is of the highest quality. If you want two for the price of one, go and check out the pre-packaged stuff in the supermarket. So here you are. This is the bill. What if I'd pestered the great Yves Thuriès with all this drivel when I went to the fabulous Le Grand Écuyer! I would have been thrown out on my arse."

The other diners are watching Àlex, whose face has gone bright red, and they can hear how boorish he's being. They can't believe their eyes and ears. They don't dare to say a word, but stare at their plates in case he turns on them as well.

All the customers have left. Àlex cleans up the dining room, puts on the dishwasher, sets the tables, sweeps up and cleans the toilets.

An hour later, when he's finished, he returns to his paradise: the kitchen. Before checking to see that he's got everything he needs for the next menu, he decides to cook a dish just for himself. In the freezer he finds some foie gras slices brought by some supplier from Périgord for him to taste, this delectable duck liver he's had stowed away for some great occasion. Well, today's the great occasion.

Àlex has had enough. Everything's so difficult. He's had enough of customers who think being coddled is more important than the food they're served. He's had enough of suppliers who won't wait to be paid. He's had enough of staff walking out on him. He's had enough of waiting tables. He's had enough of ironing chef's jackets. He's had enough of devoting heart and soul to cooking.

He must decide. Maybe it's time to close Antic Món and invest his efforts in some other job that doesn't involve so many problems, or even hire himself out as a chef to some other restaurant. Then, when he's finished the day's work, he can get changed and go home. That's it. Maybe Can Bret needs a chef… They're full up and short-staffed. Weekends perhaps?

He could also rent out Antic Món. In fact, the house belongs to him, well, to the bank, because he's got a mortgage that will keep him enslaved for the rest of his life. Now that he's thinking about that… bloody hell, he's received a couple of letters from the bank and they've been lying around unopened for days. Bad news, for sure.

Expecting the worst, he goes over to the cash-register desk, finds them and slits them open with a knife. One is a bank statement showing that the restaurant's in the red, because some heartless supplier has taken out what Àlex owed. For the last couple of months none of the money the restaurant's earned has been paid into the account, which is now inert. He's not paying it in because there's no need. As soon as it hits the cash register it leaves again because he has to spend it in the supermarket. The money doesn't have time to get to the bank.

He can't make head or tail of the other letter. Reading it makes his head spin. He hasn't understood anything, but can see it's not good news.

He reads it again and works out that the property will be foreclosed unless he gets his mortgage and interest payments up to date. In a nutshell, they're going to kick him out of the restaurant and seize his house.

Faced with such problems, the best thing he can do is tuck into some duck liver, wash it down with some Kripta, Catalonia's best cava, and forget about everything else. Today he's going to give himself a party. Just for him. We're born and we die alone, and that's life's only truth. He peels a few turnips and puts them on to boil. "Baby love, my baby love." He adores Annie Philippe and that oh-so-Sixties style of hers. He was very young, but he was a big fan and he's still got his old LP. He mashes the turnips in a little of the water they've been boiled in. "*Je ne pourrai pas deux fois, aimer de cet amour là.*" He puts a frying pan on a low flame and makes the sauce with orange juice and port, rendering it down till it's thick and syrupy. "*Pour que ton cœur efface tout?*" He places another pan over high heat and sears the slices of foie gras and, that done, he takes some slices of brioche and places them in the pan to soak up all the flavours of the duck. "*Si ton amour s'endort, si ton sourire n'est plus pour moi?*"

He then sets it out beautifully on a dish: the slices of brioche, the duck liver, the turnip purée and the orange sauce, but now, all of a sudden, he doesn't feel like eating it, or at least he doesn't want to eat it by himself.

He picks up the phone, the landline. He hasn't surrendered to the tyranny of the mobile phone, partly because he doesn't need one. He rarely leaves the restaurant, so he can almost always take a call. He phones Frank Gabo. It's ages since he's spoken to him, in fact not since he stopped supplying fish or, to be precise, since he stopped supplying it *officially*. He wants to thank him for all the boxes he's been leaving, day after day, at the door of Antic Món, and maybe Frank will happen to know somebody who can help him out, a few hours a week. Frank delivers to a lot of chefs and maîtres. He might even know somebody who'd want to buy Antic Món.

"Frank, my friend, are you anywhere near here?"

"Where's here? Your place? Bigues i Riells?"

"I'll cut to the chase: do you want to come and eat some duck liver that's as tender as a nun's tit, right now?"

"Now? And no nuns, please, I'm a Muslim."

"That's precisely why I'm not offering pork, you stupid bastard. It's now or never. Up to you."

Frank's worried. Àlex might have found out that Annette's taken refuge with his family and now wants to entice him into the kitchen. He'll make him eat heaven-knows-what, and once he's got him where he wants, he'll run him through with three of his biggest knives and then throw him in his soup pot for a bit of flavour and colour. Frank knows how Àlex's mind works...

Yet the hard-boiled truth is that he feels desperately sorry for Àlex. He has no friends. The fact that he's called him to come and share one of his most delicious dishes, a five-star treat, is a sure sign that he's more alone than a luxury restaurant's last lobster after a Wall Street crash.

The very idea of loneliness is more than Frank can stand. He's from a country where most houses have more than one family under their roofs, and people are constantly coming in without knocking and leaving when they're ready. The door is never closed and you can always find somebody to talk to or share a sunset with.

When he came to Catalonia, even though he was just a small child, he was shocked to see how people locked themselves away at home, slamming the door behind them, and how you needed a key or a doorbell if you wanted to see somebody. If it had only been a question of keys and doorbells, it wouldn't have been so bad. The worst thing, he discovered as a little boy, was how unapproachable Europeans were. If you're going to drag a "Good morning" out of them, or exchange just a couple of formal words, you have to be a "friend" and that's difficult, really difficult.

If you come from a faraway country, a helping hand is a gift from the gods. In Mozambique everyone's your friend because that's how it is. You have to do something really bad for someone to stop being a friend and become an enemy. In Catalonia, almost the reverse is true. At first, everyone keeps a distance, and you've got to work very hard if you're to be considered even as a candidate for friendship. All this is running through Frank's head in the couple of seconds it takes for him to answer, "OK, I'll be at Antic Món in ten minutes. Don't let it get cold, shithead."

Àlex rushes around to have everything ready before Frank arrives. He can't serve him his best wines because he's a Muslim and doesn't drink alcohol. He makes him an exotic fruit juice concoction which he knows Frank likes. He lights up the Josper grill, which is great for cooking with charcoal.

Frank loves meat. The mere sight of a good, thick deep-red steak, of the kind that makes you feel full just looking at it, has him slobbering, in seventh heaven. He ate very little protein when he was a kid in Mozambique. Too much gruel, a little bit of fish and lots of cassava. When he arrived in Catalonia he was shocked to see the barbecues they cooked, huge dishes piled with a variety of meats he'd never seen in his life, or even imagined. For him, a dishful of barbecued meat was the ultimate in luxury, even when the product was of the most dubious quality.

Àlex thinks that barbecues are for rustics, for plebs without the slightest sensitivity or culinary culture, a way of eating that helped to get through the long years after the Civil War, when Franco's push for development turned the Sixties into the decade of *desarrollismo*. Then, families crammed into their SEAT 600s and filed out of the city, heading for farmhouses on the outskirts where they could stuff themselves in these displays of gastronomic grossness – that's if the word "gastronomic" applies to an array of charred cuts of meat drowning in stinking aioli. Yet Àlex caters to Frank's tastes and makes him a fine barbecue with rabbit, steak, lamb, chicken... and pork.

Of course Muslims don't eat pork, but Àlex loves a grilled *botifarra*, and since he's already violating his own principles by grilling a heap of meat, he might as well give himself the treat of a couple of these glorious Catalan sausages.

"Hey, chef, can I smell burnt meat? Who are you cooking for? Didn't you tell me it was going to be a silver-spoon concoction?"

"Yes, of course. There's duck liver with port-reduction sauce. I had some meat, so thought I'd do a barbecue, but don't imagine it's for you, eh. I wouldn't cook as much as a chicken bone for you. Come on, sit down. Oh well, I've cooked it now, so I'll give you a couple of the smallest bits," Àlex says, producing an immense platter of meat straight off the grill.

"They're the smallest bits? In my country, a plateful like that would be enough to feed the whole village! If I'd known, I would have brought a nice big serving of McDonald's fries."

Fries are another one of Frank's weaknesses. He remembers the first time he went to eat in a McDonald's as if it were happening right now. He'd worked unwaged for more than three months, because his boss kept going on about his "apprenticeship", and when he finally got his first pay he decided to spend his money by going to eat in a real fast-food joint, in the most famous, biggest fast-food chain in the world, McDonald's, the Mecca of the West.

It's curious the way Frank lives, straddling two cultures. He wants to be African and seem European at the same time. He misses his country's customs and traditions, but sees himself in the mirror of Western ways of being in the world.

"Heaven help you! If you dare to cross my threshold with a potato in your hand I'll wall you up and you'll never see the light of day again. And if it comes from that rat-meat hamburger dump, whose name I'd never as much as pronounce, I'll shove you into the Josper and the coal will look white next to your ashes."

"You're weird, Àlex. What the hell's your problem with potatoes? Have you ever been hurt by a potato?"

"It will never happen, because I'm never going to eat one. They did enough damage to me when I was a kid."

"I don't get it. What on earth are you saying? Did you overeat and get indigestion when you were a kid?" Frank's intrigued.

"Mental indigestion, that's what. Come on, let's eat," Àlex says, changing the subject. "In your honour today, I'm cracking open one of the great wines in my cellar, a Vall Llach 2007. I probably won't need to hang on to it any longer. And as for you, I've made one of these papaya-and-mango juices you're so fond of."

Frank looks at Àlex and sees a face betraying infinite bewilderment and sadness. He doesn't know what it is, or exactly what it expresses, but the chef can't hide some kind of despair that's eating him up.

The phone rings. Normally Àlex flies to answer it, but today he drags himself over to see who's calling, as if his ankles are shackled, as if he fears that bad news awaits him on the other end of the line. A couple of minutes later, no time at all in fact, he returns to the kitchen, grabs the cloth hanging from his waist, flings it down on the table and opens the bottle of Vall Llach. After filling his glass to the brim, he says, "That's it. Make the most of it, my friend."

"You're right, Àlex, we should always try to make the most of it and enjoy ourselves. That's the most important thing in life – live in peace and enjoy it."

"Your advice is wise, my friend. Anyone would think you were eighty years old, and you're not even thirty yet."

"Twenty-six, Àlex... Thirty's still a long way off, because I'm only twenty-six. The richness of my culture comes from listening to the oldest and wisest people. We might not go to school, but we learn lots of things at home. They teach us to listen, which is the most honoured virtue back there. We are people with clean ears."

"Don't get carried away!" Àlex can't stand anything remotely sentimental, and instantly cuts off any conversation where the slightest hint of tear-jerking appears. "Words come cheap, and the advice you've given me is mawkish nonsense. I was taking the piss, but you don't get a joke any more than you'd eat a slab of ham. 'Live in peace and enjoy it!' You're really brilliant today. Is that the smartest bit of advice those old crocks in your village ever gave you? Don't make me laugh!"

"Listen Àlex, you're pushing it. I've got a family and they're waiting for me, yet I came here the moment you called. Do you really think I've come here to eat duck's liver? No sir, I'm here because I feel sorry for you, seeing you so alone, more shrivelled and bitter than a dried herring. I'm the only one who puts up with you and I've yet to work out why. Do you think that a white man, famous chef, restaurant owner would invite a humble delivery man to share his top-of-the-range dish if he had someone else? My wise old folk teach me this: to read between the lines, to know how to interpret a person's eyes and, above all, to be generous and hold out a hand to someone who's drowning. May Allah be my witness. You're drowning, or you've already drowned… in shit."

"Now you're the one who's really surpassed himself! But, anyway, this time I can't deny it. You're totally right. I'm finished, full of shit, and it seems I've done this all by myself." By now Àlex has drunk more than half the bottle of wine. "Listen, Frank, I phoned you today so I could ask you if you know anyone who'd be capable of working in a restaurant like mine. Someone who can manage the dining room, because I'm a disaster at that. But as soon as I put down the phone, I decided that this grilled meat, this duck liver and this special wine was going to be the best last supper for Antic Món. I've decided to close the show. One has to die so others can live. It's death that we feed on – has that ever occurred to you? We, I mean we animals, live because we kill. Bloody hell, don't look at me like that! I'm not just talking about calves, or sheep, or pigs. I'm talking about everything we eat. We have to pull up a lettuce and take its life if we want to get our teeth into it. Everything we eat is a corpse, from the inert carrot through to the cutest little quail. We have to put an end to vital processes before we put anything on a plate. Law of life. You know what cooking is? It's transforming death into sensual pleasure. That's exactly what I'm going to do. It's time to kill Antic Món and start a new life."

"Àlex, what are you saying, man? This is scary."

"Life's scary, Frank."

"So what will you do if you close the restaurant? This is your whole life. You've put everything you have and everything you are into this."

"I haven't got the faintest idea what I'm going to do, or where I'll end up, but I've had enough. That phone call I just had was from the lad who supplies organic vegetables, the only one still bringing stuff. Since he's hopeless at keeping the books he didn't realize I haven't paid his bills for three months. He tells me he can't supply me any more. Yesterday the same thing happened with the milk-and-cheese man. He said he feels let down, because he'd trusted Annette. It seems she promised him that I'd slowly pay off my outstanding bills, but he's only received a fraction of the amount of the first unpaid bill. He's been waiting to hear something about a second instalment but still hasn't been paid a cent. He says we don't keep our word. But I didn't have a clue about what Annette was up to with the suppliers. Now she's gone… You know who I'm talking about? That Canadian girl who came a couple of months ago."

"I'm perfectly aware who you're talking about."

Frank is dumbstruck. He can't come up with any piece of advice from the elders to console him. He's shocked that Àlex is going to close his beloved restaurant as he knows all too well that Antic Món's the most important thing in the world to him. It's been his whole life, but all in vain. Now he's got to close shop. Frank doesn't know what to say and opts to keep quiet, so Àlex can let off steam.

"Man, I was bloody furious when I found out that Annette was doing deals with the suppliers behind my back, but on second thoughts, I can see she was probably trying to help. Now I can't tell her off because she's gone too. Bloody hell! I want to say it and for once and bloody all: I think she's great! She was probably the best thing to happen in Antic Món after Moha left. You remember Moha, right?"

"Of course I do. How could I forget him? You were good friends, great friends, and you were always laughing, you and Moha. Have you heard from him?"

"Yes, he phoned me one day to see how things were going. I lied and said everything was fine. Since he left, it's all gone down the spout. And now, Annette. I really liked her…" Àlex has drained the bottle of Vall Llach. "I don't know where she is, poor girl. I didn't pay her, not even a cent. Where could she have gone without money?"

"What if she came back, would you still close the restaurant?" Frank tests the waters. He's trying to work out if there's anything he can do to stop what he sees as the looming disaster of Àlex's closing down the restaurant.

"I owe too much money, Frank. I don't know how I can pay off so many debts. Well, if Annette was here and if she agreed we could try to find some kind of solution." Àlex is thinking aloud. "She was on my side, a friend, but I turned her into an enemy… out of pure egoism, for the stupid bloody pleasure of ill-treating her, so I could still feel I was the boss and, to tell you the truth, because I was afraid of being indebted and feeling dependent on somebody else. I've always been a coward. Then again, I don't think I've got it in me to keep going with this bottomless pit of problems, a restaurant that gobbles up money.

Anyway, I wouldn't know where to go looking for her. I haven't got the faintest idea where she is. She won't come back, that's for sure, even if I get down on my knees and beg her. Forget it... Eat up, damn it!" he exclaims, changing the subject. "What's wrong with you, lad? Anyone'd say I cooked you up a kilo of those sardines you hate so much – yeah the ones that make your hands stink so much your wife won't let you go near her."

Frank hasn't heard Àlex's last words, as he's still pondering his confession. It's the first time he's ever heard the chef talking so intimately, so sincerely, and he's full of compassion. This is Frank's greatness. He's had a tough life, but there's not a drop of rancour in his heart. Ninety per cent of the man is generosity. The other ten per cent is ears, for listening, understanding and helping. That's why, betraying Annette's trust and friendship, he blurts out five words:

"I know where she is."

6

FLAME

*Sharp knives, of course, are the secret of
a successful restaurant.*

GEORGE ORWELL

"Why you tell him where am I?" Annette is angry with Frank. Then she
immediately feels guilty for overreacting and changes her tone. "No
worry. It OK. You no wrong."

"I know that nothing in this whole story is my fault," Frank says,
"and that I can say whatever I like. I knew you'd be upset, but even so,
I had to tell him. I felt really sorry for Àlex. That man's finished and he
needs you. He says he wants to close Antic Món. Can you believe that?
He's put his whole life into it!"

"But I no person. I no can to help him."

"I think you mean you're not the *right* person, because you're certainly
a person…"

"Pardon, I speak very bad the Catalan."

"You can say that again! You speak it as badly as Graça. I'm used
to it, so I can understand you. I fear, Annette, that you're the only
one who can help Àlex. In fact he's missing you. Yes, he confessed
it. If he knew I told you, he'd slit my throat and fill it with black
sausage."

"It's true I no have place for go, no have work, no have papers. I no
can to be here, in your house, my all life. I must to go."

"Annette, don't go back to Antic Món because you've got nowhere else to go. That would be a bad mistake, and both you and Àlex will end up burnt. Only go back if you want to, if you think you can offer something, because, by helping, people grow and are less like animals."

"You savant person!"

"Things I learnt from the wise old people back home. I'll tell you about it another time... Better still, ask Àlex about it. I told him about the wise old people in my village."

"Pardon, I no understand you nearly nothing. Maybe I go to restaurant. I think this during day."

Àlex gets up earlier than usual. It's not even six in the morning, but after tossing and turning all night he decides to get out of bed. He lets the warm water run down his back. He's always found the shower comforting. Yesterday he made a decision and informed Frank. He's going to close the restaurant. Today he has to think about how to go about it. Naturally, this is all new to him. He's never closed a business in his life.

The shower water doesn't offer any answers for the string of questions he's asking himself. The paperwork for closing down a business; what to do with the equipment; how to rent the place... Then there are the really hard questions. What's he supposed to do now? Where will he go? What can he do? The water's cleansed his skin, but his spirit is still muddy with doubts. The stains of disquiet can't be washed away.

He gets dressed slowly, looking at the old records and films on his shelves. He's more than tempted to bolt the door, lock himself in here to waste away, watching all the films and listening to all the records in his collection, over and over again, till he dies. A gradual, pleasant suicide, enjoying his treasures, that's how he'd like to go. He's always said that suicide's for cowards. His father used to like quoting Gómez de la Serna:

"Suicide can only be regarded as man's weakness because it is certainly easier to die than to endure a life full of bitterness without respite."

However, today he has to admit that he doesn't feel like he wants to continue trying to cope with the problems of the world, problems he can't understand and can't overcome. He feels like a novice bullfighter faced with a bull that keeps changing colour, form and strength, a bull that's acting in a completely incomprehensible, unpredictable way. The worst thing that can happen to a bullfighter is to feel afraid. Àlex is afraid.

He decides to go downstairs and have some breakfast. Today he'll eat whatever he feels like, the last caprice of a king who's about to be garrotted. He makes two slices of toast, liberally rubbed with a cut clove of garlic, generously anointed in olive oil and topped with a big chunk of *llonganissa*, a dry, hard sausage he loves chewing on to extract all its flavour. He adds a bit of salt and pepper. The joys of his larder. He eats slowly, washing it down with an icy-cold beer. He doesn't feel like reading the newspaper or listening to the radio or knowing anything about this incomprehensible world. He wants to fuse with the *llonganissa*, feel primitive, not know anything, not understand anything. Only chew, slurp, salivate, swallow… and top it off with a great big beer burp.

The *llonganissa* has made him feel better, or maybe it was catching sight of a few leftover bits of salt cod – scraps like dry, salty rosary beads – in one corner of the kitchen. He decides to make himself an ancestral dish his grandmother used to cook. He doesn't know its real name, but Gran used to call it *bacallà de bany d'or*. The name comes from its lovely golden colour and the fact that it's made from the humblest parts of the fish, like gold-plated tin earrings.

He soaks the pieces of *bacallà* in plenty of water, which he changes ten times, hoping to remove the salt faster, though he likes it strong-tasting. Meanwhile, he pours a generous amount of oil into a casserole and browns some finely chopped garlic. Then he adds the *bacallà*, now shredded into even smaller pieces. It has to be stirred non-stop until it takes on the oil's golden hues and is cooked through. The process takes quite a while and the action of stirring is hypnotic. This should be the time for singing, caressing the *bacallà* with one of the songs he likes, any one from his French and Catalan repertoire. But he doesn't feel like singing.

Annette's taken his enthusiasm for music with her, borne it off tangled in her curls. He can't get her out of his head – her sweetness, her smile… His brain's full of Annette. He turns the fire off and phones Frank.

"Hey man, have you got over what was bugging you?"

"Bugging me? You're the one who was as wobbly as a blancmange."

"Listen, is Annette there?"

"Yes, but I'm not sure she wants to talk to you."

"Let her decide that, will you. Tell her I'm on the phone, Mr Mozambique!"

The waiting becomes eternal. Where the fuck has he gone to find her. Quebec? What's going on? Is it true she doesn't want to talk to him? At last he hears her voice.

"Hello, Àlex. How you are?"

"Annette…"

"Yes, Àlex…"

"Can you come?"

"Where?"

"Here, the restaurant. I need you."

"You think this so easy. You talk me loud all the day and now you ask I must to come. You say I necessary. You no have help?"

"There's no lack of people who want to work for me and, if I wanted, there'd be a queue at the door. But I'm not interested in that. I want you. I'm cooking some *bacallà* just like my old gran used to make it.

83

I'd like you to taste it. Come on. I'm serious. You know how hard it is for me to say these things. I'm not ashamed to confess it. I need you."

"No possible now."

"Not possible for whom?"

"I. This, what I say you."

"It's impossible to understand your dreadful Catalan," he complains. "Why can't you come?"

"I help the Frank's wife for to cook. Many childs in house."

"OK, I'll come over then and bring lunch. This place is full of dishes no one will ever eat. Today I've closed Antic Món once and for all. I can't keep going. I don't know what I'm going to do, but I don't want to do this any more."

"Frank he explain me this."

"He told you? The man doesn't miss a beat. He honks louder than a rutting gander. So do you want me to come?"

"I ask Frank's wife."

Annette leaves the phone for a few seconds that seem endless. When she resumes the conversation her voice has changed and is now as sweet as a summer peach.

"She say you can to come."

Annette's struggling to contain her happiness, to hide it from Àlex. She's longing to see him. She's missed him since she's been staying with the Gabo family, but fears that her low spirits are an expression of the loneliness she's been struggling with since her arrival in Catalonia. She knows that confusing the need for company with love is a catastrophic error. She needs to be sure about every step she takes. She's too old to fail again. She keeps mulling over her yearning to see Àlex, which might be a result of the uncomfortable conditions of her stay with Frank and Graça, or maybe she's missing Àlex's fantastic food, or maybe... maybe, flying in the face of all the rules of logic, she's irrationally attracted to this bitter, tender, impetuous, irascible and sweet man.

Well, she'll just have to accept it. Although she hates it when her emotions take control of her actions, the truth is that she really likes, really fancies Àlex.

Àlex hangs up. He's on cloud nine, light-headed as an adolescent on his first date. He goes upstairs and applies some cologne, lashings of it. Combs his hair. Standing at the mirror, he checks one profile, checks the other, looks at his nose. A hair's sticking out. Tweezers. Gotcha! He thinks, "What a bloody fool you are. As if Annette hasn't seen you wearing any old thing, with dirty hands and hair all over the place... You're a complete cretin."

He rushes down to the kitchen, scrawls on a bit of paper, "THE MANAGEMENT APOLOGIZES. WE'RE CLOSED TODAY," and hangs it at the entrance of Antic Món.

He fills a large box with food and loads up the car. He turns the key, and the clock lights up to announce 11.35 in flashing numbers, telling him what a fool he is. Bloody hell, what on earth's he doing getting all dressed up and going out to lunch at this hour? He can't turn up so early. How can he pass the time? In the ten years since he first opened Antic Món, there's never been a day when he's had nothing to do. Without cooking, without the pressure of having to prepare dish after dish, there's no other passion in his life.

He picks up the box of food and goes back into the restaurant. Standing in the doorway he surveys the emptiness of the dark dining room and is invaded by painful, wretched feelings. He starts to cry. He's a poor sod. He wipes away his tears and blows his nose loudly into a linen napkin from one of the tables.

He goes upstairs and into Annette's room on the pretext of checking that it's clean and tidy. It's empty. He opens the wardrobe and finds a brand-new party dress and a bag containing red underwear, bought at a well-known lingerie shop in Granollers. He can't understand how

Annette could have overlooked these particular items. This woman is veiled in mystery.

He sits down on her bed and suddenly realizes he's caressing it. Damn it, it's about time he got it into his head that she's stolen his heart. He can smell her fragrance, clean, delicate with that touch of citrus, and it takes him back to the night when they sat together, very close together on his bed, laughing like a couple of teenagers at the antics of the characters in *Big Night*.

That night he'd wanted to hold her and kiss her, love her gently. More than sexual desire, it was tenderness, the same thing he felt every time she struggled so hard to make herself understood in Catalan. Or the day that immense smile appeared on her face when she saw the box of fish Frank Gabo had left at the restaurant door. He remembers how he tried not to laugh when he watched her trying to julienne carrots without being able to manage the knife, or how she literally wrestled with the chicken she had to debone. She's so lovable, Annette...

The telephone snaps him out of his reverie. He dashes down to the dining room, three steps at a time, but is too late. A girl's voice on the answering machine is requesting further information. She's seen the Friends of Antic Món page on Facebook.

He checks his watch. It's just gone quarter-past twelve, and he can't go to Frank's place yet as it's too early, even for a family with customs that are so different from the Catalan ones.

Half-bored and half-curious, he turns on the computer. It's about time he had a look to see what the hell they're saying about the restaurant on the social networks.

It takes him a while to get there, as he's hopeless when it comes to anything to do with computers. However, curiosity is a great educator and, finally, as if he's rubbed Aladdin's lamp, Facebook reveals its secrets. He's astounded. Jesus, what's this? Not only is he looking at himself stirring casseroles in the kitchen – and the photos are fantastic – but he recognizes all the dishes, although he has no recall of anyone taking pictures of them. Many recipes are given, most full of errors both in the list of ingredients and in the details of the preparation. On the page, Àlex finds some tempting items: discounts, raffles, a bizarre competition and comments by famous chefs. It's a full description of his world, of his everyday culinary existence, and he's only now discovering it.

He's so flabbergasted he's not sure whether to get angry at this usurpation of what he regards as his most intimate being, or to celebrate the effort Annette has made to pull Antic Món out of the vortex of ruination into which it is fast sinking.

Annette is a truly wonderful woman, Àlex thinks. He's got to get her back, somehow persuade her to return. In the short time she's been at the restaurant she's become very important to Antic Món… and its chef. He's more and more convinced that this woman is like the highly prized truffle that can only be sniffed out by fine, sensitive, expert noses, when not found by pure chance.

In this regard, his is not a sensitive nose, and he's well aware of that. Neither does he have any talent for finding hidden treasures. But now he's struck gold and has to know how to make the best of it… has to win her back, has to do whatever it takes to have the lovely Annette fragrance swirling round him once more.

He perseveres with the Facebook page and finds a very recent comment. He reads it avidly.

We're very disappointed. The first time we came here, Annette and Carol looked after us. We remember their names perfectly well, because we ended up chatting until very late, all of us sitting at the same table. They were charming and it was all great. Two days ago we returned very happily, but this time we were served by the owner, Àlex Graupera, who, according to your page, is an excellent chef and a wonderful man. His cooking was OK, but his manner was very brusque and quite rude. We felt very badly served and he even gave us the impression we were bothering him. We're sorry to say this, but we think he'll have to change his ways if he wants his restaurant to work. We certainly won't be going back there.

He closes the page and glares at the computer screen, itching to punch it so hard that it would fly off to some technological scrapheap ten kilometres away.

His good mood, his willingness to find a solution to all the problems, has evaporated like cognac flambéed over peaches.

He strides up and down the dining room, bristling with indignation. The joy of seeing Annette again has turned into rage. He doesn't know why the criticism on Facebook has affected him so much, but even the most amateur psychologist would be able to suss out that the cause is not the criticism of his lack of manners. Àlex has never taken any notice of comments from those mortals he calls "normal people", because he thinks they're gastronomic barbarians without any right to express their opinions. The cause of his latest hissy fit is jealousy, because he's realized that Carol, and especially Annette, could end up being even better than he is. This is anger mixed with the sad confirmation that cuisine is not enough in itself, but must always be complemented with soft-soaping the customers. He's stifled in Antic Món. He's got to get out.

He loads the box into the car again and heads off to Frank's place.

"Good morning, Àlex," Frank's wife greets him in her strong accent. "We wait you. Is honour you come to poor house here."

"An honour? Come on, woman, don't give me that corny bullshit…"

Frank's wife is transfixed and stands in the doorway gaping at him, not knowing how to respond to such rudeness.

Àlex almost shoves her aside and enters the tiny flat. Standing there, with the huge box of food in his arms, he can't see where to put it down.

"God almighty, there's not enough room in this place for a snail to stick its head out," he thinks. He catches a glimpse of bouncing red curls. Now he's weak-kneed with apprehension.

"Hello, Àlex. Graça she stay at door. What you do to her?" Annette asks.

"Hello! How are things? Are you OK?"

Àlex is so flustered he doesn't dare to look her in the eye. She's gorgeous, especially radiant.

"Yes, yes, but what you do to Graça?"

"What is Graça? A cat? A tortoise?"

"You stop! Graça, Frank's wife." Her tone is severe.

"Ah, nothing happened with the woman. I just told her to move aside as the box is very heavy. Look, I've brought everything. Would you like to taste some *bacallà* with green garlic shoots?"

"I no have hungry. I find Graça. You make food? We put the table."

Annette tries to convince Graça not to take Àlex's words seriously. He's hopeless. He can't help himself.

Frank's wife isn't so sure. She would have liked to put him in his place. However, where she comes from hospitality is sacred and Àlex is her guest. She'll have to be forbearing and steer clear of any hint of conflict.

In the kitchen, Àlex warms up the casseroles and gives the final touches to his dishes. He makes a huge amount of washing-up, not to mention a racket worthy of an advancing army. He opens a bottle of wine and pours two glasses, one for Annette, but it remains untouched, as she hasn't reappeared. He drinks as he cooks, thinking it will help him forget his wrath over the Facebook page and help him to relax a little, as he's so keyed-up about seeing Annette again. He has to behave, be nice and friendly and seduce her... but this also means a huge effort, because he's very miffed about the Facebook comment and can't get it out of his head.

After half an hour, they're all sitting at the table. Except for Frank: he's out delivering fish. Annette is silent.

The Antic Món spread is mouth-watering. The table is full of wonderful-smelling meat, gleaming salads and silky-smooth sauces. There's a crispy prawn-and-onion concoction, free-range chicken with carrots and leeks, calf's cheeks with pears, sea bass with porcini risotto, sardines with caramelized turnips and, for dessert, rice pudding with a touch of citrus.

The children don't know where to begin. Everything is strange to them. They don't understand this food Àlex has brought and have never seen anything like it. Àlex goes into "cheerful" mode, a gambit he's used quite successfully on other occasions.

"Come on, kids, this food is delicious. If you'll just taste a little bit, Uncle Àlex will be really happy."

Graça gets up from the table. She can't stand the man and still less when he has the nerve to proclaim himself her children's "uncle". She goes into the kitchen and returns with a plate of potatoes mashed together with a bit of meat, so that the children will at least eat something.

"Here, mashed potato, children. You like very good this," she announces, placing the platter in the centre of the table among the host of dishes Àlex has produced.

Àlex stares at the potatoes in disgust, looks at the children and blurts out, "If these kids only ever eat potatoes, you'll always be poor. You're doomed. You're from a culture that can only die of hunger."

Annette is so shocked she almost chokes on a chicken bone.

Graça's nostrils flare. Àlex has gone too far. She too has a sharp tongue and, despite her difficulty expressing herself in Catalan, the look on her face speaks volumes. She explodes: "Persons can be poor, but better is polite and happy than put money in the pocket. Better is be with animals than persons no love others. We no want you dirty our table. You get your food. You go. We eat potato no problems. You no hear before, this thing say some persons: 'In my misery, I the boss.'"

Annette cuts in, trying to turn the deadly duel into a peace process. "Àlex, it better you go. I help you gather the cooking."

"No, keep it. I don't want it for anything now and you can use it. If you don't want it, I'll give it away. There are plenty of needy people…"

He is dying to sound off, to explode. He's biting his tongue to block the words crowding on its tip: "Give the food to those kids and let's see if it revives their paralysed brains."

But he doesn't want to add fuel to the flames. This time, his scathing comment has been terribly out of place, totally wrong. He's just trashed his last chance, and there's no point in struggling on now.

He gets up from the table, pushes his chair in neatly and, before leaving, goes over to Annette and kisses her on the forehead. It's a friendly kiss, an eloquent kiss, a kiss that says, "Come back whenever you want. I'll be waiting for you."

In the car on the way back to the restaurant, he's still very jittery and sings loudly, non-stop: "Think of me, little one, think of me when witches of the morning make you shivery. I won't warm the cold or sweeten your coffee, but think of me, little one, think of me. Think of me when they don't pay your wage, or at eight thirty, squashed in the metro like in a cage. Take me, embroidered on your shirt with style, or painted bright red in your smile."

Without turning on any light in the dining room, he sits in the dark at Table 3 and pours a full glass of Knockando, which he slowly sips.

He feels a new sensation, a pleasurable but also disturbing sensation. Quietly savouring the whisky, he lingers in the present. He's never done that before. Not until now. Running the treadmill of life, he'd dreamt of a brilliant future which would help him smooth over the rusty nails of his tormented past. He looks at his hands. They are no longer useful. Useless hands, useless legs. His whole body, the engine he used to start up every morning to get things moving in the restaurant, is useless. He's still got a soul, but it's no longer his, because it's inseparable from the restaurant, as if the walls have sucked it in. His soul is fused with Antic Món by some inexplicable bond, and he can't escape.

He drains the glass. On a piece of white paper he writes a few stark words in big letters:

RESTAURANT FOR SALE
Tel. 65897925
(Ask for Frank)

He hangs it up at the door and phones Frank.

"I'm sorry, my friend, about my run-in with your wife. I'm heavy-handed, as you know."

"Yes, I know. You really excelled yourself. Graça and you are like a box of matches next to a fireworks factory. No problems until someone sets off a spark and… But Graça's forgotten all about it now. She's in heaven tucking into your food, but, my friend, you really hurt me by saying what you did in front of my kids."

"I'm sorry, Frank. I said I'm sorry. Listen, I'm also phoning because I've put a sign at the door of the restaurant announcing that it's for sale. I don't have a mobile, so I've given your number."

"What do you mean, man? My number? Are you completely off your head?"

"Listen to me, will you! I thought that if you'd do me this favour of getting the word around and taking calls, I could give you a commission on the sale. OK by you?"

"It's fine by me, but I want you to know that I'm not doing it for the money."

"You'll always be a loser… just like me," Àlex pronounces.

7

LIFE

*Let food be thy medicine and
medicine be thy food.*
HIPPOCRATES

Òscar's been mulling it over for several days. He has savings, not as much as Àlex's asking price, but nobody's shown any interest in buying the restaurant since it was put up for sale three months ago. He can cut a deal with Àlex for sure.

Annette's cooking dinner: courgette flowers stuffed with brandade, a superb dish. Since she's been staying with Òscar, every meal's been a feast. Cooking has become her chief interest and Òscar's delighted, although despite this gastronomic pampering he's longing for a quiet, solitary, private life.

Until he finally came to terms with the fact that he wasn't cut out for cohabitation with anyone, his attempts at domestic life had been hell. Love wasn't a good enough reason for putting up with certain things that really got up his nose like "Why don't you leave the toothpaste in the special holder?", "When you come in the door, take off your shoes and put your slippers on", "It's your turn to sweep on Tuesdays", "You should eat more greens", "Shut the door when you leave the room", "No, you can't read today because we've got to sort our winter clothes. It's getting cold."

Sort clothes! But he's only got three pullovers and five shirts! What a bore it is to share a flat. Life's much more fun if you can leave the toothpaste in the special holder one day and languishing in the basin the next. It's the last gasp in stupidity to enslave yourself to things. Objects are meant to make life easier, not to break up relationships.

Yet this is precisely what has happened with all his relationships. The first girl he lived with managed to get him to take his shoes off when he came in the door, to eat more greens and to store his three pullovers in the attic, so he could then bring down his one and only pair of swimming trunks. They spent an entire afternoon moving these clothes around, and all for nothing. By the end of it, the wardrobe was as empty as ever.

The women who came after her scored fewer and fewer wins. Finally, the last girlfriend, the company administrator, the one he was going to marry, made him see the light. Domestic life was not for him.

This revelation was such a relief that he felt as if he was floating round on a cloud of bliss and peace with whiffs of white truffle. Now he keeps his shoes in the wardrobe again, but during that first thrill of freedom he regaled himself with all the pleasures he'd been deprived of in his uxorious years. He came home and threw his shoes into the air; he didn't put down the toilet seat; he left coins scattered all over the place; he never cleaned the door handles, never ever again. This was a declaration of intent. Òscar was an indomitable rebel.

Nowadays, when he takes up with a girl, he makes sure that she has her own place and is well off. Although Annette doesn't boss him around or make him change the position of the cushions on the sofa, she's been there for three months and her presence is beginning to wear.

"Yum ... These courgette flowers are sensational, Annette. Did you take a photo before serving them? Don't forget that your followers will be waiting for today's recipe on your blog."

"Yes, yes. Of course I make the photograph before put on table. You know what is secret ingredient?"

"Let's see… today's secret ingredient must be… wow! That's hot!" Òscar yelps, and gulps down a big glass of water.

Annette loves playing the secret-ingredient game. There's always something hidden in her dishes. Today she's added a touch of wasabi to her brandade. The condiment hasn't made the slightest difference to the colour or texture, but naturally it has exponentially increased the pizzazz. Òscar also enjoys this exercise, because it obliges him to work with his taste and olfactory memory.

"No, you no drink! Water it make the hot more big everywhere in mouth. Eat bread! Bread it absorb the hot."

Although she's making progress, Annette's still a long way from speaking good Catalan.

For Òscar, on the days he gets home tired from work, these meals are like morning break time at school. The change of activity helps him to forget all about computer problems, pixels and RAM for a while. Now, however, though it may seem contradictory, he wants to have the flat to himself, even if it means a drop in eating standards. It's time to broach the subject.

"Do you know that Antic Món's still up for sale?"

"No, I no know nothing."

"Well, it is," Òscar continues. "I've driven past a couple of times and seen that the sign's still up. I've called the restaurant number but no one's answering. Then I tried the number on the announcement and was told they haven't got a buyer yet. Àlex wants sixty thousand euros for the leasehold, and the rent's one thousand five hundred. I'm sure he'll lower the price, because he must be desperate by now. Maybe you'd like it—"

"Oh, yes, I love it! Sixty thousand euros only?" she asks sarcastically. "If I find in the pocket…"

"God, Annette, your Catalan's still terrible, but you're certainly on the ball! Look, if you want Antic Món, I've got some money sitting in the bank. I don't need to use it for anything! It can be a loan."

"Òscar, we no know us so much."

"First of all," he tries to convince her, "we've lived under the same roof for three months. I think I've lived longer with you than with the girl I was supposed to marry. I know you're a good, hard-working person, and that you come from a family with excellent values. Second, don't worry: I'm not going to put the spoon in my mouth until I'm sure the soup won't burn. I mean I'll lend you the money, but with guarantees that you'll pay me back. I've been thinking about how to do it, and the best thing would be for me to pay for the lease and then you can repay the loan over a long period of time. It's as if I was a bank giving you a loan. In fact, it's quite simple."

"But I no know if Antic Món get success," Annette wavers. "It owe money, have bad name... Start again, this very difficult."

She's not convinced.

"We'll talk about profits and balancing the books in due course, when the time is right. The main thing now, the starting point, is whether you like the idea of being boss of Antic Món. Once that's decided, high hopes can move mountains. You're more than capable of managing that restaurant and getting it up and running again. You work hard and you're methodical, good-looking, a very nice person and a great hostess. You understand food and have good business sense. I'm totally convinced you'll make a good go of it. I'll be there to help you as much as you need. You know I've always wanted to have a restaurant."

"So why you not buy for you if you like restaurant?" Annette is baffled. "Is the good time now!"

"But I've got a high-powered job in IT. They pay me very well, I like it and it gives me peace and security. Running a restaurant would be a fascinating hobby for me, but that's not the way to go about it. A business like that needs full-time attention. But coming to give you a hand would be a great pleasure."

"I myself no can. I need waiter, chef… No, I no can pay!"

"You don't need to take anyone on for the dining room. Well, maybe someone at weekends, but not on a permanent basis. Well, yes, you'll have to get a chef. What about Àlex?"

"This no! Never!" She's indignant. "Àlex he go too much far."

"He went too far," Òscar corrects her.

"OK, OK. I say Àlex he no can enter Antic Món. His behave it very bad."

"Well… What about it? Do you think you can take it on?" Òscar presses, trying to drag a definite "yes" out of her.

"I no able to take this. But nice idea."

"Take it on. Repeat after me: 'I can't take it on.' That means you feel you can't meet the challenge. No one's accusing you of taking anything. Right, so tomorrow I'll go looking for Àlex and tell him about our plans."

"I no can to take on it."

"Nonsense! You'll do a great job. Listen, Annette, you've been here three months now, you haven't found a job and it's very unlikely that you'll find one. I hate having to remind you, but you're of a certain age and also without a work permit. You might get a few odd jobs, waitressing in a bar, giving private English classes, cleaning and so on, but nothing serious or interesting. This restaurant is a one-off chance for you. As for the paperwork, don't worry about that. We'll find a way. But we can make a start: I buy it. You work there. We only need to speed up the legal side of things."

"You no say *me*. You say *you*…" Annette pleads.

"What's this? You've lost me. I don't understand what you're saying."

"You no say Àlex about me. Say *you* buy restaurant. No say nothing of me."

"Right, right. OK, I'll do that. Does that mean we can go ahead?"

Òscar breathes easier. Annette seems excited about the project of reopening Antic Món, which means she'll soon leave his flat and he can have the peace and quiet he's longing for. Paying fifty thousand euros for the restaurant to get rid of Annette is a very high if not inordinate price. It would have been cheaper to rent her a flat or find her a job.

But this isn't the only reason he wants to buy Antic Món. The fact is, he's grown fond of Annette and, then again, he feels sorry for Àlex. Òscar is well acquainted with Àlex's career as a chef and admires him. Like most foodie bloggers he's made a legend of him and has glossed over his bad behaviour: a chef, if only because of the fact of sweating over a stove, must be free of any guilt. However much he "disguises" it as self-interest, Òscar's real aim in buying Antic Món is altruistic. It's his particular way of helping Annette and Àlex. He's sentimental, a romantic, and it's the least he can do. Yet he still feels mean, bothered by his conscience. He can't stop thinking that he's kicking Annette out and, moreover, paying dearly for it.

Àlex rarely goes to Antic Món, except to sleep, and that's hard enough. He spends his days in Barcelona. Frank often phones him to update him on the restaurant situation, but it's always the same thing: no news. Very few people have called and nobody's really interested. This isn't the time for buying anything, least of all an unsuccessful restaurant.

"Someone called today and he seems serious."

"Do whatever you think is best," Àlex responds listlessly.

"Come on, Àlex!" Frank chides him. "It strikes me that you couldn't care less. You say you want to sell the place and the only thing that's occurred to you is to put a tiny sign at the door. You haven't made a single phone call yourself or spread the word among your colleagues. Don't you want to sell it? How will you support yourself? Maybe you've got a stash tucked away under your pillow. I don't know how you keep going, man. You must be down to your last cent."

"I don't need much to live on. And how I survive is none of your business. Right now, I'm feeding my spirit, which was very much on the lean side. And when I'm in danger of dying of hunger I can still find a few mummified edibles in the Antic Món freezers. Who cares? Anyway, who called?"

"Some guy named Òscar. He says he's a friend of yours and is complaining because you don't pick up the phone at the restaurant. Òscar 'the blogger', he told me to tell you."

"Bloody hell! Òscar? How come he wants to buy the restaurant? He must have gone mad. I'll phone him right now."

"Remember, if you sell it, you owe me a commission," Frank reminds him.

"So the reek of money's got to you, has it?" Àlex taunts.

"You know what? I've had a gutful of you and your bad moods. Byebye. Go your own way. Forget the commission. I don't want to see you ever again."

Well, well, well, another name scratched off his measly list of friends. So what. He's certainly not going to try to patch up the damage he's just done to his friendship with Frank.

Àlex and Òscar are sitting at Table 3 in the Antic Món dining room. They're ill at ease. They used to meet up to have a good time, but today they have to talk about money, which is disagreeable, especially for Àlex.

Òscar takes in Àlex's unkempt appearance. He can tolerate a bit of dirt, but this is more than a bit. There's a centimetre or two of dust on the shelves and it all reeks of mustiness and the stale air of a closed space. Àlex doesn't seem to notice.

"Do you want a glass of Mistelle and a few almonds?" Àlex asks. "No, hang on, not Mistelle! Today we'll crack a good white, the very best, a real little gem, a Sauternes I've been keeping for a special occasion...

which never happened. I feel like drinking it today. Yes, and the almonds will go nicely with it. Sorry, I don't have any foie—"

"Don't open anything, Àlex. A glass of water will do."

"Listen young man, I'm not opening the Sauternes for you. I'm doing it for me. I feel like it and humanity can stick that up its arse."

"Rest assured, humanity won't know anything about it, so there's no need to worry. There's just the two of us here and I don't plan to tell anyone. Cool it, man. Do what you like. Let's get to the point. I want to buy the restaurant. I can't afford the amount you're asking, but I'll make an offer and let's see what you have to say."

"Just a moment, lad. I need my Sauternes. It might even happen that with the help of an exquisite, sweet, satiny white wine I'll look kindly on your offer."

"OK, OK, I'll have a glass too. I've never had the chance try the legendary wine made of rotten grapes. What a luxury."

"They're not rotten grapes. Well, slightly rotten, maybe. The wine's made of grapes affected by *Botrytis cinerea*, or noble rot if you like. It's noble rot and it doesn't stink… a bit like Antic Món, riddled with rot, but nobly so."

Àlex gets two of his best Riedel crystal glasses, which he wipes with his stained shirt tail before pouring the Sauternes. Pretending not to see, Òscar steels himself. He's feeling desperately sorry for Àlex, and it's not just the grungy dining room or the "medals" he's sporting on his shirt, but his general personal appearance: gaunt, skinny, badly shaven with dark rings under his eyes testifying to the fact that he's sleeping little and badly. The owner of Antic Món looks like a hobo.

"Out with it, lad," Àlex orders.

"I've got forty thousand euros for the lease and can offer six hundred a month."

"Listen, kid, that's much less than I'm asking for."

"Wait, I'm not done yet. The rest of the down payment will be your participation in the restaurant, by which I mean we'll be partners, although I'll have more shares than you. If you want, you can keep working here."

"Now I've put my foot in it," thinks Òscar. "Annette won't want to work here if Àlex stays." What an idiot. What's he gone and done? He's so upset by Àlex's appearance that his subconscious has taken over his tongue, which has started wagging all by itself. This wasn't his idea, and he certainly hadn't meant to say this, but the words tumbled out anyway.

"So you're telling me that you'll be my boss," Àlex snaps. "What the hell does that mean? That I'll be at your orders and will have to make prawn cocktails and barbecued lamb for degenerate palates? No way!"

"No, man, no! I mean you can continue living here and working in your own place, as you've done up to now… But some things are going to change, although with the only and laudable aim of getting this business back on its feet. Remember, you'll always have the option of selling your share if all goes well or if you don't like the way we run the restaurant."

"We?" Àlex is no fool. "Who else is behind this ridiculous idea?"

Òscar's a berk. He's always making a mess of things. First, he's been foolish enough to offer Àlex a job, and now he's blabbed the plural pronoun after Annette stressed he wasn't to mention her name in the negotiations. OK, it's done now, so what the hell. There's no way he can hide the fact that she's involved. Òscar feels intimidated by Àlex's strong personality, overwhelmed by him. The situation is making him very tense and his hands are sweating copiously, even though he's not moving. He's always been gutless. He only has to see a cop in the street and he's scared he'll be picked up even if he hasn't done anything – good or bad. And as a small boy he always had the feeling that, if the teacher called out his name, he was going to get his head bitten off.

101

Staring at his hands and thus managing to avoid Àlex's unrelenting gaze, he answers, "Look, first of all, I want to say that proposal isn't the least bit ridiculous. On the contrary, it's a great idea that will help you to keep going with the project you've given your life to – the restaurant. Then again, it's not irreversible. If you're not happy with it, you can leave. It's about trying to find a way to save Antic Món."

"Òscar Hood, rescuer of down-and-out chefs!" Àlex laughs. "But what's got into you? Who the fuck do you think you are? Do you think you can do it better than me?" He's silent for a moment, taking advantage of the pause to take in and consider the offer he's just received. "Well, let me think it over. I can't give you an answer right now. First of all I want to know the identity of this enigmatic person who's prepared to embark on such a ruinous project."

"Annette," Òscar whispers, without daring to look up from his trembling hands.

"Fuck, fuck, holy fuck! This is really incestuous. We can't break away from the circle. It's as if we're the only people who exist in this world and the rest are mere extras. Annette will be my boss? This whole damn thing's so complicated. Give me a few days to think about it."

He doesn't understand, doesn't understand himself any more and why his heart broke into a mad gallop when it heard Annette's name. Everything inside him, all his viscera have been writhing in treacherous convulsions ever since Òscar pronounced the magic word: Annette.

With his heart still in overdrive, his powers of reason kick in, trying to think and stabilize his emotions. This is utter madness and it can never succeed, which they've already proved. They've worked together before and it's obvious the venture will fail. Now, moreover, the tables are turned and he'll be the dogsbody. The mere thought is enough to make his hair stand on end.

Yet Annette has once again occupied his brain and everything has taken on a softer, smoother, more velvety appearance. He's just got another whiff of the fragrance he picked up the very first time they spoke about her, slightly acid, spicy, like fresh lemons.

Àlex looks in the mirror and sees a pathetic, lonely, morose, emotionally shrivelled old man. Diving into his memories, he finds someone made up of layers, like an onion: a happy kid, silent adolescent, young rebel, prosperous chef... and broken man. He spits copiously at his reflection and wipes the mirror with his dirty shirtsleeve.

He looks again, opens his eyes wide and glimpses a long road ahead. The joy of starting afresh with his interrupted dream prods him to overcome all obstacles. It's time to do some exercise. He doesn't want to know anything about the past. He'll pick up one of those Milan rubbers, the ones that smell like cream, and erase all bad memories from his unpublished biography. With a nice, new, well-sharpened pencil he'll make a note in his best handwriting of all the experiences that give sense to things. Yes, he wants to try again. He'll accept Òscar's offer.

"Carol? Where are you? It's been days since I've had any news of you."

"Days? Months more like it! I've haven't heard a peep out of you lot for weeks, and it's not because I haven't tried. I've phoned you both. You and Annette. Well, the truth is I've phoned her more often than you and, when no one answered, I started to imagine all kinds of situations: you'd run off to Quebec together; you'd committed suicide by diving into a cauldron of broth; you've become a Mormon and are wandering around signing up all the immigrants in the Maresme. Àlex? Àlex?... Are you there? Have you hung up?"

"I'm here."

"Why don't you say anything?"

"You won't let me. You've been ranting on to yourself for ages. Listen, why don't you come over and have dinner with me?"

"Where?"

"Antic Món. I'll defrost something."

"What 'something' are we going to eat, may I ask? You've been closed for three months. By the way, thanks for letting me know you were closing. I had to find out in the newspapers and I was gobsmacked. That lunatic Montsià saw it. That poor sod's so up himself, running round all over the place, sniffing at his wines and writing that imbecilic crap that people actually believe! Anyway, this cretin broke the story in his column. My God! That set off a torrent of articles, comments and opinions in all the media. You were the flavour of the week, my boy."

"Was I? I didn't know."

"I kept phoning you, but to no avail. Anyway, it was better like that, I assure you. They weren't remotely nice about you. They wanted to see you burnt at the stake. That gang of critics and food writers are bloody predators. By the way, how's Annette? Has she gone back to Canada? Wow, that woman is damn rude, and I was so good to her. I even bought her clothes. I haven't heard a word from her. She never even said thank you!"

"OK! That's enough. Stop. I forgot about your non-stop babble. Get your act together and come over and have dinner with me. We'll open one of those wines I've been keeping for great events, we'll get pissed, and I'll tell you about the next chapter of my life. Don't tell me that that's not a scintillating plan for this dreary Tuesday night."

"All right, I'll come. I was supposed to go to an oyster tasting in Marennes, but the very thought of it makes me retch. I can see a jamboree full of hostesses planted at the entrance, smiles painted on their mugs and asking guests to show their invitation. I love acting offended, so I can enjoy watching the PR fairy get his knickers in a twist every time he has to apologize. I piss myself laughing when I see how they squirm every time I pull a face. An evening with you will be much more fun and interesting than a dozen Marennes oysters, even if I do have to pay the price of swallowing your frozen hake."

"I didn't get a word of that. You can tell me the less garbled version later, or, with a bit of luck, you won't tell me. I'm here and dying to see you." Àlex hangs up.

He sticks his head in the freezer, a great trunk of a thing, typical of restaurant kitchens. He rummages round in bags, boxes and plastic containers, most of them empty. There's hardly anything left, which isn't surprising since he's kept himself alive on frozen food for the last three months. What can he make for Carol? Luckily, right at the bottom, buried under a layer of frosty-looking ice, he finds a bag of small prawns.

He chops up a few, quite a few, cloves of garlic. "Can someone tell me how to get out of this fix?" he begins to bellow, trying to belt it out with all Mazoni's power. He fries the garlic cloves in plenty of oil and then removes them. "There's something in you that sucks up your poetry"... He adds a touch of chilli. "It's not about wanting but knowing what you're giving up." He sings lustily, but the dish isn't singing with him. Something's missing. He needs time to finish the song. "We're not a memory or a trail, but just a lonely spot." He'd like to have a good supply of food. He misses flinging casseroles around, smells mingling in the air and pervading the whole kitchen, the thrill of cooking, the whole thing. "Happiness isn't enough; it's euphoria we need." He wants to go back to the "euphoria" of things cooking. Yes, he wants to cook, and cook with Annette.

He still has time before Carol turns up. He goes up to his room, changes, shaves and splashes on some cologne. He doesn't want her to see him scruffy and grubby and then come to her own poison-laden conclusions. She'd have him pigeonholed in no time: a poor loser. The woman's evil.

At nine on the dot, Carol arrives at Antic Món with a boxful of food. Àlex is pleased with the gift, but ashamed that he has so little to offer himself.

"I wasn't convinced by your offer of frozen leftovers so I've brought some excellent canned goodies. A dinner improvised from this stuff can be brilliant. Tins are like those friendships you don't care about, but which can get you out of all sorts of messes without moaning about being shunted aside for something more beautiful, younger and fresher. Your tins wait in the pantry, patient and uncomplaining, until you need them. Then you're full of praise for these ugly, inscrutable, aluminium cans and, when you decide to open them, you find that they're hiding a singular personality, discreet uniqueness, exquisite taste and great humility. Although they're so honest, you hesitate before presenting them in society, because they're not considered natural enough, or fresh enough, or young enough, or beautiful enough to be hanging on your arm. I have the highest regard for them because they've never let me down. I hope you value my friendship, because, like the tins, its use-by date is a long way off."

Carol arranges her collection of aluminium items on the table: tuna-belly fillets in extra-virgin olive oil, Tudela asparagus, Kalamata olives, enormous clams, Los Peperetes razor clams, Joselito ham and even some Nacarii caviar.

"You've brought all your freebies, woman!" Àlex exclaims. "Having seen the way all these salesmen grease your palm and butter you up so you'll be nice about their products, I know you haven't forked out a cent for all this. Anyway, the metaphor about cans and friendship is very fine. Maybe you picked it up from something you read?"

"Don't be so offensive. Stop hurting my feelings. Who cares whether they're gifts or I paid for them? We have them on the table here and we're going to have a feast. It's lucky I brought them. Those prawns and parsley look downright scary. Alright, lad, I don't want to get worked up. I'm too old for tantrums. I'm at a point where everything's fine and, if not, I just change the channel. I'm here today and I'm going to have a good time. You too. You've lost a lot of weight. You're a walking corpse," she says, abruptly changing the subject.

"I'm fine and I needed to shed a few kilos," he defends himself. "I like your idea of changing the channel. But right now, I'm not changing. I'm keeping the restaurant. It's sold, with me in it," Àlex says, as he opens one of the three bottles he has ready for the night.

"What's this? What do you mean? Someone's bought it with you in it?" Carol's intrigued.

"Well, my friend, that blogger Òscar, has joined forces with Annette, and they're doing their Little Sisters of the Poor thing, so they're buying it. They think they'll make me happy if they let me rattle casseroles again, and they're so lovely they'll even allow me to sleep here in my own house."

"Annette and Òscar? Well, well, well, life brings new surprises every day. This El Puntido is spectacular," says Carol, topping up her glass. "Is that all you have?"

"You've already drunk the whole damn bottle. You're a sponge. No, no, I haven't got any more Puntido, but we'll crack open an Equilibrista. Have you tried it? It's a worthy drop. This time I'm going to keep it next to me, or I won't even get to have half a glass before you down it all."

"So what are you going to do?" she resumes. "Are you going to play ball? I mean, are you going to let them turn everything upside down so Annette can be your boss? You won't be able to do that. No one can give you orders. You'd be a terrible menial."

The rate at which they're downing the wine is like a film that's been put on fast forward. In two sentences and three silences, they've just about done for the second bottle and the booze has begun to affect their conversation.

107

"I have no choice but to accept their offer. I can't find work. No one wants the restaurant. I haven't got a cent to my name. The freezer's empty. And unfortunately I've got withdrawal symptoms. There's no way I can get cooking out of my system. It's a nightmare. I dream I'm cooking, imagine I'm shopping at the market, haggling with suppliers, choosing the product, smelling non-existent aromas. I want to cook again. I have a plan and you've got to help me."

"A plan? What plan? What do you want me to do?"

"Sink them."

8

UPROAR

All mushrooms are edible, some only once.
MICHEL GÉRARD JOSEPH COLUCCI (COLUCHE)

Annette turns the key in the door of Antic Món. She moves inside and, standing in the centre of the shadowy dining room, surveys the tables, chairs, tablecloths, shelves…

The effect is stifling. There's a huge amount of work to do, so much that she has no idea how to go about it. She knows that optimism and excitement are a great source of energy, and she's not afraid of work, but she is terrified she won't be able to repay Òscar. A different way of working has to be organized, the new menu publicized, clients attracted from everywhere, expenditure supervised, different, surprising, tasty dishes cooked and the space redecorated, so that everything is gleaming, clean and tidy.

Being boss of a restaurant, all by herself, is a complex task and she's not at all sure she'll succeed. Òscar has promised to help her out in the first few months and Àlex, who's a great cook and who has run the restaurant single-handed for a long time, will be there to help her. This, however, is not really a help but a handicap. It would have been easier to start from zero with a whole new team, because old habits die hard, especially if the person who has to be "transformed" is someone like Àlex. The problems only get worse.

He's not around at the moment. It would appear that he's not keen to witness the arrival of the new owners. Annette sighs. She doesn't feel ready to cope with this all by herself.

She goes upstairs to leave her enormous suitcase there. Opening the wardrobe, she finds the party dress that Carol bought for her, and the underwear as well. Her throat suddenly constricts with anxiety. She should have phoned Carol ages ago. She's been avoiding it all these months because she wanted to get her life in order, feel calm and not get dragged into situations that might play havoc with her emotional state. She can't put the call off any longer, because Carol might think that she's upset for some incomprehensible reason. In fact, Carol has been very kind to her.

"Hello, Carol. How are you?"

"Hi, beautiful! What a lovely surprise. How are you? I hear you've bought Antic Món. Well done. I'm sure it will be a winner."

"Thank you. I'm fine. You come when you want and we talk. I have plenty work now."

"I don't doubt it. It won't be easy. I don't want to disturb you, but I'd love to see you, because we're friends and I'm the person you need. Don't forget, I'm a top food critic and this is exactly what I do, speak badly or highly of restaurants. Do you have some bright ideas for getting Antic Món up and running again?"

"I know you write food critic… I want for you to come as friend."

"I know, I know. Even though you haven't been the greatest friend yourself. You haven't answered any of my calls, which is why I thought just now that you've called me for purely professional reasons. Well, I'm sure you'll tell me the whys and wherefores of your stony silence."

"What stone?"

"Come on, girl, one of these days you're going to have to learn to speak Catalan properly. It isn't all that difficult. You might understand it a little better if somebody licked it into the depths of your ear, very lustfully, just like I would do. What the hell. The fact that you express yourself so quaintly also has its charm. You decide. If you want me to come over today to give you a hand, I'd be delighted. Tomorrow I'm off to Tokyo for two weeks."

"That very good for you. You come today if you wish this."

The last thing Annette wants is for Carol to come, but she can't say no, because it's true that she needs to have Carol on side now. She's got to keep her happy.

"I'll come and help in any way that's needed, right. You deserve it," Carol adds. "When do you want to open the restaurant again?"

"Very quick."

Just as Annette hangs up, Àlex walks into Antic Món. They stare at each other for a few seconds. They're tense. It's the first time they've seen each other in the new circumstances, because Òscar acted as intermediary in the negotiations for the sale of the restaurant. Annette's uncomfortable and she also feels terribly sorry for Àlex, who looks haggard and sad. He breaks the ice, eases the tension with the ghost of a smile, blurts out "Hello" and then heads for the stereo system to put on a CD of heartbreakingly melancholy harpsichord music. He goes upstairs to his room and is back in the kitchen a couple of minutes later wearing his white chef's gear.

"OK, Madame Boss, tell me what you want me to do." Mockery mingles with submission.

"You no talk so. We sit, OK?"

"Why do we have to talk? What we have to do is work like navvies. There's nothing here to eat and the cooking has to be done. I'm here to cook."

"Il n'y a pas the food for cook," Annette laments. When she's nervous her languages come out even more jumbled.

"Spot on. There's no food. Has Madame ordered some?"

"We sit to talk some moments," she insists.

Annette gets two beers and sits at the kitchen table. She gestures with her hand, inviting him to join her.

"Woman, if we get into the beer before we start work, this restaurant won't be going anywhere." He takes a long swig then wipes away with his tongue a spiteful remark that gets no farther than his lips.

Annette explains with great difficulty, both because of the language and her uneasiness at being confronted by Àlex, how she proposes to run the restaurant. This could well be the most difficult situation she's ever been in, and it's not as if her life has been a bed of roses so far. Today she feels as if she has betrayed Àlex: she's gone from being a helper doing menial jobs to being his boss, and this isn't easy to accept, especially by someone like him. To cap it off, she feels an inexpressible attraction for the man who's gone from being boss to underling, and the whole thing is fast becoming more and more complicated. Worse still, he used to be the owner and creator of the business she's just bought into without having the faintest idea how to run it.

He's pale and gaunt and it's very clear that he's suffered greatly. Having to give him orders and make him accept her way of working won't be easy at all.

Àlex lets Annette talk. He listens, apparently calmly, as if she has nothing to do with his work and, in short, his life. It really seems as if he's distractedly listening to the chitchat of some fellow diners, a conversation that doesn't affect or involve him, but that only interests him because it's about the future of those two people at the next table.

The new owner of Antic Món is expecting swearing, verbal abuse and crass language in response to her proposals, but his reactions are the exact opposite. He hasn't as much as raised an eyebrow. His submissive pose throws her, but also makes her feel stronger. What had begun as a timid plan for task-sharing has ended up, half an hour later, as a soliloquy, a firm statement of her intentions, a new philosophy for the restaurant.

Annette is determined to get Àlex to devise a taster menu of five dishes, all of them with her agreement, which they will offer for dinner as the

"Chef's Menu". The new cuisine at Antic Món will be more affordable and, in particular, tailored to the tastes of the local people. Their potential clients must be able to understand the dishes they are being offered and, more importantly, pay for them. At lunchtime they will offer an inexpensive set menu in the hope of attracting workers from the nearby industrial estates. At weekends they'll do a family menu.

It will be a surprising offer at an irresistible price. In order to keep the balance stable they'll cook with economical raw materials. Annette's idea is to make different, unusual chickpea dishes for example. They'll stop buying top-quality shellfish and work with frozen products and any fresh fish they use will be from fish farms, but Àlex's culinary skills will transform them into the exquisite dishes of a great restaurant. All game will be taken off the menu, as it is terribly expensive and very few people like it. Annette is aware that this is one of the contentious points, and the decision that will hurt Àlex most, because he always insisted on offering game dishes, even though hardly anyone asked for them. For him this is a distinctive feature, the mark of a good restaurant. He believes that cooking isn't classy if it can't transform the noble putrefaction of a woodcock into a sublime and sumptuous morsel. Yet, hearing Annette's announcement that they won't be offering game any more, he doesn't bat an eyelid, but keeps listening in silence. Encouraged by this, she gathers momentum and forges ahead with her list of all the changes she envisages. The menu is going to have an "International Food" section, which will include a dish from a different part of the world every day, cooked by Annette. The dessert list will be very small but of high quality. They will offer frozen home-style desserts bought from a local producer, fresh fruit, and Annette will make her carrot cake and other sweet dishes from her country such as gingerbread, berry crumble, cheesecake and apple tart. That's the kitchen plan. As for the dining room, the customers will be waited on by Annette.

In the afternoons she'll deal with management matters, mainly promoting the restaurant on the Internet and balancing the books. Her main objective is to pay off all the debts. It will be a heavy cross to bear, but they can't afford to be labelled as debt dodgers. They must work to gain a good reputation. They'll stop concentrating on customers from elsewhere, the ones that slavishly follow food guides in their quest to find top-of-the-range restaurants. They must attract local customers, town residents, people with holiday and weekend homes, office staff from the industrial estates and families on a weekend outing. Nevertheless, she'll still keep trying to spread Antic Món's fame as widely as she can, because, after all, they are on a main road and should make the most of that to include travellers among their customers.

Her monologue has been a cross between an economics class and instructions on how to harvest a field of potatoes; between a complicated spit-roasted fillet and the simplicity of bread with olive oil.

Annette takes a sip of her beer, and Àlex, taking advantage of the pause, can't resist sarcasm.

"Is that the end of the speech, Madame?"

"No, I tell you one thing more." Annette is now losing her grip and, staring at her shaky hands, realizes that she can't put it off any longer. "We will have the new name. We call restaurant Roda el Món," she whispers.

There is a tense silence. Àlex doesn't react, as if he's not affected by such a major change. Now he's just a simple worker in this rebaptized Round the World restaurant, and that's how he plans to act.

"Listen, I don't care about the bookkeeping, or your philosophy, or anything you decide. Not even about the name you've chosen for the restaurant. I'm here to work, cook and do my job well."

"But you little bit owner," she says.

"Ah, yes? A little bit? What's my share: that chair and a couple of saucepans? It's as if you're telling me you're a little bit my lover. I want all of you, not just an arm or a finger or just fifteen minutes a day. I want your whole body and your whole soul. You might think I crave too much, but I'm not willing to eat just the lobster's antennae. I want the whole thing. Today, right now, I am a cook. Just a cook. To begin with, I want a salary and, by the way, you haven't told me how much it will be yet. Second, I have the right to two days off per week, like any worker in any company. Most of all, I want to get down to the job. So move your arse and go and get some ingredients. I need some raw materials. These fridges are pitiful."

His gruff response makes Annette feel more relaxed, because the Àlex she knows is starting to appear. She knows how to cope with this character. His passive, compliant behaviour throws her off balance. She prefers the consistently cantankerous, prickly, cagey Àlex. Ignoring the sentimental part of his outburst, she hands him pen and paper.

"OK. You put list and I buy things for you start cooking."

She waits patiently while Àlex writes a seemingly endless list, then picks up the basket and, walking to the door, says, "I back after half hour." The excuse of needing to shop is a godsend. She doesn't know how to continue the conversation, and having to go out is the best way to clear away the soupy mist that is swirling around her brain. There's no doubt about it: she has an extra, major responsibility, and that is trying to keep their damaged relationship on an even keel.

It's impossible to buy everything on Àlex's list, so Annette makes a selection, a concentrated version of the food he wants. He's put ten kilos of sugar on the list, so she ignores the zero and drops one kilo of own-brand sugar into the basket. She'll only be bountiful when the supermarket has a special offer, which is the case with the hake. She buys two of them instead of the red sea bream Àlex has asked for.

115

She is sure he'll receive this cursing, swearing and trying to pick a fight, but things have changed now and she's just shown who's in charge. He can't have everything he wants. Annette will supervise the shopping and all orders must be approved by her, however many rows that causes.

Meanwhile, Àlex drains his beer. Since Annette's not around, he opens another, gets a piece of paper to write out the first taster menu he's going to cook. He stares at the blank sheet and feels like a novelist with writer's block. No brilliant idea comes to him. He always finds it hard to plan what he's going to cook. He stares at the piece of paper for quite a while then opens his third beer, which he downs in nervous swigs. He writes down one dish, then another and feels encouraged. It looks as if he's getting the yen to cook again. The doorbell rings. He hesitates before answering. After all, he's not the boss now, but just the cook, and it's not his job to open the door or attend to suppliers or even clients. But he's never been able to resist the urge to know who's on the other end of the phone call, or who's standing outside his door.

"Hi, Carol. What are you doing here? I can tell you right now that there's nothing to eat."

"No probs. Calm down. I'm interested in other things beyond your cooking, for example a gorgeous redhead. I miss that cute little round bottom."

"Don't even think about it. Keep away from her. Remember, we have a plan."

"Let me do things my way. This woman's really attractive, but don't worry, I'm not going to let her pull the wool over my eyes. I'm a big girl now and very experienced. I never mix love and business. In this case, there's no room for love. I want to have my way with her, even if only a little, and it might even make our plan work better. I'll soften her up till she's nice and tame and trusting. What are you doing?"

116

"Working out a kind of tasting menu. My boss is very demanding, but also very ingenuous, a combination that's even more horrible than vodka with gin and pepper. She wants to make lentils taste like caviar. She's crazy. There's no need to apply our plan. She's going to make a hash of this all by herself."

"Well, you certainly seem very perky. So where is your gorgeous boss?"

"She's trotted off to buy victuals with her little wicker basket," he says caustically. "Our little airhead is environmentally aware."

"Can I help you to plan the menu? I know the latest trends, what customers want. Don't forget: in most cases I'm the one who creates the fashions. I'll sort you out a winner's menu in two shakes of a lamb's tail: fresh food, lots of veggies, traditional dishes with an ethnic touch and simple desserts. You have to make it profitable, easy to cook, appealing for old folk, trendies and pimply adolescents who have barely been weaned off McDonald's."

"I'm not sure that I can."

"Of course you can. We need the place to work so you can earn a bit, keep Annette happy and, more importantly, make her think she's got it right – and then we'll hit her with your plan."

"You're a diabolical strategist. OK then, let's work out this crap menu. The fact is I'm lost. Sad, you know? I feel let down, I don't give a damn about anything and I might as well start pushing up daisies now."

"Needless to say, you've got a massive depression, my lad. Anyone can see that a mile off. Just remember that this situation won't last long. If we play our cards well, you'll have the restaurant all to yourself again, plus your dignity."

"Carol, I want to ask you something. My aim here is understandable. I'm the hurt boss, the devastated chef who wants to get back what he believes is his, and by any means possible. But you... why do you want to get mixed up in this? You keep saying you're crazy about this woman

117

and you want her for yourself... and yet you want to destroy her, see her on her hands and knees, grovelling in the mud. It's very contradictory."

"Let's see if I can put my feelings into words. They're very intense and run deep. She treated me badly. I can't stand it when people don't answer my calls. It's not elegant. I just wanted to help her. She has to learn that I'm very important and that nobody messes around with me. In addition, I admire you and consider myself your friend. I want to support you," Carol explains haltingly. "Anyway, I certainly understand my own position and consider it much more reasonable than yours. You're in love with this woman, so it's difficult to grasp why you want to ruin her. In fact, I'm sure you don't know why either. You've got a great big mess of opposing feelings in your head. You really fancy Annette and would love to share your life with her, right now, if she agreed. You'd be the perfect couple, the kind clients love to see working together."

"Where did you get this bizarre idea that I'm in love with her?"

"From your eyes. The way you look at her gives you away. And you're such a wreck, a walking melodrama. You're carrying on like a lovelorn loser."

The door of Antic Món opens and Annette appears carrying her basket with such a meagre amount of shopping it wouldn't be enough to feed a childless widow. Carol greets her effusively, like a long-lost daughter who's just returned from a gruelling voyage across many seas. While they chat, Àlex observes the scene. He's shocked to see how unscrupulous Carol is. Less than a minute ago she was talking about how to ruin Annette's life, and now she's having a lively conversation with her. Annette's explaining how she wants to manage the restaurant, the change of name, the new offers and the philosophy behind it all. Carol's all ears. They're both laughing as if they're the best of friends. Are they?

Àlex picks up the basket. He wants to start cooking, despite the wretched stock of ingredients. He puts things away in the cold room and his hair stands up on end to find, in the bottom of the basket, a bag of bright-red, explosive-red, blood-red tomatoes, the colour of horror. He'd love to hurl them out the window, so fuelled by his rage that they'd end up smashed against the front wall of Can Bret, staining it with the scarlet of shame, the crimson of insult. But he doesn't touch them, as if they were bearers of some contagious disease. He leaves them in the basket and tries to forget about them. He's got his work cut out in the kitchen. He lights the burners and the oven, gets out the chopping board and starts the ritual: he chops up all the onions, fast and expertly. He tips them into the casserole with a splash of oil and on a slow fire… It's a metaphor for the gestation of his new life. The *sofregit* – the base for his sauces – is the beginning.

Annette rushes into the kitchen, encouraged by her conversation with Carol.

"Carol say she help us very much. She love new concept of restaurant. She say name also, Roda el Món, very good. What you cook?"

"Nothing special. I'm starting with the basics. So she's going to help us?" He changes the subject. "Wonderful. I'm sure she will. When do you want to open?"

"Tomorrow."

"And the new sign, when will you put it up?" Àlex asks bitterly.

"Òscar he bring it today afternoon. He help clean also. You cook for us? I very hungry!"

"No. Chefs never cook for the staff. You'll have to do it yourself or get me an assistant to do it. Sorry."

"OK. I cook the lunch." Annette understands that Àlex isn't going to make it easy for her, but she's determined not to let this stop her. Cooking lunch for two is not exactly difficult. She makes a salad and two bits of grilled pork fillet. She's making a statement because, if she has to cook the staff lunches, they're going to be on the lean side and extremely simple. It will be home cooking, which Àlex hates so much he almost starts dry-retching when he hears the words.

They sit down to lunch. Annette's not sure what to say. Àlex remains silent and seems relaxed, as if he's eating alone. Annette would love to read the newspaper, so as not to have to deal with his muteness, but they don't get the newspaper at Roda el Món, and they don't even have something boring like a medical brochure to pass the time. She has only two options: either look at her salad or look at Àlex. In an attempt at relieving the tension, she asks Àlex what he's been doing while the restaurant's been closed, though she knows that he's hardly likely to tell her. Much to her amazement, as he broodingly chews on his pork fillet, he starts to tell her a long, harrowing story. About his son. He tells it very naturally, without the slightest hint of drama or self-pity, as if he were describing how to make the meatball for the ancient Catalan soup *escudella i carn d'olla*.

Àlex was very young, still living with his parents in Vielha, in Vall d'Aran. He wasn't a very sociable kid. He had few friends and wasn't much given to going to the disco with other boys of his age. He spent hours locked away in his room, reading.

The next-door neighbours sold their house to a big family, nine altogether: the parents, four girls and three boys. The constant hustle and bustle of the newcomers fascinated the shy, tongue-tied adolescent, who watched them and even spied on them through his bedroom window, seeing how the girls laughed, sang, studied, bickered and immediately afterwards hugged each other. This house was full of life, a place where everyone seemed happy. It was so different from the drab, leaden atmosphere at Àlex's place.

Laura, one of the two middle sisters, had long straight hair falling like a mantle to cover her whole back. She parted it in the middle and held it off her face with clips on either side, showing a wide, clear forehead without the slightest line to betray past worries. It was a forehead with all the power of a fearless, certain future. It was her job to go and buy the bread every day.

That day is engraved in Àlex's memory, the day he saw her leaving the house, immediately after which he ran to the bakery, although they didn't need bread. He introduced himself. "I live next door to you. My name's Àlex." The girl looked at him, picked up her five baguettes and the change and turned away from him without saying a word. But she did give him the merest suggestion of a smile. In Àlex's imagination, that skimpy smile widened, turned into a burst of laughter and fuelled desire. Thereafter, he sought every possible opportunity to see the slim girl with clear green eyes and long straight hair held off her face with two clips. In summer she wore floral dresses, and in winter a three-quarter-length coat. He never bought anything at the bakery, but just burbled a few awkward words. She thought he was strange but, precisely because of his elusive character, furrowed forehead and apparent austerity, she was increasingly drawn to him.

One day he plucked up the courage to invite her to have a beer with him. She accepted! In the bar, Àlex gazed at her in wonderment and adoration and, listening to her zestful, vivacious voice, instantly fell in love. Having a beer together after she bought the bread became a ritual. They drank a lot of beer, always watched over by five baguettes.

Laura talked non-stop. She told him how much she hated the subjects she was taking at the high school. She often failed and, when her father punished her, retorted that she didn't need to know how to work out stupid equations in order to be a painter. Maths could never tease out the mass of enigmatic colours of the landscape. Her world was blue when it was fine and red when it snowed, and her dream was to fly higher than the clouds crowning the mountains, go to faraway places and discover new colours. She'd never left the mountains, except for once when she was small and had an operation in the Lleida Hospital. Her imagination leapt over all barriers and that journey became a story in which she was the heroine. The hospital was the home of the White Knight who saw and struggled against the real evil: fetters on freedom. She endowed the doctor and all the nurses with magic powers, and a gang of elves and fairies set up house under her bed to defend her against all the germs that floated around looking for bodies to infect. In a little box under her pillow she kept the key, the one to open every door, the key of freedom. After her trip to Lleida, Laura wanted to stretch her wings, shake off the dingy dust and fly a long, long way away from the Vall d'Aran and its mists.

Àlex was bewitched. He wanted to give her everything: a place where she could paint, a landscape full of colours, his heart, his soul and his body. Everything, for her and her alone.

The months rolled by. They met in the bar, drank beer and dreamt of a faraway world. One day Laura asked him to meet her in the park. "I've got a joint. Let's get stoned." Àlex had never smoked hash before. He liked it and, as they clung together, he burned all his bridges.

"Laura, let's get away. We'll go to some place a long way from here. We'll live somewhere that's yellow, green and purple, in a world that's beyond blue and red, where there's no mist to drain out the colour, where we're not ringed in by mountains, where we're not imprisoned by them as if they're jailers holding us under lock and key."

Thus it was that Àlex went off to look for work in Barcelona, where he took the first job he was offered, as a kitchen hand in a good restaurant. He didn't have a clue about cooking. So what? What really mattered was that if they scraped and saved, refrained from buying anything that wasn't strictly necessary, his wages should be enough to rent a flat.

Laura announced that she wanted to study Fine Arts at the University of Barcelona. She had to work hard to persuade her parents to let her go, and they only agreed when she promised them they wouldn't have to pay anything except for the bus fare and her enrolment fees. Hers was a humble, working-class family with a lot of kids; if Laura's desires didn't represent too much of a financial drain, they'd let her go. In fact, her parents were more than busy trying to feed their family, so they didn't ask too many questions, except to make sure that she had a roof over her head that they wouldn't have to pay for.

They lived in a tiny flat in the seaside neighbourhood of Barceloneta, and Laura soon got pregnant. Àlex paid the rent and nicked a bit of food from the restaurant, which he bore off home like a treasure. Laura painted grey mountains and green lakes and, when Àlex got home, they got stoned. They kept telling their parents that the city was a long way from Vall d'Aran, so they wouldn't have to go back with the evidence of Laura's growing belly.

The baby was a boy, Laiex. They invented the name, because they were different from other people and not subject to social conventions or regulations. They didn't want to get married, or register the child, or baptize him, or give him a saint's name, as was expected of them. They wanted to be free and they became slaves: Laiex was born severely malformed and mentally disabled.

The night before mother and child were due to come home, Laura disappeared. She left while Àlex was working in the restaurant. When he arrived at the hospital, a nurse informed him that Laura had absconded. She handed him the baby with a tin of special powdered milk, saying coldly, "Here you are. Until the mother turns up again, give him a bottle with two measures of milk and four of water every three hours." It was a public hospital and nobody seemed to care. Nobody was willing to help the desperate young father.

The baby cried and cried and so did Àlex. Àlex cried in silence while Laiex's yells were shrill, ear-splitting and never-ending.

In three days and three nights of incessant crying, Àlex thought the child must be hungry and prepared bottle after bottle, too tired, too dazed to remember whether the nurse had said three measures of milk to two of water, or two measures of water to one of milk. He didn't know where to turn for help. He was alone, in despair, and he had to go to work. He'd told them what had happened, but he'd been away for three days and the boss said that if he didn't return at once he'd be sacked.

He caved in on the fourth day. Laiex hadn't stopped wailing. Àlex put the special milk and nappies in a plastic supermarket bag and, with the baby in his arms, got into a taxi.

"The Cottolengo convent, please."

When the taxi drove away, he left the child at the door and went off to work.

Twenty-eight years, twenty-eight whole years have gone by without a word from Laura. Maybe she's found a brightly coloured world, or maybe she's gone back to painting blue landscapes in summer and red in winter, or maybe her tears reflect the whole array of rainbow colours.

He visits Laiex every Monday and any other day when Antic Món is closed. He hasn't missed a single day at the Cottolengo convent these past few months. He goes there as a volunteer, helping the nuns.

He works as a handyman, painter and electrician, doing anything they ask. He feeds handicapped children, cleans up the adult residents and chats with lonely old people. It's a one-way conversation, as they never answer, not a single syllable. He gives them all his free time and is deeply grateful to them, because he's been able to see his son growing up. Laiex is a body, with arms longer than legs, a huge head drooping over his right shoulder. His mind is blank and colourless. He doesn't smile, or cry, or speak, or see, or feel. He sits in a chair, curls up in bed or lies on the floor. He never moves. Àlex, despite

124

everything, is really happy to see him so well cared for. No one there knows that Laiex is his son.

Àlex has been talking for nearly an hour. Now he stops, looks at his salad, looks at Annette and pleads, "You're the first person I've ever told this. I trust in your discretion. Please don't let this story go any further than you."

Annette has endive stuck in her throat and she can't swallow it.

9

TOMATO

*Nothing gives rich people today
more pleasure than eating what
used to be food for the poor.*
MICHEL CHARASSE

So much work! They haven't stopped for a single moment. Òscar's appeared and he and Annette have worked non-stop, the whole afternoon.
Àlex went up to his room after lunch to rest and they haven't seen hide
nor hair of him. He's calling on his privilege of being just a chef, even
if he does have a small share in the business.

Annette prefers not to criticize him for not helping, knowing that he's
expecting some kind of rebuke, but she doesn't want to give him the
pleasure of being right about that, or to light the spark that would set off
another fireworks display. He'll get used to the new situation, she thinks.

She is touched by the story of Laiex and can't get it out of her mind.
Àlex's sincerity and the horrible situation of a father abandoning his own
child have deeply affected her. He told the story unaffectedly, in a tone
devoid of feeling yet still conveying guilt, longing and utter sadness. Annette feels desperately sorry for him and wishes she could embrace him,
cradle him, give him all the love he's been deprived of for twenty-eight
years, and tell him that it's not his fault, that he's more than paid for
his decision. It's as if he now wants to become reconciled with himself,
which is why, Annette thinks, he has told the story for the first time. He

needs to get it out, to clear his conscience and to try to find a way of making up for all those years of bitterness in a quest for a sweeter future.

When Àlex comes downstairs to keep cooking, as if he's ready for the night shift even though the restaurant is locked and barred, he finds Òscar and Annette hanging up the new Roda el Món sign. He merely says hello and retreats into the kitchen, where he turns on the radio full blast. The newsreader's expressionless voice fills the whole restaurant, backed by the sound of knives chopping vegetables and the electric beater whipping up egg whites.

It's getting late, as Annette knows, because she has lentils on her mind. Emotion hasn't taken away her appetite and her brain is telling her it's dinner time. When Àlex left the kitchen free during the afternoon, she'd made the most of his absence to cook up a lentil stew which she wants Òscar to try. She'll invite him to dinner, which he deserves after all his hard work. She sets the table carefully, as if for a party, with three places.

The doorbell rings. But they're not expecting anyone. Carol! She doesn't miss a trick. How does she do it? It's as if she's been hiding behind the almond tree in front of the restaurant, watching them until the food's about to be served, and then... ring, ring.

"Hallo Carol. You give us surprise," Annette says, trying to hide her vexation at the visit. She's tired and has had enough of Àlex's hostility, so Carol's arrogance right now is the last straw.

Carol is oblivious to Annette's distant tone. It seems that she's been tasting cava all afternoon at a new winery. She's quite tanked, with shining eyes and wagging tongue. In her tipsiness she's hardly likely to discern nuances of tone.

"Hi guys! I'm heading off on my trip tomorrow, at last, and I thought, 'Emotions will be running high here today and I don't want to miss it.' How are you? Have you been fighting? Are you still friends? Are you worn out? I hate being bored and the last thing you find in this establishment is monotony. What's that? Lentils? Yum-yum. Sensible food, finally. I'm fed up with the idiocy of these newly hatted chefs. So-called cooks with titles and words, that's all they are. Their descriptions are ludicrous: silky pureed potato, subtle aromas of charcoal-grilled garlic, harmonies of truffle fragrance… Bullshit! I'm fed up with words that never appear on the plate. The silky pureed potato is cement for making walls, the subtle bloody aromas cling to me all evening and the harmonies of fragrance belong in the shithouse. What a stroke of luck, finding these lentils! Mmm, wonderful. They smell like the ones I used to eat when I was a little girl." Carol jabbers on without pausing for breath.

Òscar interrupts. "Hello. My name's Òscar. I write a gourmet blog and now I'm a part-owner of Roda el Món. I read your column and really like the way you write. I agree with almost all your restaurant reviews. It's an honour to meet you in person."

"Blogger, humph! I'll spare you my views on bloggers," she says with contempt.

"A peaceful life and good food," Àlex butts in, trying to dispel the tension that's now arisen between Carol and Òscar. "We'll feast on these lentils today and then we'll toddle off to bed. Tomorrow's going to be a hard day and these kids have to rest." Àlex wants to make things clear. They're here to work and the days of crazy partying are over.

Annette opens a bottle of wine, one of the cheaper table wines. She's tightening the purse strings. "I open this wine for to thank you Òscar, because you help me very much."

"Thanks, Annette. You know you can count on me. It's a pleasure to help you, a good experience."

This is Òscar. He always sounds pleasant and is friendly by nature, but he's also determined to get out of here as fast as he can. From now on, he'll have a heap of work whenever Annette phones and will steer clear of the restaurant as much as possible.

He used to have a ball when he visited Àlex. He'd teach him a few Internet tricks and was rewarded by a cooking lesson and a first-class meal. Now coming to Roda el Món means washing up, climbing ladders, cleaning toilets and hanging up signs. This is no party as far as he's concerned. A nightmare more like it. He's a *bon vivant*, and somewhat lazy. Jobs that require physical effort are boring and, what's more, very tiring. He's done his bit by putting his money into it. He'll find a way of not setting foot in the place again.

The four of them sit down to eat, happily tucking into the lentils. Carol praises them. She's very happy. She's raving on non-stop, telling stories, passing on professional gossip, demolishing reputations left, right and centre. Nobody is spared her vitriolic tongue. Òscar listens, fascinated, while Annette keeps getting up from the table, bringing plates, glasses, another bottle of wine and her fabulous carrot cake. Carol's drunk and not bothering to hide her lustful staring at Annette's bum. She even makes lascivious comments. She's so enthralled by her hostess's rump that she hasn't twigged that Àlex, impassive and still as a wax figure, hasn't said a word all night.

Annette has noticed. She's been watching him and she thinks she sees tears in his eyes. Àlex cries?

"Sweetheart, I'll help you as much as I can with this new venture," Carol tells Annette. "When I get back from this trip, I'll take you out to lunch on your days off. You need to know what the competition is up to. We'll analyse the menus of the best restaurants, adapt the most successful dishes to Roda el Món and detect the worst errors. It will be like going back to school. You'll have the best teacher and you have to reward me you know how." Carol's speaking to Annette, ignoring the other two. "You've got a tough job ahead in Roda el Món, but you'll do it. Especially if you're nice to me."

Annette doesn't know how to fob off Carol's barefaced propositions. She's silent for a few seconds and Àlex, making the most of this, stands up and offers a loud, clear, very succinct "Goodnight". Carol ticks him off for walking out on her when she hasn't finished what she was saying. Àlex, not bothering to respond to her belligerence, takes his plate out to the kitchen and goes upstairs.

"You two aren't going to call it a day yet, are you?" Carol wants to keep going. "It's very early and we've still got half a bottle, which is the perfect thing for a good chat."

Òscar looks embarrassed. "You'll have to excuse me. I need to get up early tomorrow to finish some work. If I don't get it done, I won't be able to come and help you, Annette. I'm sorry, Carol, because listening to you has been really interesting and enjoyable. Besides being a great critic and journalist, you're an excellent raconteur."

"Bloody hell, what a short night! You've turned into a bunch of bloody goody-goodies and gone all formal on me," she sneers. "Never mind, Annette and I will finish off the bottle. I want to tell you a few tricks for managing Àlex and getting this moribund place on its feet again."

Annette's head feels as if it's about to explode. It's getting late, she's spent the whole day running round and she's exhausted. Trying to revive a restaurant that's on its last legs is a complicated business, however you look at it, but when the task includes Àlex and Carol it's all but impossible. In the last two days, just as she's setting out on the new venture, she's been about to throw in the towel several times.

Fortunately Òscar's encouraged her this afternoon. He at least is a "normal" person in Annette's view. She thinks that Àlex and Carol are weird, peculiar, incomprehensible people. Yet they're extremely magnetic.

Annette doesn't understand herself. She wants to get away from them, but can't help feeling attracted by their singular, forceful personalities, which are full of inscrutable nooks and crannies and surprises that ambush her when she least expects them. They're compelling and very dangerous, because they create the need to keep discovering the secrets they're hiding, like the plot of a novel that keeps you awake, even if you're nodding off, until you get to the end. Like a good or bad story, Òscar's normal and comforting, precisely because you can see what the end's going to be.

"Come here gorgeous, come and sit next to me," Carol wheedles. "You look very tired." Her honeyed tone caresses Annette.

"Yes, I very tired."

"Cheer up, beautiful, and have a glass of this horrible wine you've given me. The worse the wine, the drunker you get. It'll do you good."

Annette's destroyed. She feels alone and absolutely done in. She takes the glass Carol hands her and gulps the wine, which claws at her throat. Carol blathers on non-stop, but Annette's stopped listening. She's dizzy and wants to throw up. She folds her arms and rests her head on them, her red hair spreading over the tablecloth. Carol caresses it.

Carol's drunk and the word prudence has just been erased from her dictionary. She's aroused and her hand has a will of its own, forgetting about the hair, slipping down Annette's back, and, finding an obstacle in the bra, undoes it. Annette lets her have her way: it's not just that she doesn't stop her, but she finds it comforting. She's enjoying the warm fingers caressing her nipples. She can feel Carol's panting on the nape of her neck and, all of a sudden, the tongue describing amorous scenes in the most tucked-away parts inside her ear. She's surprised to feel that she's wet between her legs. Carol takes her hand and pulls her to her feet. She leads her upstairs to her room, where they undress. Annette is like a doll, resisting nothing, accepting everything… liking it, asking for more. Carol makes her wait. "Not yet." She makes her stop. "I want you to get even more excited. I'm the boss here. You're going to come when I say so, girlie. I'm going to play with you." Annette squeals and, seeing how excited she is, how she's begging for more, transports Carol to cloud nine.

131

Carol leaves early next morning, leaving a naked Annette asleep. What a great night she's had. "Wow, this woman really turns me on," she thinks as she drives away listening to Nat King Cole: "When I fall in love it will be for ever / Or I'll never fall in love."

Yes, she'll help the new boss of Roda el Món. She deserves it. This name she's given the restaurant… yes, it has a certain charm. As soon as they open again she'll write a good review. Carol is determined to do whatever it takes to support Annette and make her happy. She's impressive, this woman from Quebec, and it's more than evident that she has latent lesbian passions.

Now that Carol has decided that this is the start of a long relationship, she's exultant, happy, because at last she can see herself with a stable partner. About time too! She's had such a collection of butterflies it's horrible to think about: married housewives about to celebrate their silver anniversary, intellectuals with airs of Victorian novelists, betrayed women who've just come out of failed relationships, adventuresses who've used her in their quest for new sensations. She's had enough of that. She wants Annette, whatever it takes.

Annette's brain is well and truly befogged this morning, the price she must pay for last night's wine. A cup of tea will comfort her. Àlex, immaculate in his chef's uniform, is already at work in the kitchen, cooking up today's menu.

"Good morning," Annette says as she makes herself a large mug of tea.

Àlex doesn't look up from the *champignons* he's cleaning in readiness for a soufflé, which is exactly the kind of cooking Annette wants to serve in the restaurant – something sophisticated with a faint flavour of mushrooms.

She sits down at the kitchen table, wanting just ten minutes for a quiet mug of tea and to think about the agenda for the intense day lying ahead and everything that has to be done. She remembers one of her father's sayings. He was a friendly, cheerful man with all the self-assurance that comes with the solid fortune of a prosperous industrialist. He demonstrated his bonhomie by hugging people tightly and cracking jokes at every opportunity. From time to time he regaled the family with lessons in his theory of life, for which solemn purpose he used a deeper and more serious voice.

Annette found it funny when, with the sober air of a Zen master, her father came out with one of his platitudes, for example: "You don't need to be a Formula One driver to get where you're going fast. It's more effective if you know the way." Then he'd go on in great detail to explain the precise meaning of his "masterly" words, so that nobody would be left in any doubt whatsoever. You can go a long way on foot. You don't need a car, but first of all you have to sit down and work out where you want to go and what the aim of the exercise is. If you start by moving, it's more than likely you'll go round in circles and end up arriving late, even if you're a Formula One driver. His cliché is very useful today. Before she starts running, she must sit down and think about what she has to do.

She puts two lumps of sugar in her tea, watches them disappear down into the depths of the mug, then stirs them in with a teaspoon. Her head is heavy and her memories of last night are like the sugar lumps sinking in tea without dissolving. Images of Carol and their conversations have turned into stones in her head, heavy stones dragging her down into the abysmal depths of contradiction, so that, rather than staying afloat, she's drowning in a sea of doubts, fear and guilty feelings. Why did she do it? Why did she let Carol seduce her? She knows the answer, but having to accept it really annoys her. She was looking for comfort in Carol's arms, an extremely flimsy excuse that doesn't absolve her of her stupidity in having got into this mess. Getting involved with Carol is the most dangerous thing she could have done. Heaven knows how she's going to get out of this. She's not a lesbian and has no intention of keeping Carol happy. Not in bed anyway.

Certainly, that was the main reason: wanting to be cherished. The anxiety of not knowing whether she's capable of running the restaurant, her tense relationship with Àlex, the feeling of helplessness in a country she doesn't know, the harrowing story of Àlex's son and the threat that keeps her constantly alert have undermined her capacity for resistance. OK, maybe she's got an iron will, which is how she likes to be seen, but her outside covering is tissue paper, which tears easily. That's when water gets in and rusts the metal. Carol's caresses were balm for her wounds, a delightful hot bath after a hard day's work in the snow.

"Hey, boss, you're turning into a dormouse! Wake up! I'm going to make *champignon* soufflé for your menu today as the *cuisine d'auteur* dish. I hope we don't get any customers with the slightest idea of good food, because they'll piss themselves laughing," Àlex says too loudly. He's trying to snap her out of her reverie.

"*Champignon* soufflé? Good idea!" she responds.

For Àlex, a mushroom soufflé is painfully, insultingly simple. Once the *champignons* are cooked, he mixes them into a béchamel sauce and adds the egg yolks. He beats the egg whites until they're stiff and gently folds them into the mixture he's prepared. He carefully butters a few individual ramekins, fills them with his concoction, ready to be kept in the fridge until some customer asks for the dish. He'll then cook them in a very hot oven until the beaten egg whites take effect and puff up the soufflé. One serving of this dish doesn't cost more than fifty cents to produce, and they can charge ten times more on the menu. Good business. If they have customers.

This is the Roda el Món's first day and they're not expecting anyone. Annette has covered the door with blackboards and signs announcing a ten-euro menu, a special offer on the occasion of the "reopening". Customers can choose from ten dishes. The culinary range is diverse and, in Àlex's view, incoherent. It's a potpourri menu to please all tastes, with everything from *cuisine d'auteur* to ethnic dishes and grilled meat. There's no clear line, as Annette's main aim is to listen to the customer, after which she'll work out which are the most popular dishes. Then they'll only cook what sells.

Naturally, Àlex doesn't agree with this jumble, but he's resolutely promised himself that he won't interfere in the "philosophy" of Roda el Món. Let them do what they like and fuck it up all by themselves. He's just a cook. He doesn't have to offer an opinion and nobody cares what he thinks anyway.

"You look tired, Annette. Haven't you slept well?" His tone is spiteful. He heard snippets of the intimate party in Annette's room. His was a long night of insomnia mixed with unspeakable nightmares in which he was the main ingredient in a dish smothered in tomato sauce. Hordes of carnivorous insects were nibbling at him. This nightmare was mixed up with another one in which some freckled redheads tied him hand and foot and, holding his nose, made him eat red and green peppers, whole and still covered with dirt from the garden.

Discovering that his beloved Annette is involved with his "partner in crime" has only heightened the effects of the nightmare, tormenting him with a feeling of irrecoverable loss. He thought, was convinced, that Annette fancied him, that he'd sown in her a tender seed that, with care and attention, would keep growing until it flowered into brilliant love. That's what he thought and now he's wounded at having been as naive as a secondary-school kid. It's not so much that he's lost the woman he desires, but he's fallen into the trap of the illusion of love. He tries to mask his disappointment in irony.

"Yes, I feel tired. I sleep little," Annette says laconically.

135

"And Carol? I suppose she hardly slept either," he insinuates. "She must have left very late."

"Yes, little bit late." Annette is serious. "You listen, Àlex. My life it for me. You, your life for you." She tries to bring the conversation to an end. "Yesterday night you no eat blueberry crumble."

"You're right. I didn't feel like it yesterday. Is there any left? I'll try some now. It's not a very beautiful dessert. The colours are too dark and it looks clunky. Do you plan to serve it in the restaurant?"

"Yes, of course. This my favourite dessert. It very gorgeous. You try. Plenty remain."

Àlex takes a mouthful, savours it, ponders it and finally pronounces, "Your desserts are very good, Madame. They have a certain appeal, so authentic, so rustic. If you'll let me, we could add some walnut ice cream. Mint sauce would go well with it too. Your style would look very English."

His tongue has run away with him. He had no intention of showing any interest in the desserts and still less in suggesting any improvements. But he's blurted it out. He thinks the recipe is very interesting, different, fun, with its juicy base of tart blueberries and the sweet crunchy topping, which holds out so many possibilities. Realizing that he's been too nice, he finishes with one of his crasser outbursts. "Be careful. I might just throw myself at you any minute. I'm sure you mixed aphrodisiacs into the flour and blueberries and Carol innocently wolfed them down. You're very cunning."

Àlex is having a great time shooting his poison arrows. He wants war, which Annette knows all too well, but she's not going to give him the pleasure. She wants mutual respect and achieving it is an extremely arduous task.

"I very tired. You no sing now when you cook."

That's true. Àlex has made his soufflés in silence, which means that for all his sarcasm, something's bothering him. Annette's words are now being replayed in an endless loop in his head: "You no sing now when you cook." He doesn't want to be so easy to read, and she's seen through him thanks to one small detail. He'll have to make an effort to sing so the boss won't be able to diagnose his state of mind. He thinks about it, concentrates on the problem, as if working out an equation with three factors dancing round: Laiex, restaurant and Annette. Now he's got to identify the hidden element, namely what's bugging him.

He's upset because, since the restaurant has reopened, he hasn't been able to visit his son as regularly as he's become accustomed to. There's no way that Laiex is aware of his visits, and still less of the fact that Àlex is his father. Laiex doesn't recognize anyone. Neither does he respond to his carer's shows of affection, which she doles out more as routine than because she really cares about Laiex. Nevertheless, Àlex is comforted by his visits to his son and feels more at peace with the world because he can help the nuns who so generously took in his little monster without asking any questions about where the poor child came from, or who he was.

Leaving the convent, Àlex drives back to Bigues i Riells in silence. He doesn't turn on the radio or even put on music. This is a time for thinking, meditating but also for praying and crying. He loves his son and that's all he can do. He feels immense sadness, endless yearning and infinite gratitude towards the people who took in the baby, when he, the real monster, abandoned him at the convent door.

He's also worried about the restaurant. Of course he is. Despite his struggle not to show it outwardly and to erase any possible sentimental bond with Roda el Món, he can't help feeling partly involved. He has to make a gigantic effort not to start cleaning, not to help the poor exhausted girl and, in particular, not to cook any more than necessary.

He'd gladly cook up miracles out of nothing, from almost no ingredients. He can do it. He has the gift. He dreams up a fantastic garlic sauce to go with the shepherd's dish of golden pan-friend breadcrumbs, *migas*, which is now a popular first course with extraordinary personality and flavour, and it costs almost nothing. But he doesn't want to fall into the trap. He has a plan and his plan is to sink Annette. He has to be strong and make sure it works.

But Annette, she's so deliciously Annette…

He's bothered by Annette. Well, not exactly. It's not Annette herself that's getting to him, but the fact that he's so attracted to her. He's thrown off balance by the battle his heart is waging against his reason. Reason is urging him to destroy her and his heart is plotting to wreck the plan and is protecting his beloved Annette, this lively, laughing, sweet, strong girl. Of all her virtues, the one Àlex most admires springs from the same soil as the great quality of the Cottolengo nuns: unconditional generosity with no questions asked. Clear, white, pure, unblemished generosity.

He isn't generous – on the contrary. Knowing that he's driven by infinite jealousy disturbs him, because it unequivocally betrays his selfishness. He wants Annette all to himself. He'd thought that it would be a matter of days, an adolescent flirtation that would lead them through stormy waters to arrive safe and sound in a safe port of sweetly drifting breezes. He'd been led to believe this by Annette's gestures, her laughter, her mild rebukes, her intentionally subtle comments and, more than anything else, because she'd forgiven all his boorish outbursts. He was completely wrong. He hadn't foreseen that she'd prefer Carol. He's been a fool. However, despite his unrequited love, he's happy about one thing: he's still able to love. He'd thought that the years had destroyed any capacity for reaction in his shrivelled heart. He's comforted by the knowledge that he's still someone who can love and not just hate, and yet he's suffering too. He regrets having let Annette go without trying to win her. But maybe he never had a chance with her. His head's all over the place, full of contradictions and conflicting feelings. The only thing he's sure about is that he's been rejected, but he never imagined betrayal would come in the form of Annette's getting together with Carol.

Àlex checks the time. He's been lost in thought for quite a while and it's getting late. They should have some lunch. The restaurant has to open in forty-five minutes and Annette's gone shopping. It seems there was no mineral water for the customers! The truth is that when the restaurant closed it had a very bad name. He has debts. A lot of debts. The suppliers don't want to come back until he's paid off what he owes them. Poor Annette's got a big pile of shit to clean up. Someone rings the doorbell.

"Hey, Albert! Great to see you! How are you?" Àlex asks happily.

Albert is a ponytailed farmer with a social and environmental conscience, as reflected in his products. He supplied the Antic Món's vegetables until just before Àlex closed it, when he realized that he hadn't been paid for six months. It went very much against the grain to stop. He's hopeless at keeping the books and absent-minded in general, but he's also a true, highly perfectionist farmer who loves growing things and driving round in his van full of potatoes, tomatoes and silver beet. He's so passionate about his work that anyone would think he's holding a work by Picasso in his hand instead of a bunch of spinach.

"Hello, chef. I was just passing by and saw the new sign. Well, man, that's a big change, but you know what I think? It's a good idea. People will be curious and want to try it. We were all a bit tired of all that swanky stuff you were doing."

"Swanky, me?" Àlex is annoyed. "I didn't cook posh stuff. I did *cuisine d'auteur*. The problem is that the people round here have ignorant palates."

"Àlex, listen, man, you live off the people round here. Look at Can Bret. They're full every day and weekends too. The people in the new estates love going there to eat their grilled meat, *calçots* and *trinxat*. That's proper Catalan cooking and that's what people like."

"They haven't got a clue what proper Catalan cooking is. But never mind. Right now I'm not in the mood for any debate about the fine points of food in this country."

"You're right, you're right. We all know that *calçots* have only been around for no more than a hundred years and that *trinxat* is like what they call bubble and squeak in England, but here we charge for it as if it's made of truffles, because that's what people want."

"Right, lad, but if we all cooked the same, there'd be no point in going from one restaurant to another."

"OK, that's true, but you don't have to go to the other extreme. One of the problems of Antic Món was the price. You made clients pay for a steak as if the animal had a PhD, or was a doctor in medicine even. And your French omelette was priced as though the eggs were made of gold."

"Look here, I was cooking—" Àlex starts.

"Listen man, cut this arrogant shit. You did what you wanted and you had to close down. By the way, you owe me money. You're in debt to half the town."

"The restaurant's not mine any more." Àlex doesn't want to know about debts. "It belongs to that redhead who used to be my kitchen hand."

"What! You mean I have to run after her to get my money? Maybe she can pay me in kind. I mean very kindly…" Albert chuckles loudly and winks at Àlex.

"Don't even think about it. Go to bed with her and you'll end up looking like beetroot juice. Watch it!"

"Wow! I can see you fancy her yourself. OK then, I'll have to keep finding my fun with the little red-light ladies in Barcelona. That one of yours, Gladys, has done me the odd favour. We should plan one of our luscious little outings like we used to. What about it?"

"That'd be good. Haven't been for a while." Àlex thinks aloud.

"While you're thinking about it, I'll leave you a box of cabbages that one of the restaurants doesn't want. I don't know what to do with it, but I'm sure you'll find a use for them."

"You're a good guy, Albert. Thanks. Look, the new boss of… Roda el Món's arriving. That's what the place is called now, I believe," Àlex says sourly.

Annette walks in with a basket full of vegetables.

"Hello Albert."

"Hi Annette. What are you doing laden down with all that stuff? Those vegetables are horrible, tasteless and full of pesticide! You should have asked me. I'll deliver them at the door."

"We owe you money so no can ask vegetables. We pay, but little bit time." Annette looks embarrassed and hurries into the dining room, so as not to have to think about debts.

"What did she say?" Albert asks Àlex.

"She doesn't want to ask you for anything, because we owe you money. She said she wants to pay you but she needs a bit of time," Àlex translates. "That girl will never learn Catalan, though she's a lot better now than she was!"

"Do what you think best. If you need anything, you know where I am. Àlex, think about my idea about getting away for some fun and games, OK?"

"I'm not in the mood right now. But of course, if I go to see Gladys, I'll let you know. We used to have fun, eh? Bye, Albert, I have to get to work. Yeah man, plenty of work. No one's going to turn up."

"Bye, Àlex. Take care and phone me, right? Oh yes, and cook up those cabbages!"

Annette's waiting for him at the table. She's reheated the lentils left over from yesterday, as she's determined not to waste a crumb.

141

"At this rate we won't need to spend a cent on gas. We can run the place on farts. How many more days do we have to eat lentils?"

"They good and the good health."

"Actually they're very good. What did you put in them?"

"Tomato *sofregit*." Freckles shimmying and waiting for him to start swearing, Annette meets his gaze.

"How revolting. I saw you had some in your basket. Listen to me, girl, do whatever you like. Stuff as many tomatoes and potatoes as you can fit into your ill-treated American stomach. Feed your customers with that shit but leave me out of it. From now on I'm not going to eat anything you cook. I have no desire to die of food poisoning. You make your own lunch and I'll have whatever I fancy. And you don't have to worry about tallying up because I'll pay for *my* lunch out of *my* pocket. I'd rather eat eggshells than your perfidious bloody food. As for that unspeakable red ball that looks like a clown's nose, the illustrious Josep Pla said it all: it's befouled the fine food of this country and spread its stench through all its traditional dishes." Àlex has worked himself up into one of his rages. His face is crimson.

"Your face it go like tomato," Annette whispers, trying to stifle an attack of giggles.

Àlex stands up, throws all the lentils on his plate into the rubbish bin and sets about chopping a kilo of onions without another word.

Annette, unflustered and apparently serene, savours her hefty serving of lentils as she tells Àlex a story. "The conquistador Hernán Cortés had obsession to bring king and queen many exotic products because they no have spices. He look indigenous people eat but he no taste. He afraid allergic problem and he think he be superior for to eat this, but he must to take to Castile and Aragon Crown new things, because they pay lot of money, big investment. He feel shame only take Aztec plant with yellow fruit they call *tomatl*. He lucky too, because he rob gold from big chief and he take to Spain. This the sixteen century and they total reject the tomato, strange plant, the exotic leaves and it from same poison family belladonna. In Italy they call it *pomodoro*, like apple of gold for form and colour. But they no like it in Peninsula of Iberia till nineteen century when Jesuits they bring it in colour red, beautiful like now. If it travel so much even with many obstacles it no can be barbaric plant."

"And how come you've got all this vocabulary in Catalan all of a sudden?" Àlex is surprised.

"I speak good when I know what I say. I study food anthropology for Catalonia in Quebec, so books I read they Catalan. I learn some paragraphs par cœur. Many things I know in history of food I know in this language. And you, why you cry last night?" She stares searchingly at him.

"Those lentils really moved me, because they taste just like the ones my mother made. They took me back to my childhood, the kitchen table where my brother and I had lunch. I still miss them…"

10

POTATO FLOWERS

All melancholy things, which may cause sadness, ought to be avoided [at the table].
ERASMUS OF ROTTERDAM

That customer loved the *champignon* soufflé. Even so, it wasn't a great day – one customer at lunchtime and nobody last night. Their total earnings of ten euros weren't going to pay Annette, or settle debts with suppliers, or start to return Òscar's money. Annette doesn't want to get worked up about it, but today's bookings are a table for two at lunchtime and one for four people that night! She's going to have to do some "business management", start a new Facebook page, get to work on some bulk emailing and get the Gourmet Club going again.

She sits down at her computer, determined to work on a more aggressive strategy in the business battlefield. As she logs on, yesterday's solitary lunchtime client pops up in her head again. This keeps happening, not that he did or said anything odd, but there was something enigmatic or mysterious about him. He sat at a corner table, made his choice, ate the soufflé, exchanged a few words with Annette, asked a couple of polite questions, paid and left.

One comment he made while savouring her carrot cake is buzzing round Annette's head. "I can see your Canadian touch here." Of course her accent gives her away as a foreigner, but it could easily be confused with a US one.

How did that man know she was Canadian?

He wouldn't have been able to find out through social media, because she uses the pseudonym of Madame Escargot, and there's nothing on the Facebook page to identify her with any particular nationality.

Maybe someone in town said something... ah, yes, that could be it, Annette thinks, although the customer didn't look as if he was from Bigues i Riells. In fact, she recalls him saying something like, "This is the first time I've been in these parts. It's a lovely corner of Catalonia." Moreover, the man has a foreign accent and she'd almost swear it was Canadian, but then again that seems unlikely because he surely would have made some comment... His remark on Canadian origins keeps ringing in her ears.

She opens her emails and is astounded. There are heaps of people wanting to make reservations. Wow, that's great! What could have happened? It soon becomes clear as she reads her emails. Carol! Oh my God! She's written an article describing the new philosophy of Roda el Món.

Àlex Graupera's cooking aims to be accessible to everyone, in terms of both price and flavours... It would be unforgiveable for any food lover to forgo the chance of trying out Roda el Món, one of the country's most attractive restaurants. An exquisite touch and the joy of food come together in this fresh project of Annette Wilson, backed up by the wide experience of our most innovative chef.

Carol has many readers and great prestige, as is evident in all the requests for bookings.

"Thanks, Carol," Annette says to herself. She's deeply grateful and would like to give her a big hug right now. But she's travelling. She knows Carol and her tastes well enough to find some way of thanking her when she gets back. Now she rushes to tell Àlex.

"We full all tables today!" Annette shouts from the kitchen door, waving the reservation book. "Carol she write about us in newspaper."

145

"What? She hasn't trashed us? Carol loves a good massacre. She's a bullfighter who'll never stop till she's thrust her razor-sharp sword deep in your heart. If she's praised you, you must be a real cunnilingus artist."

"Don't be so crude!"

"Listen to her! You get the words right if they interest you, don't you?"

"Get you cooking, you arrogant chef. We full today. We need the food." Annette ends the conversation with a command and leaves the kitchen.

She's happy. She runs up to her room and gets the beautiful photos she's brought with her from Canada, plus her mementos: the Mayan rain stick, the Quechuan mate gourd and the peanut necklace. She's hopeless at DIY, but excitement guides the drill. She hangs up the photos and places her objects around the dining room. They are her amulets, she wants them near her, and anyway they're lovely. They'll add some warmth to the space, which is too austere.

She still has to do the shopping! She rushes out with her basket. They have to open soon. Luckily the fridge is full of all the things they cooked yesterday and, since they only had one customer, they can repeat the menu. As she leaves, she almost trips over some boxes. Frank's left another gift of small fish. This Frank… he's such an angel. Next to the fish is a small box of lemons and pears. Albert! She's an atheist, but she believes in God today, because someone's come down from heaven to help her, or it could be the power of her amulets. Perhaps they've finally got to work!

"Àlex. Come! They are gifts at door. Come, get them. I must go supermarket or you no have salt you ask."

Whatever the cause, what's happening is really beautiful. First, Òscar's generosity; then a helping hand from Carol; now the encouraging gifts from their old suppliers, Frank and Albert. They're all helping. If Àlex could only be a little bit more positive, she muses, everything would be easy. But Àlex hates her, she thinks. He could never stand her, and

146

now she's boss of Roda el Món and they've changed the name of his restaurant, he detests her much more.

Yet Annette's attracted by Àlex. His brusque style, his show of youthful rebelliousness in the greying ponytail, his tattoos, the intense flavours of his cooking... She finds everything about him magnetic. She tries to get this across to him, but either Àlex is unable to interpret her messages or his animosity towards her is beyond repair. There's no hope now. Àlex knows about her "lapse" with Carol, and it's evident that he's come to all kinds of conclusions. In his clear-cut, seamless, black-and-white way of thinking, she's just joined the world of "sour lesbians". She's no longer a possibility for him, if she ever was. Annette can't stand misogynists, but for some strange reason she makes excuses for him. She can't understand her response to this obnoxious – in the eyes of others – creature. The fact that she's so confused only confirms that she's totally in love with this disagreeable man, who, at first sight, has nothing in his favour. But Annette knows that beneath his layers of hermetic concrete there are latent virtues. Bringing them out is just a matter of time... and love.

This is what she is thinking as she lugs her heavy basket back from the supermarket.

She leaves the purchases on the kitchen table. Àlex watches her take out a big bag of potatoes. He pulls a face but says nothing, focusing on his current task of grating lemon rind, after which he'll squeeze the juice. Dessert today will be made from Albert's gift. It's a very simple custard, to go with a pear sponge. The lemon will give it a slightly acid touch and perfect creaminess. You just have to mix three hundred grams of sugar with four eggs, fifty grams of flour and some lemon juice and rind, plus the same amount of water. Then you cook it over low heat until it's thick and creamy. This is a time for singing something slow, like Lole and Manuel: "Light conquers dark in distant fields where fresh bread smells fill the air, and with morning's spurs the village stirs."

"The dining room's full. Can you serve everyone? Failing on day one is like tripping on the first stair. It's a terrible fall and you can end up seriously injured," he warns her maliciously.

"Today no is day one."

"It might as well be. Don't worry about the food, because it's all under control and the dishes are very simple. I can even sing while I'm cooking. You have to remember that I'm not going to help you in the dining room. I'm the chef and, even if Carol's given me the big write-up in her article, I don't want customers to see me or identify me with the restaurant." He bites his tongue to stop himself adding: "Because this isn't the kind of cooking I like doing."

"You have part of restaurant," she reminds him. "I phone Graça, Frank's wife, so she help me."

"Well, now we're really going to have a party, what with a redhead managing the dining room helped by a black woman in loud colours! If one speaks Catalan badly, the other one doesn't understand a word. What a circus! But I don't give a damn, as long as you don't expect me to make couscous with coconut milk and serve dry lamb. While you're at it, you should get a Chinese girl to make up the UNICEF brigade. Then at coffee time you can get the customers to hold hands, raise their arms and pray for universal peace. You couldn't have found a better name for the restaurant. Roda el Món, yes ma'am, with 'Around the World' you've hit the bull's eye."

Annette wants to throw potatoes at his head, knowing that potatoes, precisely, would do more damage than a warehouse full of gunpowder. But she thinks they're too important to be wasted on Àlex's cranium. They cost money, and money is all-important. She glances round the kitchen, looking for the heaviest saucepan which, if she aimed straight, would make a nice hole in his head. Luckily for him, and for Annette too if she doesn't want to serve a life sentence, someone rings at the door. She runs out to answer it, cursing in French or English or Catalan. Who could possibly tell?

The customers are arriving. In less than an hour, the restaurant is jumping. All the tables are full. Graça has arrived late, just when Annette was about to commit suicide. There is no time even to say hello. Graça, who has no idea where the cutlery and plates are kept or how to serve soup, runs nervously in and out of the kitchen bearing off dirty plates and bringing more food.

"Annette, customer that table want speak you." Graça points.

"Which table?" All the tables are "that table".

"Table little boy."

Now they have a huge problem. The little boy wants chips. Chips! Now she won't have to commit suicide, because Àlex will boil her in oil. Obviously someone's going to get badly burnt today.

"Graça, you go kitchen for to peel potatoes," Annette orders. "Cut as like you. You put oil in saucepan on fire. You call me when it go hot!"

"Kitchen? Potatoes? Àlex he kill me!"

"You do it!"

Annette goes into the kitchen, picks up the biggest cleaver, the one for chopping veal bones, and addresses Àlex in her sternest voice. "Àlex, Graça she work in kitchen. If you no let this I kill you."

"You're getting madder by the day. I should make a recording. You'd get ten years for that. You don't have to threaten me. This place is yours, so you can do what you bloody well like, as I've said time and time again. Careful with the hot oil. You can do more damage frying potatoes than with that cleaver."

The first potatoes ever to be cooked in the history of the restaurant are carried out of the kitchen. Annette's fried them in no time as Graça has done the preparatory work. They may look like common-or-garden chips, but they're a triumph. One to Annette.

Roda el Món's last customers leave after five. The dining room is a complete mess, but Annette's more than happy. She sits at Table 3 and sighs deeply, loudly enough to be heard in Australia. Graça's still bustling around everywhere, not that she's being very productive, but she can't stop.

"Give me a break, woman! You're doing my head in, flapping around in those bright clothes of yours. It's worse than watching a merry-go-round," Àlex yells from the kitchen.

"Come, sit down you here, Graça, and we drink beer. I need rest a moment," Annette says.

Graça comes and sits down, but has tea, as she's a Muslim. They talk about their lunchtime performance in the dining room. They've made mistakes at just about every table. The girl at Table 2 ate the tuna of the man at Table 8. The man at Table 8 didn't notice that he'd been served chicken instead of tuna, because he was so fascinated by the spectacularly heaving bosom of the lady with whom he shared the table. The family at Table 6 have had red wine instead of white, but luckily the price was the same.

Graça understood that the man at Table 1 wanted white coffee, when he'd asked for an iced coffee. The people at Table 3 didn't get their bread until dessert was being served. At Table 5 they didn't get their salt, but that was OK because they obviously had blood-pressure issues. Neither did the croutons ever embellish the asparagus soup of the little old man at Table 4, but since he had no teeth he wouldn't have been able to eat them anyway. Remembering him, Annette gets an attack of the giggles, which makes Graça laugh too.

Hearing them carrying on like this, Àlex comes out of the kitchen. "You're going to have a heart attack! What are you laughing at? You should be crying. What a disaster that was! Do you want to eat the chicken from Table 7? I don't know why but it's still sitting in the serving hatch. What did that customer eat if he didn't have chicken? Bread and olive oil? What a disaster, what a bloody disaster!"

"Graça, what eat gorgeous man in Table 7?"

"He gorgeous, yes, he very gorgeous. He eat, he eat *suquet*, yes, eat fish stew. He no ask chicken."

"So what happened, then?" Àlex asks. "There's one serving of chicken in the kitchen still waiting for someone to eat it."

Annette can't stop laughing. Now she remembers. It's all because of her terrible Catalan. Rushing from table to kitchen to table, she'd gone into the kitchen and said "*C'est un pollastre*", instead of "*Quin pollastre*", an expression Òscar had taught her. She was referring to the smart-arse at one of the tables and, in the midst of all the uproar, Àlex had heard *set* instead of "*c'est*" and, thinking therefore that she'd said Table 7, had produced the chicken for the man who'd actually asked for *suquet*.

Once that mystery is explained, a scandalized Àlex can't help but laugh too. All three of them are laughing and they can't stop, because they're also letting off a lot of steam mixed up with their lunchtime stories. Suddenly Annette turns serious.

"You see dining room, Graça? It nearly six. We open nine. We must hurry. Àlex, you have ready food for this night? We full booking."

"It's all ready, Madame Learner. You never have to worry about the food in this house. You just get someone to start cleaning up. I have no intention of doing it by myself. I've cooked for thirty people, like an octopus, managing eight pots and pans all at once. And don't forget there's a saucepan full of disgusting oil that's had those revolting potatoes fried in it."

While Graça's tidying up the living room, Annette goes into the kitchen, which has stacks of dirty dishes everywhere. She whistles. Slowly, like a grandmother sitting by the fireside with a blanket over her knees and white hair up in a bun, Annette tells the surprising story how potatoes came to Catalonia.

"Tomatoes and potatoes they same family, the Solanaceae family, you name nightshades. They toxic. They come here little bit late, sixteen century, fifty years after Columbus he find America. Emperor Charles, he rule in Seville then. This plant have success because it have beautiful flower they use for to decorate palace. Eat flower also like delicacy thing or flower of courgette now. But they think the tubercle it food for pigs so it no way good, and church say people no can to eat potato because it food Devil make and only for animals, infidels, bad people or prisoners. After long time we know church put it taboo because it no decide tax farmers must to pay for to grow new vegetable."

Àlex listens, feigning a lack of interest, as he cleans the stove and collects the *mise en place* bowls containing all the ingredients he's prepared in advance in order to streamline the cooking during his shift. Annette hugely enjoys telling the story, which she hasn't thought about for ages. As she's talking about potatoes with all the élan of an anthropology lecturer, snippets from her happy student years keep popping up. If only she'd stuck with that! She wants Àlex to understand her lecture and teaches with passion and care, sparing no details and including all the juicier anecdotes.

"In the 1744, Prussia is in middle of War of Seven Years and people they hungry so start eat potatoes. The pharmacist Parmentier he in war-prisoner camp and he survive three years only eat potatoes. When he liberated he tell King Louis XVI grow potato in grain fields so they have food in war time and the King he give Parmentier land for to grow them. When they pick first potatoes he cook dinner, all plates make with the potato and the queen she decorate the hair with potato flowers. After all courtiers copy her and they have fashion of potato flowers in the hair. But people they resist still for to eat potato."

Àlex has finished his chores. Now it would be time for him to go and rest in his room, as he does every afternoon, but he's so bewitched by Annette's lilting voice and the story she's telling that he sits on the table with his legs swinging like a little boy, listening with great attention. Annette can't see him as she's labouring at the sink, washing dishes and scrubbing pots with her back to him, but she senses him. If it weren't for her voice telling the story, you could hear a pin drop. She knows he's quiet and listening, so she doesn't turn round, doesn't look at him, because she doesn't want to spoil the magic. She continues.

"The King he invent a strategy very success. He order Royal Guard they watch potato fields in day, in day only so people they get curious and fall in trap, because they think potato cost very lot money. In night they go steal. So potato enter in the kitchens."

"How do you know all this?" Àlex is perplexed.

"I tell you before. I anthropologist. I study History of Food in University of Quebec."

Àlex realizes he knows nothing at all about Annette's life. He's never asked her about Canada, if she has family there, what she did... or why she came to Catalonia. That's Àlex. He doesn't ask questions. He doesn't want to know anything about anyone, because he doesn't want people prying into his own life.

His maxim is "Silence is the shield of the troubled". His respect for the silence of others is his trick for obtaining respect for his own silence. Mixed up with this is his fear of getting too close to anyone. When you know about the troubles of others you become a fellow sufferer, and then vulnerability marches into your feelings. The result is lethal, because then the other person wants reciprocity, wants to know what you're hiding and, in Àlex's case, when he has to show his cards he always loses.

This shouldn't bother him, because he's well aware that he's a loser. However, his apparent lack of interest in the lives of others is interpreted as bad manners and lack of sensitivity, because people confuse self-protection with oafishness. And that's how everyone sees him: an ill-mannered oaf.

"This night, we full," Annette warns Àlex when she sees him going upstairs to rest.

"I told you, it's all under control. You have to get the whole dining room ready though. When you see the state Graça's left it in you're going to have a myocardial infarction."

"Myo… what?"

"Heart attack, girl. If things don't get better, you're going to have to take on a professional waiter in the dining room."

"Or waitress." Annette is offended.

"Well, well, well, so she wants to be politically correct on top of everything else. I'm really trembling. They're all going to bail out anyway. Yeah, yeah, that's fine if you prefer a cute little waitress to a man with hairs in his nose. Right, go ahead and find one who's delectable and delicious, who'll cheer up clients who are pissed off at the bad service."

Before Annette has a chance to reply, Àlex dashes out of the kitchen.

The dining room looks like a cubist painting. The tablecloths are plonked on the tables any old how, as if Graça's thrown them up into the air to see where they'll land. Some tables are set with soup spoons and others with dessert spoons and forks. The glasses have joined in the fun. There are champagne glasses, beer glasses and brandy balloons, all set out in utter disarray. The chaos is truly impressive. Annette has to redo Graça's work from scratch. She'll have to show her the ropes with huge, total patience, but her goodwill and Frank's boxes of fish more than make up for the hassle. Everything is important!

She recalls her father's words: "First of all you have to sit down and work out where you want to go." It's more effective to teach Graça exactly how to set a table than for Annette to do it all over again, so,

154

drawing on her teacher's gifts, she explains in great detail how the dining room must be readied and, like all good teachers, she leaves Frank's wife alone to work out for herself what she has to do. Annette already has her work cut out in the kitchen. She has to make cakes and the staff dinner. Moreover, she's starving.

She boils the potatoes and fries some shallots in butter until they take on a lovely golden hue, after which she mashes them up with the potatoes. Then she adds cream, a splash of water, nutmeg, salt and pepper. Parmentier potatoes must be very creamy, smooth, silky, a true delight.

Graça, Àlex and Annette are sitting at the kitchen table, spoons poised for the first mouthful when their customers start arriving. If things keep going like this, they'll end up as thin as rakes. Annette goes out to check the state of the dining room and is relatively satisfied, even if Graça doesn't know the difference between meat and dessert cutlery. The dining room is no longer cubist but has moved on to surrealism, with a few odd-looking tables where the napkins are folded in ways that would be impossible to reproduce and the glasses set out in strange clusters, but it's barely noticeable at a quick glance. Since she can do nothing about it, Annette pretends she hasn't noticed anything.

Two pairs of women's feet are flying, without a break, although dinner is slightly less frantic than lunchtime. The customers are enthusiastic about Roda el Món's tasting menu: five courses, smaller servings and a more than accessible price. Better still, the system makes work in the dining room much easier.

They close the kitchen at half-past eleven after a reasonably uneventful evening. Annette and Graça are exhausted but pleased, because there have been no mistakes. Some customers have even left tips. It takes them another hour to clean up the kitchen and dining room so they'll be ready for lunch tomorrow. Annette invites Graça to sit down and have a bite to eat.

"Thank you Annette, but I leave in my home the children."

"Of course, Graça, and you no have left restaurant all the day," Annette says apologetically.

"Graça," Àlex calls from the kitchen, "do you want to take some of this lamb casserole home with you? There's quite a bit left over and you'll find a good use for it."

Graça is very pleased to accept, but Annette isn't at all happy about Àlex's initiative. She waits until Graça has left and she's having dinner before raising the matter.

"Will you come for to have dinner? You very thin and no eat good. This make you sick," Annette warns.

"OK, I'll sit down for a moment. I'm tired too. What are you offering today?"

"Potatoes Parmentier. I know you no like but they very good."

"You know what, I think I'll try them. The dish looks tempting, and I must confess I like your potato story. It touches me that it was rejected for so many years and seen as so lowly that not even the humblest, poorest, hungriest people would eat it. After such a hard time I think it deserves to be given a chance, even though it's now been more than recompensed after its tough beginnings. No other vegetable on the planet is consumed in such quantities as the potato, which, I must point out, makes it tremendously vulgar. Anyway, let's try it." Àlex takes a large spoonful. "Yum! That's fantastic, Annette. It's really smooth and silky. I'm glad I tasted it. Congratulations. But it's one thing to taste it and quite another to eat it like other hapless mortals do. This country's brain has shrunk because so many potatoes are consumed here."

Àlex seems happy. He's made quite a long speech without swearing once or insulting anybody, apart from his sarcastic remark about the Catalan brain, which was hardly remarkable given what his tongue is capable of. Annette thinks he's behaved well today and might even come under the

heading of what she classifies as a "normal person". She still hasn't mentioned the lamb that Graça's taken home with her, but she can't ignore it
either, because this is about one of his enduring bad habits. She summons
up all her courage and says, "Àlex, I think it no good you gift away the food
of Roda el Món." She deliberately mentions the name of the restaurant,
so that Àlex gets the idea that she's talking about business, her business
precisely. "I know Graça our friend and today she work very much but is
no good you gift her food. This cost money and the workers must not to
think they always can take to house restaurant's food. If one day we have
many workers, they take all lamb, whole animal to house."

Annette speaks slowly, measuring her words, and she's very determined. She knows that it's hard being the boss, but she has to make
sure that Àlex accepts her authority. Part of his failure with Antic Món
was due to the fact that he didn't know how to manage a restaurant. He
treated it like his home. Annette wants to run the new establishment like
a proper business, so the first task is to change Àlex's way of thinking,
though she fears his reaction.

Àlex stolidly eats his Parmentier potatoes. Anyone can see from a mile
away that he's shovelling in the potatoes so as not to spit out flames.
Annette is well aware that he's swallowing an attack of rage, making a
huge effort not to blast her back to Canada on a rocket of insults. After
five more spoonfuls, he has no choice but to respond, "Very well, Madame, I'll do what you say. I won't generously make food for our friends,
or give alms to our workers, who labour away inside for hours on end
without seeing the light of day, and I won't cook anything after work
as a way of saying thank you to people who give us a hand."

"Àlex, I only want save business and for it be serious thing. I no want
for you get angry."

"Listen, curly carrot top, my life hasn't been easy. I've been kicked
out of just about everywhere – houses where I've lived and a lot of jobs

– and now I'm close to being kicked out of my own restaurant. Let me tell you straight: this opportunity you're giving me is my last chance and I have to do what you say because, in a nutshell, this is the only job I have. And since I'm here, I'll also tell you that being forbidden to give away a bit of lamb to an exhausted mother with lots of kids whom she hasn't seen all day long, and who has a husband who gives us pilfered fish, risking his job day after day, is about the least painful misfortune that's ever happened to me."

11

HARICOT BEANS

The world is a huge pot; the heart the spoon. The food coming out of the pot depends on how you stir it.
ZEN APHORISM

"Hallo Òscar. You very busy?" Annette asks. Òscar, who is working not far from Bigues i Riells that day, has dropped in to see Annette and Àlex.

"God, I don't know what's going on in the office these days, but it's like the end of the world is coming. We don't have time to scratch ourselves. And what about you two? How are things here?" Òscar hopes his I'm-very-busy strategy will save him from being roped in to clean toilets again.

"Very good. We full almost all days. Customers they so happy, but we very tired. Last three weeks I run all long day. Monday I clean a lot, do ironing and make cakes for all week."

"I've seen some great reviews on the Internet. Some of the bloggers who've been here speak very well of the place. Have you had a look?"

"Òscar, I no have time for to look Internet!" Annette laments.

"So I see. You still have the Friends of Antic Món page up and people are posting comments, but no one's answering them. Makes you look bad, Annette, especially as they're all positive."

"What they say?"

"I don't recall exactly. We can have a look now, if you like."

159

"I can't," she exclaims. "You see I make carrot cake now. I do things all the day, work all the day. I no sit never."

"OK, OK," he concedes. "Anyway, they all speak very highly of you, except for one critic who says your food is all over the place with a be-wildering mix of things. But don't worry about that, because nobody else has supported that view and he's a lone voice."

"Òscar, I want ask from you favour, because you say if we need help... I need you help with publicity, with social network, blogs, websites. You know very well and can do this. You help me very much with Friends of Antic Món page for the Facebook."

"Mmm, well, I don't know. I'm very busy, you see." He's trying to wriggle out of it. "I could do it from time to time, but what you need is regular updating and I fear I can't commit myself to that."

Annette's face is a study in surprise and disappointment. She would never have expected such a negative response, and still less from the res-taurant's real owner. The more she mixes with Europeans, the stranger she finds them.

As far as Òscar's concerned, hobbies lose their appeal as soon as they become obligations. His gourmet activities take up a lot of his leisure time and he wants to keep things like that. He evidently writes his cu-linary blog for fun, and he has plenty of readers as a result. Many of his fellow bloggers have caught on that having a lot of visitors to their pages means a lucrative opportunity and are going professional. Some have even left their jobs and are now full-time bloggers financed by food-industry advertising. Òscar is critical of this, because he thinks these blogs lose freshness and independence, so when he detects that certain bloggers have taken this step he stops following them and, if he can, boycotts them. Naturally, he'll post pieces praising Roda el Món, whenever he has the chance to sample Àlex Graupera's latest offering. But right now Annette has only asked him to work and not to have lunch, so Òscar's quite put out. Moreover, she still hasn't said a word about paying him back. He decides that now is the time to broach the subject.

"There are lots of comments online about the price, saying you're offering imaginative food at outlet prices. They also say they're happy to eat Àlex Graupera's cooking again and are delighted that the price is better suited to most pockets. Ah, yes, and speaking of costs and money, what are you going to do? When are you planning to make the first repayment? I don't want to hassle you, eh. But it looks as if things are going well and it would be a good idea for you to sort out the situation."

"This you say very truth, Òscar. I will try. I have pay already some suppliers and want for to finish debts." Annette looks contrite.

"Believe me, I don't want to put any more pressure on you," he lies, "but it would be good if you can combine things a bit. I don't need the money, but I'm not giving it away either. By the way, how's Àlex? Where is he? Before he always used to be cooking up something in the kitchen."

"He rest in room all the afternoons but he OK," she whispers. "He change very much the attitude. He help more."

It's true. Àlex accepts the business "norms" Annette keeps introducing in Roda el Món. They may look like small changes, but she knows they are great steps forward as far as Àlex's behaviour is concerned, because he no longer drinks alcohol while working, agrees to the menu in advance and – the hardest thing of all for him to swallow – doesn't interfere in the shopping for raw materials. When she comes back from the supermarket with her full basket, or brings in something she's ordered from suppliers, who are starting to trust the restaurant again, she expects some kind of put-down from Àlex. Surprisingly, he doesn't say a word. He's like a meek little lamb.

And that's not all. After the first days of refusing to help, Àlex is now contributing towards the smooth running of the dining room.

"Have you taken the Raimat Cabernet they've asked for at Table 6?"

"Have they got bread at Table 4?"

"No, that dessert isn't for Table 2. They haven't finished the duck yet!"

All this suggests that he's trying to make sure things are working well in the dining room. Sometimes Annette stares at him, looking for symptoms of illness, depression or some kind of covert rebellion, some sign that might explain this docility, but she can't pinpoint anything in particular and his attitude remains positive.

Dinner time is almost upon them and Àlex appears in the dining room.

"Hi there, lad. Haven't seen you for a while. Are you OK?"

"Yes, fine thanks. What about you?"

Òscar's not sure how to behave with Àlex. Their relationship has changed and so has Àlex, and Òscar's not overjoyed about the fact that Àlex has lost the crabby contrariness he used to find so amusing. He's not wholly delighted either that Àlex should have accepted the situation and agreed to do commercial, conventional cooking, even though the restaurant's adaptation to the tastes of the wider public has been successful.

"I'm OK. We'll have to chat another time. I've got to get moving in the kitchen. We've got a busy night ahead!"

"I'm very pleased for both of you, Àlex."

"…and for your pocket," Àlex mumbles to himself, now out of earshot.

Òscar asks timidly, "Can I give you a hand in the kitchen tonight, like we used to do?"

"You'll have to ask Madame about that. She's in charge of everything and I'm on a very short leash nowadays. Did you see we served tomato quiche on the lunchtime menu today? What do you have to say about that, eh? Of course I didn't make it. It was a success. There's almost none left."

"Yes, I saw that. Well, man, if it's good, it's not surprising that it sells."

Without asking Annette's permission, Òscar goes into the kitchen and puts on an apron. He'll do what he bloody well likes. He's the owner. He wants to cook with Àlex and that's that.

Everything goes smoothly, even though almost all the tables are full. Òscar observes the interaction between Annette and Àlex, and it's evident that something's going on because there are too many nuances. Conclusion: they're madly in love. Their struggle to hide the fact gives them away. Àlex is always badmouthing Annette, referring to her as "this woman", or "that Canadian" or "Madame". He overdoes it. Anyone can see it's a smokescreen behind which he's trying to hide his true feelings. Both are doing their best to act like professionals, but their emotions simmer on the surface whenever they speak, even in the brief exchanges they have in the middle of cooking and serving. If they shout at one another there's no sign of Àlex's former malice. If Annette makes a mistake, Àlex's way of telling her is as smooth as his béchamel sauce.

When the last customers leave, Òscar sits down at the kitchen table. "Hey maestro, that was a great success. We've earned a bite to eat."

"Sorry Òscar, but the foodie parties are a bygone thing. When we finish work these days we toddle off to bed. The boss won't let me invite anyone to the smallest breadcrumb. She's Anglo-Saxon through and through and doesn't understand how we Mediterraneans revere the table, or that we don't sit down to stuff ourselves but to share, to please, to have fun and to love. We might have to sleep in a sleeping bag, use a bowl to wash ourselves and get around on a skateboard, but we never skimp at the table. In our culture "table" means much more than a plank of wood on four legs.

"I remember one occasion, by the sea, where a family was having a picnic under some pine trees. It was in the middle of summer. They were half-naked, didn't have a portable fridge or an umbrella, but they had a full table, laden with food. I walked by and the granddad raised his hand, offering me a slice of watermelon, with a bite out of it! They asked me to join them. I didn't accept, of course, as I had to go to work, but I was grateful, not only for that, but because I saw the essence of the Mediterranean world in their offer of a wobbly table, a family and a bit of − half-eaten − watermelon. That's what they had and that's what they offered… to a stranger, a passer-by. Everything for everyone.

"This story, which is trivial but also essential, would never happen in a cold place like Quebec. The weather won't let them eat outside, they don't have watermelon and the culture of the table doesn't exist. The table is here in the Mediterranean and the house is there in the Atlantic. When they want to be hospitable they open the door. We put another plate on the table."

Although he's facing away from the door and can't see her, Àlex knows that Annette is standing just outside the kitchen listening to his words. She doesn't wear perfume, and he has a faint whiff of a subtle scent he wouldn't know how to define, the one he picked up even before being introduced to her, a fresh, lemony, tangy fragrance. Annette deliberately makes a noise, but Àlex, unperturbed, continues with his speech. However, he's no longer addressing Òscar but Annette.

"She comes from a land of potatoes, tubercles buried in the darkness of wet soil. They have to eat cakes for dessert, because the sweetest fruit they have is the carrot, and they cover everything with butter, which clogs up their arteries and brains. You can't get through to the soul of someone who lives in a place where vines won't grow."

"It seems Monsieur le chef he know my country but he never visit there." Annette is riled. "If you would make effort to visit us one day you see the kitchen is centre of house, with fire always burn for to receive visitors in comfortable way and cook many foods for table which is pride of room. Now we sit down," she orders in an almost martial tone. "Òscar he deserve his dinner and I have a special dish today."

"You're full of surprises, Annette," Àlex exclaims. "When you're worked up, you'd put the great Catalan philologist Pompeu Fabra to shame."

164

Òscar watches the conversation as if at a tennis match. Àlex has sent a hard serve, but Annette has very energetically returned the ball to his court.

She offers a small slice of tomato quiche left over from lunch and some *botifarra*, with a Penedés Merlot to drink. Òscar's enjoying watching them together. He's increasingly convinced that they're madly, desperately in love. Hearing them squabbling, one might conclude that they deeply dislike one another, even if the scorn-laden words they use are distinctly puerile. In their stolen glances, when one looks at the other when sure it won't be noticed, the candour of their gaze is total.

Àlex stares at Annette adoringly, as if her curves were the fragile outline of a Romanesque statue of the Virgin, a wonderful work of art. The unmistakable sign that he's head-over-heels is that he eats everything she serves him, reverentially, as if taking communion. *The body of Annette. Amen.*

"God, this *botifarra* is amazing. How did you do it?" Òscar breaks the mystical silence that has descended on the kitchen in Roda el Món.

"Very good, Annette. It really is," Àlex says, "but I'm sure you're tricking us and you didn't make it yourself. Where did you find it?"

"I no buy it. I give little drink of Caol Ila if you find secret ingredient." Annette is amused.

Òscar actually knows that this sausage is filled with haricot beans, but holds his tongue, because it's clear that Annette wants Àlex to make the effort to guess the secret. But Àlex has no intention of activating his taste-bud memory. He's not in the mood for playing culinary riddles.

"I haven't got a clue what you've got hidden in this *botifarra* and I couldn't care less. The main thing is that it's full-flavoured and smooth, with a slightly earthy taste that balances the pork fat. It's a metaphor for life. Flesh kindles desire, earth holds us firm, and fat is our reserve for surviving life's ups and downs."

"I no understand nothing. When you say this philosopher talk you impossible." Annette sighs loudly, as if bored to death and looks heavenwards.

"Annette's right. You're a better chef than philosopher," Òscar intervenes. "I think he's trying to say that even if we like a woman a lot we have to be rational, keep our feet on the ground and our head well stocked in order to cope with problems and always be prepared. Is that what you meant? Were you comparing the *botifarra* with love?"

"Exactly," says Àlex, staring at the *botifarra* and unsure how to continue the conversation after his absurd homespun philosophizing, which has left him fairly well unmasked. "The secret ingredient, as you like to call it, is haricot beans. I haven't eaten them for more than two decades, but the taste is unmistakable and it's branded on my memory with a white-hot iron. The clever thing is putting the beans inside the sausage and thereby making one single product out of the two things, *botifarra* and *mongetes*, which is supposedly the quintessential Catalan dish. This is totally ignorant of course, and shows how little people know about our cooking. When I hear people spouting this nonsense I feel like throwing up."

"It's long debate, Àlex. Food, Catalan or Québécois, no is inert thing but it live and it change. Cooking we do today no is cooking of yesterday. You want to keep still, you go against movement of world. It no have sense." Annette's tone conveys all the weariness of a long struggle against all the elements.

"Well, I happen to think that if we don't preserve the identity of our cuisine by establishing its basic structure, we'll end up eating sushi rice casserole with wasabi peas. What do we miss when we're away from home? Cupcakes? If we want to feel we're part of a culture, we've got to protect what we have and stop being so permeable."

"Umberto Eco he explain that incorporate new products in diet of Catalans, Spanish and Europeans it was essential for to save them. He say protein from dry beans help to make multiply European population after Middle Ages. But it also seem that people of Europe eat dry beans before America discovered, but this kind very primitive and vulgar. American bean, it very more resistant and better taste, so substitute other bean. When it arrive to Catholic lands in sixteen century, the people they reject it and it only start like them for to eat in middle of eighteen century, but now everyone they say Catalans they only know to eat haricot beans!" Annette counters.

"Yes, you're right. Catalans would live exclusively on potatoes, to-matoes and beans, whatever the order," Àlex notes. "My cooking was risky, taking a leap to maximum difficulty and a challenge that's almost impossible to meet today, because it was based on what people ate be-fore the arrival of food coming from the New World. In my resistance against using these products that are so deeply rooted, despite having such distant origins, I had a lot of fun. I wanted to see if I could avoid them in all my recipes and to test how far I could stretch the tolerance of my customers. This radicalism, in addition to my impeccable technique, got me listed as one of the most daring and best-rated chefs in Spain. I wanted to pique the curiosity of the food critics and, when I succeeded, I was acclaimed. Of course, the whole thing got me nowhere and has been nothing but a resounding failure."

Òscar and Annette stare at Àlex in amazement. He's never given such a clear and serene explanation of his reasons for rejecting New World products.

"It hasn't been such a resounding failure. Not totally. We're here, aren't we? And it seems that the restaurant's doing well." Òscar tries to tone down the drama. "In any case, you get ten out of ten for this *botifarra*, Annette. You must put it on the menu. By the way, since you're so well informed about the origins of food, do you know why beans are called *mongetes* – like the word for little nuns – in Catalan, and *judías* – like the feminine form of the word for Jews – in Spanish? It looks like a contradiction, doesn't it?"

"In the popular etymology people they say the nuns... um – how you say them? – ah yes, the *monges*, they eat always this bean they think is kind of white pea, so the people give name *mongetes*, like 'little nuns'. In Spanish they call these beans *judías* because the Jews they torture by putting in boiling water like the beans. But these no very scientific theories, and I think they no come from serious studies, but someone tell stories by fireside," she says with the solemn air of a senior lecturer in anthropology.

"Yes, Annette, you should put this *botifarra* on the menu. It'll be a winner." Àlex winds up the conversation. "Goodnight."

Òscar makes the most of the occasion to leave, in case he ends up having to wash dishes or dust shelves, or worse, Annette might ask him again for help in advertising and positioning Roda el Món on the Internet.

Annette doesn't feel like clearing up their dishes. She feels lighter somehow, and reasonably happy. The conversation tonight has been enjoyable and even civilized. She bounds upstairs and, as she goes past Àlex's door, she hears music. Haydn? How beautiful! She impulsively knocks at the door. Àlex takes a few seconds to answer. He knows it's Annette. Who else could it be? He's in his underpants.

"Anything wrong?"

"No. All good. I wanted... I wanted... Is very beautiful, the music."

"Yes, I like it too. Do you want to come in?"

"No... um yes. I no know. Yes, I think," she dithers. "I wanted... I wanted talk with you, but it very late maybe."

"It'll be a while before I go to sleep. I have a bit of trouble dropping off. You can come in, but there's just one condition. I don't want you to tell me about the history of food, whatever the kind. We'll listen to music and that's that." His gentle tone changes to brusque. "Come in, girl, come in. I'm bloody freezing out here in the passage."

What is she, the boss, doing in Àlex's room listening to classical music, and him wearing only underpants? She has no idea but it feels good.

"So, what did you want to talk about?" he asks.

"It no important. Days ago, many days you say, 'I still miss my brother.' Talk about it is good sometimes. It just this. If you want… you can to tell me," Annette stammers.

"Hmm. This could well end up late. It's a long, complicated story. I could even tell you in instalments." He laughs.

"I have time. Lot of time. And I no want sleep. You tell me please."

Àlex's older brother was what might be called a "ten-out-of-ten" kid. He had everything: good looks, brains, ambition and a pleasant nature. He was nine years older, a considerable difference. Their parents were more than satisfied with the good marks, excellent behaviour, sports medals and, in a nutshell, all their boy's achievements.

They expected very little of Àlex, however. The baby of the family was assigned the roles of clown, cuddly toy, cute kid, plaything and pride and joy of the household. Everything he did amused his parents, who cheered him on. Hence, he grew up trying to make everyone happy. He was the balance, the counterpoint and compensation for the seriousness of his big brother, who shouldered the burden of responsibility, of being the one who would eventually sustain the family.

His brother excelled at school. He wanted to study aerospace engineering, but the family had scant means to help him. However, since he was so brilliant, he got a five-year scholarship to study at one of the most prestigious universities in his field. His parents were beside themselves with joy and gazed at him adoringly. The university was a long way from home, in the United States. The boy set off and the parents cried with happiness. A son studying in the United States and all because of his own merit! A lad from Vall d'Aran was flying high, heading for the Mount Olympus of the most privileged people, going off to study in America!

It was like a dream. But it wasn't. He'd done this all by himself. No one had given him any gift. He'd studied till he was dead on his feet, with saintly devotion, as his mother said. And he'd done it. All his efforts had been recognized with the most valuable reward: the best degree at the best university. His proud mother told everyone she met in the street, in the queue at the greengrocer's or at the hairdresser's. After getting the good news she became a little vain, wanting to look good when they pointed at her in the street, saying, "There's the mother of that boy who's gone off to study in Florida." She bought a new dress and a sexy dressing gown, which she referred to as her *déshabillé*. Her husband didn't understand what she had bought. "A desa-what?" he asked, intrigued.

"Oh, Manuel, we'll never get out of this hole if you carry on like this," she sighed. "This is in all the fashion magazines. A *dés-ha-bi-llé*. I'm going to wear it in the mornings in the hotel when we go to America to see our boy. You have to look nice when they bring you breakfast: tropical fruit, hot chocolate, coffee, croissants, churros…"

Her husband burst out laughing. "Come on, girl! Churros? In America they don't eat churros for breakfast. The only Spanish dish will be you in that *déshabillé* out of the fashion magazines, and you certainly frittered away our money on that. Churros are more Spanish than flamenco."

On and on they went. "What would you know about America and what they do there? Of course they have churros! Do you think they don't eat croissants? In America they have the best of everything from everywhere, and churros are our best thing." They argued but were happy and laughed a lot.

For Àlex's mother, America was as far away as Mars, as exotic as Carmen Miranda and as glamorous as a film starring Fred Astaire and

Ginger Rogers. She packed their bags so they'd be ready when their son summoned them to come and see him, and meanwhile she dreamt of having coffee with Shirley Temple, Vivien Leigh or Clark Gable, who, she was sure, would be their son's next-door neighbours.

The longed-for day of setting out for America never came. They never saw their son again. The first year he asked them not to come and visit. His parents were surprised, but of course they agreed not to come, because, to the extent that they could, they obeyed his every command, granted his every wish. They thought he needed every spare moment for studying such a difficult course – and, moreover, in English! But that was only part of the story.

Àlex's mother never got to wear her *déshabillé* that first year and she started going less frequently to the hairdresser and eventually ended up with long hair that looked like chocolate mousse and cream: dark brown (where the dye still held) topped by white (where it had grown out).

Their son would soon be coming to spend the summer holidays in Vall d'Aran and they made a large banner with the words "Welcome home, dear son!" to take with them to the airport. Àlex's mother went back to the hairdresser's. The last letter from their son informed them that he'd be a little late arriving and instead of coming at the beginning of July he'd be there mid-August. "It would be better for me to stay a while longer in Florida. I have to do some training at the university, which will be a great help for my classes after the holidays." His parents were both sad and happy. Although they missed him and longed to see him, they also celebrated his excellent performance.

August was almost upon them. The crickets were singing their summer symphony when the phone rang. Àlex's mother ran to answer it with her usual "I'll get it!" They'd had no news from their son for days and the call was almost certainly from him. It wouldn't be long before they had him back in the bosom of the family, and they were quite on edge, but also thrilled at the prospect of seeing him soon. A few minutes later, she came back with a waxy, completely blank face, and said, "Our boy, your brother, is dead."

Àlex continued: "We only found out what happened years later. My brother studied very hard, nearly all the time, but he had also joined a far-right group, a xenophobic terrorist organization similar to the Ku Klux Klan. They went out one night on a 'clarification' mission, as they called their activities, with the aim of terrorizing a family that had just arrived from Haiti. They wanted to lay down the law and teach them a lesson – that the whites were in charge. Some members of the group were armed, but my brother wasn't, because he was too young and a foreigner. Despite his foreignness, he was seen as one of the 'good guys', because he was white and following a prestigious university course. It was good for the organization to have members with such a brilliant future as the one that seemed to lie ahead for my brother.

"The plan was simple. They were going to surround the house, leave signs identifying their organization and fire a few shots. They couldn't imagine that the Haitians had been warned and would be ready for them. There were a lot of them. They were strong and some were armed. The white kids, who were so sure of their intellectual superiority and organizational genius, were perfect – or I should say very imperfect – amateurs. The whole thing was a huge free-for-all and my brother copped it. He was hit by a bullet, and nobody knows whether it was fired by a black man or a white man.

"We only found out years later what really happened that evening in early August more than forty years ago, and my father never knew. The death of my big brother and their older son was also the death of the family. I was only nine years old, and for me it meant the beginning of a nightmare. My mother rarely said a word after that, and a few years later my father went out to work one day and never came home. I went from being the spoilt brat, the funny little clown who made everyone laugh, the Peter Pan who wasn't supposed to grow up, to being told off for everything I did. I no longer amused them. They didn't laugh at my jokes or applaud my antics. My father projected his image of my big brother on to me, but I wasn't in any way up to the standards he had set. The frustration was constant, and I felt more and more useless and pathetic, and less and less valued and loved.

"For years I believed I was entirely to blame for my parents' unhappiness, because I didn't get good marks at school, wasn't good at any sport, never said a kind word and was unable to form a structured argument. My father tried to the best of his ability, with private teachers, intensive courses, help with reading... but I didn't improve. On the contrary, I rebelled and, in particular, I completely withdrew into myself. Over the years I've learnt that I didn't have the most important things a kid needs: trust and unconditional love. Every morning when my mother came to wake me up, she said 'I love you lots', but those were only words, an empty declaration that was contradicted in her distant demeanour the rest of the day.

"We didn't know how or why my brother had died, except that it had happened in America, a country that, in the family circle, ceased to be paradise on earth and became a hostile land, full of delinquents and bad people who had brought about the ruin of my family. Anything that came from 'that continent of barbarians who killed my son', as my father constantly repeated in his attempts not to give it a name, was shunned as if it carried the bubonic plague. According to my father, it was the place, America, which had killed his boy. 'If he'd stayed here to study, this would never have happened. That country is full of barbarians,' he kept saying.

"I also had a horror of the place, and when they told us at school that the food we ate almost every day had come here centuries ago from that continent which inspired such terror in me, I decided never to eat anything from there ever again. They didn't understand my phobia at home, but didn't pay much attention either. In fact, I was almost transparent and invisible as far as my parents were concerned. We all stopped living after my brother died. My mother never went back to the hairdresser's, but wore her hair in a bun which, over the years, got bigger, heavier and more and more tightly coiled, a kind of metaphor for her pain and strength.

"That *botifarra* you made today was really good. Will you give me the recipe?" Àlex asks, abruptly changing the subject as if to banish the solemn confessional atmosphere that had been building up in his room.

"The *botifarra*, I buy it, Àlex." Annette can't think of any word of consolation. She's overwhelmed. How much can one person suffer? She kisses him on the lips and leaves his room.

12

PEPPERS

The cook's fingerprints are visible in an overly ornate dish.
PACO PARELLADA

Annette's hardly slept a wink. And when she did nod off nightmares assailed her. She can't stop thinking about Àlex's moving story. They meet in the kitchen. She makes herself a cup of very strong tea, trying to open her eyes and, blearily, to focus on Àlex as he works, totally absorbed by some courgettes, which he's hollowing out before filling them with crabmeat in béchamel sauce. He seems serene, as if nothing happened last night. Annette's surprised by his composure.

"How you are this morning?" she asks.

"As long as we can keep working, Annette, everything's fine. We're booked out today. It's amazing. Make the most of it. Keep an eye on the business, don't close your eyes to things and don't imagine this is going to last for ever."

"Why no? Can Bret always full."

"There's a big difference between Can Bret and you. They love money and you love food. Business and passion don't mix. The Can Bret people have two daughters who think they're Paris Hilton. The parents have to maintain them as such, so if their little darlings want a nice pink car, then the boss puts up the price of the *escalivada* – which nobody notices too much since it's a small percentage on the price of a few charcoal-roasted aubergines and peppers – or cuts the steak a bit thinner, or squeezes a bit more out of the immigrants he's got working for him on shit contracts. It's a piece of cake. You, however, have all sorts of inner hassles over what you need to do to get the business going or letting Graça work fewer hours. You need the pressure of a couple of kids wanting a PlayStation. Then you'll bare your she-wolf fangs and start buying the cheapest courgettes. And you'll pay more attention to what's happening with the business."

"Why you say this?" Annette is alarmed by his mysterious tone.

"Because Graça's stealing."

Àlex has discovered this bit by bit, with a missing bag of hazelnuts, a packet of rice, some chicken breasts, half a dozen eggs, a couple of lettuces… At first he thought he was getting absent-minded, forgetful. But something was always missing, trifles, small amounts of inexpensive food which would never noticeably upset the balance of the restaurant's takings. Then he started to be more watchful and to set traps, leaving things carefully set out in the fridge and memorizing the order. By the time he came back to start cooking for the evening menu some small item had disappeared. Graça was no expert, because she never covered up the gap.

Annette almost chokes on her tea. The revelation feels like a pot containing a large, very prickly cactus falling on her head out of a clear-blue sky.

"Are you keeping an eye on the till?" Àlex asks. "Have you noticed if any money is missing?"

"Yes," she admits. "Little bit. I think I make mistake with change because so much pressure, hurry at lunch, it easy for to happen."

"Graça has six kids. She's a she-wolf and can't bear seeing them going without. She wants them to have a computer, or a new sweater and Heaven knows what else. If she nicks a bit of food she saves on shopping and can put that aside for something else. If she can pinch a few euros, all the better. Don't get me wrong. She's no delinquent. She just loves her kids. So now you know, what are you going to do about it?"

"I no know. I speak with her. Try make better, hear she explain…"

"And try to help her, right? You see? You play at being a business-woman, but you're not made to manage a business. The Can Bret boss would go to the cops and make her give back what she's stolen with interest. He'd even get a court order to seize Frank's wages."

"And what you would do?"

"Exactly the same as you. First, listen to her and then get her to prom-ise it won't happen again. Ah yes, and I'd give her a raise. I suppose that option's already occurred to you," Àlex says bitingly.

"Yes. I a squatting duck."

"A *sitting* duck, it's a *sitting* duck, though what that's got to do with the price of eggs I wouldn't know. Well, if you're a duck, I'm a drake. Never mind, your decision isn't a sign of weakness but a demonstra-tion of your humanity, and in Can Bret humanity can never get in the way of business. Graça and Frank have helped both of us. That box of fish he's been leaving at the door is like all my Christmases coming at once, an incredibly valuable gift that can't be measured in terms of the quantity or quality of the goods. What counts is the message, because Frank, by doing this, is trying to encourage me and, even more impor-tantly, to show that he trusts me. Remember what I told you last night, about how my parents had no faith in my ability to get on at school? Well, trust is essential for everyone to feel strong enough to cope with what life brings. At the time, when things were going so badly with the restaurant, I didn't throw in the towel, because Frank was saying to me through those little fish, 'I'm sure you'll get through this. You just need a bit of time and a helping hand to pull you out of the hole you're in.' Graça took you in to her home without asking for anything in return.

A packet of rice and a few euros aren't enough to send her to prison, and what's pushed her to do it is love for her kids."

Annette has listened very attentively, not to say devotedly, to everything Àlex has to say. It's so beautiful and he's right: she's tidy, methodical and serious when she's working, but most of all she's humane. Thanks to his words, the thorny cactus that just fell on her head when she learnt about Graça's thieving has turned into a beautiful bunch of roses. Well, like a rose, life is full of thorns, but sensitive people don't worry about being pricked, as they prefer to enjoy the marvellous fragrance.

"By the way... do you have children?"

"I only explain you my life if you invite me for to listen classical music."

After lunch, Annette offers Graça a cup of tea, which they drink at one of the dining-room tables. It's a brief but difficult conversation. Stammering as if she was the guilty party, Annette doesn't mince her words and tells Graça what she's discovered. Graça cries. She didn't want to do it and it won't happen again, she promises.

"Graça, all my heart hope this no happen again, so we have trust in us. This surprise me, make me disappoint, but I very hopeful, because I think it episode that no will happen again. I have right?"

"My childs need things... computer. I no want they no be like other childs of school," Graça confesses.

Àlex, Annette thinks, is really savvy. He can see what people need at a glance and, following his sound advice, she suggests, "I think you must take home all the days servings clients no eat and you no spend money for dinner of childs. We do this?"

"You very good woman," Graça says.

"We must try for to be humans and for make business work, because this affect all us."

Embarrassed, Graça gets up from the table, takes her cup into the kitchen, washes it and puts it back on the shelf. It won't happen again.

Annette watches her and prays that everything will be all right now. If only everything were as easy as putting away a teacup. She really likes Graça, but also wants the restaurant to succeed, as this is the biggest project of her life. She sighs deeply, stands up, takes her teacup into the kitchen, washes it, dries it and puts it back on the shelf.

She sits down at her computer, ready to spend the whole afternoon catching up with her online publicity work. She goes to the old Friends of Antic Món page on Facebook and finds a whole heap of comments, including a debate about the pros and cons of the restaurant's change of direction. Glancing through a very diverse array of opinions, she sees that a lot of them are from Carol, all of them favourable. Wow, she's been working at this even while she's been travelling in Asia. Annette's happy, because it's clear that Carol wants to help make the restaurant work. Òscar's also contributed, saying that Roda el Món, the new restaurant run by Madame Escargot and Àlex Graupera, is excellent. Annette suddenly shivers. He's been careless and brought her virtual name, Madame Escargot, into the real world, and now anyone who cares to can seek her out. Of course he hasn't done this in bad faith, but she feels increasingly exposed and with fewer and fewer possibilities for hiding. If anyone wants to know who's hiding behind the name of Madame Escargot, it will be very easy to find out.

However, on second thoughts, she doesn't believe that anyone will want to know who she is, or who she has ceased to be, or why she uses an alias to identify herself online.

She gets to work answering each of the comments and creates a new Roda el Món page, which is full of surprising enticements. All the comments on Facebook have been very encouraging. She suggests foodie games, posts riddles, photos and recipes and also launches a promotional offer for young people: "Come and try our tasting menu. If you're under thirty, the amount you pay will be the age you are."

"Looks like business is good." Carol has just appeared online.

"Carol! Where are you?"

"I've been back in Catalonia for two days, but didn't contact you because I've had tons of work reworking some texts and publishing my travel notes. And the jet lag is hell. I'm completely done in. There's no way I can get to sleep even after a whole day dragging myself around like a snake in winter. And what about you? Are you OK? You haven't appeared even once on Facebook. Brilliant. I've been hoping to see you, wanting to chat and know what you're up to, but not a bloody word from you. Sometimes you're very disagreeable, far too reserved…" she gripes.

"Sorry. We busy, very busy. I want thank you for article in newspaper. That give us many customers."

"I was only too delighted to write it. You need a helping hand, especially when you're in such an out-of-the-way place as Bigues i Riells. But you deserve it. Are many of them coming back? I mean are you getting regulars?" Carol is genuinely interested.

"Yes. We have clients come back many times. One man he come very often and for dinner some couples they come back also."

"The owner of 7 Portes, one of the famous restaurants in Barcelona, says, 'Restaurants are not made by people who leave, but by those who come back.'"

"That very nice. Yes, we have also those who come back."

"You just have to look after the customer so he feels well attended. That's the most important thing. Then, make sure that Àlex is cooking well with clearly defined flavours and generosity on the plate. Most especially watch the prices. It's not the time now to be inventive, when the golden rule of 'good taste, good looks and good price' is more valid than ever for any business that wants to survive," Carol pontificates. "I want to see you. I'll come soon. How about tomorrow?"

"Good, that very good. You come when you want."

"You'll do it, won't you? You'll give me this pleasure?"

"What you want, Carol?" Annette asks, fearing the answer. She's a little fed up with this game.

"You'll let me take you out to dinner one day and you'll wear the dress and lingerie I got for you in Granollers. You will do it, won't you?"

What a drag, Annette thinks. Now she's in a right old mess. Carol's convinced that they're an item and going from strength to strength. Annette has no interest in continuing with the relationship, but she's also got to keep Carol on side and, most importantly, happy. It's a pain in the neck and so embarrassing too, Annette thinks. She feels soiled. She's never done anything like this – literally selling, well, prostituting herself – before. She knows that if she does what Carol wants it will be very good for business, but the price is very high.

Carol wastes no time in appearing at Roda el Món, the way she usually does, turning up without letting them know in advance. She simply walks in at dinner time, wanting to try Àlex's new dishes, or so she says, but it's hardly a secret that the real object of her interest is Annette.

The restaurant is quite full, with enough customers to keep Annette very busy and thus able to avoid her for a while. Sitting at her favourite table, Carol sips at an exceptional Mallorcan wine, Ànima Negra, and is titillated by her close scrutiny of Annette, whose busy thighs, viewed through the rosy haze of alcohol, have an extremely alluring, arousing effect. No sooner has Annette finished waiting on the tables than she literally orders her to sit down and have a brandy with her.

"I've had a very good dinner, sweetheart. Simple, interesting and natural food. I'm not surprised you're so successful, because this is exactly what people are looking for. The price is right! And the product is great!"

"Thank you, Carol... Now I must go for to clean in kitchen."

"No way! Now you're going to have another drink with me. We'll have a little chat to catch up a bit and then we're going upstairs. I can hardly keep my hands off those lovely strawberry-mousse boobs of yours – I was dreaming about them all the time I was away on that long, boring trip around Asia."

"I must to clean up," Annette insists.

"You can do that tomorrow. If you want, I'll pay that little helper of yours for a few extra hours. I've been waiting for this far too long. It's my turn now."

"Carol... um, er..."

"Don't come to me with your ums and ers." Carol is not to be deterred. "Listen, sweetie, if the problem's money, you don't have to worry. I'll pay your helper as many hours as you want. Now you have to look after me. Come on, let's go up to your room so you can put on that underwear. You haven't used it yet, have you? You're only allowed to wear it when you're with me. Understood?"

Just then, Àlex bursts into the dining room. He hasn't been able to speak to Carol yet and wants to say hello. Thank Heavens, he's saved the day, Annette thinks, and hastens to ask him to sit down with them. Carol isn't at all happy about Àlex's irruption onto the scene and is very put out by the fact that Annette has asked him to join them. She's waited long enough, what with an almost month-long trip abroad and a seemingly endless lonely dinner on top of that. There's no room for any third party in this space of tingling, itchy desire.

"How was the trip, Carol?" Àlex asked.

"Long. Tiring." She's not wasting words.

"Carol she like the menu, Àlex and I tell her the new ideas. She say they very good and we will go good." Annette does her best to keep Àlex at the table, hoping that Carol will end up so inebriated that she'll sink deep into a drunken slumber, but they need time for that, another bottle and more chitchat to make sure that Carol gets completely wasted. But she forgets that Carol is a veteran drinker and rarely gets drunk. Alcohol doesn't knock her out but, on the contrary, works in her favour by breaking down all inhibition, which means she enjoys herself even more.

Annette's nervousness gets the better of her. For every glass she pours for Carol, she pours two for herself. In order to keep the conversation going, she tells Carol about Roda el Món's first few days and the funny situations she and Àlex have had to deal with. He chimes in, describing how he saw things from the kitchen, and they both giggle like a couple of kids, not noticing that Carol neither laughs nor speaks. Annette and Àlex are talking to each other, leaving Carol out, and she's not interrupting, not at all amused by their stories or the closeness between them that she can now detect.

"That day was horrible. We are full and three more people come, but we have only two chair. You remember Àlex when customer he have table but he no have chair for to sit?"

"How could I ever forget! You flew into the kitchen, so stressed out you were bouncing off every surface like a basketball! Round and round you went. I didn't have a clue what was happening, because instead of saying 'steak', 'fruit salad' or 'fried sand eels', you were shouting 'chair, chair!' I thought you'd gone crazy or were asking for some dish in French and I couldn't understand which one. Or worse, that you eat chairs in Canada!"

"We eat chairs in Canada!" Annette laughs her head off, imagining her family about to tuck into a dishful of grilled chair at their beautifully set table.

"You know what happened in the end, Carol? The customer went back home to get a chair. Yes, he brought his own chair!" Àlex is guffawing now.

"Well, it's evident you're having a whale of a time here at Roda el Món. There have been big changes in this regard. That's all very well, but you'll have to excuse me now, because I'm very tired after my trip. Goodnight."

183

"Carol's quite uptight tonight... or maybe..."

But Annette is in no state to know. She's smashed and has passed out with her head on the table amid brandy bottles, empty glasses and breadcrumbs. Àlex carries her up to her room, puts her to bed and kisses her tenderly on the forehead like a loving father, but she's unaware of it.

The next morning, with the most excruciating hangover, she says to Àlex, "I no remember what happen last night. We finish very late?"

"Not too late," he lies. "You had a couple of glasses of brandy and then you went upstairs. I cleaned up the kitchen."

Carol phones Àlex. She wants to see him one afternoon this week, but not in the restaurant. They decide to meet today, after lunch. Àlex can tell from her tone that this isn't about a couple of old friends having a drink together.

They meet in Granollers, in a drab, rather gloomy bar not far from the station. Carol doesn't mince her words: "You and I have a plan, and that is to bring down Roda el Món, so you can get your restaurant back and get rid of that woman and her partner. Remember? I've done my bit, everything I promised. I've made sure that the restaurant's working nicely. I've done a good job. Annette's happy, trusting and optimistic. Do you want to stick to the plan or are you a little lapdog nowadays? That woman's got to you, hasn't she?"

"Whatever makes you say that?" He feigns innocence.

"The other night you were carrying on like two little lovebirds sitting on a power line. You only need to get dressed up like a knight in the Middle Ages, go down on your knees and ask for her hand in marriage. She'd be thrilled to accept, because she's got the hots for you. I can just see you both, clasped together forevermore, dancing a waltz in the Palace of Eternal Love."

On that long-ago day when Carol got Annette into bed, she'd been in seventh heaven, exultant, a new woman, and had completely discarded any idea of doing anything to hurt her. On the contrary, she was only too pleased to do everything she possibly could to help that cute little freckled girl, who was so malleable and as sweet as maple syrup. If she wanted to get rid of anyone, her target was Àlex. All her ill will was focused on how to put as many kilometres as possible between him and Annette, so that her beloved little redhead could enjoy being the undisputed boss and mistress of her own restaurant. Carol was going to look after her and get her a good chef – and there were plenty of them needing work in this crisis, dying to find a place where they could start flinging saucepans around again. She'd never anticipated any kind of sentimental obstacle in the form of Àlex, but on the contrary believed that his rudeness would completely alienate the delicate Annette.

In her idyll, Annette would work happily (under Carol's thumb) all day and Carol would come to her at night. She would find a gentle, compliant Annette, and there was no way she wanted to hear any complaints about Àlex's latest outburst or use their precious time together for therapy sessions to soothe away all the hassles caused by the testy chef. Her plan was all about placid nights, whispering sweet nothings, caressing Annette's belly, or wild sessions when Annette would cede to her most outlandish desires, all the lascivious fantasies she'd dreamt up in her eternal nights of solitude.

That evening, when Annette and Àlex were laughing about their restaurant stories, Carol saw her satiny visions of tangled sheets evaporate into thin air. It was crystal clear: there was chemistry between them and she was devastated at having missed her chance to get Annette for herself. Driving home, she decided to salvage the plot she'd hatched with Àlex. Yes, she would go ahead with it, and her revenge would be twofold, doubly juicy and interesting, with two happy futures destroyed.

On the one hand she'd shaft Annette and her dream of the restaurant, and on the other she'd wreck the only good thing left in Àlex's life: his love for Annette.

Carol runs through the script. "According to our plan, we have to organize the presentation dinner for the press. The time has come. We need to do it in about two weeks." She doesn't miss the two deep creases of worry appearing on Àlex's forehead. "What, so you don't want to go through with it?"

"No… yes… I mean…"

"You mean you're backing out, maybe? OK, if we don't stick to what we agreed, that woman's going to take over the whole restaurant. Now you're carrying on like a couple of pimply teenagers, but as soon as she tires of you – and you can be sure she will, sooner or later – she'll send you packing. No one can put up with you!" Carol's determined that Àlex isn't going to bail out now.

"I know. I'm just thinking about all the things that can go wrong. We've got to consider every detail, even the most unlikely problems. Perhaps we're rushing things, doing the press dinner so soon after the opening."

Àlex is hoping to gain time by postponing the press party, so he can think about how to get out of this mess. Of course, there's no way he'll do anything to harm Annette, but he's got to find a way of foiling Carol's malevolent intentions. Right now nothing occurs to him. Fighting against Carol is a dangerous business. She always goes for the jugular.

"You're the one who's rushing, and you're heading straight for the ditch of despair, because once you're bled dry, without a cent in your pocket, she'll kick you out." Carol is full of contempt. "Now listen, I've got the whole thing sussed. Just before the party you'll give an interview to *Dia i Nit*. Everyone reads it. I've got them to promise the whole centrefold. In this interview you have to tell them you have differences with your boss, complain that she's buying material of questionable quality

and adulterating whatever she can in order to boost profits. They'll have
the exclusive when you tell them you're leaving Roda el Món on the
very day of the party. You'll even tell them that you've refused to cook,
but you'll be there, because Annette has forced you to stay so the press
won't know anything till the official announcement that you're going.
You'll say that you've decided to take the opportunity of the interview
to make the whole thing public. They'll be ecstatic to have a scoop at
Dia i Nit and you'll make the headlines. At the party I'll spread the word
among my colleagues, confidentially and off the record, about Annette's
fraudulent practice. Nothing makes journalists happier than getting a
sniff at dirty washing. I'll do it towards the end of the evening, when
they've all eaten… the food that's been tampered with."

"Carol, it's all very well planned, but it's very dangerous thing to
poison a bunch of journalists. What if somebody gets really sick? Can't
we think up some alternative?"

"Don't worry! I've been doing my homework and have discovered a
very mild poison that only causes diarrhoea and headache. Nobody will
end up in hospital, but they'll *all* feel terrible, and that means they'll
go looking for the common denominator: Roda el Món. You'll be safe,
because the cause of the food poisoning will be the additives Annette
uses to save money. And you won't have cooked the food, which you'll
have told the *Dia i Nit* beforehand. The next day, all the newspapers
will be full of the fact that so many journalists have been poisoned. The
restaurant will be closed down and then you'll get it back and start all
over again. It's a safe, simple, watertight plan."

"Yes, it is," he reluctantly admits.

Àlex drives back feeling unhappy and alarmed. He doesn't know how to
stymie Carol's plan, but there's no way she's going to get away with it.
He worries and worries and worries. She's in control, and if she wants

to wipe them out she certainly will. Even if he doesn't say he's leaving, and even if he doesn't give the journalists a good attack of the runs by putting poison in the pot, it doesn't matter. When Carol finds out he's disobeyed her orders, she'll be enraged and will rip them to pieces in her articles. Not only in the newspapers, but on the Internet as well.

She has a horde of followers who have blind faith in her. She can make and break trends and tastes. An angry Carol is more dangerous than a large lobster which is about to be dropped into a pot of boiling water, senses certain death and breaks the elastic bands binding its claws. His brain's gone completely haywire and he feels trapped, tied hand and foot, a prisoner of his decisions. If only he could wipe from the calendar that day when, angry with Annette, he hatched the plot. But there's no going back now.

Driving back to Roda el Món, he seeks distraction by listening to Cesária Évora, humming along with her even though he doesn't understand what she's singing. Yet her silky voice is so relaxing.

He gets back to the restaurant shortly before it opens for dinner. As usual, Annette's running around, checking tables, putting the finishing touches on a cake and answering the phone. She's so graceful. Watching her, Àlex thinks, "She's the life and soul of the restaurant." As he walks past her, he murmurs, "As long as we're together no one can bring us down," but Annette doesn't hear him. Still running, she flashes him a smile – a balm for Àlex.

It isn't a great night. They make mistakes at a few tables and one customer complains that his bream is dry. Àlex is withdrawn and doesn't respond to Annette's orders, so she ends up jittery and yelling. She has to dole out a lot of free liqueurs today to compensate for their errors.

"Àlex, we must to speak," she says when the last customer leaves.

"If you're going to tick me off, leave it till tomorrow, will you? I'm not in the mood."

"I little bit tick off you. Tonight is disaster. What go wrong?"

"I'm hungry!" Àlex tries to act unconcerned.

"Something happen with you and me as well. I very nervous, because today boss at Can Bret he visit me."

"What! That shithead? The initials of his restaurant's name apply to him. CB: Cunning Bastard."

"He want for to buy Roda el Món and he pay five times more than I – well Òscar – pay."

"Bloody hell, that's a lot of money. What do you want to do?" Àlex is swamped by all the powerful emotions that have ripped through him today and he's in no condition for thinking clearly.

Annette's been distracted all evening, which is why she's made so many mistakes. She's not sure what to do about the offer made by the owner of Can Bret. It's very tempting and has to be considered, even if they're happy about the success of Roda el Món, which has been achieved by a mixture of emotional investment and gigantic effort. They've put everything they've got into it and want to lay solid foundations but, more than anything else, they must be pragmatic. This money would let them embark on a new project and not necessarily a restaurant. There are lots of things you can do in life, or so Annette believes.

Àlex is different. He thinks there's nothing else for him to do with his life. This is his home and things are looking up, so it would be a pity not to make the most of this auspicious moment.

They talk at length. Annette gets a pencil and paper and starts doing the sums, with columns of pros and cons and lists of professional opportunities. She prattles on while Àlex tunes in and out. He's doing his columns and lists, without writing them down, as the ideas themselves are enough.

In the pro-sale column, he puts the money they'll get, which represents freedom from the servitude of running a restaurant, the long hours and the constantly clinging anxiety of the immediacy of the work. It would mean the end of interminable chores and everyday hassles. He'd be able to visit his son more often, but the greatest advantage is that closing down Roda el Món would free him from Carol's stranglehold.

Yet there's one disadvantage that outweighs all the benefits put together. Selling Roda el Món would mean the end of his relationship with Annette, no longer seeing her every morning or being able to watch her incessant movement, or hear her cheerful voice and innocent shouts that some plate or other is missing, or check the freckles on her face every day in case he has to inform her that one has fallen off in the shower...

Taking all the arguments for and against into account, Àlex realizes that he can't stand the idea of having to live without Annette's hyperactive presence and indescribable fragrance.

"Well, Annette, I think we need *pebrots*."

"Peppers? We have peppers." Annette's Catalan has improved a lot, but she still doesn't understand the meaning of a lot of idioms: *hi hem de posar pebrots*, for example.

"No, no, this isn't a recipe," he explains. "If a Catalan says we need to have peppers, it means having big testicles, or being brave. Right now we need peppers. We should hang on to Roda el Món. We'll manage somehow."

Àlex takes her hand. Annette turns it round so she can grasp his tightly and, looking into his eyes, says triumphantly, "We put all the peppers in Roda el Món. Tomorrow we start. I cook stuffed peppers!" Then she can't stop giggling.

Àlex makes a face at the prospect of having to eat peppers, so Annette is quick to give him one of her History of Food lectures. The confusion between pepper and capsicum goes back to Columbus who, when he tasted a dry red pepper, was reminded of black pepper. Pleased to be able to take a spice to the Spanish King and Queen at last, he gave it the same name, pepper. Unlike the other products coming from the New World, the dried and ground red pepper was soon accepted in Spain, since it could be used like black pepper, but was much cheaper, because it was easy to grow in Spanish soil while black pepper, which had originally been imported from India thanks to Àlexander the Great, had to be shipped in from far away.

However, it wasn't just the question of price that made the new red pepper so popular. It had a wide range of uses. It was a good preservative, so food could be kept longer. As spicy and hot as black pepper, or even more so, it gave intensity of flavour and special zest to many dishes. The Spanish people were soon addicted, and all sorts of sausages and traditional recipes took on new taste and colour. How could a Spaniard survive without chorizo? What would *escabetx* be like? Soused fish without red pepper? Impossible. And what about the Catalan romesco sauce without the small round red bell pepper known as the *nyora*?

Àlex listens attentively, gazing at her with delight and stroking the hand lying in his.

"Tomorrow, when you've finished stuffing the peppers, do you want to listen to some music?"

13

VANILLA SALT

> *The gourmet never forgets the name of the deceased. Moreover, he makes express mention of it while eating, whether it's artichoke or boar, and remembers other murders and previous devourings because the pleasure of eating tends to go together with the memory of past feasts.*
>
> MANUEL VÁZQUEZ MONTALBÁN

Someone knocks at the door of Roda el Món. It's the postman with a registered letter. Annette opens it warily.

This type of letter always makes her feel uneasy. She reads it fast. It's giving notice of a freezing order unless they immediately pay off their large debt with the fish supplier.

Annette phones the director of the company and asks for an appointment in order to renegotiate the terms of repayment. Yes, they'll see her today. She doesn't waste a moment and rushes to the company offices, which are located on an industrial estate. The building isn't very big and the letters MARTÍNEZ BROTHERS are overly large by comparison. However, everything looks quite austere until she reaches the director's office, which is ostentatiously plush and in very doubtful taste. A collection of Buddhas occupies one of the shelves behind a desk carved out of a genuine ebony tree trunk. It must have cost a fortune. She is greeted by a very fat man with a round beer belly struggling to escape from the grip of his tight white shirt. The straining buttons look as if they're going to fly off in all directions like birdshot. He's not wearing a jacket or tie and the top two buttons of the shirt are undone, displaying a thicket of chest hair. He's the antithesis of elegance. Gold rings bite into sausage fingers. He looks like the biggest Buddha of all, although without showing the slightest sign of wishing to follow any religious and spiritual teachings. There are all sorts of mementos from Burma and Thailand in the office. Trying to break the ice, Annette asks what regions of the two countries he's visited and also about his devotion to Gautama Buddha.

"I've never been to Burma. But I've been to Thailand. The women there are real beauties. A lot of fun too!" He winks. "I got the collection of Buddhas from my decorator, because I wanted a nice office and he says ethnic's in fashion. I don't know about these things, but I listened to that pansy and, as you see, it turned out well, didn't it?" Mister Self-Made Man in person!"

"Lovely, yes, very lovely," Annette mocks, and then, not wanting to beat about the bush any longer, continues. "Thank you for the appointment. I come for to find way of pay debt and no have freezing order."

"You've had this debt for months now and I've been very patient. I called Àlex on many occasions and he never picked up the phone or answered my messages. The freezing injunction is already underway and can only be revoked if you pay before the end of this month."

"I no have money for to pay you all now, but can to pay instalment every month. I spoke with bank and I get promissory note so we finish debt in eight months," Annette offers, ignoring his account of the situation.

"Well, that's difficult, because the freezing order can only be revoked if you pay back the whole sum."

The fish boss is finding it difficult to have a serious conversation with Annette. He's not used to negotiating with women, and still less with such a strong-willed female. The ones he employs to clean fish are uneducated, loud and always joking. He treats them with a mixture of paternalism and despotism, constantly checking on them and considering them inferior beings, like all women. This redhead, he thinks, is quite different. She's cultured, expresses herself well and, most shocking of all, looks him in the eye. He can't handle this direct gaze so, copying a scene he once saw in some American film, swings his chair round to face away from Annette, joins his hands to form a triangle and seems to be praying to Buddha.

Two long minutes of silence ensue as he wonders what to say and how to deal with this situation. He stares at a studio portrait of himself and his family of three children and a peroxide-blonde wife with prodigious breasts. Then the solution occurs to him.

"One of my sons is a layabout. He doesn't want to study or work in the company and I don't like him hanging around in the street all the time, because he's going to fall in with bad company. He's very young, just sixteen. He might like working in a restaurant kitchen, because being a chef is all the rage now. They say girls are dying to go out with a potential Ferran Adrià! I'd be much happier if he was working and learning a trade. If you take him on I'll advance the money right now to settle the debt plus interest and you'll pay me back in the form of my son's wages each month as instalments. You understand? That way it won't cost you anything to take on my boy. The main thing, and I stress this, is that he mustn't know anything about our agreement. If he finds out that his dad's behind this he'll go berserk. It's the only solution that occurs to me."

Annette can hardly breathe. Does she have to take on this fat man's son on top of everything else? It's too much! When she tells Àlex he'll throw a fit... no, a Greek tragedy at the very least!

"Yes, we do that." She agrees without further ado. "But when we finish to pay debt we no have more obligation for your son." She wants to make it clear that she has no intention of keeping this millstone round her neck and that she's agreeing to the deal out of pure necessity.

"Very well. But remember that there are two conditions. First, you can't kick him out, which means you agree to have him for a whole year, which will cover all the instalments. Second, he must never, under any circumstances, get wind of this conversation, not as much as a whisper. Is that clear? And there's one other last condition, which is that you have to keep me informed about his behaviour and his cooking skills. If he doesn't turn up at work one day, for whatever reason, you have to tell me. Ah, and tell Àlex he has to be very strict."

The meeting comes to an end and Annette isn't sure whether she's won or lost. Maybe asset-freezing would have been preferable. But, for the time being, the reality is they're going to have to cope with a wayward kid.

She comes into Roda el Món calling, "Hi Àlex, where are you?"

"I'm cooking. This morning I thought, 'Damn it, bloody hell, I actually like cooking,' so here you have me. A change is as good as a holiday, eh? What about you?"

"You make many jokes lately, no? I come for to tell you that tomorrow a new boy he start work in kitchen," she says quickly.

"So you asked me about this? Sorry, I don't recall when." He pretends to be angry.

"I have no time for to consult but there no choice. You no ask me why. We must give job to boy. That is that. No problem for money. He very cheap. It necessity. I no meet this boy, but think he good person. He come here for to work and we must to teach him and control him."

"What a mystery! OK, you're the boss, as I've said many times. I would have preferred to choose the kitchen hand myself, which is the least I can ask, but it doesn't matter. The main thing is I'll have an extra pair of hands, and that will be a very good thing. I suppose you know what you're doing."

After turning down the offer of the Can Bret owner, they're working like navvies in Roda el Món. Àlex is doing his very best now, and instead of disappearing to rest every afternoon he cooks as if his life depended on it. The tasting menu – "Food for peanuts," he jokes – is excellent and the number of fans is growing fast. The ten-euro lunchtime menu is famous throughout the region. All the tables are taken every day and today they've done two sittings.

Annette's been cooking this afternoon. She has to make some cakes and also wants to make *biber dolması*, the famous Turkish stuffed peppers.

She'll use some beautiful, fresh medium-sized green peppers brought by Albert, the organic-vegetable supplier. She cuts off the stalks, cleans them inside to get rid of the seeds. She fries a couple of onions, adds some pine nuts and a good handful of rice, covers it with hot broth and lets the rice take it in as it cooks nice and slowly. She chops up some fresh herbs – dill, mint and parsley – which she sprinkles over the rice, after which she adds a pinch of cinnamon and a few drops of lemon juice. When the rice is cooked and has absorbed all the aromas of the herbs and spices she fills the peppers, which she then places neatly in a casserole dish and covers with water and white wine. She makes a paste out of crushed almonds and a couple of dry biscuits and adds that to the sauce. The whole thing is then simmered until the peppers are cooked and the sauce has thickened. They'll be on tonight's menu. Today, too, they have plenty of customers and the reservation book is practically jumping around on the desk.

The lone diner has come back again tonight, working slowly and thoughtfully through the menu. When Annette serves him, he asks her a few questions about the food or the cooking, and also about her professional background: where she learnt to cook, if she's cooked any of the dishes herself, how long she's been living in Catalonia, and so on. Annette is flattered and answers trustingly. When she goes into the kitchen to get this customer's order, she tells Àlex. "The peppers are for this man at the Table 2. He come many times and always put me questions. He seem very interested in restaurant and how we make the food. This man have a lot of curiosity. He look at everything in restaurant and watch me working. You think he a Michelin inspector?"

"I fear he's more interested in your buttocks than in what comes out of this kitchen on a plate," Àlex laughs.

"Now you be serious. You think Michelin guide check our work?"

"Hmm. It's strange, because, as far as I know, you have to ask them to come. I don't think they send their inspector unless you ask first. And you haven't asked. Listen, my advice is that you ignore the whole thing, even if he does turn out to be a Michelin man, because being in the guide isn't much use if you don't have a star. If you do have one, then you become a slave to their rules and regulations and way of doing things. Of course a Michelin star attracts customers from everywhere and the town would be very proud of having a starred restaurant in the guide. All the same, it's better to do things your own way and not have to end up following their instructions. It seems counterintuitive, eh?"

"Yes, totally. If customers come from far and people in town they are proud for have a restaurant with star, where is problem?"

"There are two problems. First, the people from a long way away come for a 'taste', but only once and you never see them again. Second, the locals will put you up on a pedestal, by which I mean when they're talking to people from other places, they'll boast about the importance of their town because it's got a Visigoth or Romanesque church, or a square with a crumbling stone arcade, some caves from the year dot, plus a restaurant with whatever number of Michelin stars. But they never set foot in the restaurant, just like they never gaze at the stained glass in the church windows or venture into the caves. They have to walk under the arcade when they go to buy bread, but if it weren't for practical reasons they wouldn't go there either. Michelin stars actually frighten people away. The sensation of elitism and starchiness puts them off… and they can't afford it anyway. Bloody hell! The peppers. With all this talk, they've almost gone dry!"

After they've closed up for the night, there's one serving of peppers left over. Annette invites Àlex to try them. Although he tries not to give away anything with his expression, as he still resists praising her cooking, he likes the peppers a lot and Annette can see it. This makes her so happy that she tells Àlex that this dish is reserved for special occasions in Turkey, weddings for example. Things seem to be going well at last. She pours two glasses of wine from a bottle that some customers haven't finished and asks sweetly, "Can we go to your room and listen to music?"

"We have to get to sleep early today. Tomorrow's very important for us."

"Yes, the presentation to press and the new helper he start also, you remember? It is important day, so good for us we relax a little bit."

"You make things happen to suit you… and you make me go head over heels."

"Go your head to hills?"

"You still have a lot to learn, baby," Àlex says, playing the role of a movie heart-throb.

They pick up the glasses of wine, plus another two half-finished bottles, and take the stairs two at a time in some kind of unspoken hurry to get to Àlex's room.

Àlex gets flustered trying to choose the right kind of music. Annette helps, more interested in putting on any old CD to hurry things along than expressing any clear musical preference. As they're standing side by side at the shelf of CDs, their bodies touch and Àlex feels as if he's on fire. He has already decided that tonight's the night. He wants to see her moving, touch her skin, feel her red hair against his chest, tangle his fingers in its curls, make drawings out of her freckles and find a moistly welcoming heaven between her legs.

They settle for a CD of Mayte Martín. Annette's never heard her before and is soon bewitched by the voice and the boleros that transport her to some indefinably safe place. She has already decided that tonight's the night, after too many imaginative sessions of spiriting him into her room at midnight, just as she's dropping off to sleep, conjuring up his rough hands, the castigated chef's hands that neatly tie up a rolled roast, delicately break off rosemary leaves, deftly chop vegetables and confidently shake the frying pan in which mushrooms are cooking. She wants the heaven of feeling Àlex's hand between her legs.

They drink their wine in silence, turn towards each other, still in silence, and kiss. It's a furious, wet, shameless kiss. Àlex undresses her, impatiently unbuttoning her white shirt to touch her breasts at last. Annette throws herself into his arms. They've contained this desire for so long, working so hard to hide it that it can only explode. They would have liked to make love slowly, enjoying every moment, letting the heat rise until almost melting their flesh, but they fuck urgently, trying to absorb one another.

It's taken no more than three minutes and they're both panting, not satisfied but certainly burnt, like puff pastry cooked in a too hot oven: the high temperature won't let the pastry rise so the layers can separate to acquire the crunchy texture that melts in your mouth. They sit on the bed, drenched in sweat. Annette covers herself with the crumpled sheet.

"You owe me one," Àlex says all of a sudden.

"We make now more love?"

"No, I'm fine, though I wouldn't say no to a second helping either," he jokes, imitating a customer being offered another ration. "You owe me an explanation. I want to know who I'm taking into my bed. I don't know the first thing about you except that you're from Quebec and your name. Ah yes, and you've got the most delicious vagina. But that's not what I want to talk about now."

Annette understands. She owes him an explanation, so she tells him her life story without sparing the details.

She's the only child of well-off parents. Her father was the director of a very profitable company specializing in fattening farm animals, mainly cows. She was sent to the best schools for young ladies in Canada, and her childhood could come under the "Very Happy" heading.

The young Annette grew up and met a handsome, studious, well-mannered and very ambitious American boy from a good middle-class family. Her parents were enchanted with him, as he met every requirement they'd decided on when they were raising their daughter. They lost no time in marrying her off to the brilliant young man. They had a lavish wedding and her parents bought them a flat, with everything they could possibly want, in Chicago, where Annette's new husband worked as an executive in a multinational.

Annette Chaubel, now Mrs Annette Wilson, acquired dual citizenship. They decided not to have children straight away, because she was interested in too many things and didn't want to spend all day wiping snotty little noses. She enrolled for a degree in anthropology, which she loved and kept her busy. At night, she didn't miss a single art show, or new play, or performance of experimental music. Her husband worked long hours, climbing up through the ranks in a career full of successes and recognition from his bosses. He got home late, very tired and tense after a whole day spent wheeling and dealing. At the weekend they had dinners with friends and occasionally escaped to New York, where she took lots of photos, another of her passions. They lived very comfortably and were much better off than most couples their age.

Some years after they'd embarked on this upscale life in Chicago, Annette's father fell ill and died a few months later. He had employed good managers, but without the director's supervision serious problems began to appear. Although she had neither the slightest wish nor desire to do so, Annette felt obliged to take over. Her husband left his well-paid job and they moved to Quebec to run the company.

Annette went back to her maiden name, Chaubel, and her husband slowly took over the whole management of the business, as he believed that the old system was outdated. He introduced new production systems and aggressive sales-and-marketing strategies that were very different from her father's clear, simple business style. Annette took no interest in the new management plan. She was very busy meeting her friends for afternoon tea, helping an NGO that was building houses in Mali, working with an amateur theatre group of some renown in Quebec and attending all the classical-music concerts at the Opera House.

It was around this time that she started getting interested in cooking and food anthropology, so she enrolled for a master's degree in anthropology at the prestigious University of Quebec. She was busy all day long, although she also managed to find time to go to her father's old business ATLANTIC VIANDES, mainly because there were always a lot of documents and cheques to sign, a result of the express wish of her father before he died that Annette keep the company in her name and not give power of attorney to anyone, not even her husband. She was the CEO, and nobody else could sign on the company's behalf. This power was to be her downfall. She trusted her husband so much and was always so busy with classes, meetings, the NGO, concerts, theatre, food and everything else, that she never took the time to check what she was signing. Indeed, in all honesty she now admits that she wouldn't have understood it anyway.

She and her husband were growing further and further apart. He was very busy and she had a lot of interests, so many that she didn't notice that he had quite a collection of lovers. As far as she was concerned, it was fine that he was so busy and keeping well out of her life. Moreover, he liked all the trappings of being a rich man. He travelled with his lovers to the most exotic places, took them out to dinner at good restaurants and had a marvellous flat for his trysts. He coveted wealth with ever greater avidity, obsessed in his quest to squeeze bigger profits from the company. He'd cooked up several different strategies, some of which were quite bizarre, until he came to the conclusion that the best way to make quick, juicy profits was to speed up the process of fattening the animals. He put his plan into action, resorting to fraudulent ways of puffing up the poor calves, giving them large doses of clenbuterol, a magical drug that quickly produced impressively bulky animals, which were heavy not in meat or fat, but fluids and chemical substances. The overdose he administered caused acute food poisoning in consumers. When the crime was revealed, all fingers pointed at Annette as the guilty party. After all, she'd signed the contracts and ordered the purchase of massive quantities of clenbuterol… unaware of what she was doing. She hit the headlines.

Annette Chaubel, owner and director of ATLANTIC VIANDES, has been charged with fraud after being held solely responsible for authorizing the use of the outlawed drug clenbuterol for fattening animals, causing ten deaths and widespread food poisoning affecting hundreds of people throughout Canada.

Before the case came to court, she became a fugitive, using her married name of Wilson and eventually moving as far away as possible from Canada. At first she hid out with some friends in Iowa, but she couldn't stay with them indefinitely, since she feared they might get mixed up in the scandal. And she wasn't the only one who thought so, as her friends started dropping hints about the risks they were taking by harbouring her. Wounded by their insinuations, Annette began to think about where to go. The United States was too close. She had to put a great distance between herself and Canada, so she decided on Europe and, while still unsure about exactly where, she "bumped into" Òscar online, and after that a whole series of coincidences led her to Bigues i Riells.

"Now I here. You see I become delinquent but no know it. A totally broked fugitive and my husband – yes, he still my husband – he live like king in United States because he steal company money when he see the problems that they arriving."

"Jesus Christ!" Àlex can't think of anything else to say. "We're two tormented souls, with two strange and complex stories and we've met up here in this corner of the world. We'll have our work cut out to fix things."

"We no so special. You no must think you different. All people have story but no want think about it. You no have interest for know my story until you put me in the bed. We all us alone people who share this world."

"Well, I want to be more interested. Come on, what about the second course?"

It's very early. The sun's hardly up and Annette's already at work in the kitchen. She's slept very little and is agitated and happy all at once. Last night she opened two bottles that had been languishing for too long in the cellar, made love with Àlex and finally told him her story. She feels light and floaty with relief, but today isn't the best day to get carried away with memories or drifting about like a teenager, sighing like *la dame aux camélias*. It's a very important day, crucial for the future of the restaurant.

Àlex comes downstairs, looking very spruce. He's whistling, and seems happy. They wish one another good morning, as if nothing has happened between them. They don't have a moment to sit down, have a cup of tea and talk about what they shared just a few hours ago. There's a lot of work to do before the members of the press turn up for the gala presentation of Roda el Món. Nobody will be absent, because they all know Àlex and, furthermore, Carol has weighed in by phoning up the big names. Everyone's quite excited.

Outwardly, Àlex is happy, but a terrible uneasiness is gnawing at his entrails, and this has nothing to do with all the delightful moments of his marvellous night with Annette. They made love again after she gave him her stark but complete account of her previous life, because he wanted her to understand that she had his total support and that he'd do everything within his power never to let her down.

Carol's vile plan is the cause of his malaise.

The party is tonight and, though he's been racking his brains, he hasn't come up with a plan to foil her... and to make sure that nobody gets hurt. Time's marching on, but he hasn't worked out his counterattack. Of course he's not going to say anything in the *Dia i Nit* interview about Annette adulterating the food and he certainly won't poison the food. That's for sure. He also knows that when Carol discovers he's let her down, they'll be felled by another kind of poison, and they might as well say bye-bye to Roda el Món.

"Àlex, you have eaten breakfast?" Annette asks.

"Have you seen me having breakfast? I don't think there's a bar in my room... yet. But there are definitely some empty bottles. Anyone might think there was a rave in there last night, with free drinks and all."

"Please, you taste one thing. I make you special breakfast."

"It's not a day to be tasting stuff. We've got tons of work and we'd better get down to it."

"I know, I know. But only one moment." She passes him a plate of toast.

Apparently it's a plate of toast. One slice has chopped cucumber on it, another chocolate cream and the third some slices of tomato.

"Well, if it's a feast to celebrate our first coupling, it's a bit low-key, isn't it? You might have made more of an effort with French champagne, strawberries, *bellota* ham, buttery croissants, scrambled eggs… I know we're on a tight budget but… three slices of toast, and you haven't even tried to hide the tomato! How am I supposed to take this? Are you breaking up with me already? If that's the case, there are plenty of other ways of doing so."

"You be quiet, Professor Big Spoon. I no have interest for to feed you. I want you taste a thing I keep like diamond. I have very little quantity so let you taste it mean I love you, and you know that last night. If you like this taste I make aperitif for journalists. Unfortunately, I no have sufficient for to cook, but little aperitif, yes."

Àlex tastes the toast. There is one flavour in common, despite the fact that the three toppings are totally different. He knows this flavour, tries to dredge it up from his memory, but he has to dig deep, because he's almost totally forgotten it. When he finally grasps the aromatic sweetness of the mystery ingredient, his unconscious takes him back to one long-ago summer. He's very little, with his parents and brother in a bar in Vielha, and crying, "I want an ice cream, I want an ice cream!" When he finally gets it, he doesn't like the taste, so he offers it to a famished-looking dog in the street. His mother smacks him so hard that the flavour is branded into his brain for ever. The toasts have a hint of that ice cream. He likes it, yes, he likes it very much.

"What a mystery. I don't know what you've put in this, but it's magic. It completely changes the taste of the food it's mixed with. I love it. It's some spice, isn't it?"

"Yes, it vanilla," she says.

"But vanilla is sweet and with the cucumber... well, you don't pick up that sickly sweetness."

"How long you no taste vanilla? Good vanilla, the best, like this, no is sweet. It very, very aromatic but no have taste. I need make you a vanilla class. The tongue only catch basic tastes, salt, sweet, bitter and sour. The rest of gastronomic perceptions they stimulated by aromas, and aromas give real 'taste' that tongue no catch. It olfactif that it take aromas to brain and give this information of taste of food. So this vanilla no can to be sweet because tongue no catch it. This difficult for to explain, but simple with experiment. You cover the nose. Good. Keep the nose covered and I put in your mouth this little thing and then you tell me your perception."

"Salt," he says nasally.

"Uncover nose and what you find now?"

"Ice cream." Not to mention his mother's slap that summer afternoon in the bar in Vielha.

"Vanilla. It not sweet and not salty, but what you taste now it vanilla salt I make in Canada and bring here in suitcase. It my treasure, because quality it is exceptional, so I bring this from my country as a jewel, like Christopher Columbus. When he find out he no reach to India, and he no know where he arrive, but he spend already all gold the King and Queen give him for to buy spices, so he feel very disappointed. So vanilla and red pepper that I talk about before, solve his problem. Spanish people happy with spices because they conserve very good, so food last more in time when they no have fridge. So spices they very valuable. They also give new aromas to food which have very small variety. They no have the greenhouse for to grow strawberry, so they must to eat them only in springtime and no like now all the year. The spices they give illusion they eat many different things, but the principal ingredients they the same. The vanilla tree no grow in Spain, because it need tropical place, so it different from red pepper. They must to import vanilla from distant lands, so it very expensive, only for rich people, so they think it even more better."

"So you've flavoured salt with vanilla. That's a great idea. You can make some money out of that. Set up a little stall in the market and sell salt flavoured with different spices. You can call it 'Annette's Aromas'." He's teasing her. "But till you start making a fortune selling little pots of salt at the price of spices these days, we've got to work and, in particular, cook for this show tonight. Otherwise when the journalists arrive we'll only have a teaspoon of salt to offer them, and then they'll think we're just a couple of *salt*imbanqui leaping about with nothing to offer."

Annette doesn't get the joke, as she's lost in thought, her freckles consulting the ceiling. Then she exclaims, "Àlex, what you just say for to tease me is brilliant idea. Why no? You famous chef, your cooking celebrated and many people wish to discover your secret. In home people they no have time and they cook very basic and very repeat like grill, boil, steam or sometimes vegetables in frying pan. Everyone complain that home food is boring, like we go back to the king and queen of Columbus time when they no have variety. No time, no knowledge, no imagination – it all make the food very monotonous in home. If they have your 'secret', the food very flavour and fun and they can to change taste without they change the food."

"I was joking before! You've taken me too seriously, I fear. Are you 'cooking up' some new product, perhaps?"

"I no sure if you make joke, but I very serious. We have product and it very success product. You listen me. This very simple. We aromatize salt with spices and we combine spices to make bouquet salt also. When people make the grilled chicken in home they can put rosemary salt one day, and 'Bouquet Salt One' another day or 'Bouquet Salt Two' or 'Three' or 'Four'… This salt it have taste of Àlex cooking, so it have melange of spices you put in restaurant for the chicken. We can to make catalogue of many flavours of salt. The chicken it stay same every night, but it seem different chicken because it have the new flavour."

"You're completely batty, Annette. As if we didn't have enough work in the restaurant without getting caught up in a new project. It's not as easy as you think. Who'll buy it? Our customers! All half-dozen of them?"

"I no have batty in belfry! This is very good idea. What it cost us for to make product? Few cents for the salt. Salt! It cost nothing. Salt, spices, pots we only need for to start. It no go spoil. On the opposite, salt and spices they conserve the food. Yes, we can to sell it in restaurant and try in shops also. It good business, because it cost almost zero. Listen me: ZERO!"

"Hmm. You might be right. Let's talk about it tomorrow. Let me remind you that we have fifty journalists coming here for dinner tonight. We've been here in the kitchen for half an hour and haven't as much as washed a lettuce." Àlex ties up his apron, which means serious work.

Annette's barely heard his last words, because she's distracted by someone ringing the doorbell. Eric, the fish boss's son, has arrived for his first day of work. If the father was a caricature of the self-made man, the son is a parody of the obtuse sixteen-year-old, for whom life consists of body piercing, tattoos, discos and motorbikes. Looking him up and down, Annette thinks that the difficulty won't be teaching him, but getting him to let himself be taught, and he doesn't seem in the least willing in that regard. There's no question about it: this kid isn't going to save work, but will create more.

"What do I have to do?" The boy seems to think this is a greeting.

"Work hard," Annette tells him. "Àlex, the chef, he give you the work dress and you do what he say. He the head and you the legs."

"What time do you knock off here?"

The boy's an expert in insolence. Annette chooses not to answer his question, but shows him the restaurant and explains how things work. They go into the kitchen and she introduces him to Àlex. Eric's in luck, because Àlex is in a good mood and very absorbed by what he's doing. Otherwise, the boy wouldn't last five minutes.

Annette has to make cakes, and Àlex is preparing most of the dishes they'll serve at the party. There's not a second to waste. They give Eric a box of anchovies to clean, meaning he's got to remove the heads and gut them. He gripes and grumbles that if he'd known he had to clean fish he would have gone to work with his dad, where the underlings at least treated him with all the respect due to the boss's son. But in the end he gets down to the job.

Concentration is the order of the day in the kitchen, where all three of them are busy with their tasks. Sometimes Àlex breaks the silence with an order. Graça arrives mid-morning and immediately launches into the considerable amount of work involved in setting tables, polishing glasses, arranging flowers and fine-tuning every detail in the dining room for the party.

"You got blacks working here too?" Eric asks disdainfully. "There are lots of them working for my dad and I don't like being around them. They're thieves."

"Thieves come in all colours," Àlex retorts, containing his urge to thump the boy. "Here people work. Some have dark skin, or are thin, Annette has freckles and I have a terrible temper. Graça is the wife of Frank, the distributor who works in your father's company. They are very good friends of ours, and if any idiot does anything to upset them, then we'll get very angry."

"That black, that Frank doesn't work for my dad any more. My dad kicked him out about a month ago. He was nicking stuff. A box of fish disappeared every day and my dad found out it was him. He's a thieving bastard," Eric declares with appalling serenity.

Annette and Àlex look at one another in horror. They knew nothing about this. Graça has said nothing. Maybe she doesn't know. A box of fish every day… a box at the door of Roda el Món every day. True, they haven't had any fish from Frank for more than a month, but they assumed that Frank had decided that the charity season had come to an end.

14

CHOCOLATE

*One can turn one's back on a father, a mother, a
husband or a lover, but never a chocolate cake.*
MANUEL SCORZA

The *Dia i Nit* journalist turns up just after lunch to find Àlex in the
kitchen dealing with some sea urchins, which he's going to cook in
cava, the traditional way. They're really delicious done like that. He'll
put them under the grill till they're just cooked, taking on a golden hue,
but without losing their characteristic deep-crimson colour. Chef and
journalist sit down at one of the tables in the dining room. They have
to get started at once, because the guests will be arriving in a few hours
and there's still plenty of work to do.

Àlex opens a bottle of cava to help the flow of the conversation.
The journalist seems to be a very pleasant man and, moreover, he
likes cava. They talk about Àlex's career, his culinary philosophy,
his taboo foods, the restaurant's change of direction and, in fact,
all the usual things that are discussed in a typical interview with
somebody who is eminent in his or her field. Àlex barely sips at his
cava, because he's doing the best he can to come up with intelligent
answers to the usual questions. However, when he goes to top up
the journalist's glass for the seventh time, there's not a drop left.
Bloody hell, this guy's drunk a whole bottle all by himself! They
crack a second bottle.

"Thanks very much Àlex. It's been most interesting being able to talk with you. I think I have enough now, except for one detail. What was that you said you wanted to do with Annette? Set up a business of aromatized salts?"

The journalist wants to keep chatting, as he's settled in very comfortably at Roda el Món. In fact, he doesn't have anywhere else to go.

"Yes, we want to create a new line of products so that people cooking at home can enjoy the aromas of my specialities and of Roda el Món in general."

"That's really interesting. If you want a hand, give me a call. I'm available."

Available? What does he mean by that? This question buzzes round Àlex's head after the journalist leaves. He returns to the kitchen, turns over some caramelized almonds and mulls on the journalist's words. "I'm available." Àlex doesn't like the way he said it, because there was something desperate there, the tone of someone clutching at straws.

He expects anything from Carol but ingenuousness. She's as sharp and cunning as a fox. Very perceptive too. He finds it strange that she hasn't turned up for the interview to make sure he's done what he promised, namely condemning Annette's way of running the business and insinuating that she adulterates the food for fatter and faster profits, which was supposed to be the sensational exclusive: Roda el Món was guilty of fraudulent practice, because Annette's only concern was money. He'd also been ordered to say that he had no longer had any connection with the restaurant, he'd been sacked and he hadn't cooked any of the dishes that were being served at the dinner.

That was what Carol had decreed, but he's gone along with his own plans, following the dictates of his heart, telling the journalist that the Roda el Món food is wonderful, made with the region's best-quality products and that Annette is an exemplary boss. To add insult to injury, he's also let the cat out of the bag by talking about their future project of producing salt aromatized with spices, because this will bind him to Annette for ever, God willing.

He's got work to do, but he can't let this go. He sits down at the computer, goes to Google, types in the journalist's name and that of the newspaper. There are hundreds of pages, thousands of articles, interviews and reports he's signed. Yes, he's prolific. He looks at the dates. There's no recent article. The last one is from the 20th of last month. A journalist who writes nothing in a month? Àlex smells a rat and calls the newspaper, asking to be put through to him. The very helpful receptionist informs him that this man no longer works there. They've cut back on staff and the man's now unemployed. Unfortunately she can't give contact details.

Àlex's head goes into overdrive. An out-of-work journalist comes to do an interview for a newspaper where he no longer works. What's this all about? It can only be something nasty cooked up by Carol. "Now I get it!" It's so devious it's like the worst kind of B-movie. She knows he won't stick to the plan, so she's paid a fake journalist, a hatchet man who won't publish the interview in which he so highly praises Annette.

Carol had foreseen his reaction and was determined to thwart him at any cost. She might have saved herself the comedy of the journalist and interview, but she probably thought she'd be more certain of his trust by putting on the show. But her crystal ball hadn't shown the journalist downing almost two bottles on an empty stomach and letting slip, with childlike naivety, that he no longer works for *Dia i Nit*, or that, in consequence, Àlex would deduce that Carol wasn't honouring her part of the bargain. Knowing that the interview is never going to appear, Àlex feels lost. He can't begin to imagine what kind of plot Carol is hatching. He's going to have to be extremely watchful. And the whole night long.

* * *

Carol's very pleased with herself. That loser of a journalist has told her that the idiot cook has fallen into the trap and has been more than willing to waffle on the whole interview, because he's so thrilled at the idea of having the centre spread all to himself in a newspaper with such a big circulation. Her subterfuge couldn't have worked better. After that night when she'd registered how much Àlex and Annette secretly fancied one another, she'd correctly guessed that Àlex had no intention of doing anything that might harm his precious freckled redhead.

Carol was incensed when she realized that her sentimental plans were just a pipe dream. Rage boiled in every cell of her body, building up an insatiable thirst for revenge in her brain. She wasn't going to wipe out Annette alone. Àlex would go down with her. Carol wanted both of them dead. There were many ways she could annihilate them, but the most painful and effective one was to make them see their darling Roda el Món project in ruins. This would be lethal for them both, economically and emotionally speaking. She could burn the place down, but that would be too unsophisticated. It wouldn't be much fun either and, worse, people would feel sorry for them. She could just see the newspaper reports:

Chef Àlex Graupera is distressed by the fire in his beautiful restaurant in Bigues i Riells but says, "We'll come out of this stronger than ever and shall build up Roda el Món all over again, with the very latest in technology and tremendous commitment."

No, she doesn't want to give them any chance to tug at society's heart-strings with their misfortunes. She wants to destroy them by killing the restaurant's good name.

"Hi, lovelies!" Carol sweeps into the restaurant, a jabbering tornado swirling in all directions at once. "My God, what an incredible amount of work.

214

I can guarantee this will be a huge success. Everyone's dying to find out about what Roda el Món's up to and what you're offering. Talk about great expectations! Oh, Annette, what beautiful flowers you've got in the dining room. Congratulations. And Àlex, how did the *Dia i Nit* interview go?"

"Very well, thanks Carol! Thanks very much for setting it up. That journalist was very thorough," he says, without looking up from the veal fillet he's getting ready to roast. "Sorry, I can't attend to you now. Time's running out. But do help yourself to a glass of cava."

"Hallo Carol!" Annette calls from the other side of the restaurant. "It too long since we see us. I want to call you, but I run out all time very much."

"Run out? What have you run out of? I'm perturbed to hear this." Carol feigns interest.

"Annette still gets her idioms mixed up. Her Catalan's impeccable, apart from not knowing the gender of things or set phrases. I think she means she's been running around a lot," Àlex says, adding: "And that's indeed the case, as we've been running around non-stop these last couple of months. What about you?"

"Hmm, so she doesn't know the gender of things," Carol mutters to herself, "but I bet she knows the gender of your dick when it stands up to salute her. The bitch may not know about gender but she knows plenty about sex."

"What was that, Carol? I can't hear a thing with this beater turned on." Àlex looks up from the mayonnaise he's now making.

"Nothing, sweetheart, nothing at all. I think I'll take you up on that glass of cava you just offered me. Come and keep me company for a moment. I want to tell you a juicy bit of gossip about one of your colleagues. People for miles around are pissing themselves laughing."

"Wait for me. It like me to hear also." Annette starts taking off her apron.

"No way, darling. You're such a delicate little thing and some things are not for your ears. You'd probably faint, and I'm sure there are no smelling salts in this very modern establishment. Off you go. Get yourself upstairs. Go and make up those cat's eyes of yours because you have to look gorgeous tonight. You're the star, after all."

Annette obeys Carol, as she feels indebted to and guilty about her. She hasn't phoned her once and neither have they chatted on Facebook, but Carol's helped them so much by phoning up all the journalists to make sure they'll come to the party.

Carol makes the most of her absence to show Àlex the dose of poison he has to put in the casserole, just enough to give the journalists an upset – slightly upset – stomach.

"Don't worry, they're not going to kick the bucket, but they will have a nice belly ache. Imagine, that journalist you saw will be writing up his interview now and tomorrow all the online newspapers, which are must faster than the old-style ones, will be talking about it and highlighting the food poisoning. We've got the whole thing under control, and the result will be perfect. Did you tell the journalist everything we agreed on?"

"Yes, yes, I did." He averts his gaze.

The first guests are starting to arrive and the place is filling up with TV cameras, microphones and notebooks at the ready to jot down statements made by Àlex and Annette. It looks like a kitchen set for a film. Annette's nervous. She wants everyone to have a good time and feel well looked after. She wants the dishes to be served hot and perfectly cooked, doesn't want anyone to end the night still hungry and, most of all, she doesn't want to die of embarrassment when she has to make her speech. Oh, and she doesn't want to forget any of the acknowledgements and the messages she wishes to convey. If it all goes well, she'll sleep like a log tonight.

Òscar comes in puffing.

"Sorry I'm a bit late, Annette. I wanted to come and give you a hand, but I had a lot of work," he apologizes.

"Don't worry. Graça and I we can to do dining room because Àlex he have now helper in kitchen."

"A kitchen hand? Great. That must mean that things are going well. I'm happy about that, because it also means you can start paying back what you owe me…"

"Yes, yes, Òscar. We plan this. After party we give you first payment."

"As long as you're planning to do so, that's fine by me. The only thing that worries me is that you're spending money on unnecessary things or you're overstepping your limits, which is why Antic Món crashed. But let's leave this subject for now, because you've got the big party now and I'm here as a journalist. My blogger friends would give an arm and a leg to have this experience. I'll write something that will have the whole world drooling and dying to come here to meet you."

Annette jokes, "Well, for whole world will to come you must to write in English, Chinese, Japanese and Urdu in addition of Catalan, Spanish and French. You have big job here!"

"No probs. I'm going to use the universal language of images without writing as much as a single line. That's old-fashioned! I'll post a video. It'll be really cool, eh? I'll work out how to do it. It's going to be experimental."

"You will pass all party for to make film? But you like so much eat and drink, in ten minutes you leave camera on tray… then… where it is? And we find in dishwasher with champagne glasses and dirty forks," she teases.

"Me? Film? No way! I'm going to give my total attention to this fantastic menu you've come up with. This is an experimental video, as I told you. No one's ever done anything like it. I'll leave the camera filming above the kitchen door and it can do its own thing. Then it will show what's being cooked and how, Àlex's movements, waitresses going in and out, friends and journalists saying hello to Àlex, the atmosphere at the stove… It will be the ultimate reality show. I'm going to edit it, eh. Make it about ten minutes long. I love the idea. This will be my first foodie short based on a real-life situation," he explains, looking very pleased with himself.

There's chaos around the stove. The journalists, some of them good friends of Àlex's, come in and out of the kitchen, making themselves too much at home. They greet Àlex, try a mouthful directly from the pot and exchange gossip and secrets among the saucepans. Although the dining room has been made ready with their maximum comfort in mind, they prefer to be behind the scenes in the kitchen. The stove provides an ideal cosy atmosphere for their hush-hush exchanges, taking them back to the days of fireside chats and grannies who added new details to their stories night after night. They complain that they have to attend too many boring social functions, but they never say no when Àlex or Carol calls, because they always know it will be fun. This time they don't know the half of it, as tonight's show is going to be really over the top.

Àlex is very alert, expectant, monitoring Carol's every move. He's certain that she hasn't given him all her poison and that she's kept some – or a lot – to use herself, waiting until Àlex is distracted by something to drop it into one of the saucepans. Àlex and Eric are coating some pork spare ribs with soya sauce and honey before putting them in the oven to cook. Three journalists are in a huddle alongside them, buzzing into each other's ears. Àlex catches snippets.

"I've had it up to here with Carol. She doesn't leave space for anyone else."

"She's the spoilt brat of the newspaper. They'd even print her farts."

"She's lost any taste she ever had. Now she can't tell a lemon from a mandarin."

Àlex hasn't been talking to his journalist friends recently, so he's not up to date with their current frame of mind. So they're pissed off with Carol. Now that's really news!

"Eric, come here a moment. I want to show you the wines we're serving tonight." Àlex wants to get Eric away from the journalists' sharp ears.

"But, boss, I haven't finished this and, anyway, I hate wine. It's disgusting. Give me beer any day, and right now I'd drink a whole bottle."

"Come with me, you blockhead. OK, you deserve a beer." And Àlex, who's starting to get tetchy, drags the boy into the dining room.

"Listen, lad – that's if you've washed your ears a few times these last fifteen years and can still hear me – I want to give you a mission tonight and hope your brain can register two orders at the same time. First, forget about the kitchen. I mean from now on you don't have to help me with getting the food ready. Second, I want you to keep very careful watch on one woman, the one who was the first to arrive. You know who I mean? That one, that tall, older woman with long black hair who's throwing her weight around."

"An older woman? I'm only interested in the hot ones my age. What about the beer, boss?"

"Will you kindly pay attention! The woman I mean is wearing a long, flower-patterned dress, and you can pick her out because she's talking to everyone and carrying on like she's the queen of the party."

"There are plenty of women with long hair here."

Àlex continues, ignoring the boy's callowness. "All the guests will go to the dining room now. It's highly likely that this woman will hang around in the kitchen and fiddle with the pots and pans. That's when you've got to watch her, but you have to dissemble. Do you know what that means?"

"Course I do! I've spent the last ten years dissembling when I'm supposed to be studying!" He sniggers.

"Well, you have to watch everything she does, OK? And tell me later."

"Right, boss. And what about the beer?"

Àlex takes a warm beer from a crate, opens it and hands it to Eric. "Here, you can have a swig at this, but only one mouthful. If you do a good job, I'll let you finish it later on. If you don't do as you're told, you'll still get your beer, but with the bottle too, right on top of your head." He's under no illusions about Eric, but he's the only person who might be able to help him.

When he goes back to the kitchen, the last journalists are on their way to the dining room, Carol taking up the rear. She whispers to Àlex, "Which is the star dish? Which is the one I'd better not eat, so there'll be enough left for the others?"

"The sea urchins. They're fantastic," he murmurs.

The plan was that Àlex had to tell her which dish he's poisoned, but she's going to eat them all, because she knows he hasn't used her product. But she'll certainly use it, and has enough of it in her bag to make an elephant extremely ill.

A television crew is waiting for Àlex in the kitchen, ready to ask him some questions. The sound technician asks him to move away from the stove and background noise, but the cameraman wants to have the pots and pans in the background. It's to be a short piece, without too much talking. Àlex loves being interviewed, though he'd never admit it. Indeed, whenever it happens, he tends to describe the journalists in his usual "affectionate" way: "that idiot journalist", "that cretin" and his favourite of all, "that starving hack".

However, when he's with the interviewer it's a very different matter, with a beaming Àlex offering glasses of cava to facilitate the conversation and, should the journalist bring out a camera, his performance is worthy of a psychologist's scrutiny. Before a television camera, Àlex becomes Julio Iglesias, Mick Jagger and Cindy Crawford all rolled into one. His coy glances and the way he preens and pouts for the camera are hilarious. He completely forgets himself, forgets about the world and surrenders himself body and soul to the journalist and, in particular, the camera.

Eric is still at work, washing herbs to be added for a last-minute touch of freshness just before serving. He's annoyed and he doesn't see why he has to watch this old woman. His first day of work is very strange. He's been taken on to help with the cooking and, after working non-stop all day long without even time to go for a piss, he's now been told to stop cooking and keep an eye on this woman. He's not at all keen on the idea of becoming a detective, but it would be worse to have a bottle of beer broken over his head... This chef has a foul temper.

Àlex is busy playing to the camera, and Carol is in the dining room drinking cava with the journalists. But hey, Eric sees her sneaking into the kitchen and going over to a pot of cream-of-watercress soup to which the mascarpone has been added, as it's about to be served. The woman with long black hair puts her hand in her bag. Eric feels very nervous and does his best to pretend he's engrossed in cleaning the herbs. Carol tips the contents of a small packet into the watercress soup, stirs it in with the wooden spoon, and pretends to taste it, looking at Eric and winking. She returns to the dining room just as Àlex is answering a couple of questions from the hostess of a TV food programme who's interviewing him.

The guests are getting impatient. They've been waiting at their tables for a while and nothing seems to be happening in the kitchen. Annette looks in several times to see if they can bring out something to eat. Eric is clueless and Àlex is still being interviewed, but if they wait any longer they'll have a disaster on their hands. Annette sees that the easiest thing to serve now is the watercress soup.

"Come on, Eric. You put plates make line and I put soup in all them. You know what go on top?"

"These herbs and truffled cheese."

"OK, we do it. Àlex he still with interview and guests have hungry."

Annette and Graça serve the soup to their guests and then clear up the bowls and spoons afterwards. Surprised by its intense green colour and silky texture, they all pronounce it an excellent first course and are full of praise for Àlex. "He's really shone with this soup." Carol hasn't tasted hers.

"You are OK? You feel bad?" Annette asks. "Àlex he make this especial for you, because you write always that good meal it must to start with the soup."

"I'm fine, really fine. I must confess I was in the kitchen, like the other journalists, and couldn't resist serving myself a cupful because I was very hungry. You've made us wait a long time, sweetheart. If I have any more I won't be able to enjoy the other wonderful delicacies you've prepared for us, let alone your dessert."

Àlex finishes the interview. He's had a great time and has been asked exactly the kind of questions he loves answering. He revels in telling the story of how he learnt the trade, the high point of the interview for him, in which he can play the victim recalling the tough times of being cold and hungry, working fifteen hours a day for a pittance.

"You couldn't have been too hungry," the interviewer challenges him on his slip, because, well, actually, the one thing cooks don't suffer from is hunger. But overall he's really shone. He goes back to the stove.

"Shit! Have you already served the watercress soup? Are you crazy or what? How dare you! Why didn't you tell me? What did you put in it? Did you remember to serve it with the truffled cheese, you imbecile?" he yells at Eric in alarm.

"Yes, yes, I put in the truffled cheese. We didn't wait for you, because Annette decided to go ahead, because people were hungry, but they said it was fab, yeah, great," the petrified boy answers.

Àlex sticks his head out to see what's happening with the journalists. They seem happy. Phew! He hates not being able to keep an eye on every last detail, since he knows how much attention the gourmet press pays to the finer points of the appearance of the dishes, which must look beautiful, as they take photos and may even publish them. He can't afford to take the risk of letting a sixteen-year-old kid with his brain addled by drugs, beer, heavy metal and the obnoxiously loud exhaust of a souped-up motorcycle serve his food. He can see Carol's black mane of hair from the doorway. She's surrounded by the best-known journalists and tossing down the wine like it's going out of fashion. This woman never leaves a drop in any bottle, he thinks. Then, he almost has a seizure. Fuck! Carol! He's totally forgotten about her because of the bloody interview.

"Eric, Eric!" he shouts.

"What's the matter, boss?"

"That woman, Carol, did she come into the kitchen?"

"Yeah, while you were doing that interview. When are they going to show it? Wow! When my mates see it I'll be more famous than Michael Jackson."

"Shut up, will you! That's enough of your nonsense. Tell me what she did. What?" Àlex is almost hysterical.

"She put something in the pot."

"What pot?"

"The watercress soup. The pot's in the sink now."

"Bloody hell!"

He paces round the kitchen. He's desperate. What can he do? And Annette – please, please, no, don't let her have tasted it, he begs some deity.

* * *

The party's been a great success. The journalists have left more than happy after eating and drinking to their hearts' content, and the write-ups will certainly be fulsome, Annette thinks. She's very tired, that's for sure. She could never have imagined that a formal opening could be so much work and cause so much stress, especially when she had to make her little speech. She didn't say everything she wanted, but she didn't do badly, given that she was trembling like a reed in the wind and, in her nervousness, she spoke half in French, half in English, providing the journalists with the anecdote of the night. She would really have stolen the show if she'd finished off in Graça's languages, Portuguese and Swahili! Graça and Eric have gone home, as has Òscar, who, after reclaiming his camera from its perch, is thrilled with his film, although it's going to be difficult to make a short out of it when he has enough material for a feature.

Annette and Àlex sit down at the kitchen table and drink a bottle of cava. Although they're both doing the same thing, their moods are very different. Annette savours her cava with delight, sighing contentedly over the bubbles and gabbling on non-stop. Àlex sips his in silence, also sighing, but it comes out more as whimpers from the depths of his heart and mind. Annette's so thrilled she doesn't notice his silence at first, but then she stares at him. "What happen you? You no are happy? It go very well and they love menu you make, especially sea urchins, and Carol she praise very much the watercress soup."

"Bloody bitch…" he mumbles.

"What you say?"

"Nothing, nothing. Yes, it went very well… Annette, listen…"

"Yes?" She's intrigued.

"We have to work on the aromatic salts. I think it's a brilliant idea and I'm sure they'll sell very well. Maybe the business will let us forget about the restaurant, and you know what I'd really like to do? Close the place down and go somewhere else, a long way from here. How about accepting the Can Bret offer?"

"But what you are saying? This is our dream now be true and we get plenty advertise of journalists. We must to use this good chance."

"Listen Annette, journalists are two-faced. They tell you one thing and mean the opposite. They're hypocrites. I think we should go and see the Can Bret man tomorrow and accept his offer. Yes, tomorrow. If he comes up with the money, I'll sell the building and sign the contract immediately, and you and I can get away and start a new life together."

He's desperately seeking strategies to convince Annette, although he knows his arguments do not hold water.

"You no must think this," she says. "We work here very hard and we keep with idea of new business because it very good. Now my very good idea is celebrate good party tonight. You invite me for listen music in your room?"

Àlex isn't really up to sexual feats tonight, but agrees anyway. In bed, Annette's happiness is evident, but Àlex is unresponsive. She believes he needs time to unwind after all the effort he's put into cooking and fretting about the party. She unbuttons his shirt, removes his trousers and gently finishes undressing him. His tattoos leap out, begging for attention. She caresses them with her fingertips, stopping at one on his back with a heartbreaking message: "I want to be with you, brother." She licks it and then all the rest of him, leaving no centimetre unexplored, from his toes to the soles of his feet, up his legs, calves, thighs, buttocks, moving towards her goal. Then she stops.

She wants to make him wait, suffer, go mad with desire, beg for more. She wants to make him implore her to hurry, to lick his penis and surround it with her lips. She caresses his chest with her curly hair, tickles him gently under the arms, wanting to hear him laugh. She climbs on top of him, leaning over till their lips touch, gently kissing him. Àlex is miles away, absent. Annette's done her best, wanting this night to be doubly magic, but she can't turn him on. They remain in silence. She's tired too, and goes to sleep like a baby in the shelter of his arms.

He wakes up to the sweet smell of something hot exhaled from a cup. Annette wants to surprise him with breakfast in bed, but Àlex is distraught. He can't bear the idea of hurting his beloved Annette. If only he could wind the clock back like a video film, he'd just press rewind and go back to the day when they started to plan the party. He'd tell her to forget all about the idea of putting on a show for these cynical people and just get on with their life in the restaurant, working until they'd had enough. But he can't. He's blown it. Now he has to tell her that he's betrayed her, that he's a bastard and that all her hopes will be shattered today.

He dips a slice of sponge cake into the cup, letting it greedily soak up the satiny hot chocolate perfumed with cinnamon and vanilla. He loves the intense bitter warmth of the chocolate on his tongue. When he was a very small boy he once covered his white shirt in hot chocolate at the first-communion party of one of his brother's friends, but his mother didn't get cross with him. On the contrary she laughed and, still giggling, said, "You look like a chocolate-and-cream zebra." Now, forty years later, he's drinking it again. It was sweet when he had it at the first-communion party, but today it's bitter, quite bitter, although Annette has added quite a lot of sugar.

"The Aztecs they beat chocolate with two sticks and it make the sound 'choco, choco'. Then they put the water, in Aztec is word *alt*, so make this name *choco-alt*, what very same like today name, maybe only Aztec word we use still today. In sixteen century the people in Spain they crazy for chocolate and in *Le Grand Dictionnaire de cuisine*, Àlexandre Dumas he say everyone know that Spanish they have no need more than chocolate, chickpeas and bacon."

"Thank you, Annette. It's been wonderful to know you."

"We no die now! We have plenty time. Many experiences they wait for us together."

"That chocolate, which was so sweet when I was a child, is bitter today, because circumstances have taken away the sugar that made everything easier. Growing older means getting used to the bitter taste and learning to find pleasure in it," Àlex muses, looking out the window so as not to have to meet Annette's gaze. "Did you try the watercress soup last night?"

"Sorry, Àlex, I no have time. Everyone they say it very good, but if remain any I have today."

"No, beautiful, I don't want you to eat it. It's too bitter for you."

Àlex's eyes light up with happiness. He gets into his best clothes: shirt, tie and jacket. He rushes downstairs, out into the street, where the cold air reddens his cheeks and abruptly wakes him up, even though it doesn't banish the fog taking over his brain.

He marches into Can Bret, where the boss receives him. The transaction lasts a few minutes. Àlex signs away his home and also a commitment to transfer the business.

He walks slowly back to Roda el Món, crunching plane tree leaves underfoot. He looks at his property and is suffused by a mix of nostalgia and happiness. He wants with all his heart to go somewhere a long way from here.

15

MAIZE

*To eat or not to eat is a question of money. To
eat well or eat badly is a question of culture.*
MANUEL VÁZQUEZ MONTALBÁN

All the newspapers are full of the story of poisoned journalists and other
guests at the party. The more charitable pieces speak of error, but most
are harsh, speculating about inadequate hygiene, negligence, poison and
so on. A quick glance indicates the strength of Àlex's degree of friendship with the journalist concerned: the measure is malice.

Annette has read all the reports with great attention. The grim reality
is that the restaurant's image was already terrible, and all it needed to go
right under was to be the cause of mass food-poisoning, which is what
the headlines are screaming, loud enough to be heard in the furthermost
corners of the country. There's no denying the evidence. They're done
for. It will take years to win back the confidence of clients, and Annette
will need centuries to recover. She's as tough as an old maple tree, but
being blamed for a second episode of food-poisoning which she hasn't
caused is more than she can handle.

Cleaning up after the party and reading the newspapers, she hardly
notices the morning flying by. She's decided not to open for lunch. Friday
is the slackest day, because most people from the local factories only work
in the morning, so they've practically begun their weekend, while the
city people with holiday homes haven't arrived yet. They plan to open

for dinner, but after the newspaper reports Annette's not expecting too many customers today.

She goes to the door for a breath of fresh air and to look at the sun. Still holding the newspaper, she sees Àlex walking towards her. If she didn't know that wild horses wouldn't drag him to Can Bret, she would almost have thought he was coming from there.

"Almost all journalists they sick because they get poisoned and say it because of our dinner. What will happen us now, Àlex?" she almost shrieks.

"Right now, we're going inside to have a cup of coffee. I need to talk to you." Àlex looks hangdog and can't meet her eye.

"Àlex, we finished. We no can recover now. I destroyed. I no know what can we do." Annette's crying and sobbing.

Àlex fears that Annette's tears will wash away her freckles, but now he has to inform her that he's just sold his house to the Can Bret people. He can't find the words, because this will be even more devastating for her. He should also tell her that he knows that the journalists are suffering from food-poisoning, but he can't bring himself to do it.

"Listen, darling, let's forget about the restaurant. We'll use our money to set up our vanilla-salt business."

"We no have money. I use money we get for to pay debt with suppliers, and the party it was very expensive. I was thinking the journalists write good things and we get more customers, more money for to pay Òscar the money he lend. We no have money!"

"I have money. I just sold the house, and we have the option of selling the restaurant too, but I need your agreement. But we have to do it immediately, today in fact."

Annette is really alarmed. "What you have done? You sell the house? Who you sell to? Who want restaurant that all newspapers they attack? You must to forget this idea. You say silly things."

"I sold the house to the Can Bret people this morning, and they want to buy the restaurant too. I've signed a commitment to sell the restaurant as well." He still can't look at her.

"With permission of who? To Can Bret, never! You crazy. We finished, yes, but we must to keep the honour. You no ask me. You son of the bitch, you betray me!"

She's so hurt her despair turns to rage. Transparent tears are little magnifying glasses on her freckles, making them flash like red lights.

"We can't afford to talk about honour. This is an extreme situation, and the Can Bret boss is willing to pay. We've been struggling in vain. Now we have to put all our efforts into vanilla salt. We'll find a small place where we can live and work." He tries to sound reasonable.

The phone interrupts them. It's Carol, wanting to know how Annette's taken the news. She tries to calm her and invites her to lunch, saying she wants to help her with this terrible situation and the future of Roda el Món. Annette thinks this isn't the best day to leave the restaurant, but her feelings are mixed and she's very confused. Even though she senses that going to see Carol would be like tightrope-walking across Niagara Falls in a storm, it also seems that she's the only person showing fortitude and determination. Nothing is clear in this murky situation, but at least Carol is offering warmth and Annette needs a change of scene. Carol finally dispels all doubts by dropping the bombshell: "I know what happened yesterday."

Life seems much easier in Carol's car than it does when she's hanging around Àlex. It's clean, there are no papers scattered on the floor, the petrol tank is full and it smells nice. When they stop at a toll gate the barrier opens immediately, a small detail which Annette finds comforting. Life with Àlex is full of barriers that block and complicate everything, a continuous succession of gates that don't let them through and conspire to thwart all their dreams.

Carol stops at the entrance of a restaurant in Arenys de Mar on the Maresme coast, where they are effusively greeted by the woman who owns it. Carol tells Annette to get whatever she wants.

They order an array of Catalonia's splendid sausages, haricot beans, potatoes with lobster and cannelloni. Carol seems happy. Her chief concern today is to find the restaurant with the best cannelloni, and the ones she's ordered are exceptional, especially when washed down with French wine.

When their second course has been served, Carol decides that it's time to raise the subject. "This is a terrible thing to have happened. But you can come out of it brilliantly, because you're wonderful in the dining room. I can help you find a good chef, because with this crisis there are plenty of them looking for work."

"Àlex he very good chef. We have bad luck, because if this thing happen with other people who no are journalists we say sorry and nobody know. The problem it is big because they tell it in all the media."

"Yes, it's everywhere, that's true. This is very tough, but the journalists like you. They think Àlex is a madman, a temperamental artist. They admire him, but also fear him, and some of them can't stand him as he can be very crude at times. I think that if you get rid of him, we can start again from square one. I'll organize a couple of interviews for you in the mainstream newspapers and TV programmes, and I'm sure you'll come out of this."

"I no think I need kick Àlex out. You get interviews in newspaper for him and he explain and have new chance. Carol, I want ask if you OK. You no have problem with dinner?"

"Actually, I'm not a hundred per cent today, but at least I'm not in intensive care. I didn't eat much yesterday, because I desperately wanted everything to go well and was very nervous. And look how it all turned out… Do you think the food-poisoning was just bad luck?"

Annette, surprised by the question, asks, "What this mean? Of course it bad luck. Some ingredient it was bad."

Carol runs her index finger round and round the edge of her bread plate as if trying to hypnotize Annette. "Well, it's just that… Àlex said something weird a few days ago and it made me very uneasy. Have you noticed anything strange about him?"

"Strange? We so busy I no give attention."

Looking condescendingly at Annette, as if struggling to convey to her that this is a dangerous world where babes in the wood get gobbled up by wolves, Carol, apparently drained by the most crushing weariness, sighs loudly.

"I shouldn't be the one to tell you this, since you should have worked it out for yourself, but Àlex wants to wipe you off the map. He hasn't told me so himself, but I can see from a mile away what he's up to. Poisoning the journalists meant destroying your last chance of getting the restaurant up and running again. If you are ruined he can then get it back for himself without paying a cent. Once it's in his grasp again he'll find a way to start all over again."

"You are telling me Àlex he sabotage the food? This no have sense. Impossible. We start new business… together. You make mistake, Carol. No, this all wrong because he give up and sell house to Can Bret. It impossible he want get restaurant back."

"I adore your cute innocence, sweetheart! Look, I'm an old hand and I've been keeping an eye on him for a while now, waiting to see what he'll do. Àlex wants to hurt you. It's a matter of pride, nothing to do with wanting to be the owner but with his waning popularity. You were becoming the queen of the place, people know who you are, they're asking for you and feel let down if you're not there. Your work in the dining room is very important, because you're the visible face of the business, and it doesn't matter who cooks, as long as the quality and appearance of the dishes is excellent. The chef is anonymous and you're the real boss. This is too much for Àlex's ego. I'm telling you this because I love you. If not, I'd leave you to deal with it all by your sweet little self. I don't know how he managed to poison the journalists, but I'm certain it was him. Think about it and work out how you're going to pay him back."

Roda el Món is in darkness when Annette gets back, and Àlex's car isn't in the garage. So much the better. She doesn't feel like finding him there and having to confront him, although she knows that she'll have to sooner or later. She's upset and can't get Carol's words out of her head. The restaurant will be opening in a couple of hours, and she has to make a couple of cakes. If she concentrates and works fast, everything will be ready when the customers arrive. Actually, there are no reservations, even though it's Friday, usually a busy night.

She gets the ingredients and utensils ready, but can't find the beaters from the hand mixer. She looks everywhere, opening all the drawers... but what on earth is this? A transparent envelope with the remains of some bluish powder in it. She's never seen this before. She picks it up and hides it in her pocket just as she hears Àlex's car arriving. Her heart is thumping loudly, tolling like an old church bell. It's amazing she can hear anything else.

He comes inside and puts on his apron without as much as saying hello to Annette. He goes into the cold room and reappears with about ten onions bundled in his apron. He gets a chopping board, spreads a damp cloth over it, tucks it in underneath to make sure it doesn't move, picks up a knife and starts chopping them. Annette knows this will take almost an hour, and that he's doing it because something is bothering him, filling him with sadness.

Meanwhile she breaks eggs into a bowl, adds sugar and beats the mixture well, watching Àlex out of the corner of her eye. She sees tears pouring down his cheeks and, for some inexplicable reason, she feels sorry for this bastard who's trying to destroy her – has destroyed her in fact. Two men have ruined her life with poison. Now she's crying too.

Nobody has come for dinner. Àlex has spent almost the whole evening chopping onions and Annette has made cakes. She's increasingly convinced that Carol's story is true, and there's no doubt that Àlex is acting very strangely, as if he's guilty of something.

Annette can't sleep, so she spends almost the whole night at her computer reading the latest reports on Roda el Món, as well as seeing what the bloggers are saying. Everyone's talking about the poisoning. It's terribly depressing, because they all mention both their names. They've been judged and sentenced, and she has no idea how to redeem the situation. Carol's words are still ringing in her ears: "I think that if you get rid of him, we can start again from square one. I'll organize a couple of interviews for you in the mainstream newspapers and TV programmes."

She goes down to the kitchen before sunrise, makes herself a cup of tea and, with the sole aim of ridding herself of this obsessive mulling over everything, she decides to make some cornbread, just like she used to do for her girlfriends in Quebec. They came to have it for breakfast, as they loved the taste of a good cornbread sandwich with cottage cheese. They would chat away and laugh, without a care in the world because they were all from well-to-do families and never missed a wink of sleep, unless they were fretting over what to wear to the opening of some art show or other. They said they wanted to eat cornbread because the cob was a great metaphor for their tight little group. They always giggled at the witticism.

What are her old friends doing now? She misses them. They've lost a member of the group – Annette – but she's sure that their conversation is the same, still naughty and racy in her absence. She and Àlex are two lost kernels of a cob that was once strong and whole. Life brought them together and the need for company united them, but the only thing they have in common is the wish to be left alone, which is hardly a strong bond.

We are social animals, but excessive dependence on a group weakens us. Annette tells herself she has to be strong, has to learn to live alone, as this is the last option open to her. She must cling to solitude like a drowning sailor clings to a bit of flotsam. She is that drowning sailor, lost in the immensity of the world, about to go under… swallowed up in the hatred and envy of the human beings around her.

"The smell of bread woke me up," says Àlex, standing in the kitchen doorway.

"We no open today, because I receive email from Health Department. They send inspector to discover why journalists sick. I make cornbread. You want breakfast?"

"No, I'm not hungry, and I don't eat maize."

"You so chic you no can to eat humble thing like is corn?"

Àlex makes himself a cup of coffee, talking to Annette with his back turned to her. "I don't think anything. You know I don't eat that kind of stuff, and you also know why. Don't push me. I'm not in a very good mood and have no wish to try to decipher the hidden meanings in your enigmatic words."

"The Indian people in the Americas they worship the maize. It the basic part of diet." Annette is teaching again. "It result from many years experiments and study, one of first crops where they use genetic selection, which mean the people that they live in this territory no primitive, but they have the high level of the culture. They never eat maize alone, but put with it meat, legume, vegetable and fish, so they get balance of diet.

"Spanish people they no like maize, and they say it food for poor people, like what happen with big part of food from New World. The poor people they eat it alone, like also they do with wheat, but no can to eat more things with it, so it insufficient. The wheat it have gluten that is protein, and vitamins also, but the maize it have only carbohydrates, so the poor people they get sick and the rich people say it no good for to eat because it make sick the poor people.

"Fifty years the maize take for to arrive to Germany, and there the famous artist Hans Burgkmair he make it immortal with woodcut print, which make the rich German class they get interest and start to eat it. It very strange that simple thing can to change perception of all the social class, but it happen like this today also." Annette muses aloud on the culture of food as she makes a cornbread sandwich with slices of tomato, cottage cheese, a few kernels of fried corn, a gherkin and some leek mayonnaise.

"I haven't eaten for three days. Looks like I'll have to force myself to accept your sandwich. Thank you." Àlex's tone and expression are blank.

Annette glances at him as he grudgingly eats her sandwich. He looks like a wounded animal, vulnerable, sad, hurt and broken. He couldn't have poisoned the food. Not Àlex. But why did Carol accuse him? Maybe pride, envy or jealousy led him in a fit of fury to poison the journalists, but if that's the case, why is he behaving so oddly now? He's hardly said a word these last two days. When he's worried about something he resorts to sarcasm; when angry he turns to insults; when sad he starts drinking and eventually tells her why. But he never goes mute. Annette doesn't understand it and she's suspicious.

Àlex finishes the sandwich and leaves, saying that, since they're closed today, he'll make the most of the time as he has a few things to see to.

* * *

It's late. The Health Department inspectors are leaving Roda el Món. They've spent ages checking the cold rooms, the kitchen and also the toilets. Annette helped them as much as possible and showed them the little packet of blue power, as she, more than anyone else, wants to know the cause of the poisoning. Rat poison, they conclude. In certain doses it can cause intestinal problems in humans. Annette is increasingly bewildered. They've never bought rat poison or any other pest-control product, because they employ a company to look after the health and hygiene aspects of the business. So what was a bag of rat poison doing in the drawer with the spoons? Although she is disconcerted, Annette starts joining up the dots and seeing a pattern and connections emerge.

Àlex comes back quite late that night. Annette is in her room, still awake. As soon as she hears the front door squeak she runs downstairs. She can't wait a moment longer to find out what really happened. Àlex is sitting at the kitchen with a beer in his hand.

"Àlex, I must to speak with you."

"You want a beer? It's been a bad day. I don't want to do anything, but if you like we can go to my room and listen to some music." His eyes are red and his voice slurred. He's very drunk.

"No, I no want the beer and no go to your room. You drink enough the alcohol."

She joins him at the table, serious and severe. "I arrive to point. The journalists no suffer upset from food. Someone *poison* them. You understand? This deliberate. It seem you have relation with this."

"What are you saying?"

"I say that, if I look at all people who make the party, you from this win most. We know you do it."

"'We'? Who knows this? You and who else? Who's behind this stupid accusation?" He's very nettled now, with angry, red, swelling veins standing out in his neck. "What proof do you have? I've never heard anything so ridiculous. What possible interest could I have? Professional suicide maybe? You're crazy."

Annette takes the packet of blue powder from her apron pocket and throws it on the table.

"I find the rat poison in drawer with spoons. We no buy this never and no use it. I open this drawer every day for making the cakes. It no was there before party. The symptoms they suffer the journalists they the same as give the rat poison. I cannot know why you do this, but I know you are speaking lies to me all the time."

"I haven't lied to you! I haven't poisoned anyone. I see Carol's tentacles behind all this, because she was the one. It was this bloody woman who poisoned the journalists."

"I no believe you!" Annette retorts angrily. "Why she want to poison the colleagues? What is good it make for her?"

"She didn't want to hurt the journalists, but was aiming at me and, in particular, she wanted to destroy our love. I can't believe you don't see this. This woman is an evil fucking bitch. She gets pleasure out of being malicious and harming people and, more than anything else, she loves her own power of destruction. And she wants you. She wants to have you totally in her thrall. You're a pushover for her, especially as she knows how desperate you are."

"This no is true," she protests. "She no need be so extreme for to get what she want. Carol no do this. You manipuler. She no have access to kitchen, and now there is the proof of crime, the rat poison."

Annette doesn't know what to think. Both versions are incoherent and seem implausible. And both suggest sick minds at work.

"Think what you like, girl. You've been in bed with both her and me. Maybe you're the crazy one. I didn't put poison in the watercress soup."

"It was you, Àlex! I no sure for a moment, but you just betray you because how you know poison in watercress soup? You sick, you murder and I have fear. I no want you here. This restaurant it belong to me now and I want make it good again. I will do this, but I no want you here."

"Don't worry. I'm leaving. Not because you're making me leave, but because you don't believe me. Your lack of trust in me is the worst poison you could ever have fed me. I'm very sad to be leaving, because I love you, Annette. You're the only person who makes me believe in life and you're all I have in my life."

Annette watches Àlex closing the restaurant door. He has a small bag in his hand, far too small for his music and film collection.

Annette has been running Roda el Món by herself for four weeks. Each week has brought a new cook and each cook has brought new problems. Carol carries on as if she's the owner and is in her element. Graça gets ticked off because her earrings are too big; the suppliers get ticked off because she considers that their products are not good enough for a first-rate restaurant like this; Eric gets ticked off because she can't stand his standard vocabulary of "hey man", "cool", "awesome" and "dork". She berates the chefs until they walk out and takes Annette to task because she's always too tired at night to "reward" her for all the effort she's so unselfishly putting into the restaurant.

The four chefs have left, not only because of Carol's tongue-lashings but also because they consider that Roda el Món is far too humble for a place that aspires to *cuisine d'auteur*. Annette can't stand this stupid way of thinking and is fed up with Carol. The suppliers' bills are rising with the new, increasingly exquisite products they're bringing day after day. She has to put the prices up and the customers soon voice their complaints.

"Annette, these tomatoes are excellent, but not worth the ten euros you've charged me for them. I've never paid so much in all the time I've been coming here," complains an executive from one of the nearby factories who often comes for lunch.

"Excuse me, miss," one of the summer holidaymakers complains, "I asked for a fillet of the 'fresh fish of the day', but you've charged me for the whole fish!"

The solitary customer has come for lunch today. He's not the only one who eats alone, but his watchfulness and his questions always put her on edge. She now knows he's not a Michelin Guide inspector, but that's the whole extent of her knowledge. It's not that he seems particularly interesting, but the other customers who eat alone always end up talking about their work, where they come from, their families...

A person who eats alone isn't necessarily a loner, but usually someone who is circumstantially lonely, which means he or she wants to speak, begin a conversation with the owner which, while usually consisting of the most trivial chitchat, does give some idea of the person sitting at the table. The mysterious "solitary" customer, however, is quite another story. This man, the "loner" as Annette calls him, is skilled at extracting information, while never revealing the slightest detail about himself.

"How are things, Annette? Have you recovered from the problem with the journalists? That must have been tough. Are you coping OK? Has that ever happened to you before?"

"Not exactly like this." She is sincere with him. "But life it is full of surprises and they not all good. A person no can use always what she learn from experiences that they happen before."

"You're a philosopher. So are you saying you had a similar experience before this, but you can't use what you learnt to sort out the new problem?"

"Exactly! 'Avoid scandals,' the people say, but if you experience a scandal, learning it is no good if you no can to apply it when it arrive the next scandal."

"I've run into Àlex a couple of times in Barcelona. He doesn't look good. He told me he lives in the Raval. I guess I'll see him quite often, as I tend to be around that area. I understand you're not working together any more."

"He no here now. He needed to change. He not feel good?"

"What isn't good is the food you're serving here now. I don't want to offend you, but I do want to warn you. This food is too pretentious and too expensive. It's lost the authentic taste you had before. It's dressed up as something else now."

It's true. The cooks Carol has found all want to be celebrity chefs and have no idea of what the public in this part of the world expects. Accordingly, the takings have dwindled considerably, and the pages of the reservation book are verging on immaculately white once more.

Annette can't cover their excessively high costs with what they're earning. It's not only a matter of paying suppliers and the staff's wages, but she also has to pay rent on the house. The Can Bret owner is implacable. Annette's resolve is shaky.

Tomorrow is Monday and Roda el Món is closed. Carol has decided to go and have lunch in some fashionable place in Barcelona, because she has to write about it for her newspaper. The idea of spending her day off with Carol is unbearable for Annette, but Carol will never take no for an answer. She's the boss and makes or cancels decisions as she pleases. Annette is her puppet and must satisfy her every whim. She hasn't left Annette alone for a single day since Àlex left. Now Annette only wants to have a day to herself, with time to think about how she can get out of this prison in which she's now trapped. She believes that the bars have been forged by Carol's possessiveness, but the real prison is her own brain, which keeps forcing her to recollect Àlex's words: "I'm very sad to be leaving, because I love you, Annette. You're the only person who makes me believe in life and you're all I have in my life."

* * *

Furthermore, she's starting to see in Carol's behaviour some other words uttered by Àlex that night: "She didn't want to hurt the journalists, but was aiming at me and, in particular, she wanted to destroy our love"; "She wants to have you totally in her thrall. You're a pushover for her, especially as she knows how desperate you are." A few remarks made by Carol – and one of them in particular: "It'd be better to take the watercress soup off the menu, because the clients might think we want to poison them" – have again made her doubt that Àlex is the guilty party.

How did Carol know the poison was in that particular dish? The inspectors couldn't analyse it, because not a drop was left. They never discovered how the journalists were poisoned. The Health Department couldn't fine Roda el Món because they found no negligence in the cooking procedures and all the spaces of the restaurant observed the most rigorous standards of hygiene. Àlex had said it too: "I didn't put poison in the watercress soup." Now Carol has mentioned it. Annette's head is spinning. How did they both know which dish was poisoned?

16

TURKEY

*Pleasure is like food. The simpler it is
the less you tire of it.*
FILIPPO TOMMASO MARINETTI

Carol has drunk a lot tonight and, snoring rhythmically, is hogging most
of the small bed. Annette, kept awake by the unlovely noise, is looking
for Òscar on Facebook, because she hasn't spoken with him since the
party. She's been avoiding him for weeks, as she's afraid he's going to
ask her to repay the loan, but she also needs to talk to somebody who
understands her and knows the characters in this show, which is more
twisted than anything any author could ever dream up. She wants to
suggest that they have lunch together so they can chat without hassles
and she can also get out of Carol's clutches for a while.

"Òscar…"

"About time you contacted me! I've written, phoned and was about
to turn up at Roda el Món to see how you are. I see you haven't made
any attempt to pay me back. I imagine there's not much coming in."

"No, we no do well, as you can to imagine. After the scandal in all
newspapers it very hard to keep going. And you, you are OK? I no ask
you still if you get poison also."

"I found out about it in the newspapers, but I felt very sick. I didn't
know what it was, because it wasn't the usual kind of stomach ache
you get from overeating or eating something that's gone off. It was a

strange sensation. I had diarrhoea and a terrible headache for two days. I couldn't leave home, but it stopped all of a sudden, and now I barely remember it. What caused it?"

"We no know, really. I have some signs, but it is all big mess. I need talk with you, because you involved also. I no have money, but we find cheap restaurant for to eat. What you say?"

"I'm delighted with your proposal, but I'm working, so it can't be lunch. Come here for dinner if you like. Then we can talk and I'll also show you the video I made that night. What with the stomach upset and all my work I haven't had time to post it online yet. But it's great. It was a fantastic party, even if we did all end up poisoned."

Annette is already hard at work in the kitchen very early in the morning. Sharing a room with Carol is a nightmare and she gets up at dawn. Carol comes downstairs a few hours later, as happy as a sandboy. She pours a glass of cava and makes herself a plate of different kinds of cheese. Annette doesn't know how she can start drinking so early.

"Carol, you drink cava at this time?"

"It's your day off, isn't it? It's a big day and we're going to have fun. Now we're going to have a few drinks, then we'll go up to your room and, while everyone else is working, I'm going to have my way with you. You've been very mean to me lately and ignoring all my caresses for days. I want to touch you, see you opening up, feel how wet you get and watch you coming. I want you to be all mine this morning. Then we'll go out for lunch and, if you're a good girl, this afternoon I promise you'll see stars... of pleasure. I want you all to myself today, sweetheart."

"Well, this morning I must to go for talk with this man of Can Bret. He ask many times for to talk and I no can postpone more." Annette doesn't want to see Carol's sex-induced stars. "Oh and I sorry, but I no can to have lunch in this restaurant because—"

"Because nothing!" Carols snaps. "You're having lunch with me. We arranged this and you're not going to spoil my plans. You can go to Can Bret this morning, OK, but after that we're going to have lunch in the restaurant I've chosen especially for you and then we'll spend the afternoon in our room. You've kept me waiting too long and I'm fed up. It's my turn to be pleasured by you today. It'll do you good too, because you're very tense. Sex is what you need. Believe me, you'll come out of it relaxed, full of energy and ready to face anything next week may bring."

Annette can't find any good excuse that might let her off the hook. Without answering, she takes off her patchwork apron and leaves Carol alone in the kitchen with her cava and cheese. It's time to go to Can Bret.

The meeting is an ordeal. The Can Bret boss insists she has to sell the restaurant, showing her a document signed by Àlex in which he agreed to transfer the business. He's paid Àlex an advance. Either she sells him the restaurant or Annette must return the advance with interest, plus a fine for "financial loss and damage". This is more than she can handle. There's too much money involved, not to mention all the stress, much more than she can take either physically or psychologically. She asks for time. He gives her thirty days, after which she has to sell him the restaurant or pay back his money.

Why is she so principled? She should sell the place and forget about everything and everyone: Àlex, Carol, Òscar, the Can Bret man and the fat fish supplier. But this would mean throwing in the towel, and her father brought her up to be a fighter. Making a success of the restaurant is a challenge she's ready to accept. She doesn't want to give up now. It's not a question of proving anything to anyone, but simply a goal she's set for herself, to show she can succeed with a big project like this. One is always one's own harshest critic. Anyway, she'll only have a few cents left over after she's paid back Òscar, the fish man and what she owes the other suppliers, because she's now behind with those payments again.

What can she do with her measly few cents? She must keep trying to succeed with Roda el Món, as a matter of pride, survival and showing she's not going to give up so easily.

Carol's waiting for her upstairs. She makes her put on the clothes she bought that long-ago day in Granollers. Annette is too weary to protest. She puts on the red dress and gets into the car and they head off for a stylish restaurant in Barcelona. As often happens in these chic places, it's full, and the stuck-up employees look like peacocks with ruffled feathers, ready to hiss rebukes at you if you don't behave like a good client. When you go to these "in" places, you have to dress up, in order to fit in. Carol decrees that the food isn't bad. She's not going to rip them to pieces but plans to write something friendly – that's if the two bottles of Verdejo she's downed don't make her forget what she's tasted. On the way back to Roda el Món, Annette prays that she'll fall asleep as soon as her head hits the pillow.

This doesn't happen. Carol is euphoric as she enters the room ready for her sex session, which is intense. She begins slowly, undressing Annette, taking her time. Carol wants to play and makes Annette pretend to be a painter's model, so she can paw her with the excuse of getting her into the best pose. Annette finds it ridiculous at first, but eventually relaxes and starts to play too. Carol strokes her, caresses her, licks her all over and Annette likes it more and more. After all these days of tension, Carol's fondling feels good. After the initial poetic tone, Carol changes her tune and starts manhandling her, insulting her and making her pose in uncomfortable, humiliating positions.

The heat rises and Annette is more excited than she's ever been. She doesn't want this, but trying to get some control over the situation and to resist turns her on even more. She finally surrenders and lets Carol take her well beyond all limits she had ever imagined possible.

"That was great, Annette, and I can see you were revelling in it too. You needed that, because I've found inside you the power you need to keep fighting. It was out of action, stymied by all your worries. Sex limbers you up and then you feel powerful. Believe me."

"You have right, Carol. This it has been fantastic."

"We'll do it whenever I say. You're my toy. I'm the one who puts in the batteries and takes them out. I'm the one who makes you move, who stops you in your tracks, who lights you up and switches you off. Your body is mine and I'm going to take over your mind as well. In a few weeks you'll be like a dog running after me. You'll be begging for sex and I'll be the one who decides if and when. I'm doing this for you, because you need someone to guide you and to help you unwind. I'm like the masseur who might hurt you when touching damaged muscles, but who also helps you to move more freely. Now I'm going to get to work on you by making you come up here whenever I see you need it. But not always... I don't want you to expect it, take it for granted or guess when it's going to happen. I want the surprise factor to make you really hot."

Annette listens, wide-eyed, her freckles dancing. She trusts Carol and feels safe and calm with her.

Her phone rings. Òscar's waiting for her at the Granollers bus stop. They're supposed to be having dinner at his place tonight. It's getting late and, since she wasn't on the last two buses, he's wondering if she's forgotten. Yes, she has forgotten, and now she's going to be terribly late. She wonders if she should go or not, decides that she should, invents some implausible excuse for Carol and rushes out before she has time to object.

She'll use the time she has to herself on the bus to think about her relationship with Carol, because right now she's totally confused. She's enjoyed her experience this afternoon, but now the intense pleasure also revolts her. Carol is extremely controlling and always gets what she wants. In fact she's doubly victorious now, because Annette's revelled in it. She still has a pleasurable sensation, but there's also bitterness mixed in with the sweetness. And there's a memory that jabs at her almost painfully. Uneasiness has lodged in her spirit.

The bus reaches Granollers and Annette is no less confused, but dinner with Òscar should help to sort out the mess in her head.

Òscar's worked hard and has prepared a dinner worthy of being posted on his blog, so he says. It's one of those dinners that must be eaten cold because the photos have to be taken beforehand.

Seeing the exquisite spread he's produced, Annette feels even worse that Carol's skilful hands made her disconnect so much from the real world that she forgot about her friend's invitation. They drink an Abadal Picapoll, a white from the Bages region, and what with the wine and her seething emotions, Annette almost forgets why she wants to see Òscar. He, however, is direct.

"So what's going on at Roda el Món? Where's Àlex?"

Annette gives him a detailed account of the incredible story of the clashing versions of the poisoning incident. She wants him to know for two reasons. First, Òscar presently owns a good part of the business, so he has the right to know, and second, Annette needs to talk to someone. Three weeks ago she was convinced that Àlex's pride led him to put rat poison in the watercress soup, and for the last week she's thought that Carol's insatiable ambition led her to do it. Today, both options seem possible, she can't see the wood for the trees and feels completely bewildered. She knows Òscar won't be able to help her and isn't the best person to drag into this.

"Who you think do this?" she asks.

"I'm astounded, Annette. How could someone deliberately poison the food? This is utter madness, the act of some lunatic. The strangest thing is that both of them know which dish was poisoned. What about you? You're hanging around with two psychopaths, so how come it hasn't rubbed off on you?"

"It no is easy with two personalities so strong and so tortured."

"It could be… maybe it started out as a plot they hatched together? They agreed on it, but at some point they fell out and one of them tried to stop the plan while the other one went ahead with it?"

"You see too many films. No, I no believe this. Why they make plot? Both they say they want to be with me… so if they hurt me it no have sense. If also the love messages they tell me make part of this plan, I no know, but it seem very bizarre. I no think they two make a plan. This thing it is for novels and films."

"Hey! Speaking of film! I want to show you the film I made in the restaurant. It's great. Here you have the party more or less live. I want to make a short out of it and enter a competition, but it's very hard to cut down. It really looks as if it was based on a written script. So many things are happening and there's such a lot of movement!"

"Oh… the film… I no sure I want see this now. OK, we see it because I come here for this, no? First I finish this fig carpaccio with ginger ice cream. It fantastic, Òscar, this recipe."

They watch the film. Òscar thinks it's amazing, but Annette is quite bored. He is ecstatic to be hobnobbing with so many well-known journalists, food critics and celebrities. Annette's never been interested in this world and still less in a few journalists she'd never even heard of six months ago. It's also painful for her to relive the scenes of the party, which, after all her efforts, turned out to be such a disaster.

Òscar is chuckling continuously when not making comments.

"Look, look, that woman is Carme Cassanyes. She's so elegant."

"I can see that fat pig Martí Peris over there. He's such a freeloader and would never miss a free meal."

"There's Xènius Agut, drunk already and the party's just begun. You should have seen him at the end!"

"Did you know that the party was the start of an affair between the chef Albert Camot and that journalist from the afternoon programme, what's her name? Ah yes, Elena Sanchis... Incredible!"

What with the darkness in the dining room and the boring film, Annette keeps nodding off, despite Òscar's salacious comments about all the guests.

Suddenly she grabs Òscar's arm. In one wakeful moment before dozing off again, she sees it! She makes him stop the film. Go back. Stop. Òscar doesn't understand.

"Look!" she shouts. "You no can see?"

"What? I see the kitchen, yes. I see Carol in the background and that new boy you've taken on. What else am I supposed to see?"

"The arm of Carol, the hand, the saucepan of watercress soup. Go back. We look careful. What she do?" Annette is shocked and babbling.

"Calm down, Annette, please."

"How I can calm down? You no know the headaches, worry, the nights I no sleep these weeks, and it worse this doubt that make big hole in my brain. I no would want that my most biggest enemy suffer this. Now we find the key for all we talk about tonight. The truth it is in this film. Now we know at last and we can demonstrate this to the persons who want the proof. And there is witness also. Eric! We look careful again, all number of times we must."

The image is distant, in the background, but Carol is perfectly visible, as is Eric behind her. Carol's peering into the saucepan. Then she dips a spoon in and tastes the contents. She takes something out of her bag and seems to wave her arm over the saucepan as Eric watches.

Annette's heart is skittering around like a ping-pong ball. They have their proof. It was Carol, because Òscar's camera also shows Àlex being interviewed by the TV journalist. A few minutes later it records Annette entering the kitchen and, with Eric's help, starting to serve the soup. Àlex is still being interviewed.

"These images are impressive, but they don't constitute irrefutable proof, because the soup could have been poisoned earlier, and don't forget Àlex knew which dish was poisoned. Carol could claim she added herbs or spices," Òscar muses.

"The journalists no bring charges, because they no go to hospital, but they do more worse than take us to the court because they write this in the newspapers and tell all the people, we no have customers now we no have customers never. If they no make complain with police, Carol she no go to the prison. That is certain, but we can destroy her, like she do to me, if the press see this video."

"Don't underestimate Carol's incredible power. You already know how manipulative she is. Let's work out a plan. The aim is that everyone should know that Carol set out to sabotage you in this way. We don't know why and probably never will, because, as you say, there will be no official inquiry. We can only present facts, but there is one problem here, a kind of dark cloud of doubt over the whole thing and this bothers me. We can't be certain that what Carol put in the saucepan was rat poison. We still have the possibility that the soup was poisoned beforehand."

"I taste the soup when Àlex finish to make it. I had hungry and I think I no will to have chance to eat after, so I drink a bowl of this soup before guests come, because this very quick. You no need spoon and fork or napkin or sit down. I finish bowl and drink one more big spoon. I drink big quantity, but when Àlex ask if I taste the soup I say no, because he always complain the kitchen staff 'rob' him the food. I no get poison. And Carol she no taste this soup. She send plate full back to kitchen. This one more sign that she guilty."

"Yes, but you can't prove it. You can look for witnesses, but no one will remember whether Carol tasted the watercress soup or not. Anyway, nobody will dare to accuse her because she's so powerful," Òscar argues. "People can also say that bit was filmed some other day, not the day of the party. Carol is often at Roda el Món and we could have filmed that any day and edited it in."

"Come on! This is more pervert than the brain of Carol. And the television camera and your camera they film same thing, so the other camera for sure film it also. That film show Carol guilty. We must get this part of the television film. I no know these journalists and no have access to the television producers. How we can do this?"

"Let's see… we have to be fast, surgical and get it right. First of all, we have to find Àlex. Hang on, let me think… no, maybe that's rushing things. We need to get our hands on all the material proving that Carol poisoned the soup, and then we have to go and find Àlex." Òscar, who would love to be the detective starring in a crime series, is thrilled with this role of chief investigator.

"I very certain now who is the guilty person. We need discover how Àlex know the soup had in it the poison. How he know this? Did they make this plot the two? I think this nearly impossible. We must to find Àlex."

"You don't know where he is?"

"I no know, but one customer say he see him often. I no know who is this man, his name or telephone number of course. He say Àlex live in the district Raval of Barcelona."

"In the Raval? I'm afraid I know who he's with then. Phone Albert the fruit and veg man and he'll take you there. I warn you: don't be shocked by what you find."

She gets back to Roda el Món very late. Carol has gone home and Annette's delighted. She couldn't stand having to see her now. Carol will be away all this week, at some congress in San Sebastián. At least something's going right. She can work on her inquiry into the food-poisoning without having to deal with conflicting emotions. If Carol were here, it would be much more difficult to concentrate. She'd been mulling it over all the way back from Granollers to the restaurant. She wants justice, wants to make a success of Roda el Món, wants to get out of this mess, and wants to know what happened. But she would have preferred to have kept her friendships with both Àlex and Carol!

She's tortured by these contradictions. They've both hurt her, deceived her and manipulated her, but she can't help being attracted to such strong personalities, each so different from the other and from everyone else as well.

People don't have a fixed, clearly defined nature. Different kinds of behaviour are often immediate reactions to circumstances. It's not so much character as environment that shapes us and guides us. Trying to understand the complexity of the human brain is a colossal and very often futile task.

Carol isn't such a witch as people say. She's eccentric, it's true, but she also has a heart. Àlex isn't an oaf on two legs either. He has his tender moments and strong values. Both of them have taken her in, both of them have loved her... in their own ways. Carol would certainly have been a good friend, with all her mysteries and contradictions, if the poisoning incident hadn't spoilt their relationship.

Life has taught Annette that even the most improbable characters in novels are less complex and less difficult to understand than real-life people. The novelist has to create a clear, comprehensible character that the reader can situate. In real life, people say they know where they're going, but somewhere along the way they come up against an obstacle and arbitrarily take some other direction. They keep evolving. Life is multihued.

Annette phones Albert early in the morning.

"Good morning, Albert. I am Annette, and I phone you because people say you know where is living Àlex."

"Me? No, I haven't got the faintest."

"He live in Raval."

"Ah, yes, then I know where he is."

"You can to take me there? This night, please?"

"OK, I'll take you, but it's no place for girls like you."

Annette's intrigued. This is the second time she's been told that Àlex is living somewhere that might upset her. So where has he hidden, then?

Albert comes to pick her up at Roda el Món early that evening. For the first time ever, Annette leaves the restaurant in the hands of Graça and Eric. She can't count on the chef who started on Friday and thinks he'll last three days at the most. But Eric now understands much more about how the kitchen works and the dishes made in it than some of these other young men who have graduated as qualified chefs.

Albert parks in a dark street, and they're assailed by the reek of piss as soon as they get out of the car. Some Filipino kids are playing football, using two tins as their goalposts in a patch of waste ground. It's supposed to be a kind of urban park, but there are no trees except for a few bare trunks and the ground is dusty and dirty. They go up a narrow alleyway lit by a few small Pakistani shops, each one with a man sitting on a chair waiting for some customer to come inside.

A grubby tabby cat brushes against Annette's leg as it goes past. She screams in fright.

They go up a high, steep, bare stairway decorated only by a few dim bulbs, half of which have blown. It smells of spices. Albert thinks of how things have changed. Only a few years ago there was a disgusting stench of cauliflower, and now it smells like garam masala. The old people have died and newcomers have moved in.

"The Barcelona locals shun this neighbourhood. Not even the pros want to know about it. There are only a few old whores plus a few of the most desperate ones. The flats are a health hazard and the pros want places where they will at least not die from some kind of infection," Albert tells Annette. By the time they get to the third floor she's puffing, short of oxygen. Her nervousness, the smell of spices, the semi-darkness, what's in store for her when she sees Àlex again and her mixed feelings of fear and desire are almost too much to cope with.

A tall, dark, plump woman opens the door. Albert introduces her. "This is Gladys, a good friend of ours. She works as a prostitute. How are you, beautiful? It's been such a long time and you're as sexy as ever. This is Annette. We're looking for Àlex."

"Hello Albert. You're looking very handsome. As usual! I don't have much time to talk, because I've got to work," Gladys says very naturally, as if she's selling buttons. "Àlex usually arrives around now. Wait here and make yourselves at home. Or if you prefer you can wait in the bar downstairs. They do a good rum and coke."

They decide to wait in Gladys's tiny living room, which is dominated by a television set. There are photos of three boys, one in military uniform, on a coffee table. They must be her sons. There are also faded Christmas cards and a calendar full of notes. It looks as if Gladys would hate to forget the birthday or saint's day of any of her nearest and dearest.

He has keys. He opens the door. He looks first at Albert and then stares at Annette. He's completely flummoxed. This visit is totally unexpected. Barely bothering to say hello, he starts yelling abuse at them for having taken him by surprise by lying in wait for him like this, his swearing, shouts and accusations a sure sign that he's completely unnerved and doesn't know how to react to the shock of finding them here in Gladys's flat.

They go down to the bar for a rum and coke. Àlex still hasn't worked out whether he's pleased to see them or pissed off because they've found him. In any case, he doesn't complain too much. The two men are hungry and there's not much to eat here apart from some tripe, which is good, and a more than edible green-pepper omelette.

Annette is still digesting Òscar's gourmet dinner, so she asks for sautéed turkey breast and likes the way they've cooked it. It's different from the usual way of treating it like any old slab of meat. They dice it and sauté it with honey and lemon. Then they put the plate in the centre of the table so they can all pick at it.

"Taste it, Àlex," Annette urges.

"It turns my stomach," he responds.

"Why?" Now it's Albert who has his say. "It's very subtle. Don't you like chicken?"

"Of course I like chicken. But this white stuff turns my stomach. If you want to try to convince me that turkey and chicken are from the same family and therefore if I like one I should like the other, I would remind you that roses and raspberries belong to the same family and you'll never catch me chewing on a rose, however lovely I think it looks."

"Well, edible roses are great – in fact, I'm growing them. You wouldn't believe how well they sell. People make jam out of them and even use the petals in salads." Albert never misses a chance to tout the products from his garden.

"You know the old saying, 'Only madmen eat flowers'?"

Annette listens to the conversation and, while they're talking, slips a bit of turkey onto Àlex's plate. He's so distracted he sticks his fork into the first thing that gets in its way and eats it. Annette giggles.

"The turkey, the *guajolote*, they call it the Mexicans, was the product more successful of the New World in Europe. The colonizers they were so determine to give the Spanish reference to these products, so they call it *gall dindi* in Catalan, because they think it rooster of Indies. In Spanish they call it *pavo*, like *pavo real*, because it look like peacock. Spanish people like very much this delicate meat, so they domesticate the turkey, which very quickly they eat everywhere of Europe, so it become luxury food that they serve as main course at Christmas. Most of the food of the New World they think is low category and no for eat by nobles and rich people in Europe. But the turkey it break this prejudice, because it big bird. The birds for table have prestige then, and especially chicken, but now they have this very big roast bird on the table and it good for image of the rich house. The Spaniards they make a party in Mexico, in the square of Tenochtitlán in 1538. They serve the best exquisite food from Peninsula then: ham, quail, partridge and stuffed chicken, plus the only local food the Spaniards think can share table with their food: the turkey. They have very high opinion of this food."

"That's all very interesting, Annette, but I'm not going to try it," Àlex declares.

"Sorry, but you eat some already. You no realize it, you eat it and you no get the disgust look on your face."

17

PINEAPPLE

> *We should look for someone to eat and drink with before looking for something to eat and drink, for dining alone is leading the life of a lion or wolf.*
>
> EPICURUS

Àlex feels very emotional when he walks into Roda el Món. He tries not to show it, but the expression in his eyes gives him away. The poisoning affair was a devastating blow. Now there is a huge amount of work to be done, but he has Annette's support, which is what matters most.

The fifth chef to occupy Àlex's job in one month is working in the kitchen, together with Eric. Seeing his *sanctum sanctorum* under the command of this brat so beautifully decked out as a chef, complete with manicured fingernails and peacock strut, saddens him immensely. In an attack of nostalgia and rebellion, he makes himself a great slab of toast, takes some anchovies from a dish and puts them on top and bolts down the lot, not minding greasy fingers and lips. He can't work in the kitchen. There's no place for him there. Now there's a proper qualified chef, who's learnt the trade at school and from textbooks, staring haughtily at Àlex.

They're opening in a few minutes. Not that they expect many customers. There have been very few these last weeks. Feeling a need to remove himself from the scene, Àlex goes up to his room. Witnessing the new chef ruining the dishes he makes so superbly is more than he can bear.

He phones the television journalist who interviewed him on the night of the party, praying that she still has the complete recording. Hearing her voice on the phone, happiness starts welling up inside him.

"Hi. How are things?"

"Busy as usual. Àlex, we haven't spoken since the party, and I owe you an explanation. We didn't show the interview because the bosses killed it after the journalists came down with food-poisoning."

"Bloody hell. Well, it wasn't our fault."

"I know you're not responsible but that's what television's like. All the newspapers are full of the story, so we can't show a report of a wonderful restaurant that has poisoned all its guests. We had it edited and all ready to go."

"Have you thrown away the whole recording? And the report?" Àlex starts feeling desperate.

"The whole recording, yes. We never keep the originals as they take up too much space on the computers. I don't know about the report. I imagine it's still in the files. But there's no point in going on about it. There's no way we're going to show it."

"I don't want you to show it. I don't give a damn about that. I just want to see it. Please, I beg you, let me see it. This isn't an ego trip. It's really important for me. I think the report can reveal the cause of the poisoning. You can help us to get out of this mess."

"Hmm. I'm not sure if I can promise anything, but I'll ask the programme director. Come over here and we'll talk about it."

"There's no need for you to ask anyone. I don't want any fuss and, for the moment, nobody needs to know about it. Get it, please, and let me see it. I promise I won't bother you any more."

The journalist agrees to help.

Àlex puts his foot down on the accelerator of his clapped-out car. He's driving with his eyes fixed on the road, as if possessed by some demented spirit. He's desperate to see the film. Right now.

The journalist is waiting for him in the reception area. They go up to the editing room, a small, dark space which, if all goes as Àlex hopes, will become the most luminous spot on the planet, the gateway to hope, freedom and life itself.

They watch the film. "Look, that's it!" Àlex shouts. The film clearly shows Carol adding something to the saucepan of watercress soup. No problems now. The TV station can find time to broadcast this, and then the whole country will learn how the famous food critic poisoned her colleagues. It would be easy, yes, but the TV bosses aren't willing.

Carol works on one of the channel's programmes, one of the most successful, with the most viewers and lucrative ads. The bosses don't want to kill the goose that lays the golden eggs. She's the linchpin of the programme, and they won't gain anything from this. Indeed, they have a lot to lose. Àlex tries his best to convince the bosses that the truth will sell, since it's a sensational story that unmasks a well-known personality, but they think it's too risky and are terrified of losing their advertisers in these difficult times. They're not keen to cover a story about the ruin of a small-town restaurant, a matter that has no importance for the country as a whole. They're sorry, but things will have to stay as they are.

Driving back, he's dying to tell Annette what's happened. He's disappointed, but is certainly not going to give in. He's more determined than ever. They have to hurry and go for it right now, as Carol will be back from the congress soon and won't be at all happy to see that Àlex has returned to Roda el Món. Halfway back, he has an idea, turns sharply and drives into the Montcada industrial estate. He vaguely remembers the way but, shit, he thinks, all these roads look the same, half lost in the sea of factories.

He drives round and round and, when he finds himself on the same road for the fourth time, is about to give up but, just as he is promising, swearing and assuring himself that the first thing he's going to do when he finds a "civilized" place is buy himself a mobile phone so he can call Òscar and ask him where the hell the IT company he works for is located, he almost crashes into him.

"Hi, Àlex! What a surprise. What are you doing here? We were worried about you. I imagine that Annette's put you up to speed."

Àlex doesn't answer any of his predictable questions and gets straight to the point. "We've got to hurry. I've already wasted too much time looking for your hideaway. Coming to see you is worse than running an obstacle race."

Àlex tells Òscar the whole story: the film with the images of Carol putting something in the saucepan, the refusal of the TV station to show it and therefore discredit Carol. It's clear that some people in the media have a high opinion of her, half fearing her and half admiring her, which makes her untouchable.

"We can't count on the media, then," he concludes, "so we have to find another way to get the story out. We'll have to work alone, David versus Goliath, and it will be a hard-won fight. You know all about social networks and all this Internet stuff, and its immediacy gives us an advantage. We've got to get this around before she returns from the congress. We've got four days at the most."

"Àlex, I'm working now. They'll kill me if they find out I'm doing something else in company time."

"Listen Òscar, you're all I have, and it will only take a day. It will be good for you too if we can keep the restaurant going, because, as you'll recall, we owe you a tidy sum. You're the only one who can do this."

"OK. I'll get the bit of film showing Carol putting something in the pot. You two can write the item, as if you're journalists reporting what happened. In particular you mustn't show that you're upset or suggest that this is some kind of revenge. Information must be objective. Once you've done that, I'll get it out to the food blogs and put it on Twitter and around the other social networks. I'll post it for the 5,000 friends on my Facebook wall, but it all has to come out at the same time, so that we make a splash in all the social media at once. The story needs a sensationalist title which can be picked up by all the newspapers that follow the social networks, something like 'Identity of Roda el Món Poisoner Revealed: Carol Amigó', or maybe: 'Famous Gourmet Carol Amigó Poisons Colleagues in Attack of Jealousy'. I can't do anything till you write the text. Send it to me by email this afternoon and I'll get it out to everyone tonight. It has to be written in Catalan, Spanish and English. Annette will do a good job with the English. Keep it short and shocking. It's very important to draw attention to Carol's motives and how she did it."

"I have no idea how to write this…" Àlex groans.

"You'll find out. I'm not a journalist either. Remember that many pieces by journalists aren't exactly gems, or maybe they're some kind of gem when you consider how brilliant they are at messing up the story of two and two make four. I'll polish it when you send it this afternoon. The most important thing is that people can understand it. If I can understand it, everyone else will. The style is secondary."

"When do you want to post it?"

"As soon as I get it. Tonight at the very latest, so when everyone gets up tomorrow morning it will already be in the online editions of newspapers. The scandal will be splattered everywhere. And, moreover, I can email it directly to all the journalists," Òscar offers.

"How can you do that?"

"It's my job and I have a few little tricks. Leave that to me and my keyboard."

"Hang on, hang on, I've just thought of something. Wait two days. I'll phone you. I'll tell you exactly when to get it out. Give me a copy of the video, please. Now I'm going to look for a church."

"You! What are you going to do in a church?"

"You're an IT man and totally trust your technology. You only believe in computers, because they're your truth. I'm just a poor cook who still wonders at the transformation of an egg into meringue, so imagine me when faced with a computer. It all looks like the most obscure kind of magic. I'm going to light a candle to the Virgin of the Impossible, since it's the only way I can think of to get help and win this battle. Then I'm going test my faith in our institutions for the very first time, because I'm going to the police to report Carol for poisoning the soup. I'm going to knock at every door in my efforts to defend the honour of Roda el Món."

Although they haven't seen each other for ages, Àlex and Pérez-Salvat, the chief organizer of the San Sebastián Gourmet Congress, one of the most important on the whole Iberian Peninsula, are good friends. The congress is a jamboree for people in the restaurant business: chefs, food journalists and suppliers. A large number of people from the sector attend it and the lectures given by chefs are a highlight of the show. Àlex hasn't done one for ages, although in the early years of the event he spoke on several occasions about his unusual way of working. In recent years, however, he hasn't been invited to attend – not that he has been interested in going. It's time to put in an appearance.

Pérez-Salvat is happy to hear his voice. "Hi, man, how are you? I thought you'd kicked the bucket."

"Can't you speak Catalan yet, you blockhead? You spend all the time sucking us Catalan chefs dry and you can't even say hello in our language," Àlex berates him.

"*Hola*? I think it's the same, isn't it?"

"Yeah, man, yeah. It's the same. I was joking. Listen, I want to give a lecture at your congress. I have a few things to say and I'm sure you'll enjoy listening. Will you give me half an hour on the last day, please?"

"You're mad! Tomorrow is the last and most important day. Adrián Ferrero is speaking and the hall will be chock-a-block. You know he's announced his retirement as a chef and he's going to give us the scoop on his future plans."

"Trust me. Just an itsy-bitsy half an hour or twenty minutes. Put me on before Ferrero… and then tell me how I can return the favour."

"Bloody hell, do you have to be so crude? I don't want anything in return, and you couldn't give it to me anyway. I'll see what I can do. I can't guarantee you a slot before Ferrero, but maybe I can find a few minutes for you. Well I guess you'll liven up the show. The last few congresses have all been the same, a syndrome we critics call Ferreritis. Everyone wants to be like him."

"Is Carol around?" Àlex asks.

"Carol? That witch! Your friend. Yes, she's here, bullshitting as usual. If only she'd piss off to a nice little place in the country as she's been threatening to do for years, and disappear off the gastronomic map. We need new voices. The stuff this harridan produces is completely old hat."

"I see you still worship her."

"I can't stand her and she's getting worse. She's dreadful. One of these days I'm going to tell her so."

"Don't worry. She'll get what's coming to her. I'm sure I'm going to make you very happy."

* * *

He shuts down the computer. He's sent the news item to Òscar and it looks good. He throws a few things in an overnight bag and rushes downstairs. He'd love Annette to come with him to San Sebastián, but someone has to keep an eye on the restaurant. In any case, he's encouraged by the fact that, if everything turns out well, their future will be bright. It's also coming closer and closer. He kisses her on the cheek.

"Where you go now? I no understand nothing," she says as she grates the carrot for her cake.

"Trust me. I'm going to sort everything out and get what I need to build our future."

Annette is uneasy about the immediate future, but also because of a question she's put off asking for too long. Now's the time to ask it. She needs him to explain how he knew the poison was in the watercress soup.

"Annette, I wanted to tell you later, when we have a bit of peace and quiet, when our relationship isn't plagued by feelings of doubt and resentment. But you want to know now and you have a right to know."

They sit at the kitchen table and have a cup of tea. Àlex takes almost an hour to confess all the details about his feelings when he agreed to Carol's plot.

"There was one factor I didn't foresee: I fell in love with you. I wanted to stop the conspiracy, but Carol wouldn't have any of it. She saw that we were in love and anger got the better of reason. She acted out of spite, not because she'd gain anything from this – indeed, as we can see in the end, she has a great deal to lose. She exploited your innocence and her power. She knew that nobody would dare to contradict her and, again, that nobody would believe my version. How was she supposed to benefit from this, in fact? Of course, she couldn't imagine that her skulduggery was going to be filmed, that the camera would expose her in all her treachery. Mysterious are the ways in which life looks after the weak," he concludes.

"But I no understand still how you could to know that the poison dish was the watercress soup."

"Well, since you want the whole story, I'll tell you, although the detail is irrelevant. From the very beginning I didn't trust Carol. I knew she'd stab me in the back me the moment I turned around. So I went and got someone to be my spy: Eric. I asked him not to let her out of his sight, to watch her every movement, but not to stop her or say anything. He only had to watch her and then inform me. And that's where my plan failed. That was your fault. Eric did a good job but, since he didn't know what it was all about, he couldn't imagine that what Carol put in the soup was rat poison. You said the first course had to be served while I was being interviewed and, by the time I was through with the TV people, the journalists had already finished the soup. It was pure bad luck. I want you to know that I'm still in love with you," he adds, as if remarking on the weather. "Goodbye. I'm off to San Sebastián. If they don't lynch me I'll be back in a couple of days."

Àlex drives to the Basque country without resting. He knows that this is the last trick up his sleeve. If things don't go as planned he'll lose everything: credibility, restaurant and Annette. If he doesn't act, he'll also lose everything.

All the crème de la crème of culinary journalism is gathered at the congress. The prospect of Adrián Ferrero's keynote speech has attracted a large number of professionals and various other hangers-on. The hall is jam-packed: the five hundred seats are occupied and another hundred people are standing, but it's not just about numbers. It's the quality that counts. Among those six hundred people are all the bigwigs, all the top food critics in the world and all of Ferrero's colleagues, the most prestigious gourmets in the country. The perfect audience for Àlex's plan.

He phones Òscar.

"Get the news out this afternoon, at six on the dot."

He takes a few deep breaths, trying to absorb whatever molecules of self-confidence might be floating round the hall. His own stock has run out. He gets up on stage. He needs to look serene, but his legs are wobbly. Everything has to be right: script, technology and, of course, resolve.

He begins his presentation by praising the return to traditional cooking, the cuisine which links people and territory, illustrating his words with dishes based on time-honoured Catalan tastes but using cutting-edge techniques and Asian aesthetics in their presentation. They are monochrome, austere dishes, using only a few ingredients.

Àlex realizes that his selection is hardly daring and that his approach differs little from that of many other chefs. However, he is all for a return to a traditional emphasis on flavour, arguing that this is the only way that many restaurants whose success is founded on good food – unlike those of celebrity chefs who sign contracts with the food industry – can combat the impact of the crisis without jeopardizing the quality of the raw material or any detail in the preparation of the dishes. This is a decent, sensible alternative to all the staff cuts restaurants have had to make in recent years.

"Now," he tells his audience, "I'd like to show you a very short video. I'd be grateful if you'd give me your attention for just two minutes."

The baffled audience has been listening to this speech, which seems trite in its obviousness, without giving the least cause for optimism. They don't understand why Pérez-Salvat has given such a prominent slot to Àlex Graupera. Many of them have been contemplating walking out to enjoy a beer and some ham at one of the advertisers' stalls, but fear of not having a seat when Ferrero comes on makes them stay put.

It's five to six. Àlex asks the technician to show the video. On the giant screen, some members of the audience recognize images from the gala launch of Roda el Món and see themselves leaving the restaurant's kitchen. However, they don't understand what on earth this is about. Àlex addresses them in Spanish.

"Ladies and gentlemen, here we have the party we held to launch the new image of Roda el Món. Some of you came to enjoy the dinner and you praised the menu we prepared. However, the following day, suffering from food-poisoning, many of you bad-mouthed the restaurant. Although this lamentable event had no serious effects on the health of our guests, it did mean the end of all our hopes in the new Roda el Món. Our management team was held responsible by all the media. It is now time to reveal to you what really happened that night. I am sure you'll enjoy the images you are about to see."

Right on cue, Carol appears in the screen, walking into the kitchen. She goes over to the stove, rummages in her handbag and throws something into the large saucepan, the contents of which aren't visible, but it's easy enough to imagine that it's full of soup. As if by magic, the pips, peeps, buzzes, beeps, tinkles, dings and dongs of many mobile phones resound around the hall. Their owners, embarrassed by not having silenced them, grab them as fast as they can. The uproar begins. They've just received the news: Carol Amigó poisoned the watercress soup.

"There is no doubt about this. We have the film that clearly demonstrates it, and you have just seen for yourselves how Carol Amigó added rat poison to the watercress soup with the sole aim of destroying our restaurant."

"That's a lie!" Carols shrieks from the third row. "That's slander!"

"It isn't slander. It's the truth, and it's time to reveal what you did and your sick reasons for doing it."

Pérez-Salvat leaps onto the stage. He is loath to stop the show, because he feels like a kid enjoying the clowns at a circus, but he must stop the congress from degenerating into a bloodbath. Adrián Ferrero is waiting backstage, but the congress director has his work cut out trying to calm down the audience. In fact, the pandemonium is more like a parliamentary debate than a circus.

"Ladies and gentlemen, what we have seen just now in the video that Àlex Graupera has shown us is truly shocking, and unfortunately it reveals how low a person can stoop for reasons that are totally indefensible. Ms Amigó will have her chance to defend herself, but it will not be at this congress. Àlex, I should be grateful if you'd leave the stage now, as we must now welcome the great Adrián Ferrero, who will give the closing address. Thank you very much for your contribution."

Adrián Ferrero wastes no time in taking over the stage as Àlex leaves, waving his thanks to the audience. Backstage he stops in his tracks, panic-stricken. Carol is powerful and a lot of her colleagues will support her. However, he also knows that she has serious enemies among the chefs, as she has done a lot of harm by ruining promising careers.

The Internet and the social networks are abuzz with the news and the video that show Carol for what she is. Her own notoriety, rather than any benevolent angel smiling on Roda el Món, has ensured that the news is now spreading like wildfire.

The phone is ringing non-stop back at the restaurant. Journalists from all over the country want to speak to Àlex, but Annette is alone. She answers their questions inexpertly, not knowing exactly what has happened, except that everyone is now pointing the finger at Carol. They've won. Justice has been done. She opens a bottle of cava and drinks as if she's at a party surrounded by a host of friends. She talks to herself. Shouts. Dances, Sings, Weeps.

Escorted by several chef friends, Àlex gets to his car unscathed. He did well not to underestimate Carol's fury. Surrounded by her acolytes she has insulted, vilified, cursed and threatened him. He breaks all speed limits on his way back. He turns on the radio and listens to the news, where tonight's exclusive is the story of the food journalist who, out of sheer malice, has poisoned a hundred of her colleagues. The whole country knows now.

It's been a very long trip. Annette is asleep when he enters her room. He undresses, gets into bed with her and holds her tight. "Everything's fine now, my love," he whispers. She moves, but doesn't wake up. Àlex is exhausted and goes to sleep with Annette in his arms.

The phone wakes them up at eight. It's a television station, chief competitor to the one for which Carol works. They want to do a special in which Àlex can tell the whole story. It's a very tiring morning. The phone doesn't stop ringing. The media, clients and other chefs are all calling. They're deeply happy but, for all that, they must be careful, sensible and not miss any more opportunities. And the most sensible response is to keep working hard and forget about any feelings of triumphalism. They have to start from square one – with a certain advantage, it's true, but it's still square one.

Annette prepares breakfast. She dices a pineapple and makes turkey-sausage and tomato sandwiches. Àlex eats this reluctantly, looking up from his sandwich at a radiant Annette, thinking, "I'll never be apart from you again, wherever you go." He realizes that his priorities have changed. The restaurant is no longer the most important thing, although he's struggled for it body and soul for so long, the best years of his life, but things are different now and it no longer matters. All this time he's spent coping with one problem after another hasn't been in vain because he has his reward, his Annette, who is the most important part of his life.

"This pineapple it very sweet," she says, savouring a bite.

"It's really surprising. In fact it's delicious."

"I no can believe you never taste it before. You exaggerate this fanatism."

"No, I've never tasted it before and now I have. It's OK. Don't look at me like that: it's no big deal and I'm not a delinquent because I never tasted it before today." He's a little defensive.

"You know what *ananas* mean? In language of Indians who live in country today we call Brazil it mean perfume. The Spaniards give it new name *piña* because they want put names of Spanish food for all the food they eat in New World. The form of American pineapple remind them maybe of the pine cone, but with this logic then you say the egg it look like chestnut. Except the form they no have nothing in common, not taste, size, texture or way of to eat. The pineapple it is the most popular of all foods they bring from America to Spain, and more and more rich people they eat it like luxury food. It no good for to cultivate here, so they only have it sometimes and keep it for big festivals. The chronicles of New World they say it most famous fruit in Indies for Indians and Spanish, so they also make it success. One of them say it have such intense aroma that where there is ripe pineapple, all the room it smell like peach. I like always pineapple and when I discover the Catalan expression *fer pinya* when they 'make a pineapple', the tight group for to work together, I like it more. It very beautiful metaphor and we… we… all us – Òscar, Graça and even Eric – we make a good pineapple for to save the restaurant."

"Listen, Annette, I don't know what I like more, the pineapple or your explanation. You should work at this. We have no idea here about the history of the food from the New World, and you can earn more out of this than you would from the product itself."

"I have job. I have lot of work! OK, we work now." She suddenly stands up and rolls up her sleeves ready to cook.

"I'm serious. You should write a book about the origins and meanings of the foods we eat every day. It would be really interesting."

"You very innocent, Àlex. First, you no can write book in few afternoons. Second, I no know publisher have interest in this. Third, there are many books on this subject in market. Fourth, we have lot of work here. You no agree?"

"First," Àlex replies, "you don't have to write it in a couple of days. Second, we can find a publisher or publish it ourselves. Third, the book could combine the history with my – I mean Roda el Món's – recipes. Fourth, we always have a lot of work, with or without a book."

"I no know how you do this, but you convince me always. You euphoric and I also. You know what? I no think of a book but little booklet and, well, I see a way for we to publish this."

Annette goes up to her room and comes back with a box full of small glass jars, about a hundred, each one containing white powder speckled with different colours. These are the first samples of flavoured salt for the company Vanilla Salt.

The catalogue is divided into four kinds of salt representing four cultures: Mediterranean salt with oregano, rosemary and cinnamon; Asian salt with turmeric, ginger and cardamom; American salt with red pepper, vanilla and nutmeg, plus Mexican salt with hot chilli, powdered garlic and coriander; and, finally, the queen of them all, vanilla salt, made from Annette's precious American vanilla. Each kind of salt has its own label and is packed in a box designed by Annette. It even shows the price and a catchphrase: "The aromas of Roda el Món in your own home". Àlex is astounded. This is really impressive, but when has she done this? The product is ready to go on the market!

"Here, Àlex, we put the little booklet here. You see? We wrap up salt in your recipes of Roda el Món that we adapt them, so the people can to make them at home and use the salt. I put a comment, the history and some words about ingredients with every recipe. It will be a perfect product for to use at home and for nice present also."

"This is wonderful, Annette, but how are we going to sell it?"

"Now things no are done like before. Today we no need the shop. Of course we can sell our Vanilla Salt products in restaurant but… I make also a website. It ready now. The customers can consult about products before they buy direct from restaurant, and like this maybe we make new customers too! We can to send also by post and, on this new page, we offer transport service."

"So far so good, but this idea of home delivery of the product is crazy. If you sell the Vanilla Salt pack at the price you say, the transport alone will cost twice as much. And who will deliver it, anyway? Me? I can see it in your face… No, no, no, I'm not going to do that. I'm not going to deliver it. Me, going to Sant Feliu de Buixalleu to take a little packet to Senyora Maria? No thank you."

"Calm you, calm you, Àlex. This no is problem. You work in kitchen. I think about this. The customer pay for cost of transport, but less than messenger service, but first time customer buy Vanilla Salt product we deliver it no charge, because this investment for to advertise our product."

"You haven't told me who will deliver it." Àlex is slightly rattled by Annette's calm self-assurance as she presents the business. "Seeing how you have everything planned, I'm sure you've given it a lot of thought. But I'll just repeat that there's no way I'm going to be running round the country in my old bomb of a car. No bloody way!"

"You no worry. I tell you already that you no do this, of course. I think of one professional man for to deliver. You know who? His name is Frank and he lose job because he help us. Now it time we give him back favour."

"Frank hasn't got a car! And we can't employ him, because we're broke too."

"You got that bomb car. No is fantastic, but this what we got and no, we no can give him contract because we no have money. But think, because he no have job now and the way economy of this country now, he no will find job. So we give him this little job that no is much, I know."

"It's less than not much. It's nothing, because, until we sell a pack, we can't ask him to take it to the middle of nowhere to some client who will never repeat the order. It might be ten years before Frank can be paid something."

"Listen, I explain you it in little bits. I do web page before I prepare jars and boxes. My time very valuable for me and especially since I work here with you. I want first discover if people interested for to buy the product. I very surprise that I get many orders and, I must say this: it because they know your name. So I start quickly work and prepare the little jars. Then we have scandal of poison and this stop business. But, it lucky thing, customers with interest in product no think bad of me because I send them letter for to explain the incredible story. Today I look at web page and orders they go up like rocket. I think this because of revelation about poisoning, so, I sorry for say this, but it give us big publicity."

"You've really planned it very well, but do you know how long one pack of salt would last in a family of four? An eternity! It will never be finished inside a year. Frank won't ever earn a cent!"

"I know and I think this also. You have reason when you say it difficult they repeat when salt it last long time. But the customer can buy more for to make gifts, for example. It very nice gift. But I want we include Frank in our business. He no have to be partner, but we pay him percentage for every pack he sell. Frank very nice and attractive man and he help us with publicity. If he take pack to Sant Feliu de Buixalleu like you say, he can use journey and take product to shops. We only need sell few pots and free journey will make for us profit."

"You've got an exemplary business head on you. But there's one thing. Have you forgotten that Frank's as black as a Kalamata olive?"

"So?"

"Well, people are very prejudiced about immigrants in this country. And it might be difficult for us to get the product into shops if we have a black salesman."

"I will not even think this. This country have prejudice, but we help to break it with way we act. We do what we believe, always sure, firm and consistent. This is how we fight this stupid thing."

18

AVOCADO

Acorns were good enough until bread was invented.
DECIMUS JUNIUS JUVENALIS, 125 AD

This is day two of the new era, as Annette likes to call it. They have an enormous amount of work today but, in contrast with other times, she doesn't find it a chore. She goes about her tasks happily. They need to cook, answer a host of journalists who are overjoyed with the prospect of flaying Carol alive, meet Frank to offer him the job with them and find time to do serious work updating their Facebook page and engaging in other social networking. Naturally, she hasn't had a moment to start writing the booklet that will be included in the Vanilla Salt pack.

She doesn't want to admit it, but she's thrilled at the idea of writing her small history of food. After spending so long studying the subject, it's wonderful to have this chance to make good use of her efforts and share her knowledge with others. It looks as if everything's going well at last, a beautiful time for them.

Àlex is in the kitchen with Eric and, in a fit of rage, has just tipped into the rubbish bin all the "dreadful" culinary efforts of "that little shit", as he defines the last chef, decorated with all sorts of school certificates, who was sacked yesterday. Annette comes in to make her raspberry crumble, which is to feature on the dessert menu today. What she likes most about this dish is being able to recycle their leftover bread, now crumbled, mixed with butter and sweetened with brown sugar to make a crunchy top for the caramelized raspberries. Even in her earlier life, when she was a rich woman living in Canada, she hated wasting food. Now, when she's totally broke, she finds it even more terrible to throw away food, so, seeing the bin full of the dismissed chef's efforts, she almost faints.

She calls Àlex over and berates him. "The same old story!" she exclaims as she criticizes his bad habit of wasting food. Eric watches on in amusement. He loves conflict and hopes the knives will start flying. He'd be in the middle of some mêlée or other all the time if he could, and thinks it's a shame people usually behave well when it's so much fun winding them up. Annette sees that he's enjoying the show and says, "Àlex, we go and have a cup of tea and talk. Eric he will finish to clean the clams."

"Tea, tea! What kind of poncey thing is this now? Don't come to me with all this Pu-erh, green tea and healthy infusions bullshit. If Madame likes it, that's all very well, but it's not my thing. I don't drink tea, OK?"

"When you ready, come to table with me. It important and you have what you think good for you. I have tea," Annette says, completely unperturbed.

If Àlex's tantrums terrified her before, she's immune now and even finds them funny. If too many days go by without explosions, she misses them. He doesn't seem to realize how childish they are, like a kid whistling in the dark, and they add a splash of colour to the otherwise sterile whiteness of the kitchen. Hence, with today's outburst when she offered him a cup of tea, she's let him sound off as much as necessary and, to goad him just a little more, she's made herself a blend he particularly detests – passion fruit and vanilla.

"Pooh! That stink is terrible. Only Indians and Anglo-Saxons – the former dirt-poor and the latter illiterate in all things gastronomic – could drink that shit."

"You a cliché walk around on two legs, Àlex. No all the Indians of India they poor. On the contrary, everyone know the rajas of India they live like kings."

"You can count them on the fingers of one hand. The rest live in the direst poverty."

"Listen, we no can to lose time with stupid conversation. We have very big problem. In few words, we no have money. I know you get scared when you do books, so I give you this summary of our business. In the beginning we survive problems because Carol write good articles about us."

"Don't mention that woman's name. It's prohibited in this restaurant!" he interrupts.

"OK, I no call this cat a cat, but I continue. In good times we pay your debts and have party with money remaining. After scandal we get less and less money."

"I don't understand why you're telling me this when I already know. Everything will be fine now. Look at the reservation book. We've got quite a lot of work."

"Yes, we maybe can recover, but we have many debts accumulated. The Can Bret man he phone today and tell me he take us to the court if we no pay rent – two months of rent I no can to pay him. He remind me also that you sign him document to sell restaurant and deadline is near now and we must finish this deal or give back him the advance he pay to buy this business. We have problem, a very big problem, and you make it for us, all yourself."

Àlex huffs and puffs. "Everything's always my fault. Stop talking so much about problems and looking for guilty parties. Let's think positively and find solutions."

"Yes, is what I try to do now, and the only solution I can think is: you sell house already, so you have money. You return advance with interest and invest you in business, or we must to find other solution. We no have more possibilities, no time and no can wait more…"

Àlex stares with glazed eyes at her cup of tea. He is silent.

"You no say something?" Annette's expression is serious.

"I don't have the money. I haven't got a bean."

"The money of the house?…"

"I don't have it. I gave it away."

Now she's angry. "What is this you say? This is crazy thing. What you do?"

The day after the party, the day Annette had lunch with Carol, Àlex went to Barcelona. He hadn't been able to visit his son in the Cottolengo convent for some months owing to all the work at the restaurant. He felt guilty, sad and lost. He went directly there. The nuns were overjoyed to see him, as there was a lot of work for him to do, which he set about immediately, unblocking a toilet, fixing a pipe, changing light bulbs and tiling one corner of the kitchen. It had been ages since he had done any work for the nuns. He couldn't find his son. He wasn't in his usual room and the question was eating away at him, filling him with a feeling of helplessness until one of the nuns confirmed his fears. Laiex had died some weeks earlier. "This is to be expected," the nun told him. "People with conditions like this don't usually survive beyond thirty. Now he is with God."

Àlex asked for an appointment with the Mother Superior and made an exceptional donation: most of the money he'd got from the sale of his house. He felt enormously happy at being able to contribute something to the community of nuns who had taken in his disabled son, the son he had abandoned. However, despite his generous donation, guilt still gnawed away at him. Money can't neutralize pain or feelings of meanness, but at least his spirit felt lighter.

He didn't give the whole lot to the nuns. The small amount that remained would have been enough to get the restaurant going again or set up the flavoured-salts business.

"When, believing that I was the one who poisoned the journalists, you threw me out of Roda el Món, I felt very hurt, extremely hurt and alone, dreadfully alone. I had nowhere to go and my life didn't make sense. I loved you and you didn't believe in my innocence. I could have spent the first night in a hotel, rented a flat with the bit of money I had left and then looked for a job. But I was totally destroyed. Having to spend the night alone in a hotel room would have done me in. In fact, I didn't want to live. I went into a bar and stayed there till they kicked me out at closing time, dead drunk. I went to sleep in a doorway, and the next morning the concierge yelled at me and made me leave. I spent all day wandering around the streets of Barcelona, literally without a roof over my head until I ended up in the Raval."

This story goes back to earlier times. After Laura left him alone with Laiex, Àlex began hating women and became a hardened misogynist. He hated his mother, hated Laura, hated anything to do with the female sex and promised himself that he would never again have any dealings with any woman, neither in his personal nor in his professional life. He gave himself body and soul to cooking. But he was still a man and his craving for sex made life unbearable.

One Monday, some eighteen years earlier, after spending the whole day working at Cottolengo, he was walking around the city and had a few drinks to wind down afterwards. He ended up in the Raval, where he saw a young prostitute soliciting men on the street. She reminded him of a daisy, a childlike, white and delicate flower. He went over to her, paid the trifle she asked for in advance and went upstairs with her to the room she rented by the hour, a bare, dirty, dark space. Àlex didn't speak to her, but roughly undressed her, entered her and brutally fucked her till he came.

"Darling, please, my love, be gentle with me, please," she begged in a strong Brazilian accent. He filled her mouth with his penis and obliged her to swallow his semen until she almost choked. Then, in a primitive, animal rage he began to beat her, shouting, "Fucking whore, pig, bloody bitch."

Cowering in a corner of the grotty room, the terrified woman sobbed. Mute with fear, she couldn't say a word. Seeing her so defenceless, Àlex kicked her hard in the back. He closed the door, leaving her alone, naked and crying, curled up on the dirty floor.

On the way back to the restaurant, Àlex had been about to drive off the road. He wanted to die, crushed by twisted metal, in the River Tenes. He had to pull over and stop the car, and he immediately threw up all the hatred he'd accumulated over so many years. He felt relieved, totally vile and disgusted with himself.

He had to wait a whole week before he could return to Barcelona, enduring seven days of being almost asphyxiated by remorse. Finally Monday came around and he drove into the city centre, obsessed with finding the Brazilian prostitute. When he approached her she shrank away, looking around for help. She went pale and, just as she was about to start running, Àlex grabbed her arm. She screamed and shook her head, but he showed her a handful of notes and said, "This is for you, princess. Let's go to a bar and talk." She couldn't resist the temptation of the money he was offering and, since he'd suggested an open space, surrounded by other people, where he'd have problems if he attacked her again, she agreed to go with him.

She asked for a Fanta and they started talking, although it ended up being a kind of interrogation in which she hardly dared to speak, except for timid answers to his questions. Her name was Gladys and she'd arrived quite recently from Brazil, where, as the second of twelve brothers and sisters, her chances of bettering herself were less than remote. She had a baby son, whom she'd left with her parents. She wanted to study and become a nurse, but at present she was hard put to get enough to eat every day. The night he attacked her, she'd been in Barcelona for just two weeks and had only begun working as a prostitute a few days earlier. She was nineteen years old when he invited her to a Fanta in the bar.

After that Àlex went to see her every Monday. He always paid her double the agreed rate, saying, "Half of that is for food and the other half is for your nursing studies. Save it."

Their relationship had little in common with the typical whore-client encounter. Àlex treated Gladys like his girlfriend, his sweetheart, his friend. Of course they had sex, and a lot of it, but they also talked and freely exchanged confidences. Monday was a delightful day. Until early afternoon Àlex busied himself with all sorts of jobs to help the nuns at Cottolengo, which he left happy and satisfied at having been able to see his son and do something for the nuns. Gladys was waiting for him towards evening, with the sweet, chocolatey, delicious, firm breasts he'd been dreaming about. He loved listening to her melodious voice, rich with the music she'd learnt on the streets. They talked and talked and Àlex slept naked in a bed which Gladys rented by the hour, in the disgusting room, in dirty sheets in which at least a dozen men had wallowed.

"The day you threw me out, the day when I wanted to die, after wandering round the streets not knowing where to go or what to do, I went to see Gladys, who took me in. Life is full of surprises! I was taken in by a whore! A few months earlier she'd been able to rent a tiny flat two doors away from where she worked, so now she could live alone and was at last spared the farts of the old pros in the house where she'd had to share a room because she couldn't afford anything better. What with the rent and having to buy food, Gladys didn't have enough to pay the fees for her nursing studies, the only course that didn't require a certificate in primary education. I felt indebted to her, so I gave her the rest of the money from the sale of the house and the advance. Now you know everything," Àlex concludes. "If you want to get something back, you'll have to take on a whore and several nuns. I wouldn't advise it."

"What you tell me is very typical with you. I can imagine this. I really sorry for death of your son. You no tell me this before. But I remember the day you come back after party you chop many onions and close you inside you. I understand this as clear sign that you guilty for the poison, but you silent because Laiex die. I make big mistake."

"I didn't tell you because you didn't ask me what was wrong."

"We no start argument round and round same track now, because it no lead us nowhere. We have this situation of no have money and problem of debts. We have scenario: we must pay rent and loan of Òscar. If we no return advance pay for business, plus fine, we no have restaurant in two weeks. We must make decision. We go and speak with bank for credit or—"

"We'll sell the restaurant." Àlex is categorical.

"But, Àlex, this your life, and now it my life also."

"Our life isn't in this restaurant." He's categorical.

"But… you cooking. You love this most."

"What I love most is you and I don't want to lose you. We can do lots of things together. We have plenty of experience, ideas, energy, dreams and time. Let's not blow this chance by getting into debt up to our ears, fretting our lives away in one small corner of the planet when we have a whole world to discover."

Caught up in their conversation, they haven't been watching the clock. It's late and they have less than an hour before they open. They have tables reserved and Àlex hasn't had time to cook all the dishes featuring on the lunchtime menu. He dashes into the kitchen to throw together whatever he can to save the situation.

He looks around and is dumbstruck. While he was talking with Annette, Eric has done the cooking. It's not exactly what Àlex had in mind, but he's done a good job. All by himself, with the few ingredients he's found in the fridge, the scraps of culinary knowledge he's managed to pick up from Àlex and the arrogance of youth and inexperience, he's produced six dishes. Àlex is pleasantly surprised. The kid's got talent. He's acquitted himself very well.

Annette and Graça get the dining room ready. They're expecting quite a few people today. Annette's troubled, upset by her conversation with Àlex and saddened by the prospect of selling Roda el Món. She barely speaks. The Can Bret people are only concerned about making money and couldn't care less about good cooking, culinary culture, gastronomic sensibility and fine products. When they look at a customer, they only see the bulge of his wallet. She imagines what they'll do to Roda el Món. They'll wreck the place, reduce the kitchen to half its size so they can cram in more tables, change the format of the menus, smothering them in plastic so they'll last for ever, send back the fine wines so they can offer cheap ones with a high mark-up, and sack Graça because she's black. Annette can't bear the awful reality of what will happen in less than two weeks if they sell to the Can Bret people.

She grabs the phone and calls Eric's father, the fish supplier, to ask for an appointment. He immediately agrees, since he fears that this must be about his son's less than satisfactory behaviour, although he's had the impression for a while now that the lad has stopped hanging round with those pothead friends of his. He tells her to come later this afternoon.

Annette takes the bus to the industrial estate and Eric's dad is punctual in receiving her. It's clear from the sweat pearling on his forehead that he's worried. Annette reassures him.

"Please you no worry about your son. Eric he work very well and he even like his job. He prepare today all the menu, himself alone. We are happy with him. His attitude also change, and now he not so aggressive but more tolerant. It hard for him to control the impulses of young person, but he try."

Eric's father is greatly relieved. This is the best news he's had since he signed the deal with the biggest hotel chain in the country. If his business is booming and his kid's not getting up his nose, he's the luckiest man on earth. As long as his wife lets him go to see the young ladies in Thailand a couple of times a year then life's a bed of roses.

"I'm very happy to hear that. In fact, he's a good lad, and I can say it even if he is my own son," he boasts. "He just had to find a job that interests him. I really had a great idea when I had to decide what to do about your debt. Sometimes I surprise myself with the things that occur to me," he says, glancing in the enormous mirror covering a good part of one of the walls in his office and rearranging the remaining few strands of hair across his bald dome.

"Yes, he is very good boy, and true also that he like cooking. But your son he would not be fine in any restaurant. The good principles in Roda el Món, the workmates, the freedom Àlex give him to create new dishes, the discipline in timetable… all these things important for your son so he can to work well." She employs all her shrewdness to save the business. "There are many different kinds of restaurants and most too big or impersonal or not enough disciplined… some are incredible. Depending on kind of cooking you need lot of serenity and many skills to deal with the tension. It very important for Eric to have good training before he try other restaurants."

"But why are you telling me all this? Do you want to sack him? Remember, this is impossible, because you signed a contract that is very clear about this. You can't sack my son." His tone is now threatening.

"No, no, for Heaven sake! No, I no want to sack Eric. We love him like he is our son." She looks at the ceiling, trying to hide the fact that she's lying, although it's true that they've grown quite fond of Eric.

"So what's all this about then? Why are you telling me it would be better if he didn't leave Roda el Món?"

"We no have money for to pay a debt from when we start the restaurant and that get worse after scandal of poison food. I think you know we were not responsible. You know that?" She's speaking slowly, to make sure he gets everything she says.

"Yes, of course I know. I have followed the case with great interest – after all, my son works with you! I've read all the newspapers and my son's even told me a bit… well, a bit, because you know what these young people are like. They don't talk much."

"Well, he talk very much in restaurant. He feel happy with us. I want to tell you we cannot pay the debt and we must sell restaurant. Can Bret make us very good offer, so in fifteen days Roda el Món will belong to them and we all lose our job: Eric, us and the waitress. We have two weeks only. Unless—"

"Unless what?" Eric's dad is clearly irked.

"Unless you buy restaurant."

"Now you're floored me, girl. You mean you think I should buy the restaurant. Then what?"

"Everything go on like now. You will be owner and Eric will have safe job. You can think about it this night and telephone me tomorrow? We do not have time, because the Can Bret man he is pushing us, every day more."

A very determined Annette hands him a document showing all the conditions of the sale of the restaurant: the price, the deadline for payment and the clause clearly stipulating that the new owner must respect the way the business is being run by its present owners. Annette's sure she's won the day. Eric's dad is bound to buy the restaurant and, since the only thing he wants is to make sure his son learns some kind of trade, keeps busy, stays out of trouble and stops giving him headaches, leaving him in peace to get on with his trips to Thailand, he won't interfere in the running of the restaurant.

That night, after they close, Àlex and Annette have a frugal dinner at the kitchen table. Wanting Àlex to try the foods that came to Spain from the Americas, she has made guacamole. He doesn't want to be rude, but he doesn't like it. The texture and taste put him off. She tells him that the main ingredient, avocado, was the last of the American foods to be accepted by the Spanish people, who, like Àlex, didn't take to it at first. It didn't grow well in Spain and, since it ripens fast, it spoils very easily when transported, so it was never widely distributed and didn't appear even on the tables of rich folk, although it was a staple in its natural environment. The Aztecs believed that it was an aphrodisiac because of its shape, which is why the tree was called *Ahuacuatl*, testicle tree.

"You need taste new food at least ten times so you get used with it. I no surprise you no like it the first time, because it have really a strange taste. But if you try more times, I am certain you will like it in the end."

"And if I insist that you come upstairs to our room now, I am certain I will like you in the end," Àlex mocks her affectionately.

Annette has given Eric's father until the end of the morning to respond to her offer, and he doesn't make her wait. At one minute past eight the phone shrills hysterically. She flies out of Àlex`s room, leaps down the stairs and gets there before it rings off. In her mad rush to take the call, she shouts "I'm coming, I'm coming", as if the person on the other end of the line could hear her.

As she imagines, it's Eric's dad and, unsurprisingly, he accepts all her conditions. She hangs up, and the argument between her head and her heart immediately begins. She's really happy, of course, but she's also deeply sad. She knows how hard it will be to recover Roda el Món, but at least it won't fall into the obnoxious hands of the Can Bret man.

With the money from the sale, they'll be able to settle their debts with the suppliers, pay back Òscar's loan and return the advance of the Can Bret man plus whatever they are fined. They'll have enough left over to get the flavoured-salt business off to a good start. Only one small detail remains. She has to break the news to Àlex.

She doesn't beat around the bush. "Àlex, I sell Roda el Món to the father of Eric."

She expects shouts, a bawling-out and a heap of arguments against her plan, but he is perfectly calm and thinks it an excellent idea. The only surprise for him is the identity of the buyer.

"We're not leaving. Like this we can to work peacefully and put this money in Vanilla Salt," she adds.

"Yes, yes, I get it, and if everything goes to plan we'll never again be slaves of our overheads as we are now. We've got to make sure that everything works well, because our income depends on it, but at least we'll be relieved of that never-ending pressure. You've done very well, Annette."

A very cheerful Àlex gets to work on the day's menu and, listening to him singing, Annette hears the tender tones she heard when she first came to work here. Everything will be easy today at Roda el Món. She starts getting the dining room ready, but then, on the spur of the moment, she rushes outside and gives Can Bret the finger. She's learnt that this silent but eloquent "Up yours" is called a *botifarra* in Catalonia, and doing it makes her feel even more relaxed. She goes into the kitchen and, inspired by the cheerful atmosphere, makes a large, generous apple cake, like the ones she used to make when she was a rich woman in Canada. She's like a cat on hot bricks, excited and relaxed all at once. While she's waiting to take her cake out of the oven and for the future owner of Roda el Món to arrive, she amuses herself by dusting the wine shelf and then decides that a drop of Priorat red would be a good thing, so she pours herself a glass from an open bottle of Embruix. "To the eternal good health of our love," she toasts, all by herself. She's got till mid-morning before Eric's dad comes in his Porsche Cayenne and takes her to the notary's to sign all the papers.

At the notary's, the fish dealer opens a briefcase, takes out the money and pays cash. No problems. The papers are signed. Annette phones Òscar. She wants to invite him to dinner, pay off her debt to him and celebrate the new, calm, less complicated journey they're embarking on in such style. As she waits for him to answer, her hands are trembling. What does the future hold?

She gets back just before the first lunchtime customers start arriving. Even the reservation book seems to be bustling round the desk as the bookings come in, and there are already quite a few tables reserved. Everything will run smoothly today and they won't even notice the time passing.

Graça is just putting the final touches to the tables when a well-dressed man arrives, asking if he can speak to Annette. She sashays off to the kitchen and calls, "Annette, fashion man, he desire talk with you!"

Annette comes out, wiping her hands on a tea towel, thinking it must be one of the usual wine salesmen, but to her great surprise she finds that the "mysterious customer", as she and Àlex call him, is waiting for her. What on earth could he want?

He suggests that they sit down to talk at an out-of-the-way table, because the matter is delicate and he doesn't want anybody to overhear.

"How can I to help you?" she asks, intrigued.

"My name is Alain Dumaine and I work for a big Canadian insurance company."

The expression on Annette's face speaks volumes. She shifts in her chair and Monsieur Dumaine continues in French, "I've been sent to Catalonia to discover your whereabouts and inform the Canadian authorities where you are hiding. It hasn't been difficult, because you're not very discreet. I found you here a few months ago thanks to an article in a mainstream newspaper signed by a famous food critic, Carol Amigó. I am sure you will know who I am talking about. My mission wasn't very risky, but it was important, and I couldn't afford to make any mistake in identifying Annette Chaubel."

"My name is Annette Wilson," she replies, now very anxious.

"Yes, of course, Annette Wilson, I know that everyone around here knows you by your husband's name and that you use an American name in an attempt to cover your tracks. But this was very ingenuous. It may have been effective in keeping the Canadian police at bay, because when they come up against the first obstacle they call off the search and slap a great big red 'MISSING' on the file, but there are also economic interests involved. This means there are people who will move heaven and earth to track you down. For example, the insurance company I work for had to pay out a fortune to the people affected by the clenbuterol you fed to your calves. You will know what I am referring to."

"Yes," she whispers.

"Well, I had to find you. And I've done that."

Annette sees her whole world falling apart in a microsecond. This is the end. When the scandal broke in Canada she feared this would happen, and now it has. She's finished. She listens impassively to Monsieur Dumaine, without fear and without sadness. She feels nothing at all, as if all her emotions have escaped from her body and left her sitting there like a machine, nodding and shaking her head as if by remote control. Her features are frozen and her eyes are staring into space. Alain Dumaine is completely unperturbed.

"My job was to find you, and I did find you, but I didn't notify the Canadian authorities. I've been watching you all these months. I was never in any doubt about your identity and I could have put an end to the matter a couple of weeks after arriving here. It was so easy to find you. But Catalonia is a lovely place and, as a humble employee in the Frauds Department of an insurance company, I don't get too many chances to enjoy this wonderful Mediterranean world. So I decided to deceive the company and stay on here for a few months. From time to time I came to the restaurant to make sure you hadn't escaped – and, I must say, the food is great here. I was softening up. I saw that you are a very vulnerable, noble, hard-working woman who is attentive to the well-being of her clients, and I began to feel sorry for you."

Annette listens carefully, without the slightest idea of how all this is going to end. He continues, "Yes, I got fond of you and Graça. Àlex too. You make a great team. So I decided not to write the report I should have written to the authorities. Instead I said that it was impossible to find you, and that, deeply regretting that I had failed in my mission, I would soon be returning to Canada empty-handed. I must confess that I only have a few months left with the company before I retire, so I haven't taken a huge risk. On the other hand, this was my chance to offer a new life to a girl who deserves it. I felt magnanimous, pleased and proud of my decision. But then the food-poisoning story broke in all the newspapers."

"It wasn't our fault. We have proof that this was the work of Carol Amigó," Annette says, clutching at straws.

"I know, I know. I'm well informed about everything concerning Roda el Món and Annette Wilson. Let me finish, please. When I read in the papers that you were accused of poisoning the journalists, I believed that I had got carried away by all the good Mediterranean vibes and misinterpreted what I thought was your open character. If you were guilty of two large-scale poisoning crimes, there was no way you could be a good person. Angry with myself for being so naive and for my professional lapse, I wrote to my company telling them your exact whereabouts."

Alain Dumaine needs a sip of water, as he's upset, despite his serene appearance. He is sure that this woman is a good person who has been greatly harmed after being deceived twice, but it is his job to send her to prison. And that would be very unjust.

"You were in luck, though. There was some kind of computer glitch and the email didn't go through. Three days ago the company phoned me to ask what was happening. Surprised by this, I told them I'd already notified them as to your whereabouts and also gave them the details on the phone. Then I re-sent the email with the precise information. Some hours later I read the denouement of the poisoning story on the Internet, and learnt that Carol Amigó was guilty of poisoning the journalists. It was too late. I felt like a traitor. I've been trying to come here and warn you for the last two days, but problems and work commitments kept cropping up. I'm getting old and everything's too much for me. But you've still got time. You must leave today. Go to some place far away from here. They won't find you. They'll get tired of looking for you. Listen to me, please. Leave now. Don't let them catch you with your hands in the dough... of that gorgeous carrot cake."

19

SUNFLOWER

> *My definition of man is a "Cooking Animal".*
> *The beasts have memory, judgement, and all*
> *the faculties and passions of our mind, in a*
> *certain degree; but no beast is a cook.*
>
> JAMES BOSWELL

Annette races down the street. One of these days, she thinks, she'll have to stop leaping around like a little girl. She runs into the house calling, "Àlex, À-a-a-lex!"

"What's up? Anyone'd think you've just seen Dracula with a garlic necklace round his neck like a rosary."

"You say crazy things! Look, look at the newspaper. We have won at last!"

"What?"

"I was having a cup of tea in the bar with time to read all the newspaper, even the smallest things. Like this."

Àlex reads the brief item:

A court has begun hearing evidence against Carol Amigó, who is accused of poisoning food served in a Vallès restaurant. There is considerable public interest in the trial, because the accused is a well-known food critic.

At last! They've been waiting for months to find out how the food-poisoning story would end, both of them fearing that Carol would spread her tentacles and try to pervert the course of justice. However, it seems that sometimes justice is justice in this country, and Carol hasn't been able to manipulate it in her favour. She will pay for her deeds. Whether she has to pay a lot or a little is not the main issue. The important thing is that justice is done.

They had to leave Roda el Món with nothing but the clothes on their backs, so to speak, the very same day that Monsieur Dumaine came to visit Annette. They only had time to go to and see the Can Bret man and repay the advance, plus the fine that had been imposed because they hadn't sold him the restaurant. All above board. Immediately after paying, they packed up whatever clothes they could, a few CDs, videos and some chef's equipment, loaded it into the car and set out without really knowing where they were going.

The person who was most affected was Eric, who still doesn't understand anything. Àlex took him aside, telling him, "We have to go. Right now. We didn't expect this, but we have no choice in the matter."

"What time will you be back?" Eric's not very interested.

"Sorry, I haven't been very clear. We're not coming back."

"What do you mean? Are you crazy? Who's going to run the restaurant?"

"You. The restaurant is yours."

"But I can't do it by myself. I don't know how to!" Now Eric is distressed.

"Listen to me. To begin with, you can do it. I've seen that you can. You've got a good gastronomic sensibility and you're very smart. That's what you need to run a kitchen. Moreover, you're a fast learner. You're a sponge, soaking up everything, immediately. You only have to do what you've seen me doing – and, in fact, I've been watching you these last few days and have noted that you've adopted my routine. Don't forget it. That's important. It's true you're very young, but you can make up for inexperience with discipline. I have great faith in you. You've never missed a day and you're always punctual, which is an extremely important aspect of good cooking. Finally, you have to remember that the restaurant is yours and the success or failure of the business depends on you and you alone. If you understand that, the mechanisms of ambition and effort will kick in and help you get through the moments of exhaustion."

"Your advice sounds all very nice, man, but me, by myself... it won't work." Eric is unconvinced.

"You won't be alone. You'll have me. You can always phone me whenever you need advice. And if you have an especially busy time or feel out of your depth, let me know and I'll come and give you a hand. In fact, I was thinking that I could drop in from time to time, but not on any day in particular. I don't want you to be dependent on my help. Try to do it yourself. The satisfaction is greater and the feeling of pride is deeper when you achieve something through your own efforts. Lots of young guys would love to have this chance you have now, to know that success lies in their own hands. Be brave, determined and tough on yourself, and enjoy your small triumphs. Don't go hankering after what the other lads have, but take pleasure in what you've got. You already know that taking over a restaurant means you can't do the things other young people do. Bye-bye weekends! But this in no way means that your wings will be clipped. On the contrary, you'll be free to make your own decisions. Go for it and do a good job. Plenty of young people will never be able to make their own professional decisions. You'll do a wonderful job, Eric!"

"I'm shitting myself. You've given me a great sermon, but it's only words. I'm going to be left here all by myself, lonelier than a nun's vagina!"

"OK, you need a kitchen hand. But you're the chef and you have to give the orders. I know a good, reliable girl. You'll have to teach her how to make our dishes, but she's like you. She learns fast. Since she's from Barcelona, she'll have to sleep here. She can also help you out with cleaning. Here name's Gladys. I'll phone her today and ask her to start tomorrow. I'll bring her here myself. She's been working as a prostitute."

"Bloody hell! A pro in the kitchen. That's just what I need." Eric clasps his forehead in despair.

"So? Let's see if you're capable of getting it into your head that not all engineers are smart, not all cops are good and not all whores were born to be whores. Gladys never had the chance to choose. That's all. She's clean, clever and she wants to get out of the mess she's in. She'll be eternally grateful for this chance you can give her. She'll never let you down. An opportunity is the most valuable gift you can give anyone. You got your chance and now Gladys can have hers. I've also got a new opportunity right in front of my nose and I have to grab it before it flies away to someone else's house."

"So, you mean a pro in the kitchen and a darkie in the dining room. That's wonderful," Eric says contemptuously, staring upwards and sighing noisily.

"Not a pro and not a darkie. People. Remember that, Eric. People. The difference between you and them is about age, the country you come from and the family bank account. So far, they've proved to be a lot smarter than you. If they'd had your dad's economic security and the support he's given you, they wouldn't be doing the work they're doing. They have a lot to teach you: to struggle till you drop, to respect differences, to value what you have, to love the people who help you... Open your eyes and ears and learn the values they uphold. Right here, you'll have a couple of very good teachers in the subject of Life. Make the most of it."

"Can I fuck the pro for free?"

"Listen, lad, if I hear from Gladys that you've overstepped the mark with her, I'm going to cut off your balls very slowly, skewer them and then grill them. Look at me now. I'm telling you very, very seriously, that these two women are very important in my life and I love them as if they were my daughters. A father will kill for his daughters. Is that clear?"

"Yes." Now Eric is deferential.

"I'm convinced, well let's say absolutely certain, that you couldn't have a better apprenticeship than you'll get with these two women. Learn to put their theories into practice and you'll end up discovering what the word 'dignity' means. Get on with the job, lad. You can do it. Oh, and one last thing: don't give my phone number to anyone. Annette and I 'have disappeared'."

"All these mysteries…"

Eric has phoned only a few times since the day they fled leaving him dumbfounded and assailed by doubt. Thanks to Graça's experience and Gladys's willingness to learn, Roda el Món is doing very well. Annette's got an unemployed niece of the Can Bret man to help out.

The whole thing's like an absurdist comedy.

Today they have a meeting with Frank to go through the Vanilla Salt orders. The business is booming. Although there aren't many online sales to individuals, a range of small businesses all around the country, from gourmet shops and village bakeries to small supermarkets, are starting to sell their products. The little book of recipes with ideas about how to use the flavoured salts is quite an attraction. In brief, they're happy with the way things are going.

It was a good idea. Frank happily accepted the job as a Vanilla Salt salesman, not so much for the money he expected to be paid because, to start with at least, he didn't have a fixed salary. Basically, he was tired of hanging around doing nothing all day. Àlex and Annette were generous. They gave him a share in the business – their way of thanking him for the help he gave them in the form of boxes of fish on the doorstep all those months.

"Good morning, family," Frank calls as he comes in the door. "I've got a big delivery today. Have you got it ready? That family in La Garriga loved the meatballs and now they want sautéed black-eyed peas and veg. Two servings."

Annette has had the good idea of offering home-cooked dishes on the Vanilla Salt website. Once they'd got through all the upheaval of finding somewhere to live, moving into a house on the Maresme coast and settling in, Àlex started to get restless. In other words he was being a pain in the neck. He needed some action and wavered between starting a vegetable garden in the backyard, which was impossible, because there was only enough room for one tomato plant, or setting up a couple of tables in their tiny dining room to have a miniature restaurant of sorts. An inactive Àlex is like having a full butane gas cylinder right next to a blazing fire. Annette was terrified that if she didn't find a way of calming him down, she'd find customers at a table in the toilet. But no bright ideas occurred to her.

Then, one day, she was clearing the table after lunch, in despair because she couldn't find a space in the fridge for the enormous quantity of marinated salmon with apple and ginger that Àlex had prepared. All of a sudden her brain lit up. Yes! She didn't have to look for ways to amuse a retired Àlex. She just had to get him working as a chef again.

Àlex can't live without cooking. He went off to the market early every morning and came back loaded with supplies, after which he spent all morning in the kitchen cooking their lunch. But when he sat down at the table he wasn't hungry and hardly touched his food, while Annette was piling on weight. Her trousers were tight. She felt terrible about throwing food out, but there was no way she could finish what he served. Impossible! Àlex cooked for ten. The fridge was groaning under the weight of cooked delights: bits of this and that, bowls of leftovers and near-full saucepans. Seeing the fridge in this overstocked state gave her the brilliant idea.

On the Vanilla Salt website she added a section of accessibly priced takeaway dishes cooked by the great chef Àlex Graupera. "Take Àlex Graupera's art and skills into your own home," her slogan urged. "Luxury meals at everyday prices," she promised. The response was more than satisfactory, with orders flooding in as soon as they posted their new products. They had to rush out to buy takeaway containers and the fridge was now liberated... and Annette even more so.

In their small house by the sea Àlex is now cooking up the customers' orders, plus a little extra so they can have a stock of dishes. They're getting plenty of work. The only investment they've had to make is a vacuum-packaging machine, so the dishes will last a little longer. They've designed some labels for "Àlex Graupera in Your Kitchen" and Annette works hard, writing up the ingredients in every dish, the use-by date and how to serve the dish at home. Now they're preparing Frank's order for La Garriga. They also have to deliver some Vanilla Salt packs in the village and takeaway dishes to several homes.

"Bye, my friends. This is going great." Frank sets out again.

Now is Annette's time. She sits down at the computer. She likes surfing the web, reading her friends' blogs, looking for ideas for her cakes and new flavours for the salts. Best of all is having time to write her book on the history of food. Àlex has finally convinced her to share her anthropological knowledge and she's enjoying herself enormously. She hasn't found a publisher yet, but that doesn't matter. The most important thing for Annette right now is that she's having fun writing it. In order to make her account more appealing, she's embellishing the text with recipes by the chef she loves most: Àlex Graupera.

As she writes, she takes a break to gaze out the window. She can see a tall cypress tree and, behind that, the dark-blue spread of the Mediterranean. She feels privileged, aware that sitting by a window overlooking the sea is a huge gift and, more than anything else, that she's here by the skin of her teeth…

The phone interrupts her musings. Òscar. They've been trying for days to find time to meet up. They've invited him to dinner several times, but he's too busy. Now he says he has some good news, but they'll have to meet up this weekend if they are to see each other at all.

Àlex and Annette are intrigued and also delighted that Òscar's coming to see them. They plan an exquisite dinner. Àlex gets into the car and goes off on a pilgrimage (as he puts it) to find the best products in the region. He buys the vegetables from a farmer friend and lamb at the Mataró market, then heads off to the fish auction, to get the fish straight off the boats.

He comes home as happy as a sandboy. This is going to be a memorable dinner, worthy of a five-star restaurant and with no skimping on ingredients: teardrop tomatoes from Girona, ratte potatoes, bell peppers… they'll lack for nothing. He'll also make guacamole to go with the salt-cod salad. It's a complete menu with all the ingredients that Annette has helped him to rediscover and love.

MENU "In Celebration of Òscar"
Salt cod salad with watercress and guacamole
Vegetable and foie gras terrine with black chanterelles
Marinated fresh anchovies with green-olive hollandaise sauce

Oven-baked baby monkfish
Powerhouse chocolate and hazelnut cake
Soupçon of sublime carrot cake
by Canada's best pastry chef

They've spent all afternoon working together, calmly, without stress and with all the time they want. Just the two of them, cooking whatever they feel like. Àlex is concentrating on his black chanterelles, treating them like the jewel in the crown. Annette, making her *sablée* pastry, which has to be done by hand, is touched to see how tenderly he deals with every single mushroom. Her hands are coated with the butter-and-sugar dough, which is unavoidable. Like a serial killer, she sneaks up on Àlex from behind and wipes her hands all over his face.

Àlex yells and, when he turns round to get his revenge, sees her running upstairs. He races after her, yelling, "You'll regret this, really regret it!" He corners her in the bedroom, hurling himself on top of her, and they fall on the bed. Annette struggles in Àlex's strong arms and then gives up. Their eyes meet.

Annette uses the only muscle that she can work at present. She starts licking the sweet dough off his face. Happy, loved, cherished and serene, he lets her. He adores this bloody woman who likes playing such childish games as covering your face in *sablée* dough. He raises her floral skirt and starts caressing her. She whispers, "What about your black chanterelles? You haven't finished cleaning them."

"Don't you worry about the black chanterelles. They can wait." Àlex, very aroused, has other priorities now, and they make love, coated in sweet, buttery dough.

They whisper, as if keeping secrets from the spider watching them from its corner of the ceiling. They're in heaven in their small, bare, inconspicuous room. No one knows that they're here, in this tranquil, humble oasis, decorated only by two naked sweaty bodies, ecstatic at having found, after so many years of struggle, someone with whom to share a double bed three hundred and sixty-five days of the year.

"We're two loners cohabiting for the sake of convenience," Àlex often says, to annoy Annette. Certainly it suits them to live together, but it's about finding themselves, being fully human, and recovering all the self-esteem that was lost in all those difficult years.

They don't notice the time passing. They can no longer see the sea. It's dark outside. The doorbell rings.

"Shit, Òscar!" Annette shrieks, as she throws on some clothes.

"Your skirt's inside out," he warns, too late, as she's already running downstairs.

The superb dinner is only half ready. They wanted to receive their friend with a beautifully set table, candles lit and a well-chilled Godello in the fridge. The dining room's a mess. The shopping basket's on the floor in the middle of the room with its haughty pedigreed vegetables peering over the edge. The kitchen's completely topsy-turvy, with the sink full of half-cleaned chanterelles, a chocolate cake waiting to go into the oven and the hostess with her skirt on inside out.

"Well, well, well, so this is the glorious dinner you promised me," Òscar smirks.

Judging by his hosts' appearance, he imagines that only two things could have happened. Either someone's beaten them up or they've been wallowing in sensual raptures, and since there are good vibes everywhere, he opts for the latter explanation.

They look at each other and burst out laughing. OK, no problem, they'll have the over-the-top dinner tomorrow. Today they'll open up a few servings of "Àlex Graupera in Your Kitchen" and enjoy a good drop of Penedès red, a Mas Comtal Petrea.

They sit at the unset table, onto which they've thrown a few pieces of cutlery, the uncut bread on its board, the unopened bottle, paper napkins and vacuum-packed takeaways fresh from the microwave, all scattered round the table.

Annette and Àlex are keen to hear Òscar's news, but he makes them wait till dessert, a few slices of watermelon and a half-eaten box of chocolates which Annette produces from a drawer. Now, at last, he's ready to talk.

"So, I've come to tell you that I'm going to work in Cupertino, in California. I've got a job with Apple, an IT man's dream. I'll be working in their research department. The best of the best. I can't believe it. Next Friday I have to show up at the office of Jonathan Ive, the boss of the department where I'll be working.

"That's amazing, Òscar! Congratulations. But... you don't speak a word of English, so what are you going to do about that?" Annette asks.

"They're arranging a teacher for me and I'll be doing an intensive course. I'm not going there on some scholarship, you know: I'm going in big-time. Jonathan Ive himself sent me an email. But here's the most incredible thing about this story... It's all because of the fuss we kicked up when we showed that Carol had poisoned the journalists. They heard about it at Apple, and now they see me as a possible hacker, someone worthy of their respect."

"A hacker? But you didn't hack anything. You did a great job sending out the news, of course, but you didn't do anything fraudulent," Àlex says.

"Well, it was a bit... mmm, well... very fraudulent actually. Àlex, do you really believe that anyone would have taken any notice of the story if I'd sent it out from my computer? Of course the video proved that Carol did it. There's no doubt about that. But the whole thing could have been a home-made set-up job."

"What did you do, Òscar?" Annette sounds like a teacher who's ticking off some wayward boy in her class.

"Please don't be cross with me, Mademoiselle," he mocks. "I got into the office of the Spanish News Agency."

"What! What do you mean you got in there? How? Are you mad?" Annette screeches.

"You don't always need keys or a picklock to get into an office. You need a key, yes, but a virtual one. I got in through the Agency's software, working from home, take note. Nice and warm, with the heating on and in my pyjamas. The news was sent out as if it were coming from the Agency, with all the authority attached to it," he explains.

"But that's serious fraud. They'll get you for this. They'll get all of us!" Annette is really alarmed.

"Don't worry. There's no problem at all. The news was signed 'E.D.' Who the hell is that? Esther Duran, maybe? Or Elena Dorca? Or Eva Donadeu? Or Eugenia Díaz? All of them work in the Agency, but not one of them sent out the item. And, anyway – the logo that heads the news, guarantees it and testifies to its authenticity – wasn't the exact logo. One letter was missing. It's practically imperceptible. So no one noticed. I fiddled with the logo and also the name. If you look carefully, you'll see it says 'Spansh News Agency'. Just one little i is missing. No one can blame them, and they'll never find us, since I worked through their computers. The police won't come looking for us because no one's reported it. But the guys in Apple did find me. They know all the hackers and they like the ones who aren't delinquents, as in my case. They see us as highly skilled and daring."

Annette gets up from the table heaving a big sigh of relief. Phew. She's always unwittingly getting caught up in something illegal. She'll just have to get used to it, she thinks. What else does life have in store for her?

She comes back with something to go with the coffee. Àlex is still chatting with Òscar about his American adventure, and they're so carried away with the subject they don't notice what Annette has served them. They munch away automatically. This is something sweet, crunchy and tasty. After polishing off quite a few, Àlex asks, "What's this, Annette?"

"Caramelized sunflower seeds. From the beautiful, spectacular flower that greatly impressed the Spanish. They planted it in their gardens for show. But many, many years passed before they planted it as a crop. Today it is the most important industrial crop of all the foods that came from the Americas. The edible seeds are just a little bit of the story. They make oil from them, and people consume quite a lot more of this than olive oil."

Àlex gets militant. "Not here. This house uses olive oil, and will use only olive oil!"

"Don't worry, we don't have one single bottle here. Òscar will have to get used to it though. In the United States, olive oil is more expensive than Périgord truffles."

Òscar leaves very late. Annette starts to clear the table. "Leave it. We'll do it tomorrow. We're too tired now," Àlex says affectionately.

"The kitchen's a disgusting mess, Àlex, and the black chanterelles are still sitting in the sink waiting for you to clean them."

"You seem on edge. What's up? Ah, I think I can guess. This story of Òscar's about how he made the news credible – that's it, isn't it? You don't like these messes, I know."

"You're right. I don't like them. I feel like a sunflower. Just when I start enjoying the sun, and the stronger and happier I feel, things I can't control come along and slap me down so I have to feel guilty for something I've never done."

Àlex comforts her, half-joking. "Sunflowers are beautiful, resilient, and they observe nature's cycles. It's not a bad thing to be like a sunflower. I've always been called a cactus. So what would you prefer to be?"

"A cactus. That's not a bad idea. Did you know it was one of the plants that most impressed the Spaniards in America?"

"Don't start now! Come on, let's get some sleep. Tomorrow you can fill my head with your cactus stories, but now I'm tired and I want to love you to bits."

Once they're in bed, Annette murmurs, "Well, the conquistadors were so keen to Hispanicize all the plants they found in the Americas that they called the cactus fruit *higo chumbo*. They added the adjective 'prickly' to this 'fig', because it wasn't as delicate as the Mediterranean one, which it resembled."

"You don't miss a chance, do you, when it comes to doing American proselytizing? I like it when you tell me these things, as you know, but the bedroom isn't the most suitable classroom. I want you to tell me about juicier things."

"Juicy things are not for talking. They're for doing. OK, let's refrain from talking."

"You've turned into a real little Catalan-speaking beast. So where did you pick up 'refrain from' then?"

"From Frank! You know, we foreigners will end up speaking better Catalan than the locals, because you don't care enough about what you consider belongs to you."

"She huffs and she puffs... so besides being an anthropologist, teacher, writer, businesswoman and cook, she's turned into a Catalanophile as well. Bloody hell!" He grabs her wrists and tickles her with her own hair.

"Stop!" she cries, laughing uncontrollably.

"I won't stop till you desist from lecturing me about food in bed and succumb to my bestial pre-Columbian Catalan desires."

"By the way, did you know horses don't come from America?"

"Enough! Enough! Enough!" Àlex fondly orders.

They make love, slowly and gently. They've found their little corner of the world, a place where they belong. They're happy. They know that nothing will happen to them on this small island, within the walls of this house in the Maresme, surrounded by friends like Frank, Òscar, Graça, Albert, Gladys and Eric. They feel as if they're living in a bubble, but their experiences along life's winding paths have taught them that threats are always lurking outside the bubble, lying in ambush, ready to attack, like a huge envious needle poised to prick the bubble in order to drain out the happiness inside it.

Lying there side by side, they gaze at one another. Annette doesn't want anything to spoil this miracle which has given her a home, a place in time and a family. Àlex has learnt to read her freckles, and knows that despite their happiness, she worries about the fact that they're not in charge of their own destiny.

"Tomorrow we're going to have the salt-cod salad I started making for dinner. It's been left half-done in the fridge."

"We've just made love, and the only thing that occurs to you is to talk about what we're going to eat tomorrow. What a romantic conversation," Annette complains.

"When I was breaking up the *bacallà*, I noticed a very aggressive stink. There must have been a bit that had gone off in the batch we bought. Bloody hell, what a stench!"

"Aha, the sweet nothings are getting sweeter! So we make love and, afterwards, not only do we decide what we're going to eat tomorrow, but we also go into all the details of the rotten fish we bought. Who on earth would want to get involved with a chef?" she laughs.

"I removed the rotten *bacallà* and the rest is perfect, smelling like sea and salt, and absolutely delicious. If I hadn't got rid of it, the whole lot would have gone off."

"Yes, yes, you're right. But I want some romantic words, some words of love, an 'I love you' and a few caresses. And all you can talk about is salt cod. What a disaster."

"Annette, we need to keep our noses on the alert to pick up any pong of putrefaction that gets inside things and taints everything around it. You and I have to be very attentive, so we can keep our love and save it from anything that might harm it. If we make sure that nothing rotten comes into our house, and we prevent any possibility of spreading decay, we'll be fine. The threats come from outside, not inside."

"I love you, Àlex. I want us to travel together in search of the sun, defying the darkness. We won't let any bit of rotten fish spoil our happiness. We'll struggle against anything bad that comes along. Let's be rebel sunflowers."

Àlex is in paradise watching the freckles dancing all over the body of this woman he loves so much.

GLOSSARY

Abadal Picapoll: A Designation of Origin (DO), fresh, slightly fruity white wine made with Picpoul (*Picapoll*) grapes from the Pla de Bages region of Catalonia. It is best drunk young.

Ànima Negra: An aromatic, flavourful, oak-aged red wine made from Callet grapes from the village of Son Negre near Felanitx, Mallorca.

Aromes de Montserrat: A herbal liqueur, containing thyme, juniper berries, lavender, cinnamon, cloves and coriander, inter alia, supposedly invented by the Benedictine monks of the Montserrat Monastery.

bacallà: The Catalan name for the Atlantic cod. Salt cod has been popular in Catalonia since the latter half of the seventeenth century and there are literally hundreds of *bacallà* recipes in Catalan cuisine.

bacallà de bany d'or: The name Àlex's grandmother gave to her dish of salt cod and garlic, emulsified in golden olive oil.

bellota (Spanish): In the context of ham, this word meaning acorn refers to Spain's highly prized ham made from free-range, acorn-fed, thoroughbred Iberian pigs.

Bonet: This well-known brand of herbal liqueur is made in the Bonet family distillery in Sant Feliu de Guíxols on the Costa Brava.

botifarra (1): This famous Catalan sausage made from raw pork and spices is based on ancient recipes going back to Roman times. It comes in several shapes, forms and colours.

botifarra (2): An obscene gesture, the Catalan equivalent of the *bras d'honneur*, a silent but eloquent "Up yours".

botifarra amb mongetes: Sometimes known as *botifarra amb seques*, this dish of grilled *botifarra* served with white beans cooked with garlic and parsley is often regarded as typically Catalan, although it only dates from the nineteenth century.

calçotada: A popular gastronomic event held in Catalonia in late winter or early spring, in which green onions (*calçots*) are grilled and served with *romesco* sauce.

capipota: Stewed calf's head and foot, said to have originated in the Barcelona municipal slaughterhouse where it was cooked by the workers in the early hours of the morning.

cava: A sparkling wine, mainly produced in the Penedès region of Catalonia from the Macabeu, Parellada and Xarel·lo local grape varieties. Of Designation of Origin (DO) status, it is produced in the Champenoise traditional method but, under European Union law, cannot be called "champagne" as Champagne has Protected Geographical Status (PGS).

chorizo (Spanish): A spicy pork sausage made with paprika, known as *xoriço* in Catalan.

churro (Spanish): A fried-dough pastry which is popular as a breakfast snack, dipped in hot chocolate or coffee.

Conca de Barberà: A region in the Province of Tarragona, well known for its fine wines and with its own Designation of Origen (DO).

Embruix: A full-bodied oak-aged red wine made from Carignan, Grenache, Shiraz, Cabernet Sauvignon and Merlot grapes in the Vall Lach winery, established in the 1990s by the singer Lluís Llach in the Priorat region of Catalonia.

Equilibrista: An oak-aged red wine with hints of ripe red fruits and chocolate, made from Carignan, Shiraz and Grenache grapes in the Ca N'Estruc winery near the mountain of Montserrat.

escabetx: A traditional form – going back to the fourteenth century – of conserving food (usually fish or fowl in Catalonia) in a vinegar-and garlic-based sauce, usually flavoured with bay leaf, thyme, rosemary and paprika. It seems that the name is derived from the Perso-Arabic word *sikbāj* (vinegar stew).

escalivada: The name of this appetizer dish is taken from the Catalan verb *escalivar* (cook in hot ashes, *caliu*). The two main ingredients are aubergine and red peppers, which are served in strips with a touch of garlic and olive oil.

escudella i carn d'olla: The word *escudella* means bowl and *carn d'olla* is meat cooked in a saucepan. Deemed by the author and gourmet Manuel Vázquez Montalbán (and many others) to be the *Summa Theologica* of Catalan cuisine, this rich, complex broth is made from root vegetables, cabbage, chickpeas, meatballs, chicken, sausage, etc., simmered for hours and usually served with large shell pasta. In many families it is considered the *sine qua non* of Christmas lunch.

Figueres onion: Excellent in salads, this mild, sweetish onion, slightly flattened in shape and with purple skin, is typical of the Figueres and Alt Empordà region of Catalonia.

Foraster Trepat: A young oak-aged red wine produced in the Montblanc area of the Conca de Barberà region by the Mas Foraster winery. Trepat is a grape variety that is unique to Conca de Barberà.

Godello: A variety of white wine grape grown mainly in Galicia, in north-western Spain. Fine white wines are produced from this grape, notable amongst which are those from Valdeorras.

gratapaller: Literally meaning "haystack scratcher", this is a particularly prized free-range chicken.

higo chumbo (Spanish): The fruit of the cactus *Opuntia ficus-indica*. Some common English names for the fruit are Indian fig opuntia, Barbary fig, cactus pear and prickly pear.

Joselito: *Jamón Joselito* is considered by many famous chefs to be the best ham in the world. The acorn-fed pigs are raised in Extremadura and the ham is cured in the Guijuelo factory, in the Province of Salamanca.

Kripta: A fine brand of *cava* made in the Penedès region of Catalonia by the Agustí Torelló Mata winery.

Lepanto: A brandy made by the company González Byass in Jerez de la Frontera in Andalusia and notable for its golden colour and the toasted almond, vanilla and caramel notes in its flavour.

'L'estaca': A song by the Catalan composer and singer Lluís Llach. The word *estaca* means "stake" which, in this case, is extrapolated to mean "without liberty". Composed during the Franco dictatorship, it is a call for unity of action to achieve freedom.

llonganissa: A very popular long pork sausage, typically made in the Osona region of Catalonia.

Mas Comtal Petrea: A prize-winning oak-aged red wine (Merlot) from Avinyonet del Penedès (Designation of Origin Penedès) in Catalonia.

migas: (Spanish: crumbs) a typical dish of Spanish cuisine using leftover bread, soaked and cooked in olive oil with paprika and, depending on the region, spinach, pork ribs, chorizo, bacon and sometimes grapes.

mongetes: A generic word for beans, qualified by an adjective, for example *mongetes tendres* (green beans). In this case (*botifarra amb mongetes*), the reference is to white beans, often served with *botifarra* and *bacallà*.

Nacarii: A brand of caviar from sturgeon raised in the Vall d'Aran, 700 feet above sea level in the Pyrenees.

nyora: A small, round variety of sweet pepper, usually used in its dried form.

patxaran: This liqueur made from sloe berries and coffee beans and flavoured by a vanilla pod, is popular in Navarre, the Basque Country and the Pyrenees. It is usually served chilled or on ice.

pebrots: The Catalan word for peppers (and also testicles).

Los Peperetes: A Galicia-based (in Vilagarcia de Arousa) brand of high-quality tinned foods.

Périgord truffle: This valuable black truffle (*Tuber melanosporum*) is named after the Périgord region in France where it grows with oak and chestnut trees.

pernil de gla: Ham made from acorn-fed pigs (see *bellota*).

picada: A unique element of Catalan cuisine. Used since at least the thirteenth century, this thickening and flavouring agent is made of such ingredients as nuts, garlic, fried bread, olive oil, herbs, spices and sometimes a touch of dark chocolate, pounded together with a mortar and pestle (one of the meanings of the verb *picar* is "crush"). It is usually stirred into the dish a few minutes before the end of cooking.

pijama: An over-the-top Catalan dessert, typically including tinned pineapple and peaches, crème caramel, ice cream and cream.

Priorat wine: The Priorat, a region of Catalonia with unique black slate and quartz soil, is famous for its full-bodied red wines. It is one of only two wine regions to receive (together with Rioja) the highest Spanish qualification for a wine region (DOC). The main grape variety in the region is Grenache but Carignan, Shiraz and Cabernet Sauvignon grapes are also grown, together with four authorized white varieties.

El Puntido: An oak-aged red wine (100 per cent Tempranillo) made by Viñedos de Páganos in the Rioja region.

Raimat Cabernet: Named after a locality in the Catalan Province of Lleida, the Raimat winery produces wines that have been granted a Designation of Origin (or Protected Geographical Status) under the name of Costers del Segre. The Raimat Cabernet Sauvignon is oak-aged and greatly appreciated for its satiny palate with forest-fruit touches.

romesco: This sauce from Tarragona is typically made from any mixture of almonds, pine nuts and hazelnuts, roasted garlic, olive oil, hot peppers and *nyora* peppers. Roasted tomatoes and red-wine vinegar may also be added.

sardana: A circle dance, originating in the Empordà region, going back to the sixteenth century according to some scholars, which became popular and extended throughout Catalonia with the *Renaixença* cultural revival movement which began in the Principality of Catalonia in the first half of the nineteenth century. The music is played by a *cobla*, a band consisting of ten wind instruments, a double bass and a small drum.

Sauternes: A sweet wine from the Sauternais region in Bordeaux. It is made from Sémillon, Sauvignon blanc and Muscedelle grapes that have been affected by "noble rot" (*Botrytis cinerea*), which causes the grapes to become slightly raisin-like, giving the wine a concentrated, distinctive flavour.

sofregit: A simpler Catalan version of the Spanish *sofrito* and the Italian *soffritto*, is made of onions and (usually) tomatoes and cooked in olive oil to a jammy consistency. It may also include garlic and other vegetables, for example leeks or red peppers. It is used in hundreds of Catalan dishes.

suquet: A fish and potato stew from the Empordà region. The name comes from the verb *suquejar*, meaning to seep or exude, suggesting that the fish flavours ooze into the sauce. The quality of the ingredients is very important in this delicious simple dish.

Terra Alta: This Designation of Origin (DO) wine-making area is in the western part of the Province of Tarragona. The name means "High Land" and the region is known today for its Grenache Blanc white wines and a growing red-wine production.

Les Terrasses: An oak-aged red wine made from Carignan, Grenache, Cabernet Sauvignon and Shiraz grapes by the Álvaro Palacios winery in the Priorat region of Catalonia.

trinxat: This dish from the Cerdanya and Alt Urgell regions, and Andorra, is made from boiled potato and cabbage, which are mashed together, mixed with pork belly and fried in olive oil.

Tudela asparagus: The white asparagus from Tudela de Duero in the Valladolid region. It is so famous that the town holds an Asparagus Festival every year, on the last weekend of May.

Vall Llach 2007: The year 2007 saw an excellent vintage in Porrera, in the Priorat region where the Vall Llach winery is located. With black currant, ripe berry and toasted almond overtones, and a silky finish, this red wine is made from Carignan, Merlot and Cabernet Sauvignon grapes.

Verdejo: A very old variety of white-wine grape which was brought, probably by Mozarabs, to the Rueda region (Castile-León) in Spain, which has Designation of Origin (DO) status. Wines labelled "Rueda Verdejo" must contain 85 per cent of the grape but they are often 100 per cent Verdejo. They are aromatic and full-bodied. The grapes are usually picked at night to avoid, thanks to the lower temperatures, oxidation or browning.

Vichy Catalan: A well-known brand of mineral water of high mineral content and natural carbonation from Caldes de Malavella, which was known for its hot springs in prehistoric and Roman times.

Xarel·lo: A sweet, small and compact white-wine grape variety, typical of the Penedès and Camp de Tarragona regions, used in the production of cava.